SPACE BANDITS

MARK MILLAR
WRITER

MATTEO SCALERA
ARTIST

MARCELO MAIOLO
COLORIST

CLEM ROBINS
LETTERER

MELINA MIKULIC
DESIGN AND PRODUCTION

RACHAEL FULTON
EDITOR

LUCY MILLAR
CEO

Matteo Scalera's covers
colored by **MORENO DINISIO**.

IMAGE COMICS, INC. • Robert Kirkman: Chief Operating Officer • Erik Larsen: Chief Financial Officer • Todd McFarlane: President • Marc Silvestri: Chief Executive Officer • Jim Valentino: Vice President • Eric Stephenson: Publisher / Chief Creative Officer • Jeff Boison: Director of Publishing Planning & Book Trade Sales • Chris Ross: Director of Digital Services • Jeff Stang: Director of Direct Market Sales • Kat Salazar: Director of PR & Marketing • Drew Gill: Cover Editor • Heather Doornink: Production Director • Nicole Lapalme: Controller • IMAGECOMICS.COM

One

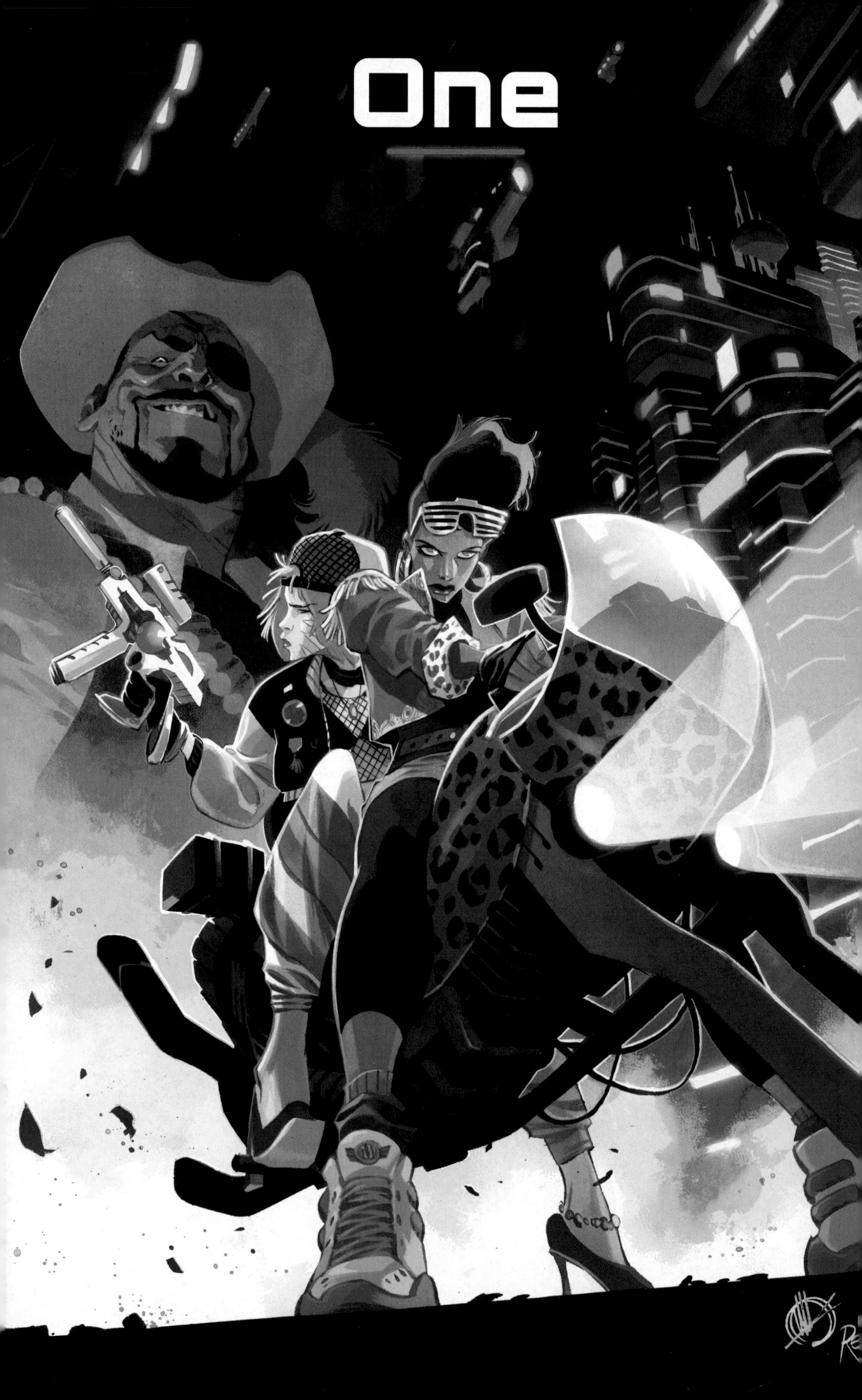

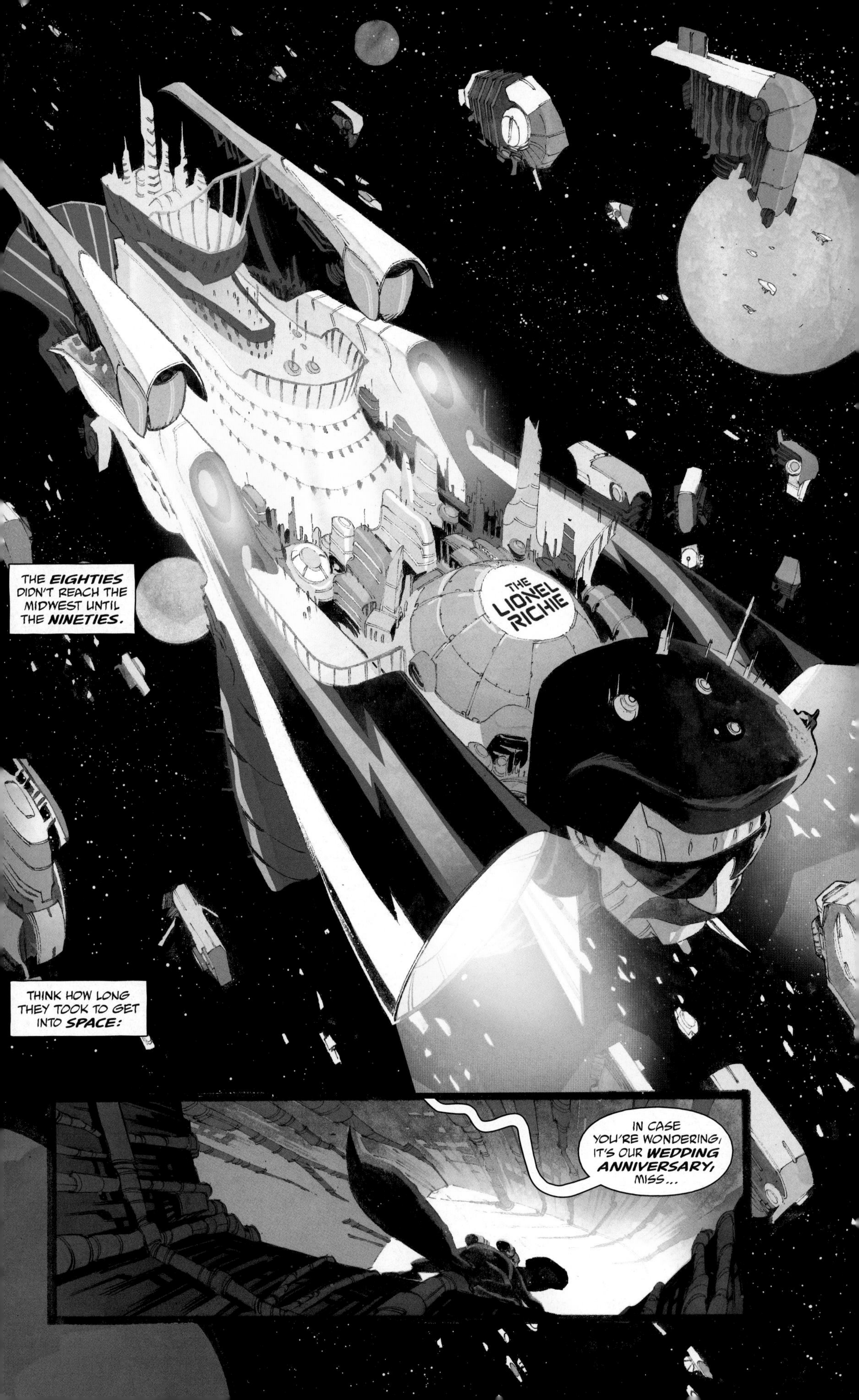
THE EIGHTIES DIDN'T REACH THE MIDWEST UNTIL THE NINETIES.
THE LIONEL RICHIE
THINK HOW LONG THEY TOOK TO GET INTO SPACE:
IN CASE YOU'RE WONDERING, IT'S OUR WEDDING ANNIVERSARY, MISS...

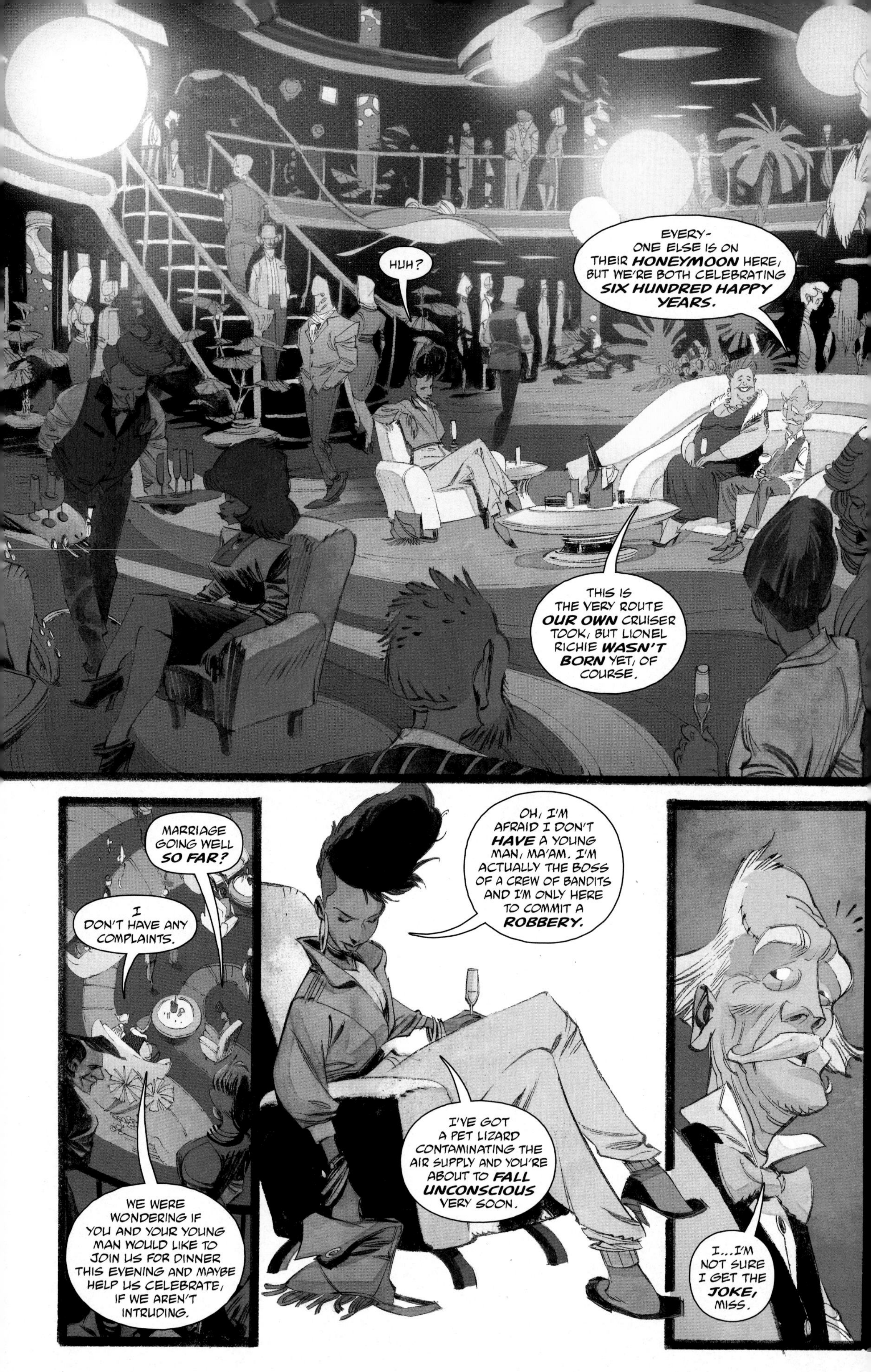
HUH?
EVERY-ONE ELSE IS ON THEIR HONEYMOON HERE, BUT WE'RE BOTH CELEBRATING SIX HUNDRED HAPPY YEARS.
THIS IS THE VERY ROUTE OUR OWN CRUISER TOOK, BUT LIONEL RICHIE WASN'T BORN YET, OF COURSE.
MARRIAGE GOING WELL SO FAR?
I DON'T HAVE ANY COMPLAINTS.
WE WERE WONDERING IF YOU AND YOUR YOUNG MAN WOULD LIKE TO JOIN US FOR DINNER THIS EVENING AND MAYBE HELP US CELEBRATE, IF WE AREN'T INTRUDING.
OH, I'M AFRAID I DON'T HAVE A YOUNG MAN, MA'AM. I'M ACTUALLY THE BOSS OF A CREW OF BANDITS AND I'M ONLY HERE TO COMMIT A ROBBERY.
I'VE GOT A PET LIZARD CONTAMINATING THE AIR SUPPLY AND YOU'RE ABOUT TO FALL UNCONSCIOUS VERY SOON.
I...I'M NOT SURE I GET THE JOKE, MISS.

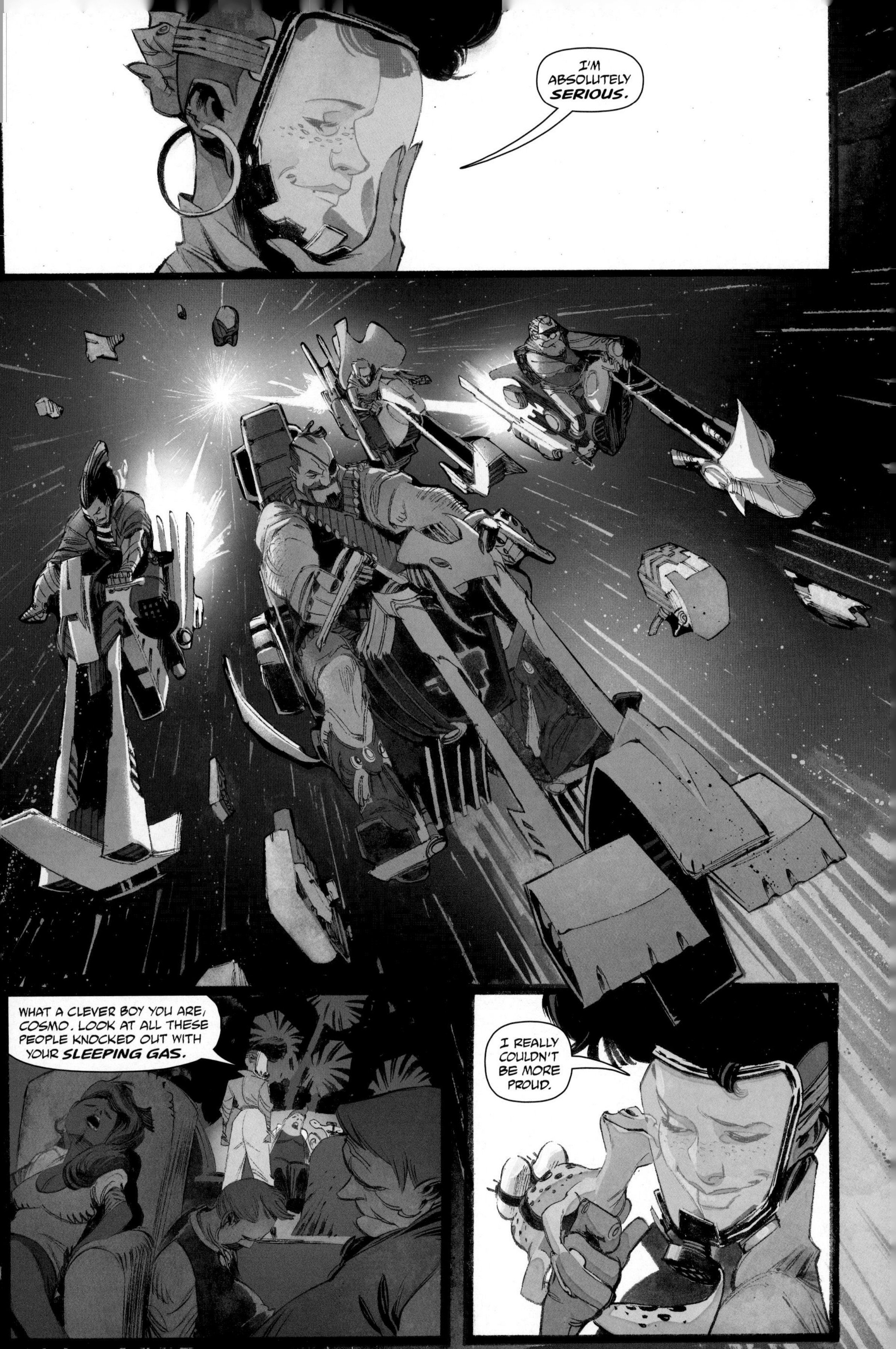
I'M ABSOLUTELY SERIOUS.
WHAT A CLEVER BOY YOU ARE, COSMO. LOOK AT ALL THESE PEOPLE KNOCKED OUT WITH YOUR SLEEPING GAS.
I REALLY COULDN'T BE MORE PROUD.

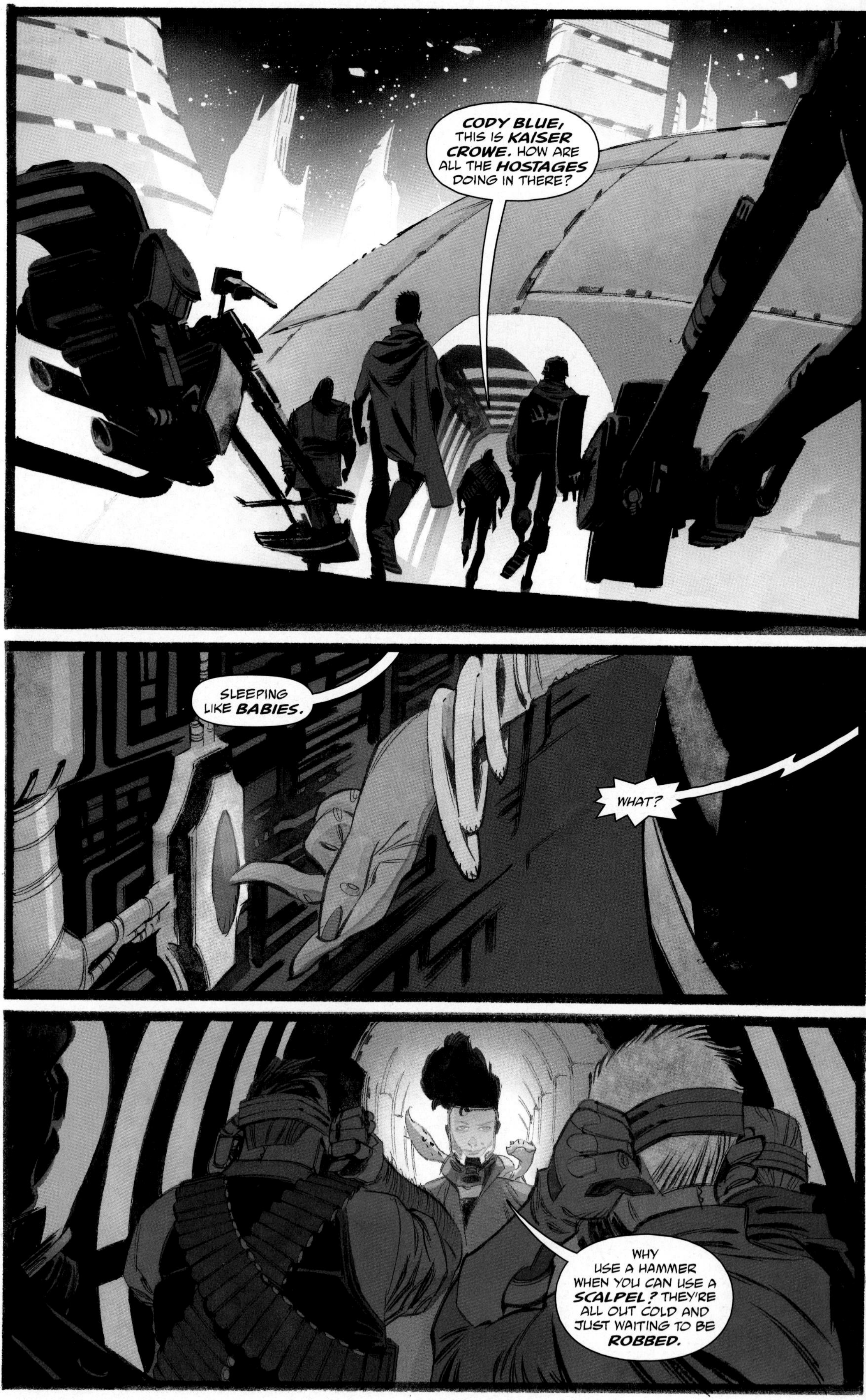
CODY BLUE, THIS IS KAISER CROWE. HOW ARE ALL THE HOSTAGES DOING IN THERE?
SLEEPING LIKE BABIES.
WHAT?
WHY USE A HAMMER WHEN YOU CAN USE A SCALPEL? THEY'RE ALL OUT COLD AND JUST WAITING TO BE ROBBED.

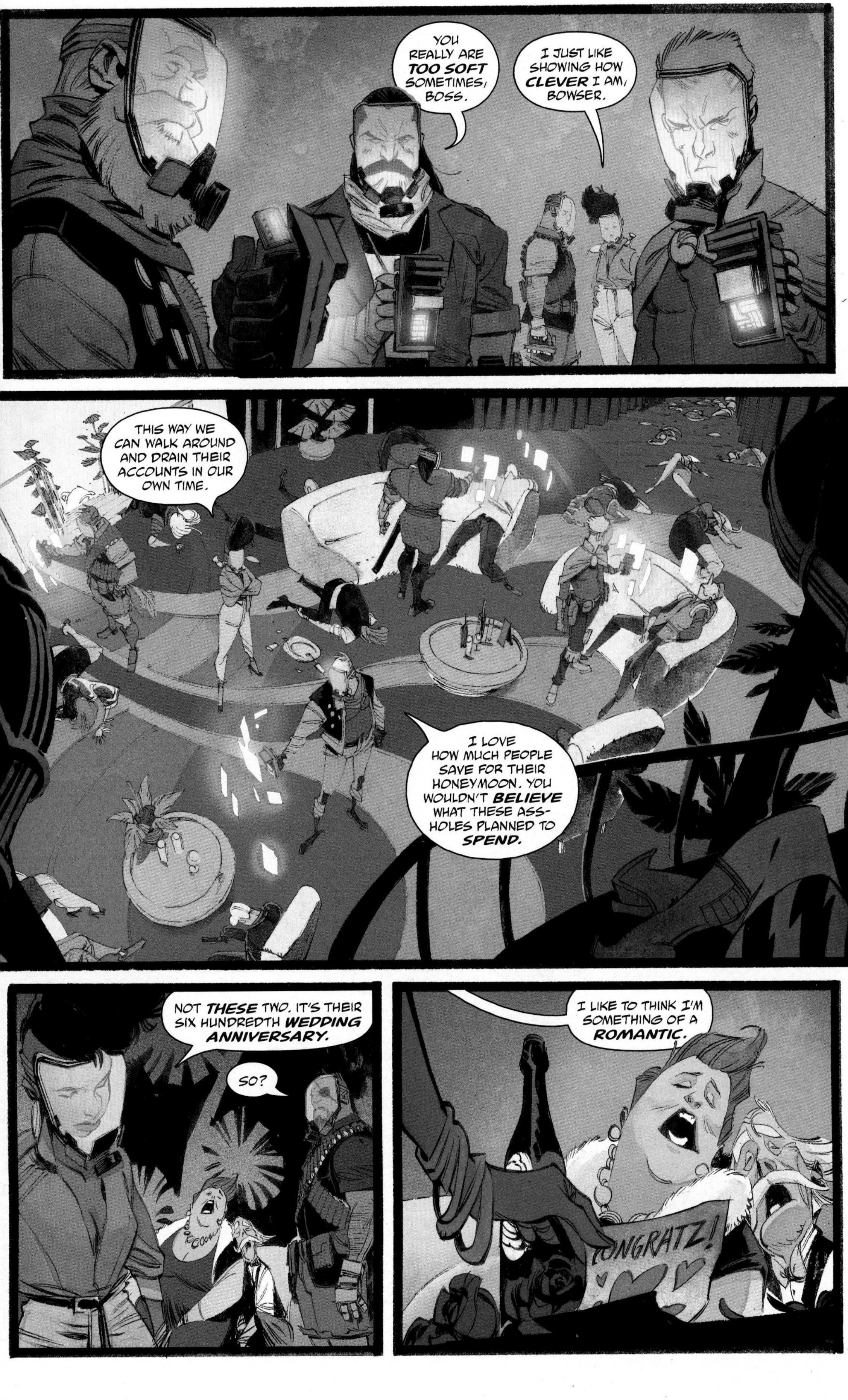
YOU REALLY ARE TOO SOFT SOMETIMES, BOSS.
I JUST LIKE SHOWING HOW CLEVER I AM, BOWSER.
THIS WAY WE CAN WALK AROUND AND DRAIN THEIR ACCOUNTS IN OUR OWN TIME.
I LOVE HOW MUCH PEOPLE SAVE FOR THEIR HONEYMOON. YOU WOULDN'T BELIEVE WHAT THESE ASS-HOLES PLANNED TO SPEND.
NOT THESE TWO. IT'S THEIR SIX HUNDREDTH WEDDING ANNIVERSARY.
SO?
I LIKE TO THINK I'M SOMETHING OF A ROMANTIC.
CONGRATZ!

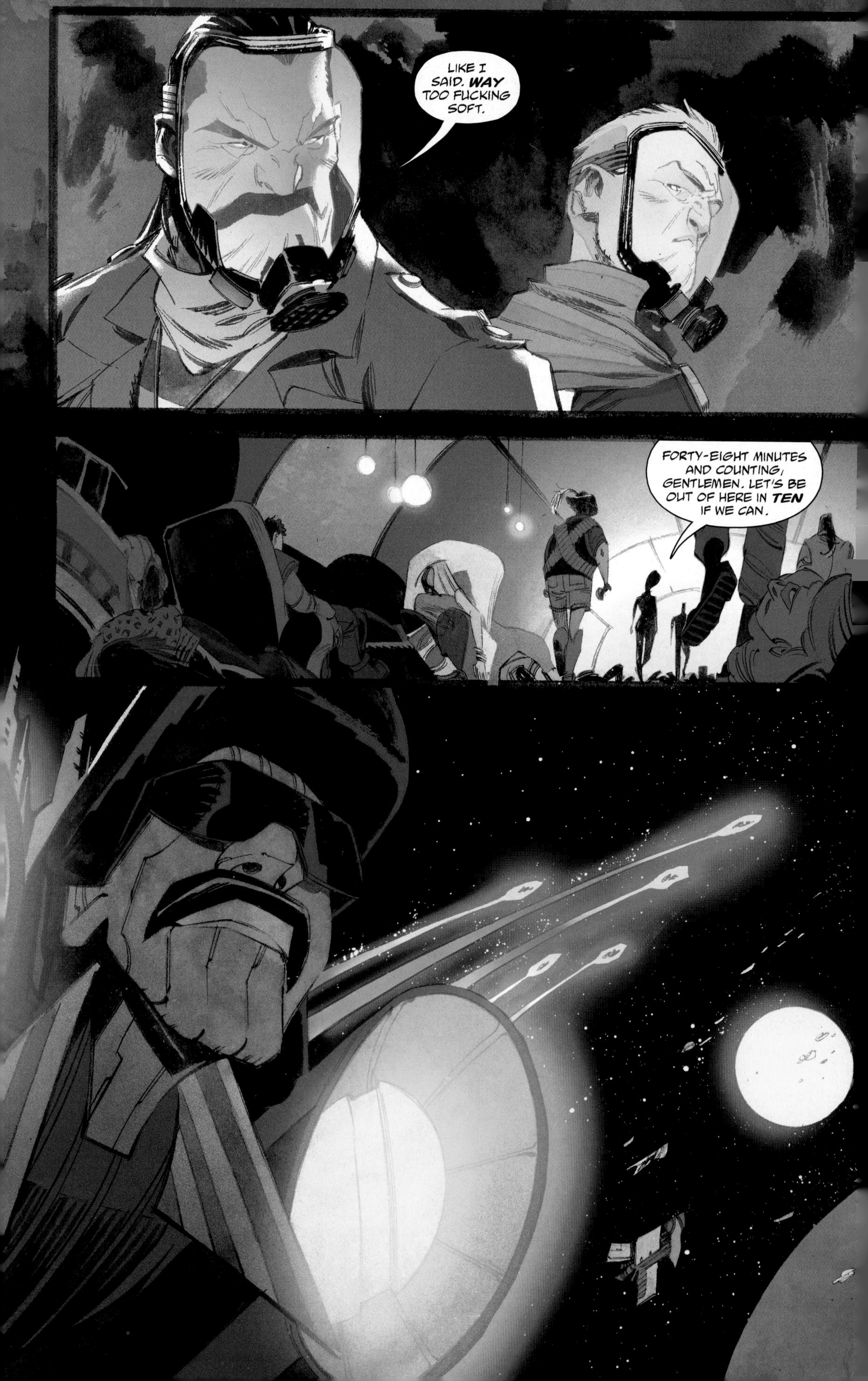
LIKE I SAID. **WAY** TOO FUCKING SOFT.
FORTY-EIGHT MINUTES AND COUNTING, GENTLEMEN. LET'S BE OUT OF HERE IN **TEN** IF WE CAN.

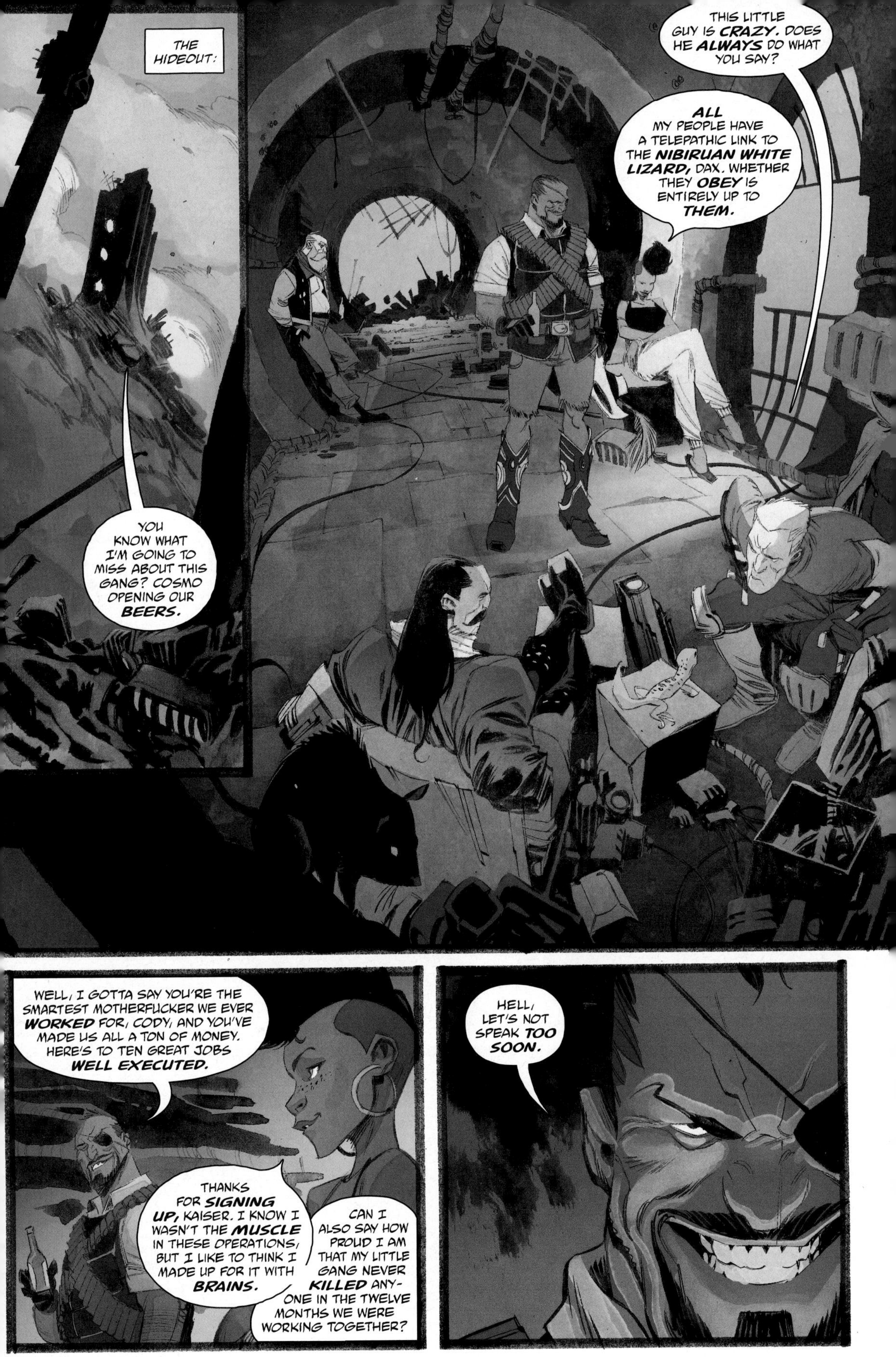
THE HIDEOUT:
YOU KNOW WHAT I'M GOING TO MISS ABOUT THIS GANG? COSMO OPENING OUR BEERS.
THIS LITTLE GUY IS CRAZY. DOES HE ALWAYS DO WHAT YOU SAY?
ALL MY PEOPLE HAVE A TELEPATHIC LINK TO THE NIBIRUAN WHITE LIZARD, DAX. WHETHER THEY OBEY IS ENTIRELY UP TO THEM.
WELL, I GOTTA SAY YOU'RE THE SMARTEST MOTHERFUCKER WE EVER WORKED FOR, CODY, AND YOU'VE MADE US ALL A TON OF MONEY. HERE'S TO TEN GREAT JOBS WELL EXECUTED.
THANKS FOR SIGNING UP, KAISER. I KNOW I WASN'T THE MUSCLE IN THESE OPERATIONS, BUT I LIKE TO THINK I MADE UP FOR IT WITH BRAINS.
CAN I ALSO SAY HOW PROUD I AM THAT MY LITTLE GANG NEVER KILLED ANY-ONE IN THE TWELVE MONTHS WE WERE WORKING TOGETHER?
HELL, LET'S NOT SPEAK TOO SOON.

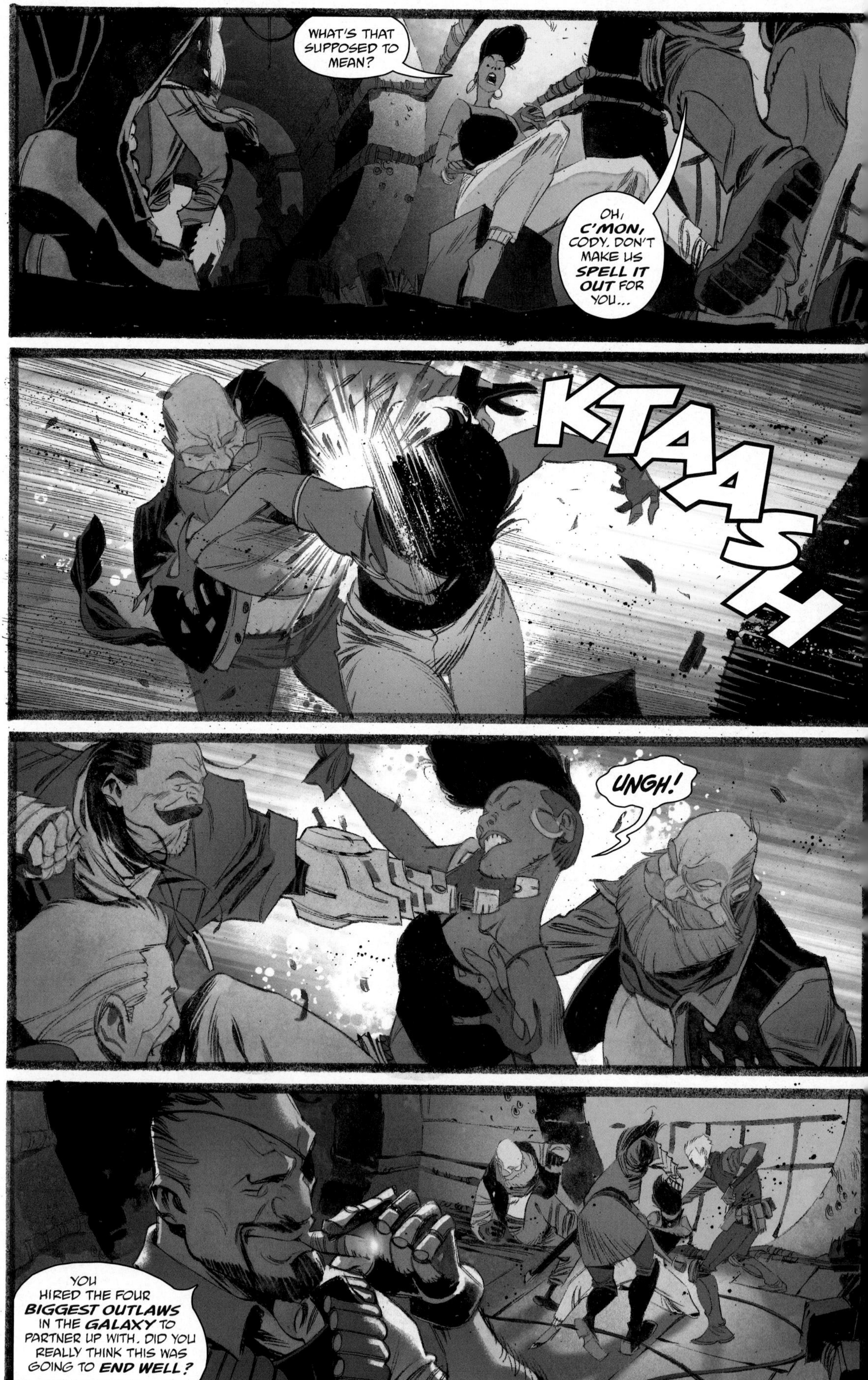
WHAT'S THAT SUPPOSED TO MEAN?
OH, C'MON, CODY. DON'T MAKE US SPELL IT OUT FOR YOU...
KTAASH
UNGH!
YOU HIRED THE FOUR BIGGEST OUTLAWS IN THE GALAXY TO PARTNER UP WITH. DID YOU REALLY THINK THIS WAS GOING TO END WELL?

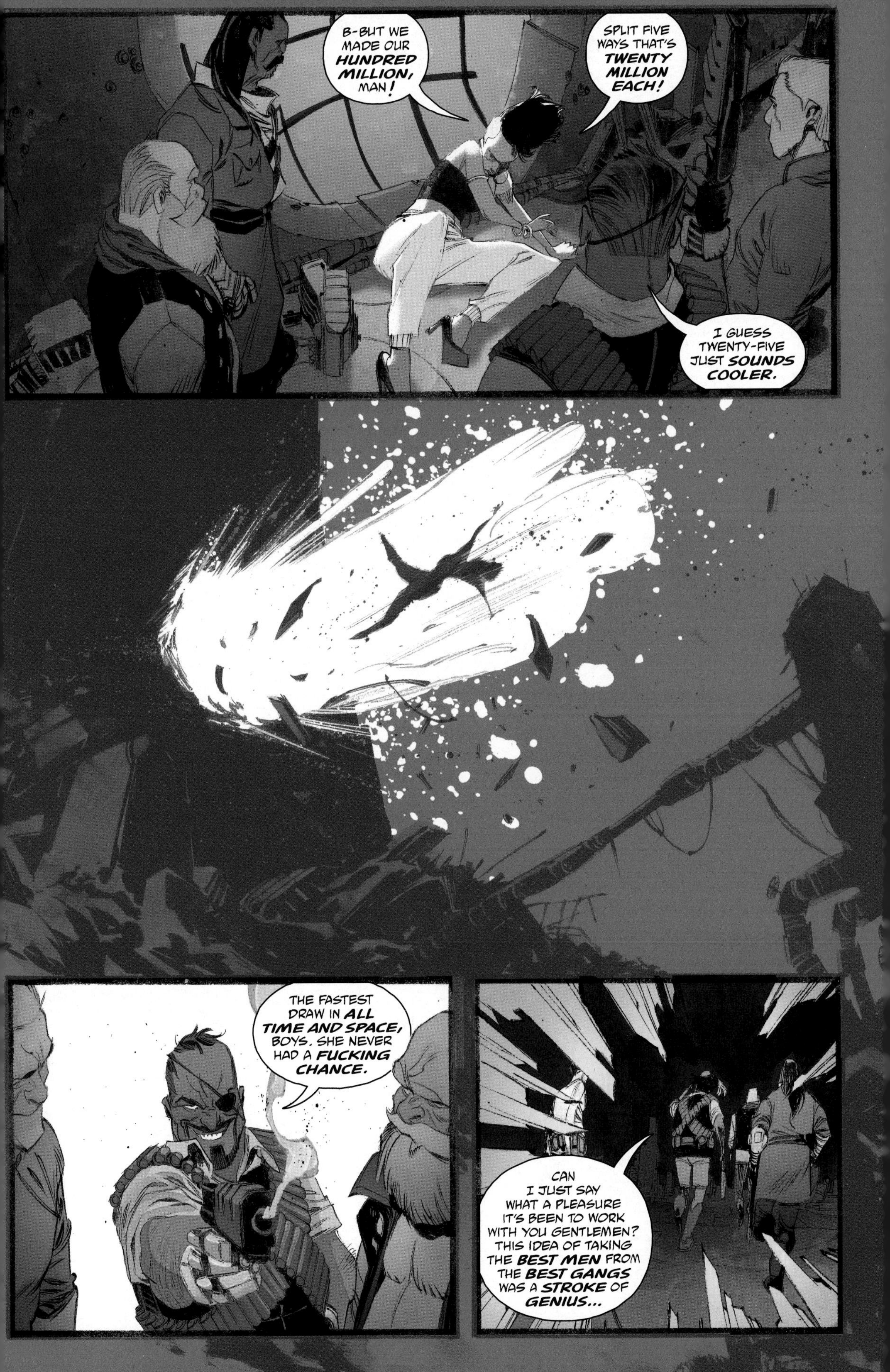
B-BUT WE MADE OUR HUNDRED MILLION, MAN!
SPLIT FIVE WAYS THAT'S TWENTY MILLION EACH!
I GUESS TWENTY-FIVE JUST SOUNDS COOLER.
THE FASTEST DRAW IN ALL TIME AND SPACE, BOYS. SHE NEVER HAD A FUCKING CHANCE.
CAN I JUST SAY WHAT A PLEASURE IT'S BEEN TO WORK WITH YOU GENTLEMEN? THIS IDEA OF TAKING THE BEST MEN FROM THE BEST GANGS WAS A STROKE OF GENIUS...

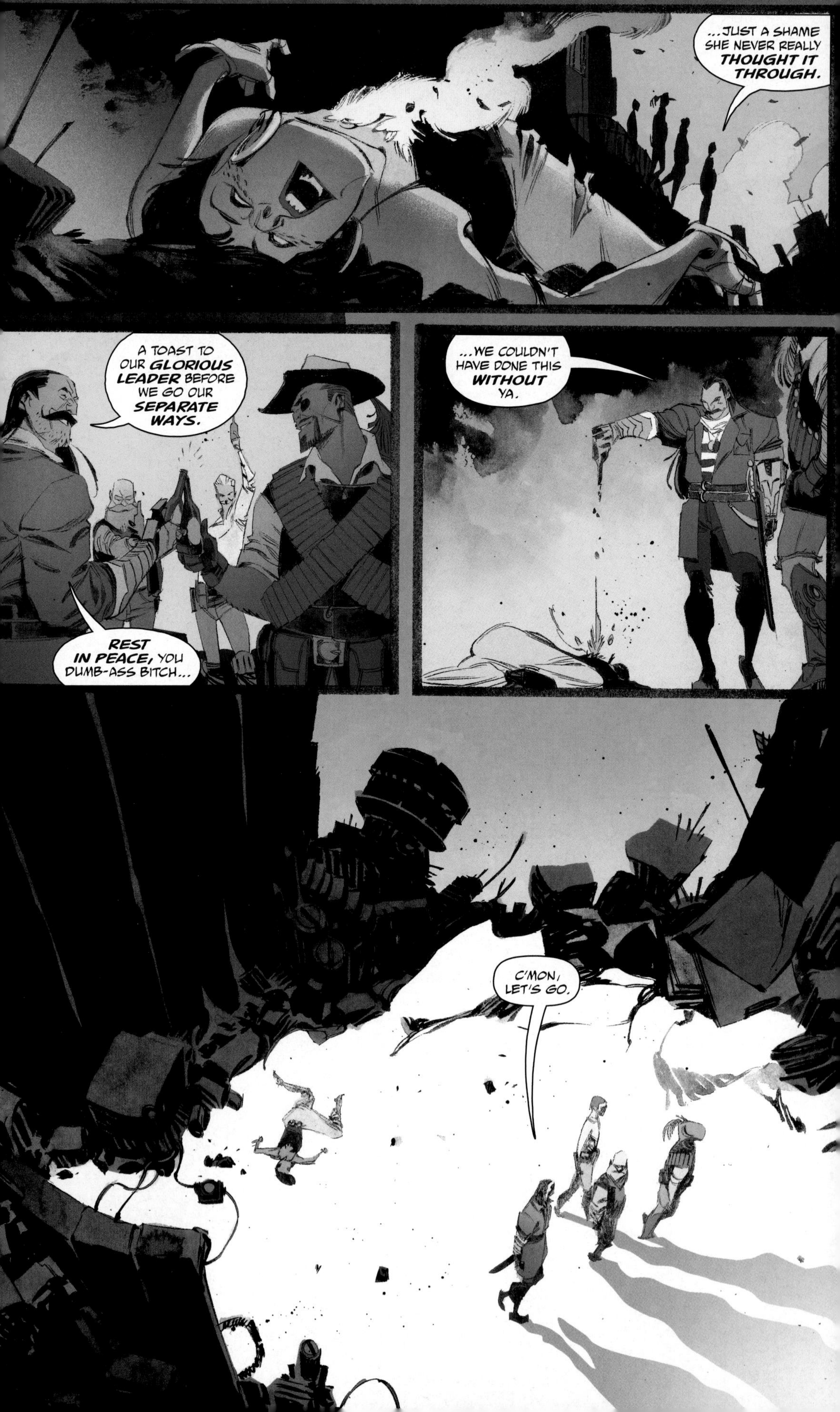
...JUST A SHAME SHE NEVER REALLY **THOUGHT IT THROUGH.**
A TOAST TO OUR **GLORIOUS LEADER** BEFORE WE GO OUR **SEPARATE WAYS.**
REST IN PEACE, YOU DUMB-ASS BITCH...
...WE COULDN'T HAVE DONE THIS **WITHOUT** YA.
C'MON, LET'S GO.

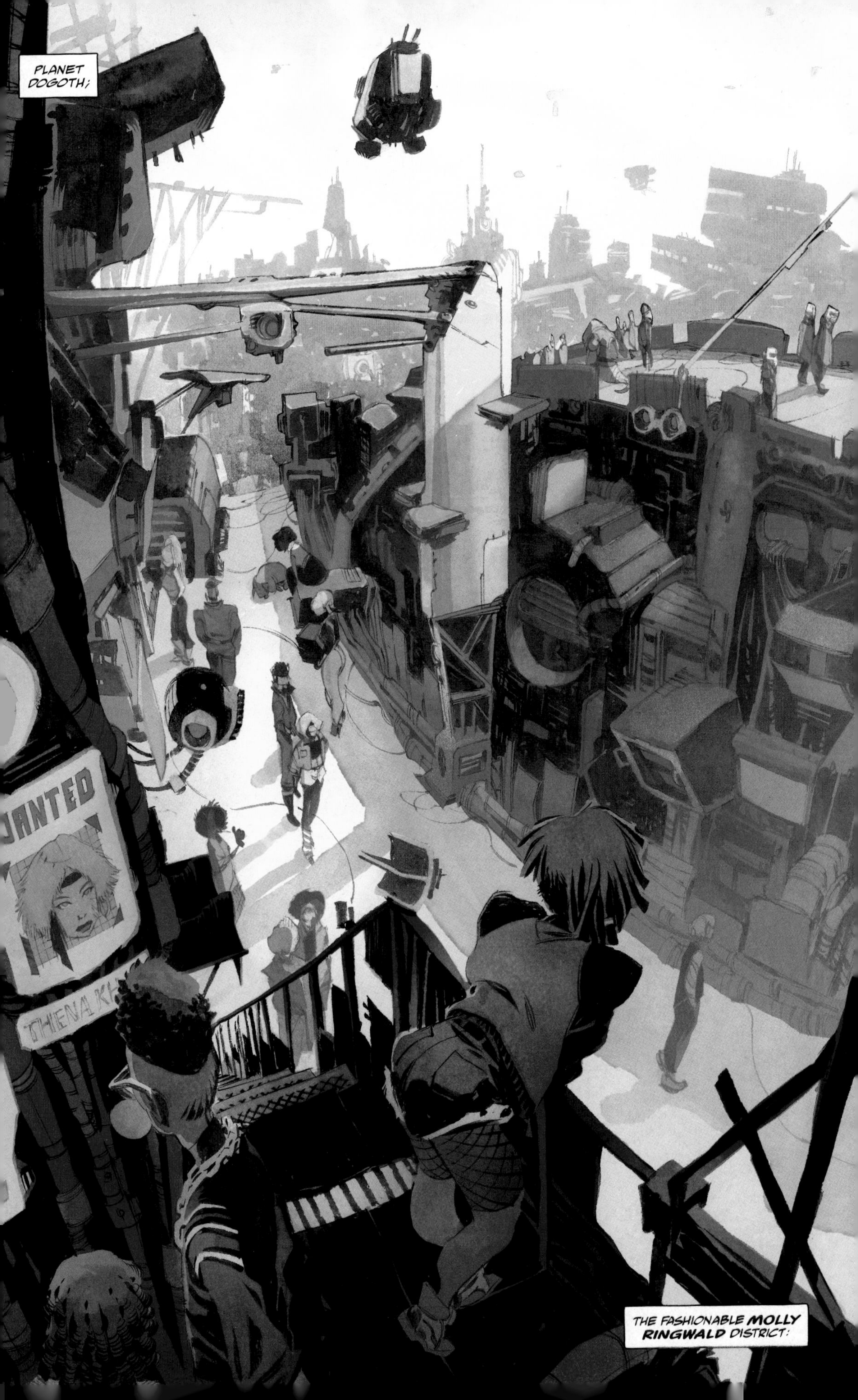
PLANET DOGOTH;
THE FASHIONABLE MOLLY RINGWALD DISTRICT:

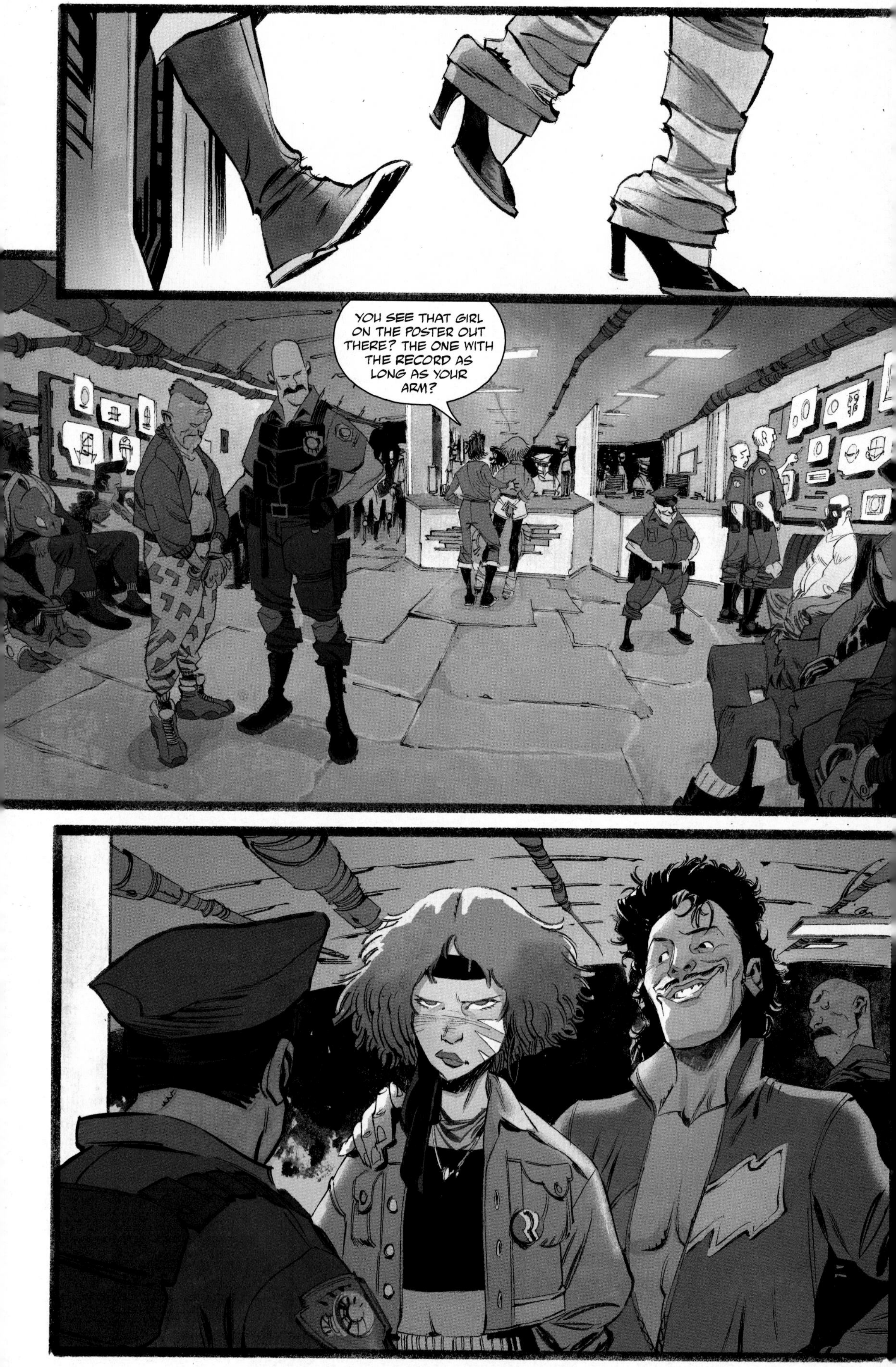
YOU SEE THAT GIRL ON THE POSTER OUT THERE? THE ONE WITH THE RECORD AS LONG AS YOUR ARM?

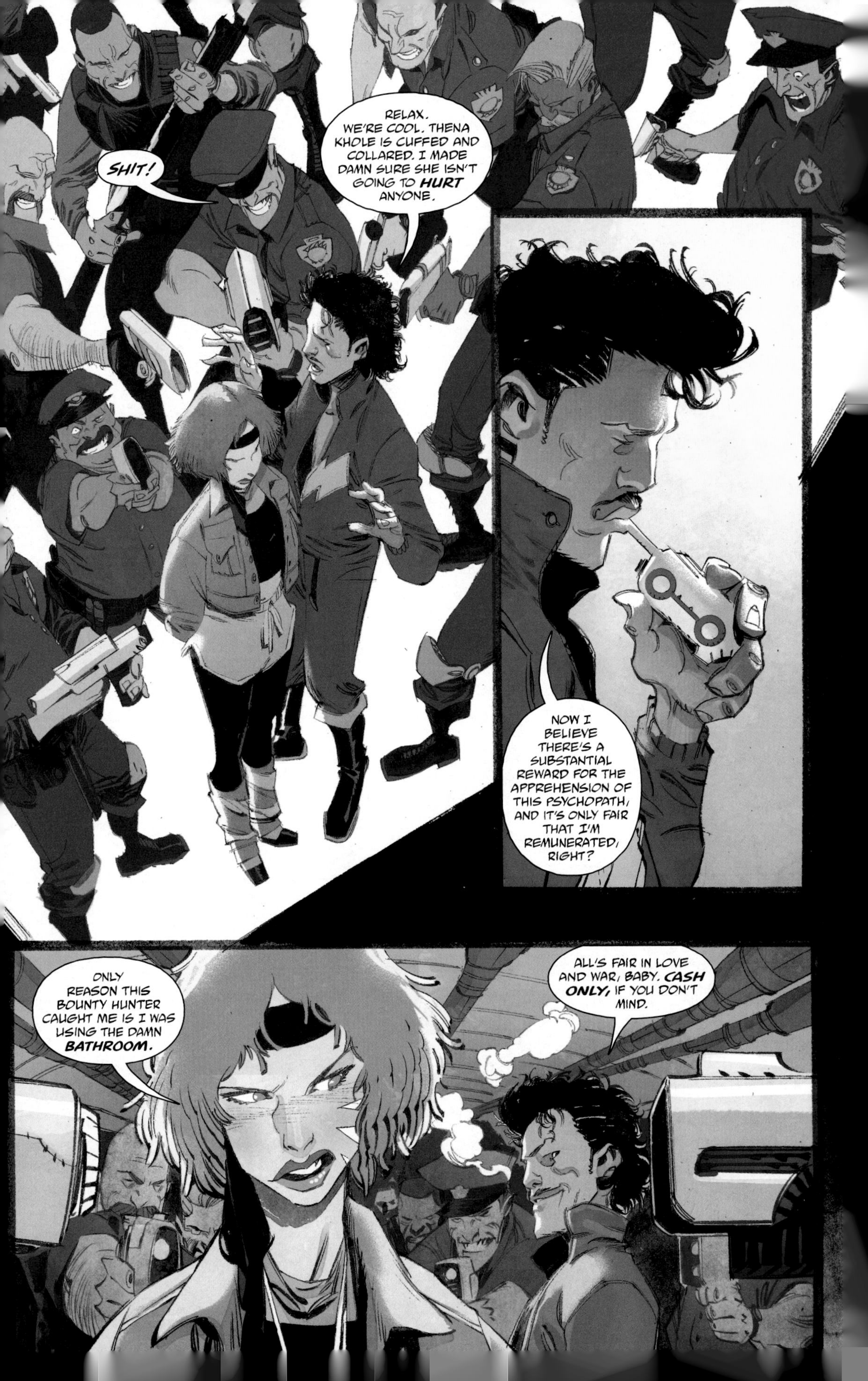
SHIT!
RELAX. WE'RE COOL. THENA KHOLE IS CUFFED AND COLLARED. I MADE DAMN SURE SHE ISN'T GOING TO HURT ANYONE.
NOW I BELIEVE THERE'S A SUBSTANTIAL REWARD FOR THE APPREHENSION OF THIS PSYCHOPATH, AND IT'S ONLY FAIR THAT I'M REMUNERATED, RIGHT?
ONLY REASON THIS BOUNTY HUNTER CAUGHT ME IS I WAS USING THE DAMN BATHROOM.
ALL'S FAIR IN LOVE AND WAR, BABY. CASH ONLY, IF YOU DON'T MIND.

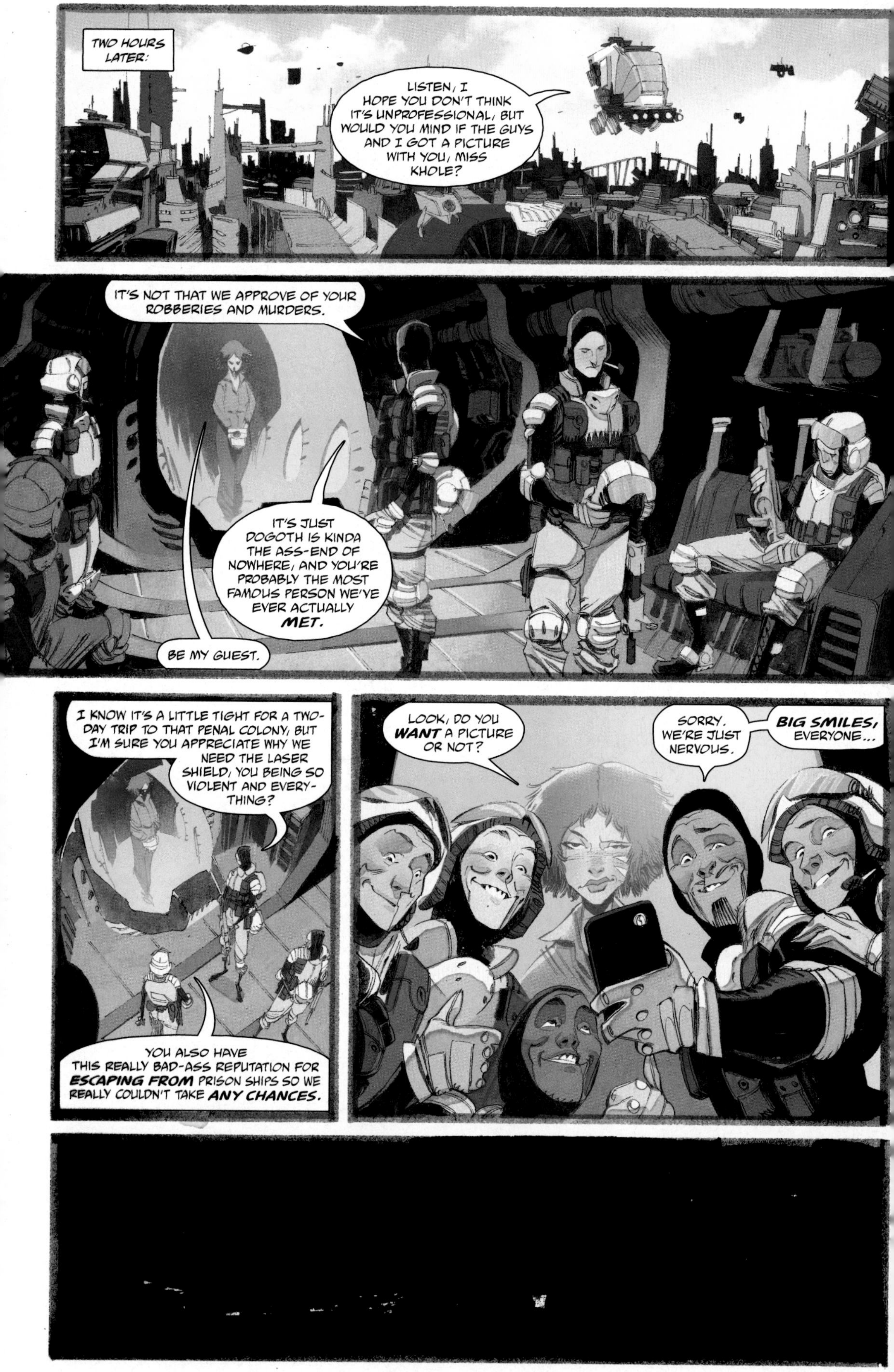
TWO HOURS LATER:
LISTEN, I HOPE YOU DON'T THINK IT'S UNPROFESSIONAL, BUT WOULD YOU MIND IF THE GUYS AND I GOT A PICTURE WITH YOU, MISS KHOLE?
IT'S NOT THAT WE APPROVE OF YOUR ROBBERIES AND MURDERS.
IT'S JUST DOGOTH IS KINDA THE ASS-END OF NOWHERE, AND YOU'RE PROBABLY THE MOST FAMOUS PERSON WE'VE EVER ACTUALLY MET.
BE MY GUEST.
I KNOW IT'S A LITTLE TIGHT FOR A TWO-DAY TRIP TO THAT PENAL COLONY, BUT I'M SURE YOU APPRECIATE WHY WE NEED THE LASER SHIELD, YOU BEING SO VIOLENT AND EVERYTHING?
YOU ALSO HAVE THIS REALLY BAD-ASS REPUTATION FOR ESCAPING FROM PRISON SHIPS SO WE REALLY COULDN'T TAKE ANY CHANCES.
LOOK, DO YOU WANT A PICTURE OR NOT?
SORRY. WE'RE JUST NERVOUS.
BIG SMILES, EVERYONE...

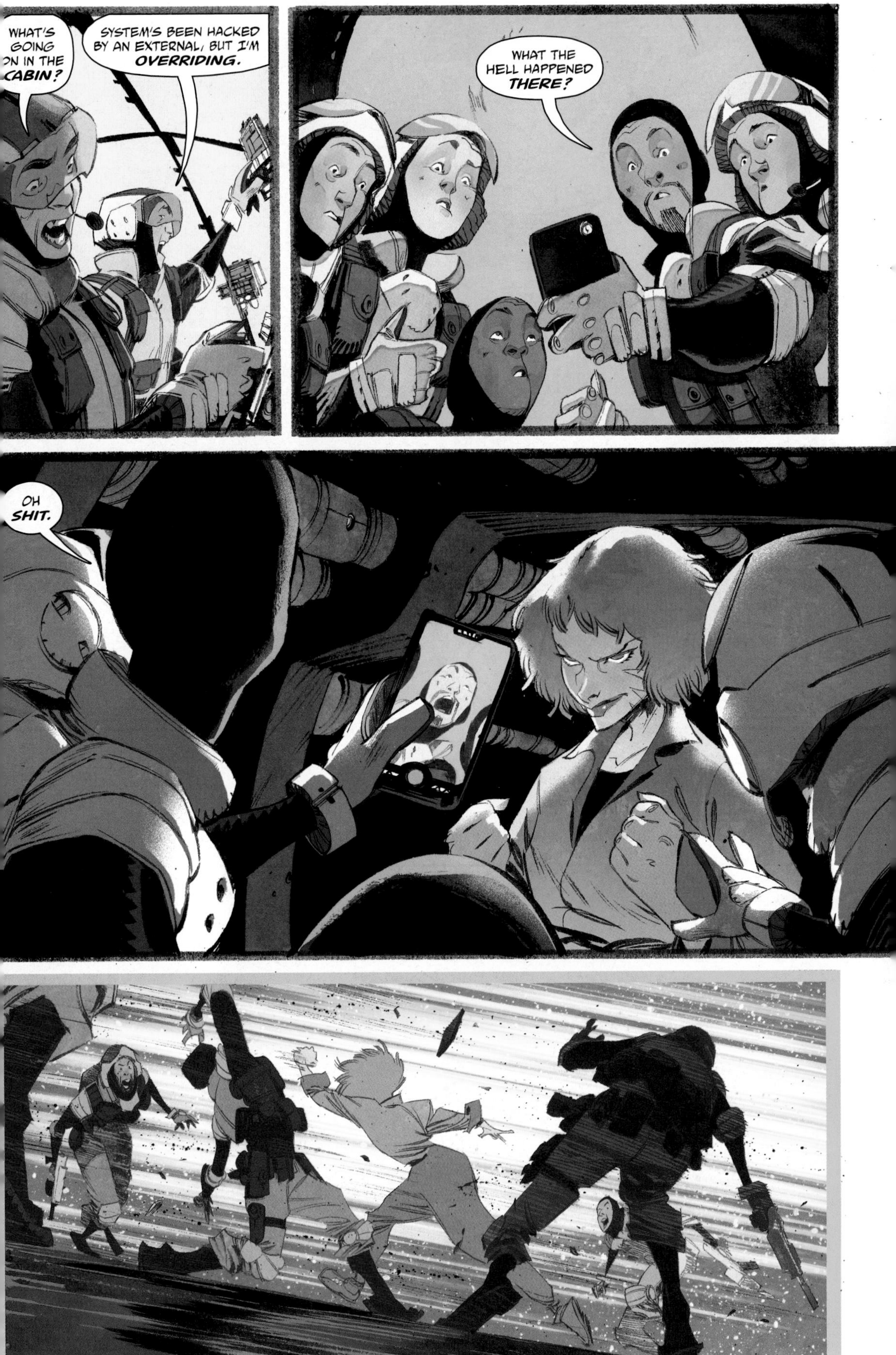
WHAT'S GOING ON IN THE CABIN?
SYSTEM'S BEEN HACKED BY AN EXTERNAL, BUT I'M OVERRIDING.
WHAT THE HELL HAPPENED THERE?
OH SHIT.

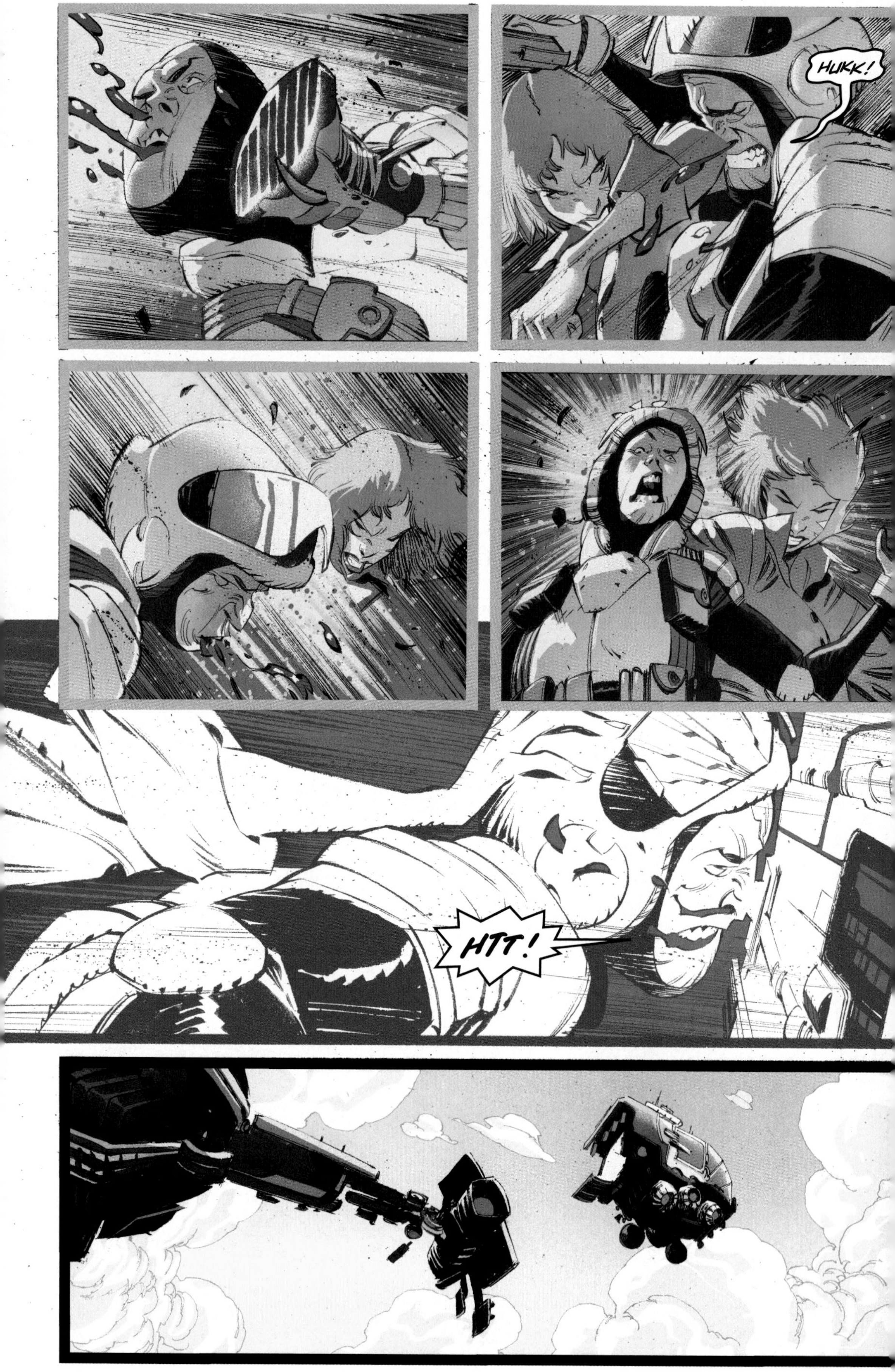
HUKK!
HTT!

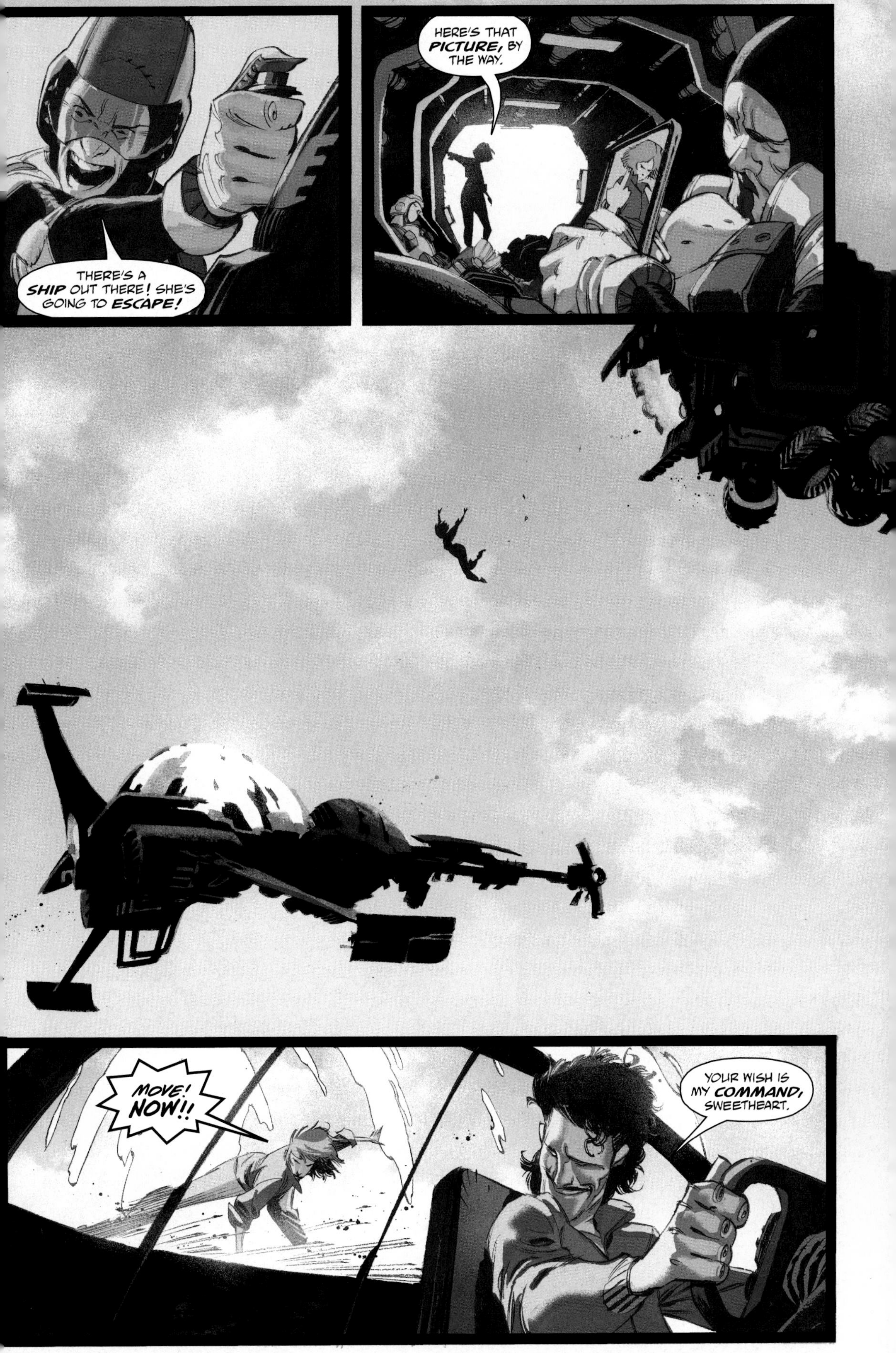
THERE'S A SHIP OUT THERE! SHE'S GOING TO ESCAPE!
HERE'S THAT PICTURE, BY THE WAY.
MOVE! NOW!!
YOUR WISH IS MY COMMAND, SWEETHEART.

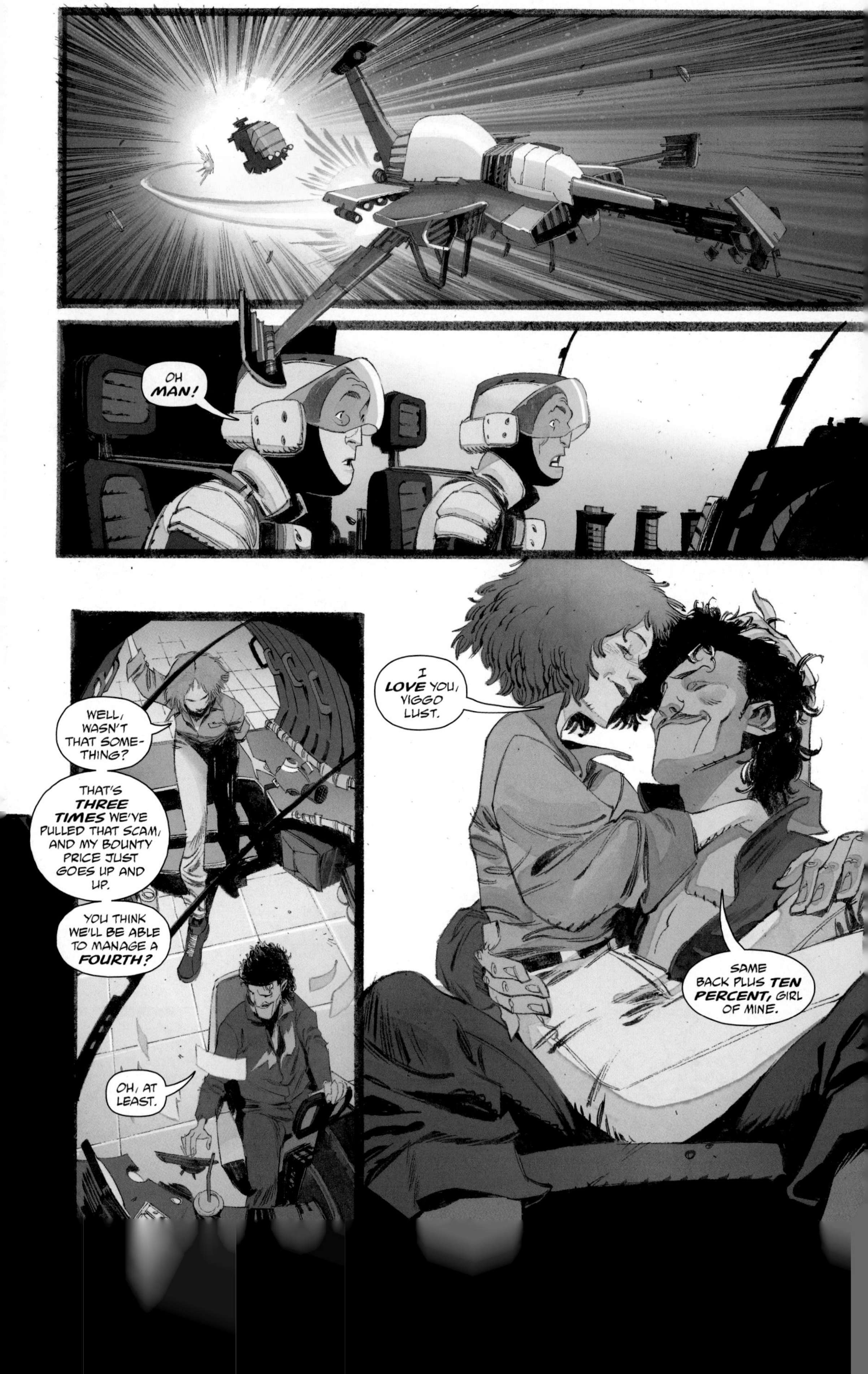
OH MAN!
WELL, WASN'T THAT SOMETHING?
THAT'S THREE TIMES WE'VE PULLED THAT SCAM, AND MY BOUNTY PRICE JUST GOES UP AND UP.
YOU THINK WE'LL BE ABLE TO MANAGE A FOURTH?
OH, AT LEAST.
I LOVE YOU, VIGGO LUST.
SAME BACK PLUS TEN PERCENT, GIRL OF MINE.

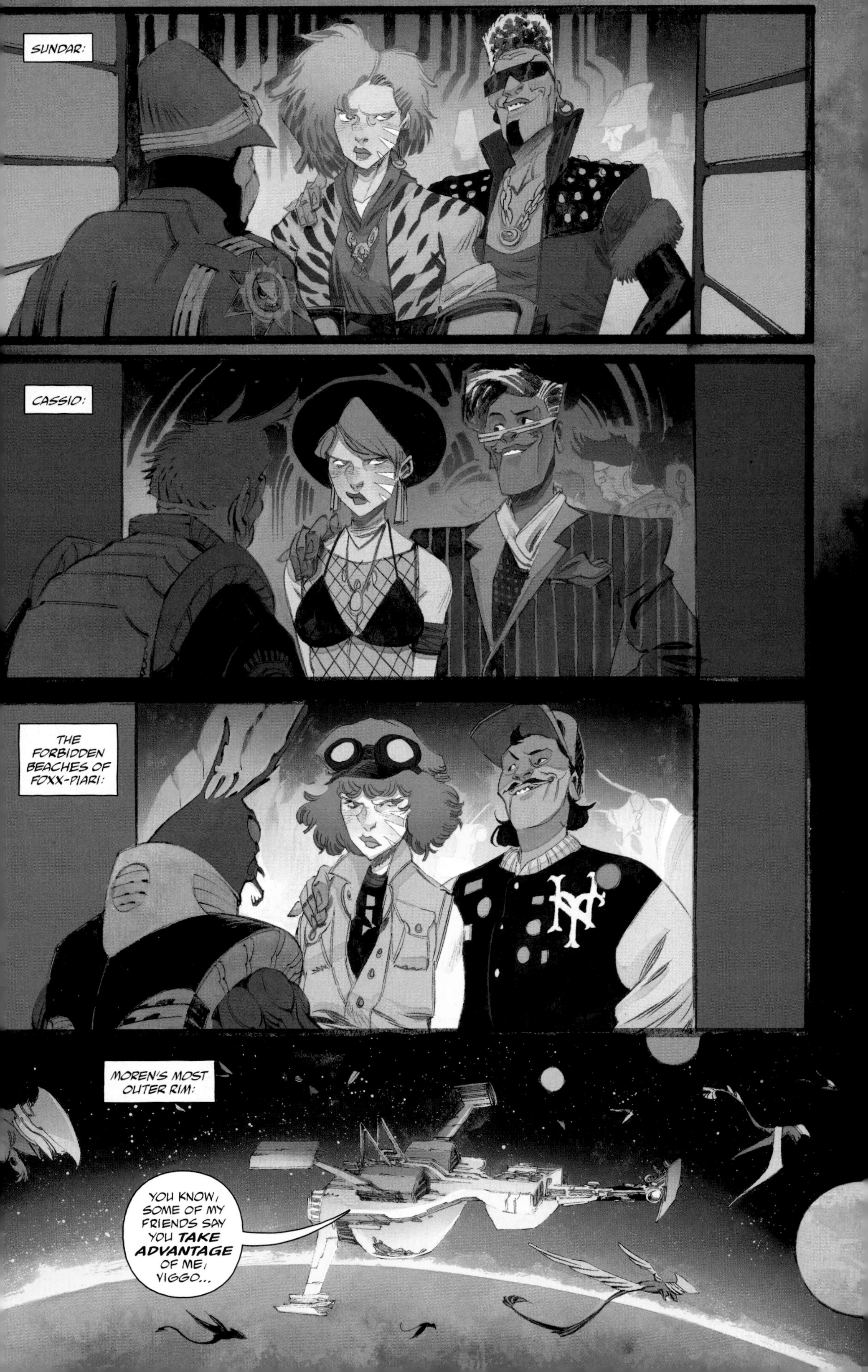
SUNDAR:
CASSIO:
THE FORBIDDEN BEACHES OF FOXX-PIARI:
MOREN'S MOST OUTER RIM:
YOU KNOW, SOME OF MY FRIENDS SAY YOU **TAKE ADVANTAGE** OF ME, VIGGO...

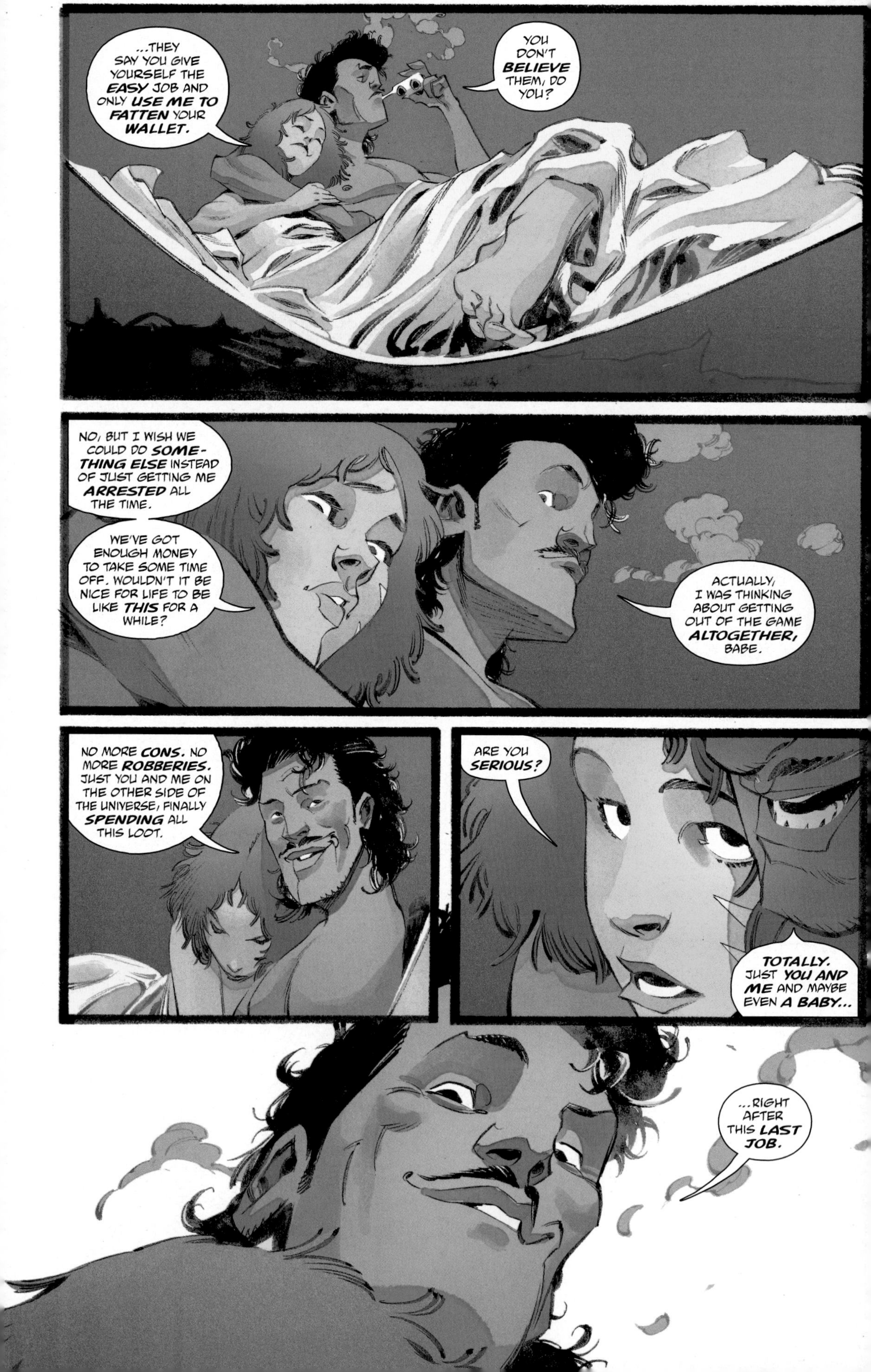
...THEY SAY YOU GIVE YOURSELF THE EASY JOB AND ONLY USE ME TO FATTEN YOUR WALLET.
YOU DON'T BELIEVE THEM, DO YOU?
NO, BUT I WISH WE COULD DO SOME-THING ELSE INSTEAD OF JUST GETTING ME ARRESTED ALL THE TIME.
WE'VE GOT ENOUGH MONEY TO TAKE SOME TIME OFF. WOULDN'T IT BE NICE FOR LIFE TO BE LIKE THIS FOR A WHILE?
ACTUALLY, I WAS THINKING ABOUT GETTING OUT OF THE GAME ALTOGETHER, BABE.
NO MORE CONS. NO MORE ROBBERIES. JUST YOU AND ME ON THE OTHER SIDE OF THE UNIVERSE, FINALLY SPENDING ALL THIS LOOT.
ARE YOU SERIOUS?
TOTALLY. JUST YOU AND ME AND MAYBE EVEN A BABY...
...RIGHT AFTER THIS LAST JOB.

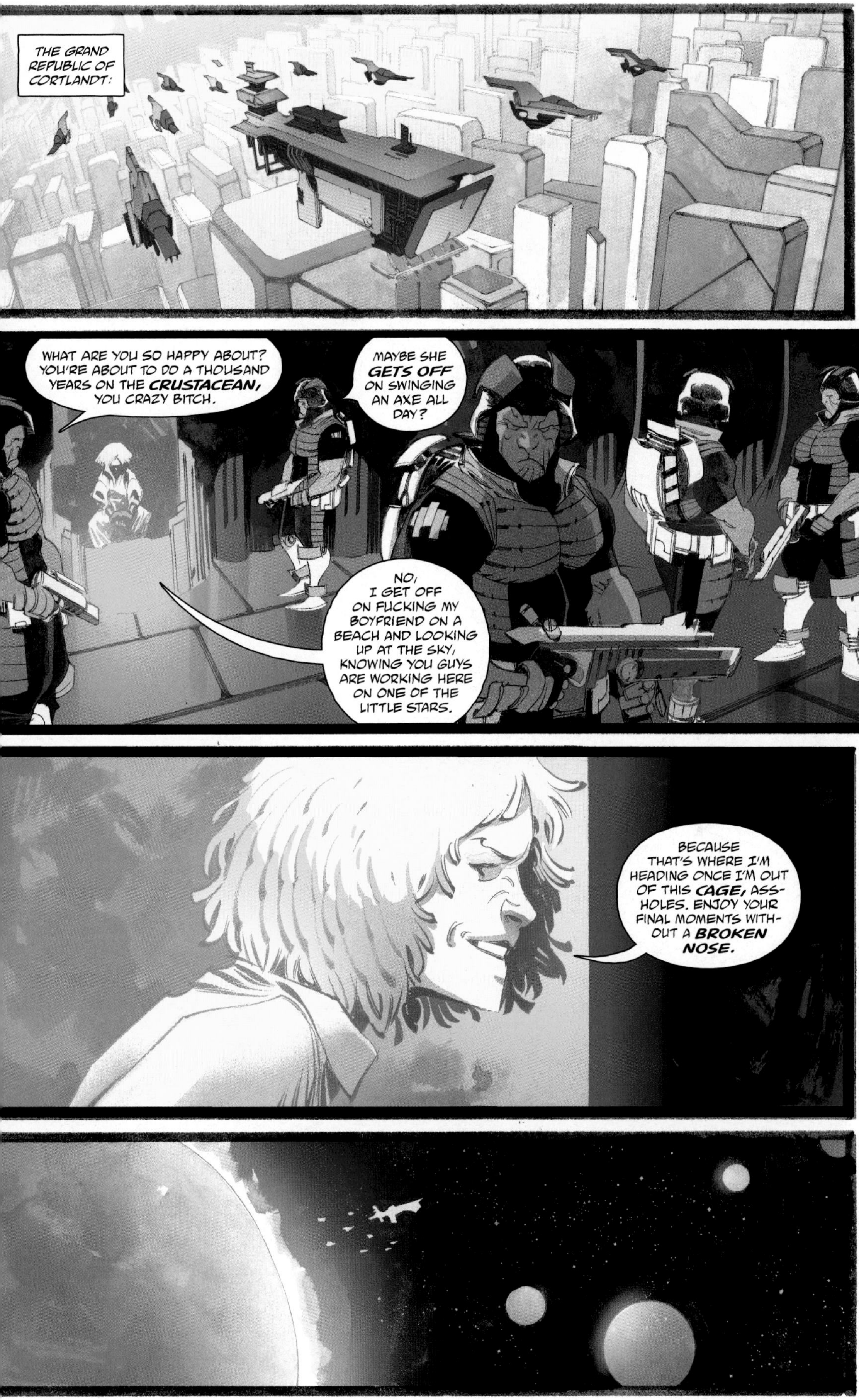
THE GRAND REPUBLIC OF CORTLANDT:
WHAT ARE YOU SO HAPPY ABOUT? YOU'RE ABOUT TO DO A THOUSAND YEARS ON THE **CRUSTACEAN,** YOU CRAZY BITCH.
MAYBE SHE **GETS OFF** ON SWINGING AN AXE ALL DAY?
NO, I GET OFF ON FUCKING MY BOYFRIEND ON A BEACH AND LOOKING UP AT THE SKY, KNOWING YOU GUYS ARE WORKING HERE ON ONE OF THE LITTLE STARS.
BECAUSE THAT'S WHERE I'M HEADING ONCE I'M OUT OF THIS **CAGE,** ASS-HOLES. ENJOY YOUR FINAL MOMENTS WITH-OUT A **BROKEN NOSE.**

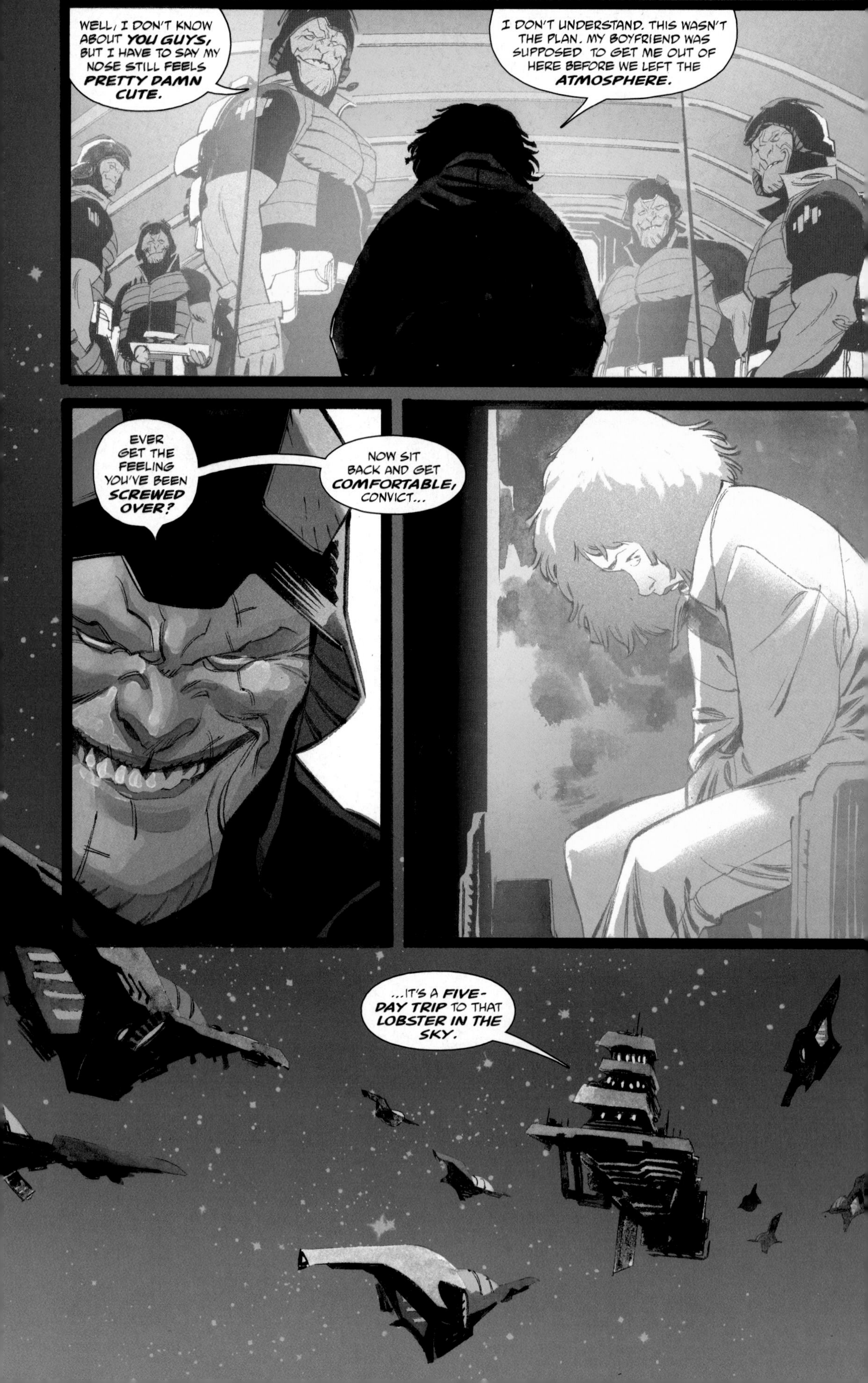
WELL, I DON'T KNOW ABOUT YOU GUYS, BUT I HAVE TO SAY MY NOSE STILL FEELS PRETTY DAMN CUTE.
I DON'T UNDERSTAND. THIS WASN'T THE PLAN. MY BOYFRIEND WAS SUPPOSED TO GET ME OUT OF HERE BEFORE WE LEFT THE ATMOSPHERE.
EVER GET THE FEELING YOU'VE BEEN SCREWED OVER?
NOW SIT BACK AND GET COMFORTABLE, CONVICT...
...IT'S A FIVE-DAY TRIP TO THAT LOBSTER IN THE SKY.

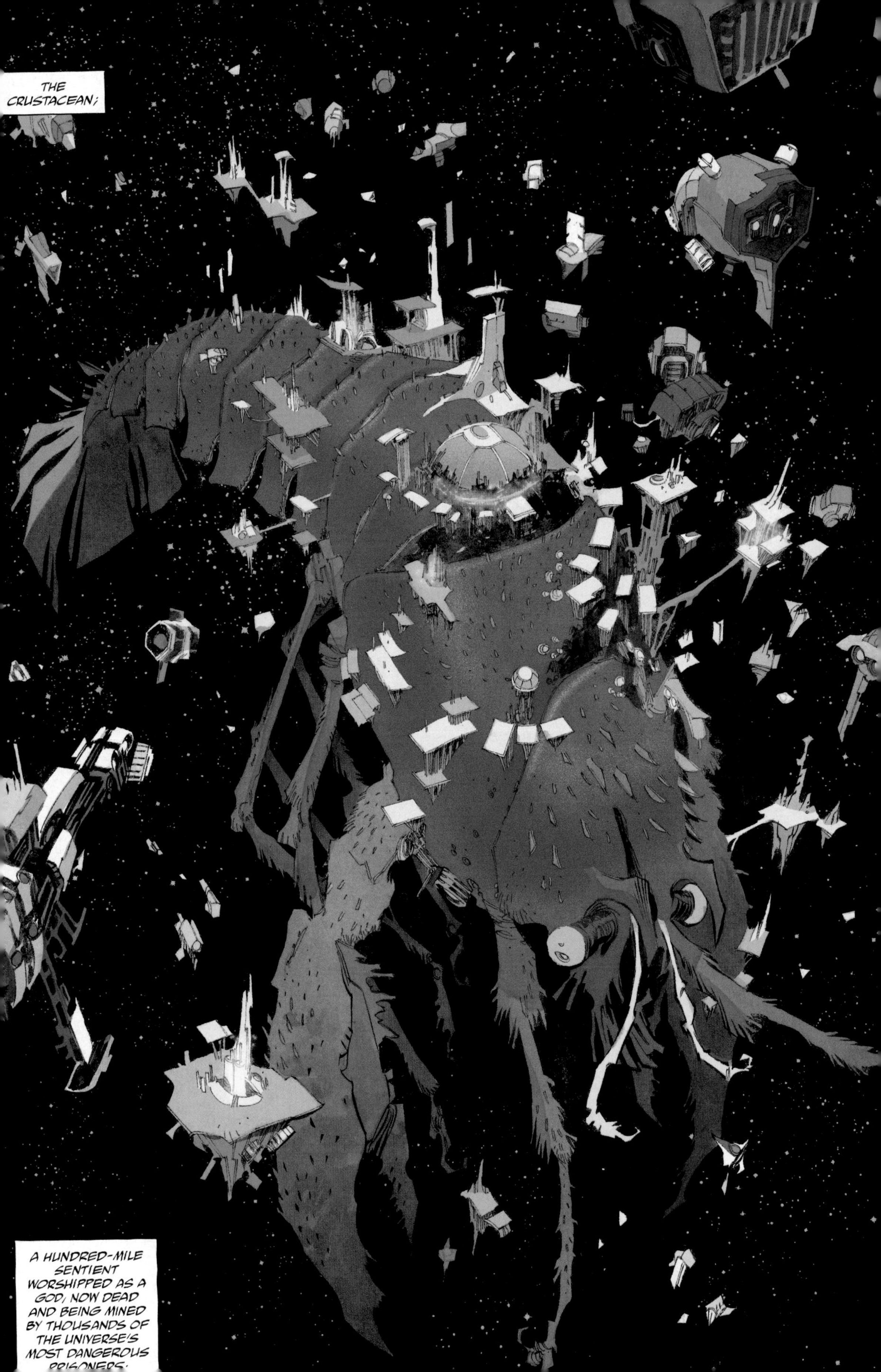
THE CRUSTACEAN;
A HUNDRED-MILE SENTIENT WORSHIPPED AS A GOD, NOW DEAD AND BEING MINED BY THOUSANDS OF THE UNIVERSE'S MOST DANGEROUS

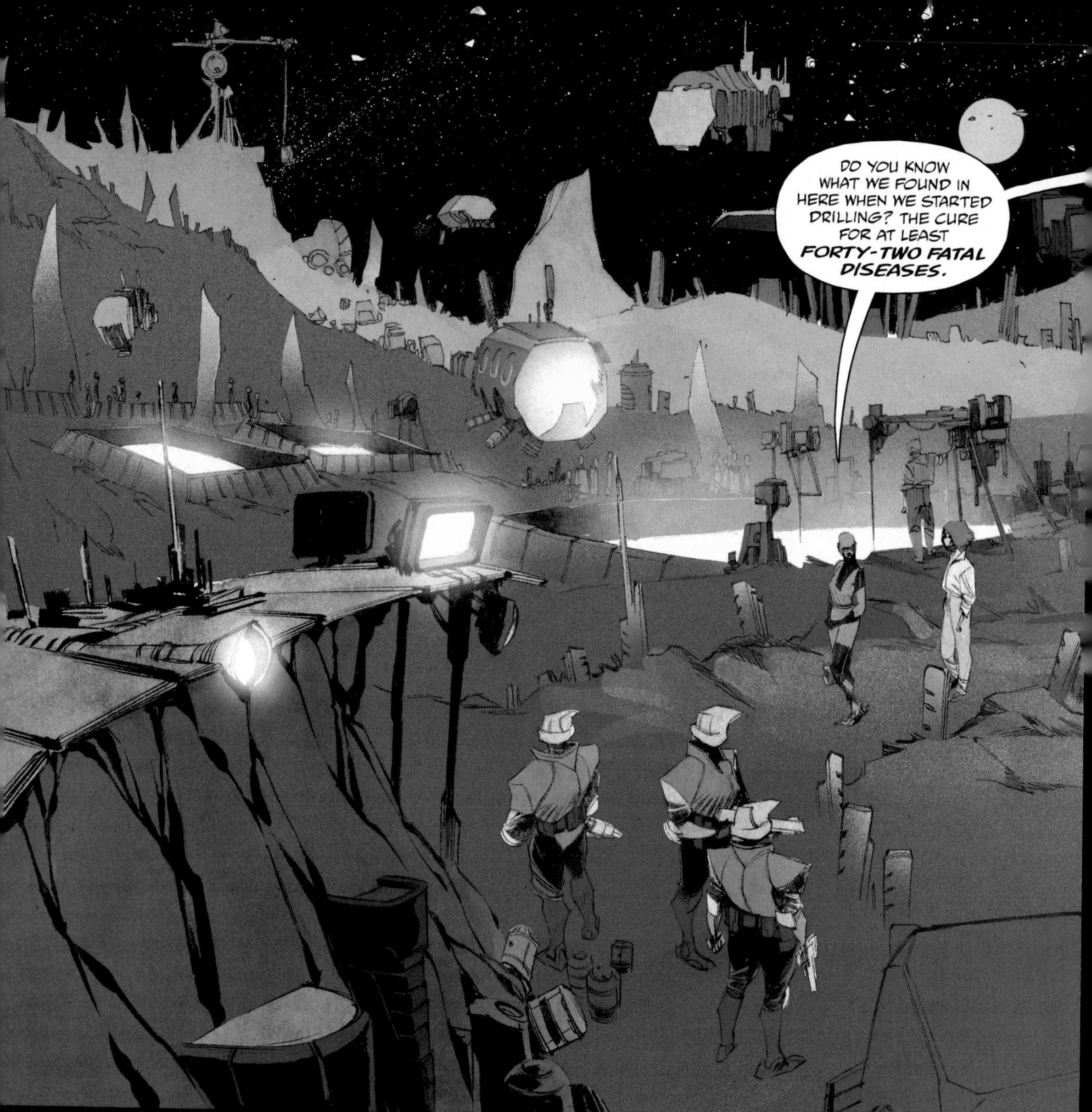
DO YOU KNOW WHAT WE FOUND IN HERE WHEN WE STARTED DRILLING? THE CURE FOR AT LEAST FORTY-TWO FATAL DISEASES.

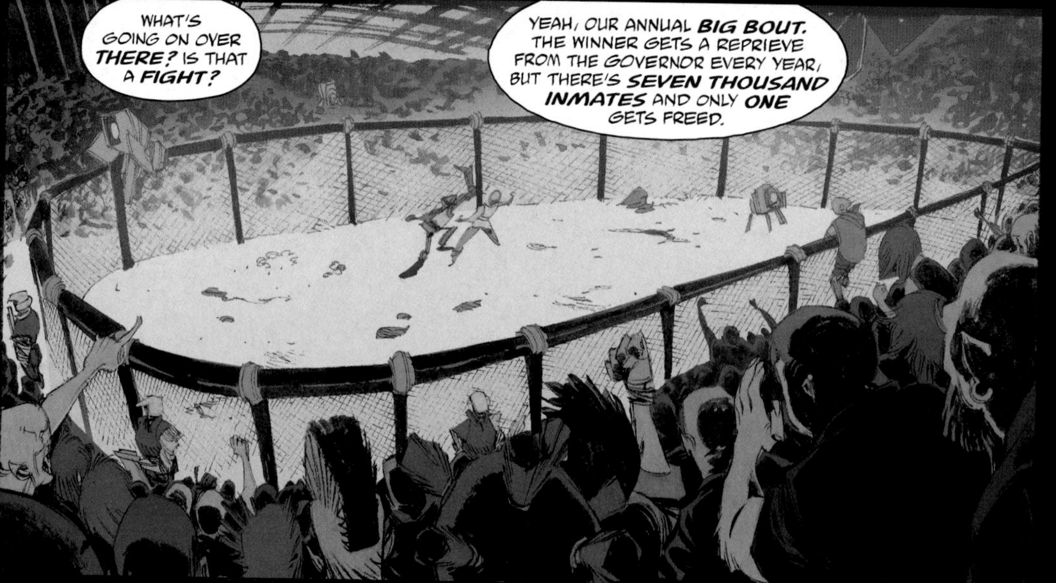
WHAT'S GOING ON OVER THERE? IS THAT A FIGHT?
YEAH, OUR ANNUAL BIG BOUT. THE WINNER GETS A REPRIEVE FROM THE GOVERNOR EVERY YEAR, BUT THERE'S SEVEN THOUSAND INMATES AND ONLY ONE GETS FREED.

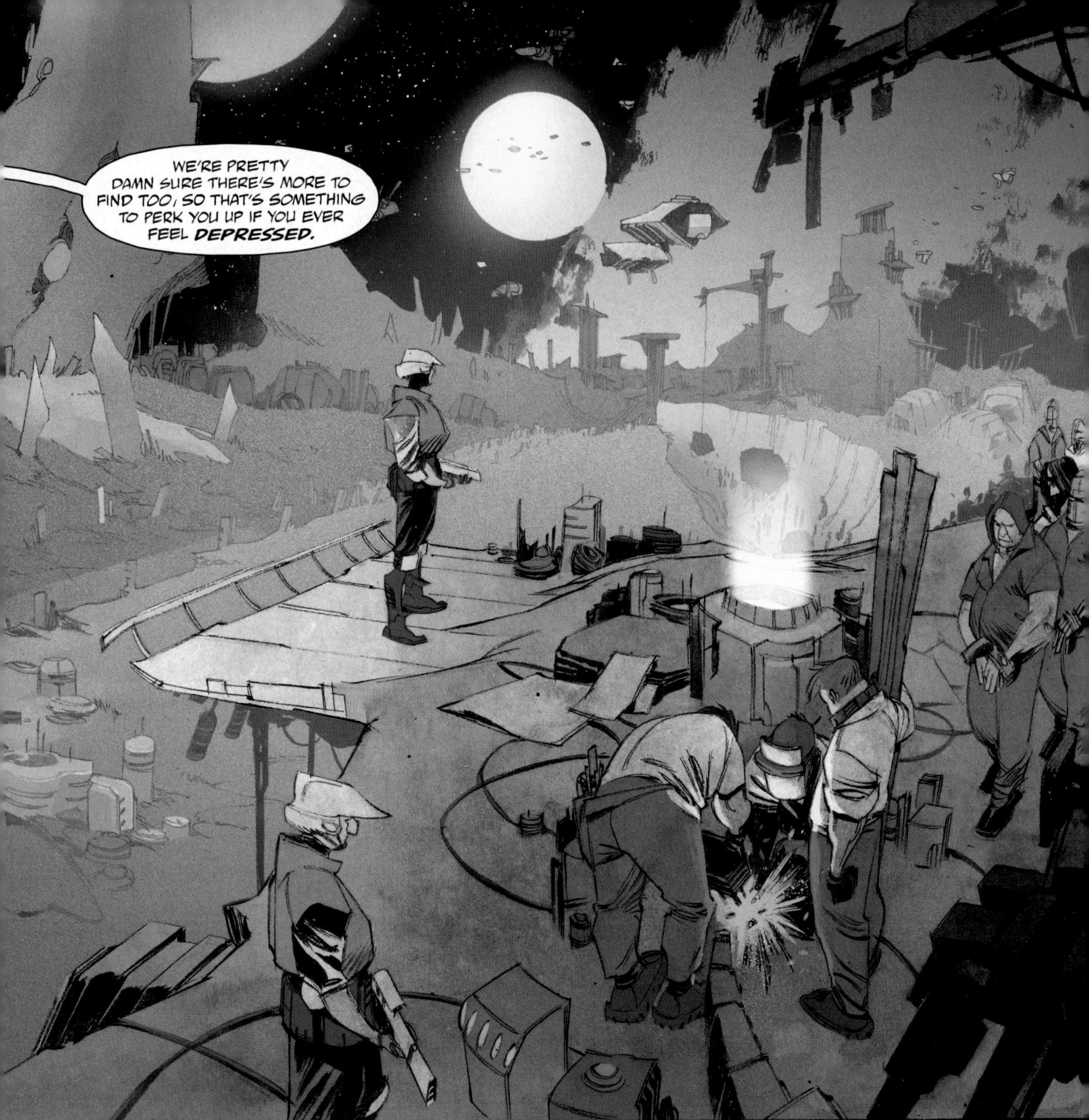
WE'RE PRETTY DAMN SURE THERE'S MORE TO FIND TOO, SO THAT'S SOMETHING TO PERK YOU UP IF YOU EVER FEEL DEPRESSED.

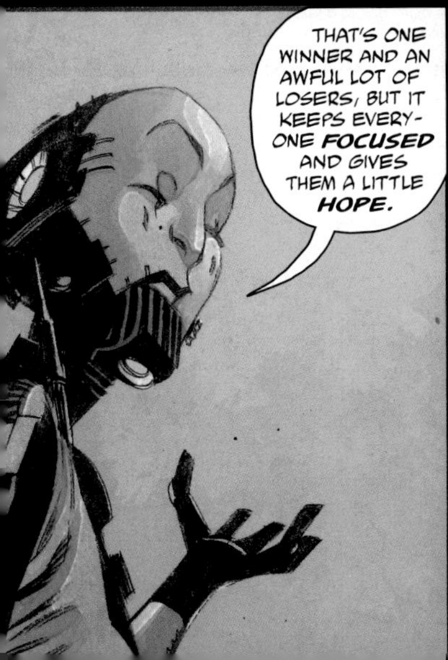
THAT'S ONE WINNER AND AN AWFUL LOT OF LOSERS, BUT IT KEEPS EVERY-ONE FOCUSED AND GIVES THEM A LITTLE HOPE.

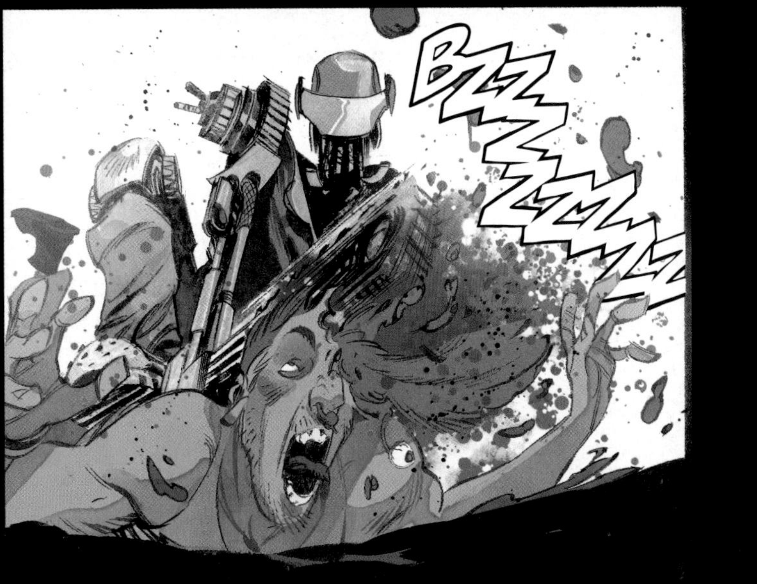
BZZZMMM

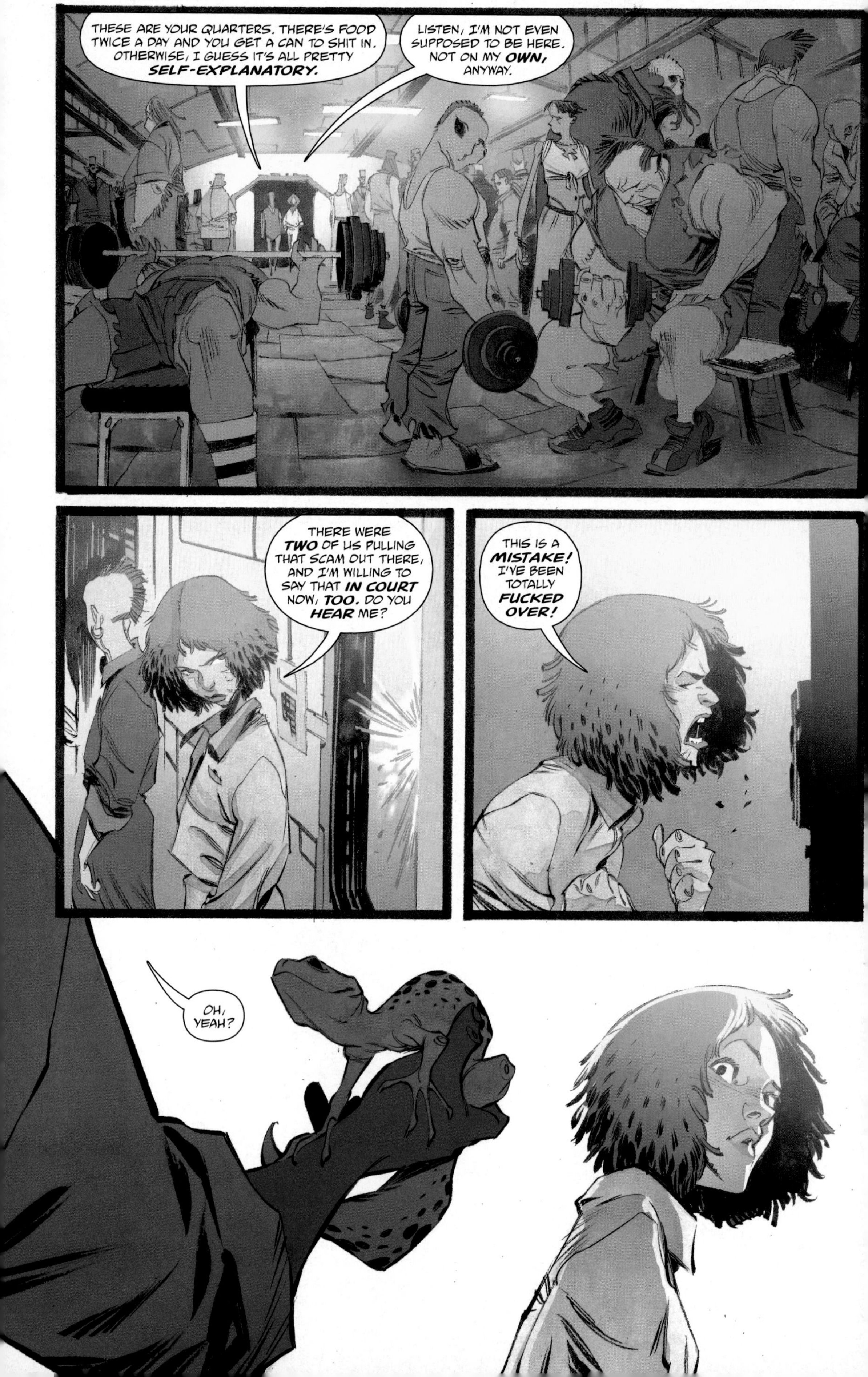

THESE ARE YOUR QUARTERS. THERE'S FOOD TWICE A DAY AND YOU GET A CAN TO SHIT IN. OTHERWISE, I GUESS IT'S ALL PRETTY **SELF-EXPLANATORY.**
LISTEN, I'M NOT EVEN SUPPOSED TO BE HERE. NOT ON MY **OWN,** ANYWAY.
THERE WERE **TWO** OF US PULLING THAT SCAM OUT THERE, AND I'M WILLING TO SAY THAT **IN COURT** NOW, **TOO.** DO YOU **HEAR** ME?
THIS IS A **MISTAKE!** I'VE BEEN TOTALLY **FUCKED OVER!**
OH, YEAH?

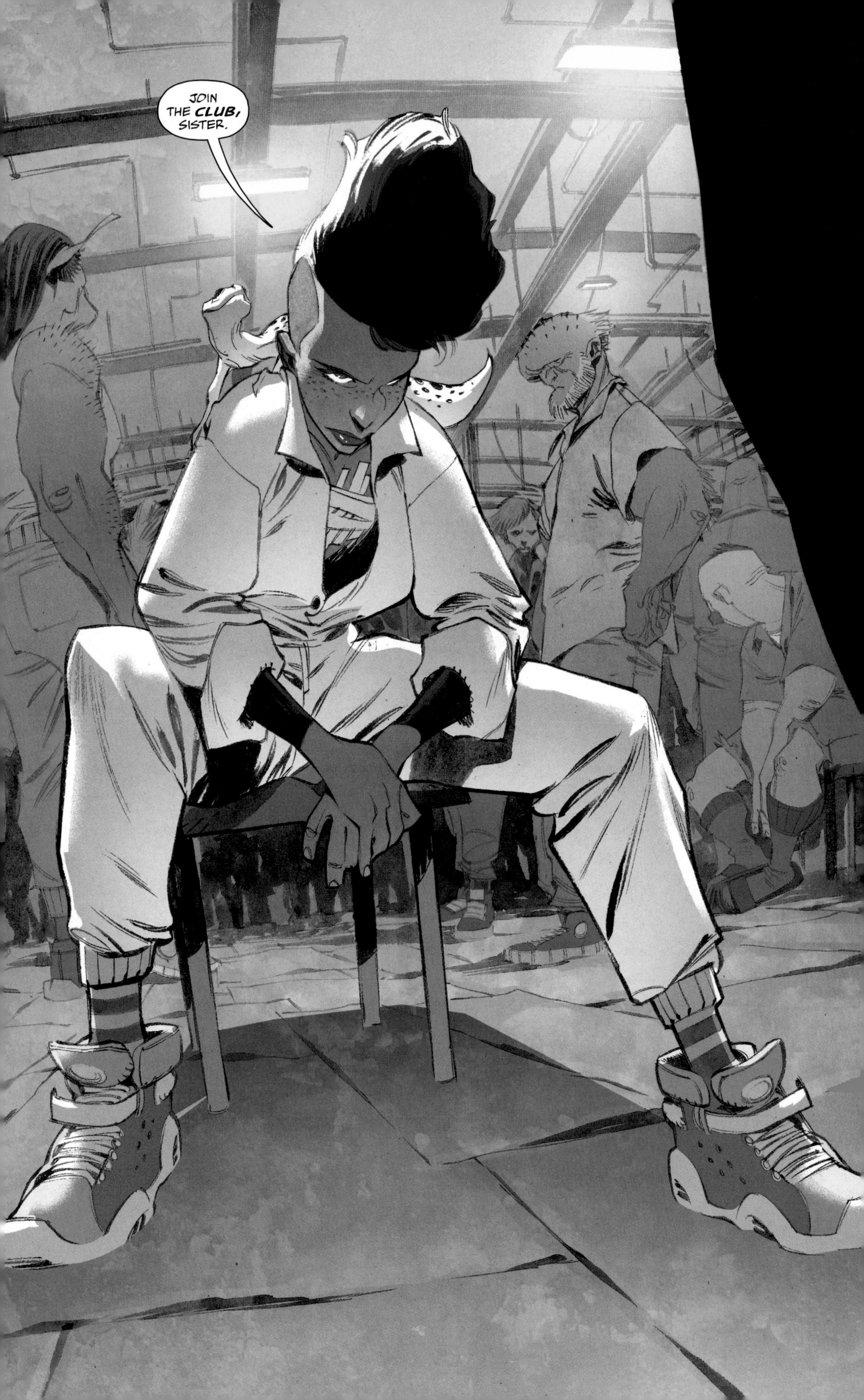
JOIN THE CLUB, SISTER.

Two

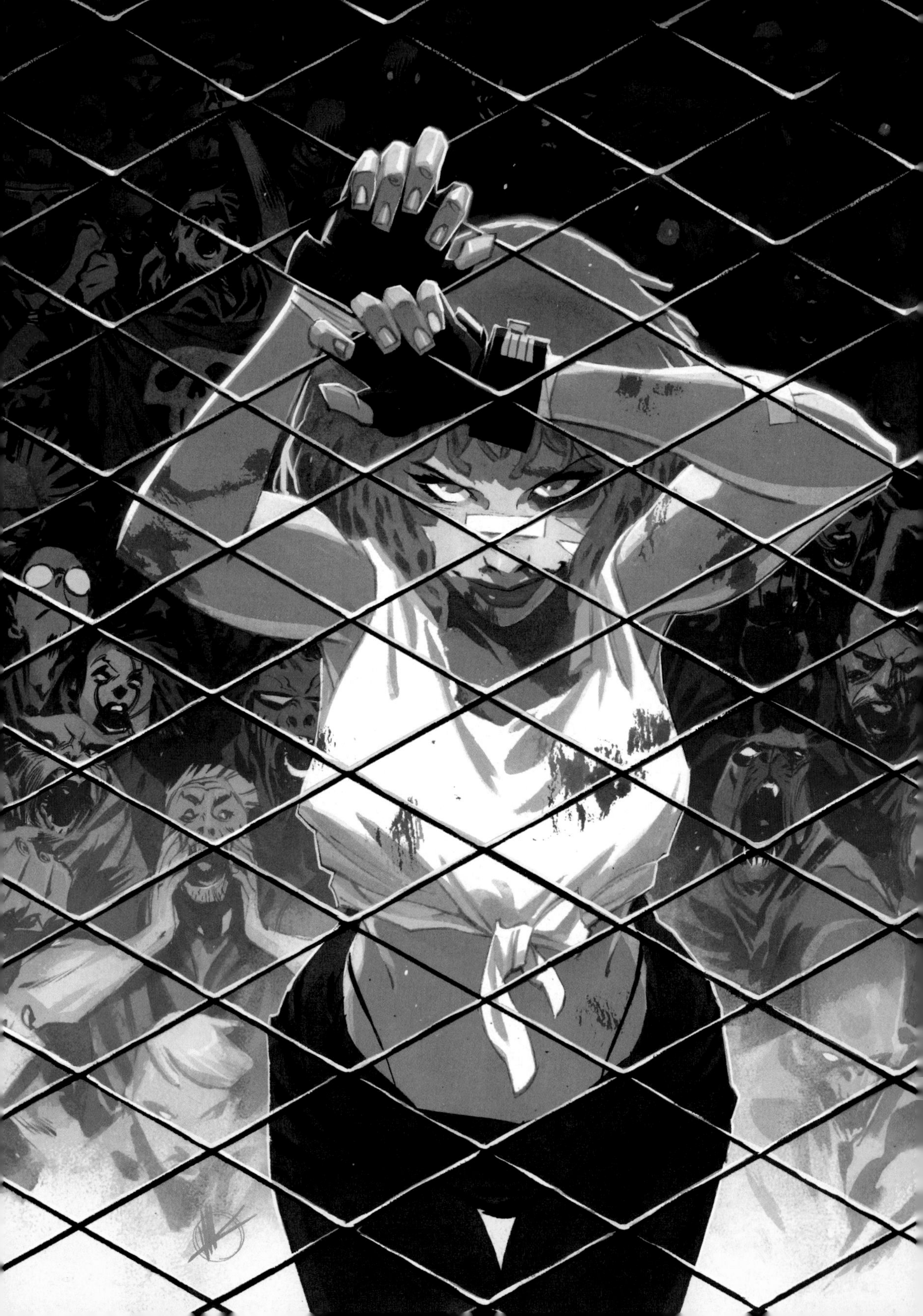

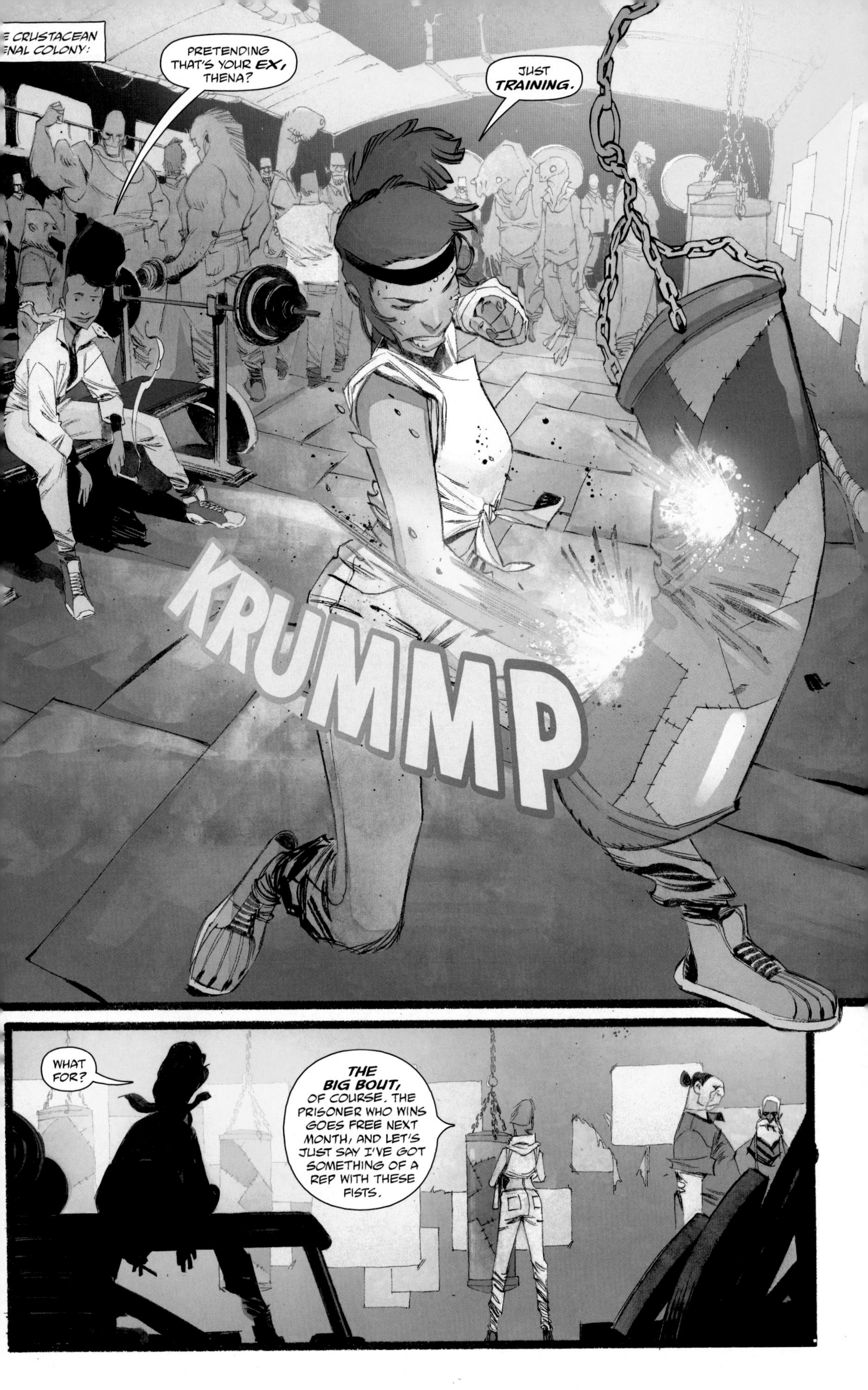
E CRUSTACEAN
ENAL COLONY:
PRETENDING THAT'S YOUR EX, THENA?
JUST TRAINING.
KRUMMP
WHAT FOR?
THE BIG BOUT, OF COURSE. THE PRISONER WHO WINS GOES FREE NEXT MONTH, AND LET'S JUST SAY I'VE GOT SOMETHING OF A REP WITH THESE FISTS.

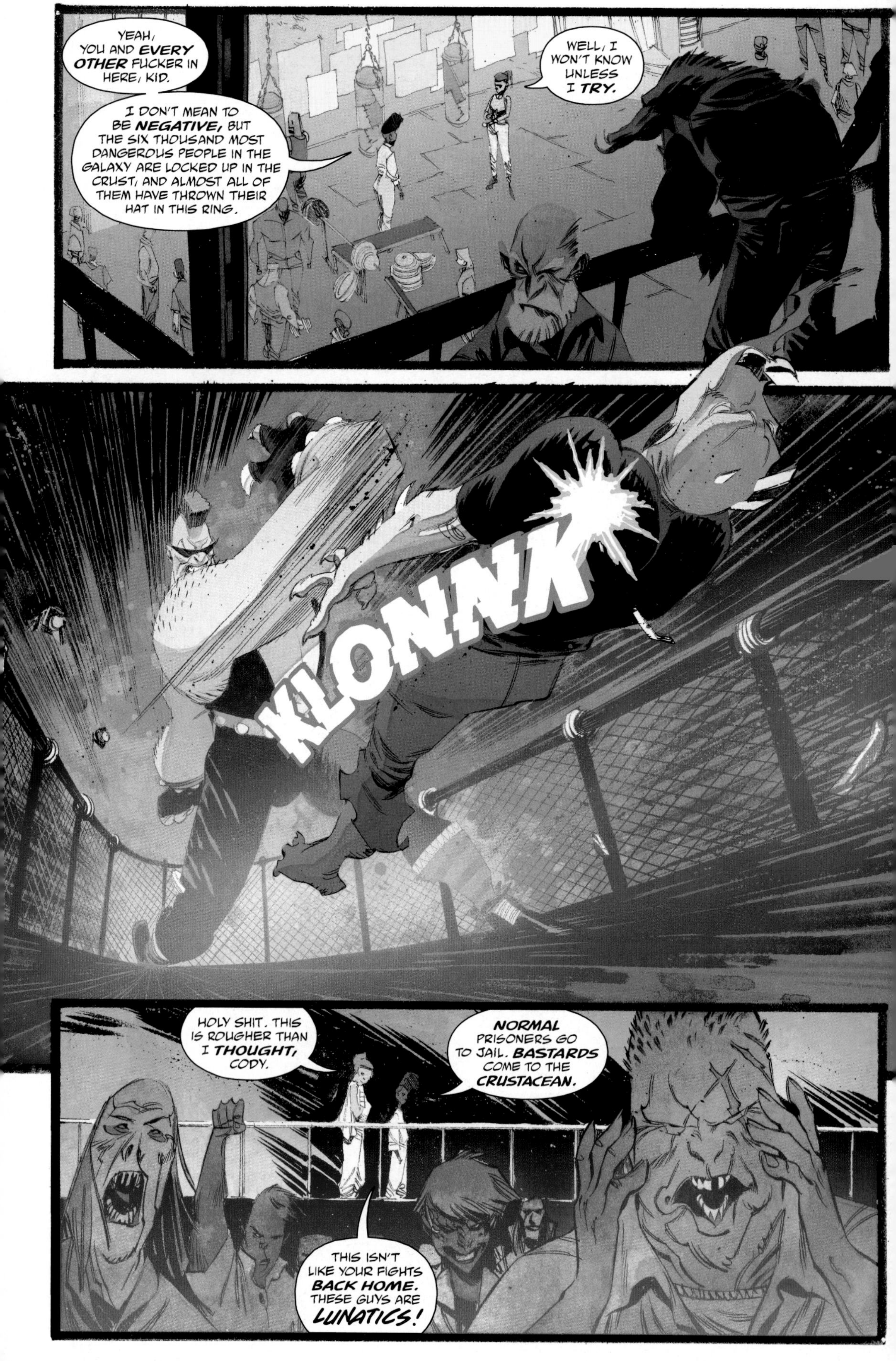
YEAH, YOU AND EVERY OTHER FUCKER IN HERE, KID.
I DON'T MEAN TO BE NEGATIVE, BUT THE SIX THOUSAND MOST DANGEROUS PEOPLE IN THE GALAXY ARE LOCKED UP IN THE CRUST, AND ALMOST ALL OF THEM HAVE THROWN THEIR HAT IN THIS RING.
WELL, I WON'T KNOW UNLESS I TRY.
KLONNK
HOLY SHIT. THIS IS ROUGHER THAN I THOUGHT, CODY.
NORMAL PRISONERS GO TO JAIL. BASTARDS COME TO THE CRUSTACEAN.
THIS ISN'T LIKE YOUR FIGHTS BACK HOME. THESE GUYS ARE LUNATICS!

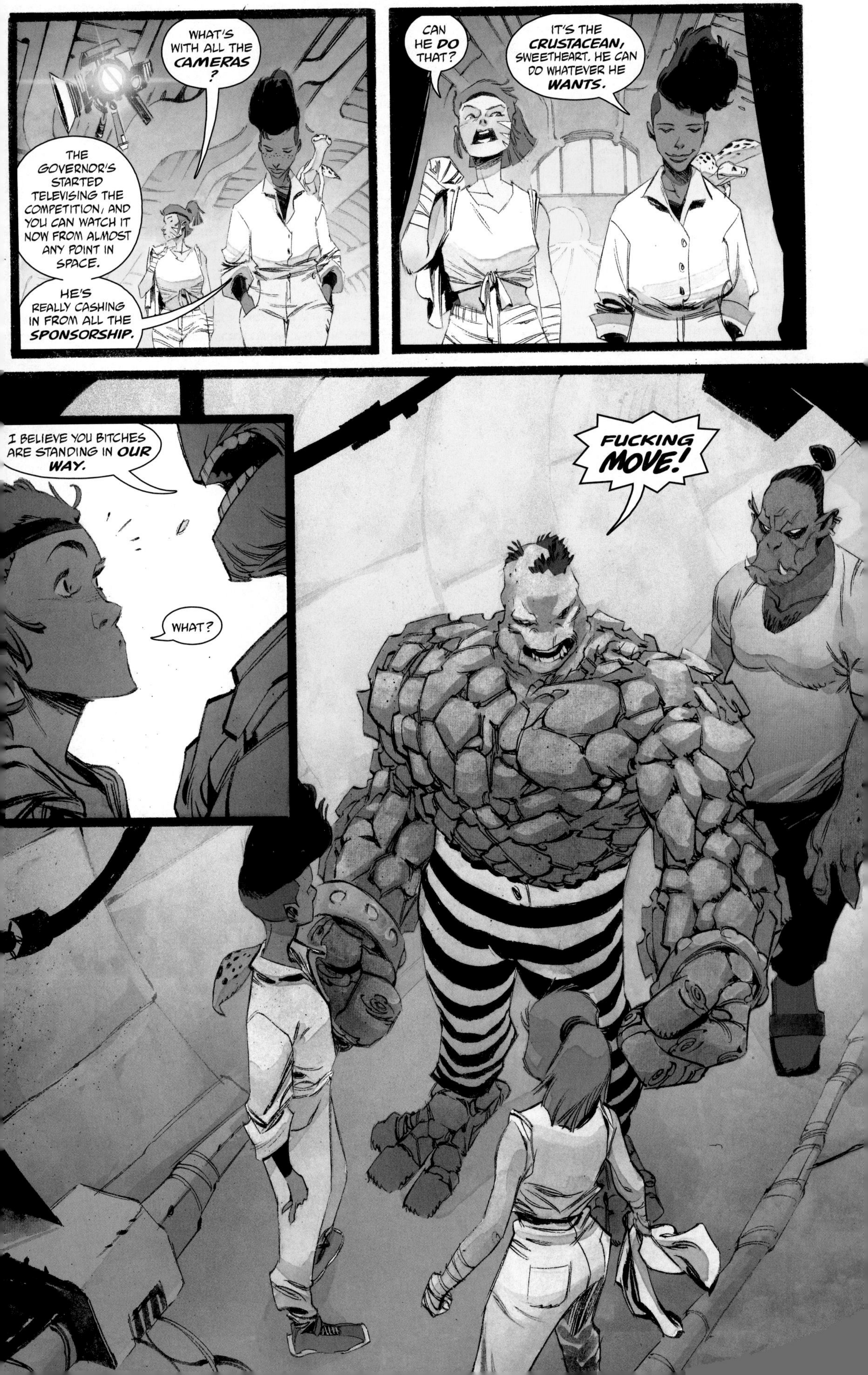
WHAT'S WITH ALL THE CAMERAS ?
THE GOVERNOR'S STARTED TELEVISING THE COMPETITION, AND YOU CAN WATCH IT NOW FROM ALMOST ANY POINT IN SPACE.
HE'S REALLY CASHING IN FROM ALL THE SPONSORSHIP.
CAN HE DO THAT?
IT'S THE CRUSTACEAN, SWEETHEART. HE CAN DO WHATEVER HE WANTS.
I BELIEVE YOU BITCHES ARE STANDING IN OUR WAY.
WHAT?
FUCKING MOVE!

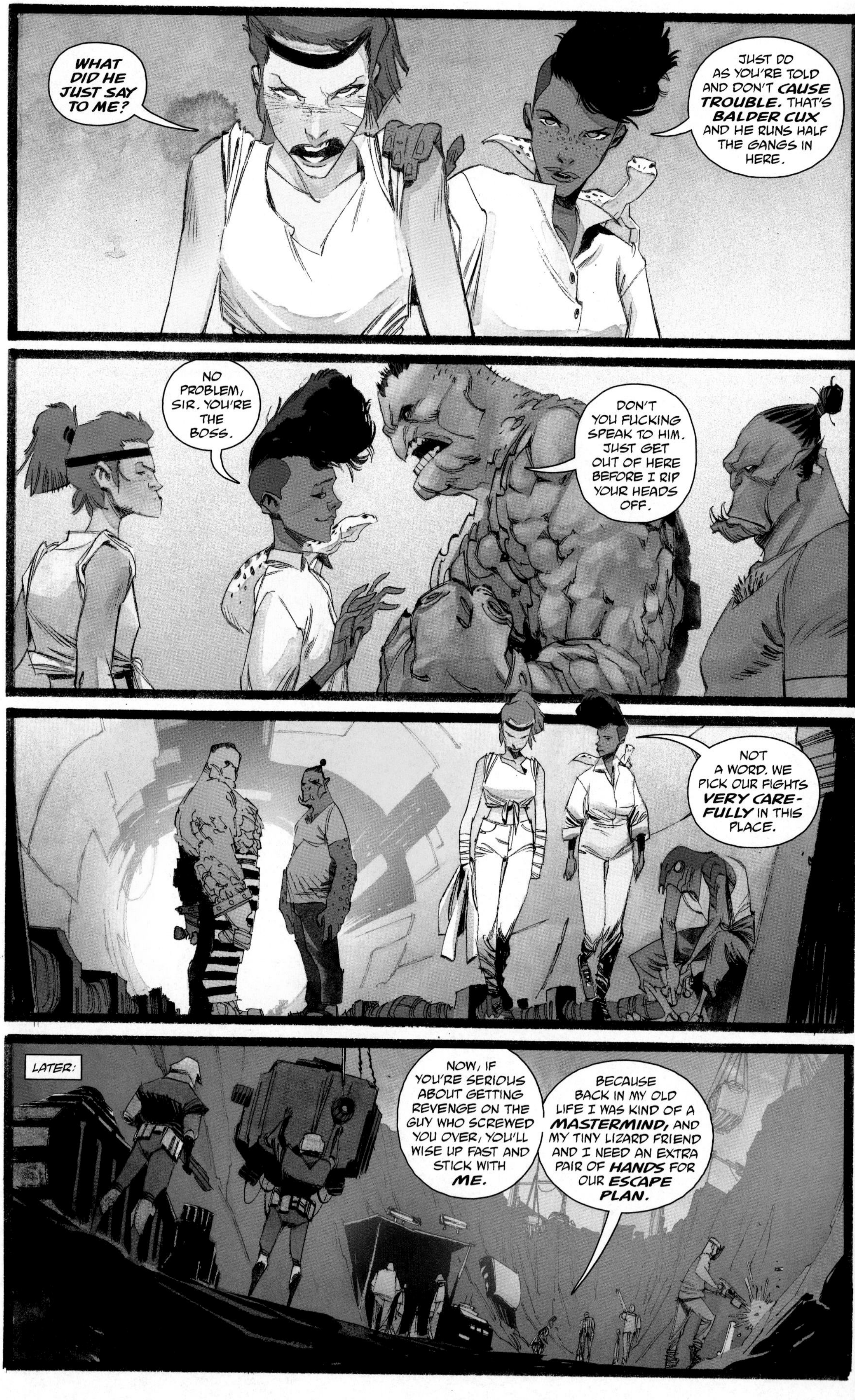
WHAT DID HE JUST SAY TO ME?
JUST DO AS YOU'RE TOLD AND DON'T CAUSE TROUBLE. THAT'S BALDER CUX AND HE RUNS HALF THE GANGS IN HERE.
NO PROBLEM, SIR. YOU'RE THE BOSS.
DON'T YOU FUCKING SPEAK TO HIM. JUST GET OUT OF HERE BEFORE I RIP YOUR HEADS OFF.
NOT A WORD. WE PICK OUR FIGHTS VERY CARE-FULLY IN THIS PLACE.
LATER:
NOW, IF YOU'RE SERIOUS ABOUT GETTING REVENGE ON THE GUY WHO SCREWED YOU OVER, YOU'LL WISE UP FAST AND STICK WITH ME.
BECAUSE BACK IN MY OLD LIFE I WAS KIND OF A MASTERMIND, AND MY TINY LIZARD FRIEND AND I NEED AN EXTRA PAIR OF HANDS FOR OUR ESCAPE PLAN.

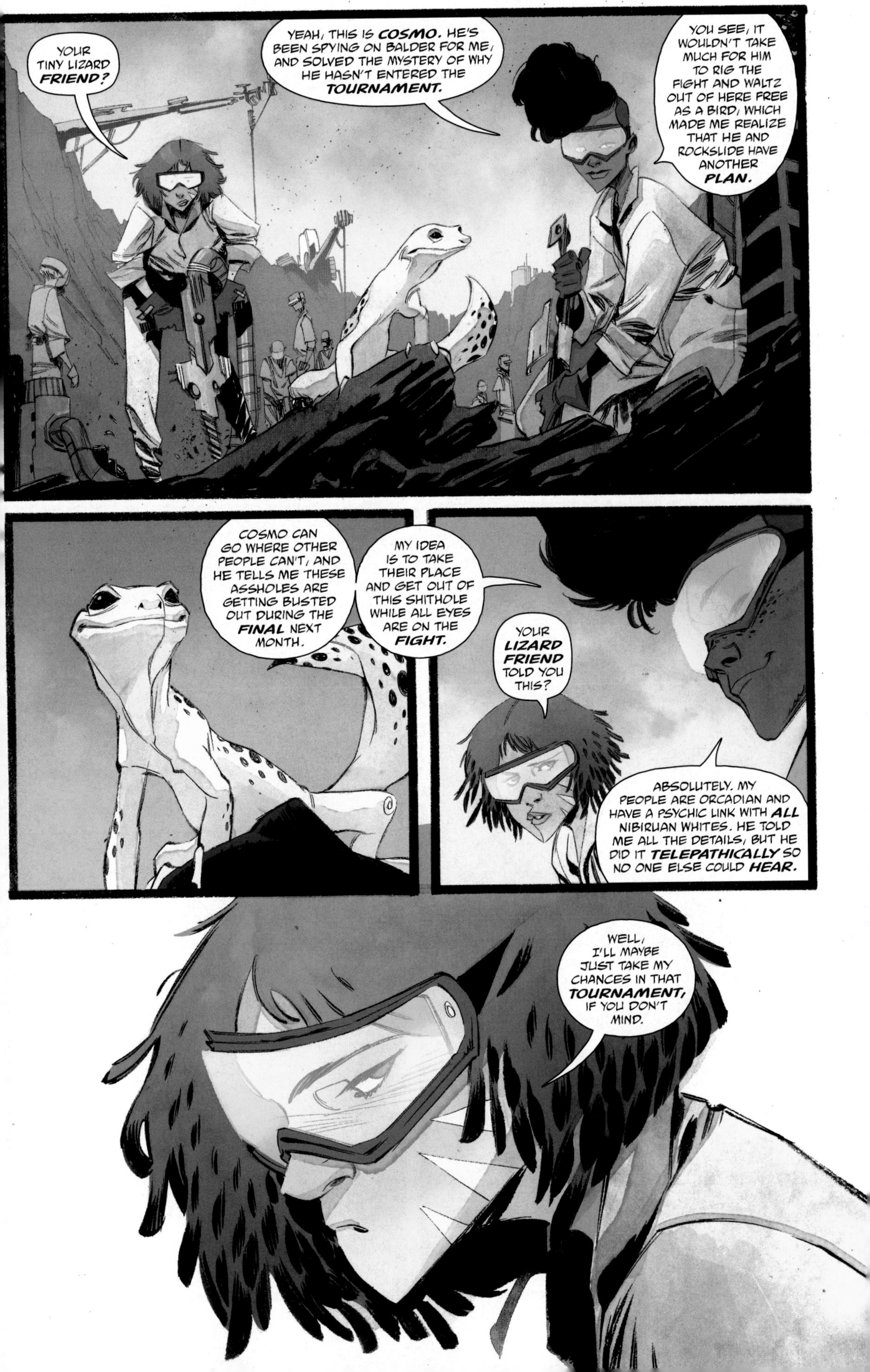
YOUR TINY LIZARD FRIEND?
YEAH, THIS IS COSMO. HE'S BEEN SPYING ON BALDER FOR ME, AND SOLVED THE MYSTERY OF WHY HE HASN'T ENTERED THE TOURNAMENT.
YOU SEE, IT WOULDN'T TAKE MUCH FOR HIM TO RIG THE FIGHT AND WALTZ OUT OF HERE FREE AS A BIRD, WHICH MADE ME REALIZE THAT HE AND ROCKSLIDE HAVE ANOTHER PLAN.
COSMO CAN GO WHERE OTHER PEOPLE CAN'T, AND HE TELLS ME THESE ASSHOLES ARE GETTING BUSTED OUT DURING THE FINAL NEXT MONTH.
MY IDEA IS TO TAKE THEIR PLACE AND GET OUT OF THIS SHITHOLE WHILE ALL EYES ARE ON THE FIGHT.
YOUR LIZARD FRIEND TOLD YOU THIS?
ABSOLUTELY. MY PEOPLE ARE ORCADIAN AND HAVE A PSYCHIC LINK WITH ALL NIBIRUAN WHITES. HE TOLD ME ALL THE DETAILS, BUT HE DID IT TELEPATHICALLY SO NO ONE ELSE COULD HEAR.
WELL, I'LL MAYBE JUST TAKE MY CHANCES IN THAT TOURNAMENT, IF YOU DON'T MIND.

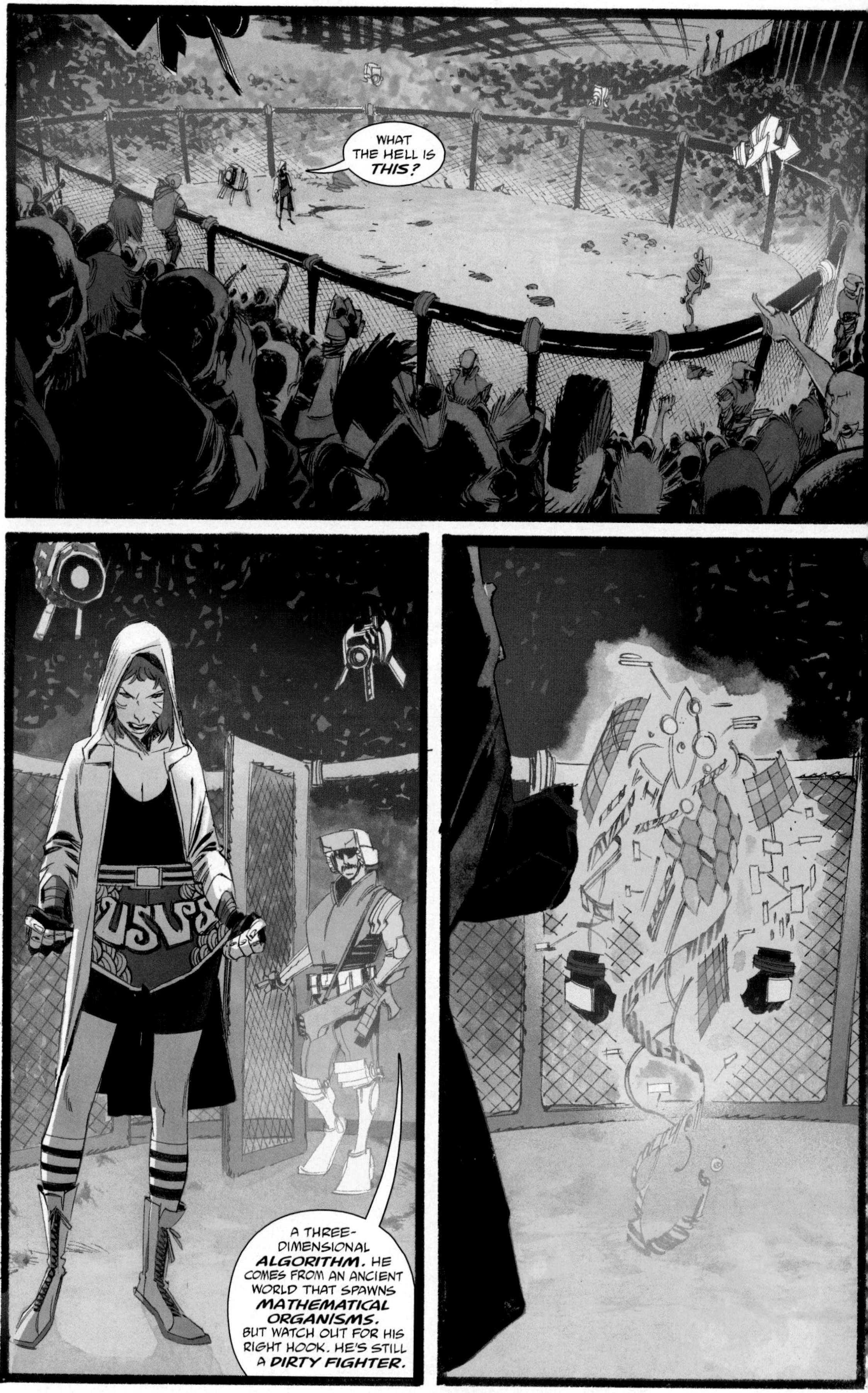
WHAT THE HELL IS *THIS?*
A THREE-DIMENSIONAL **ALGORITHM.** HE COMES FROM AN ANCIENT WORLD THAT SPAWNS **MATHEMATICAL ORGANISMS.** BUT WATCH OUT FOR HIS RIGHT HOOK. HE'S STILL A **DIRTY FIGHTER.**

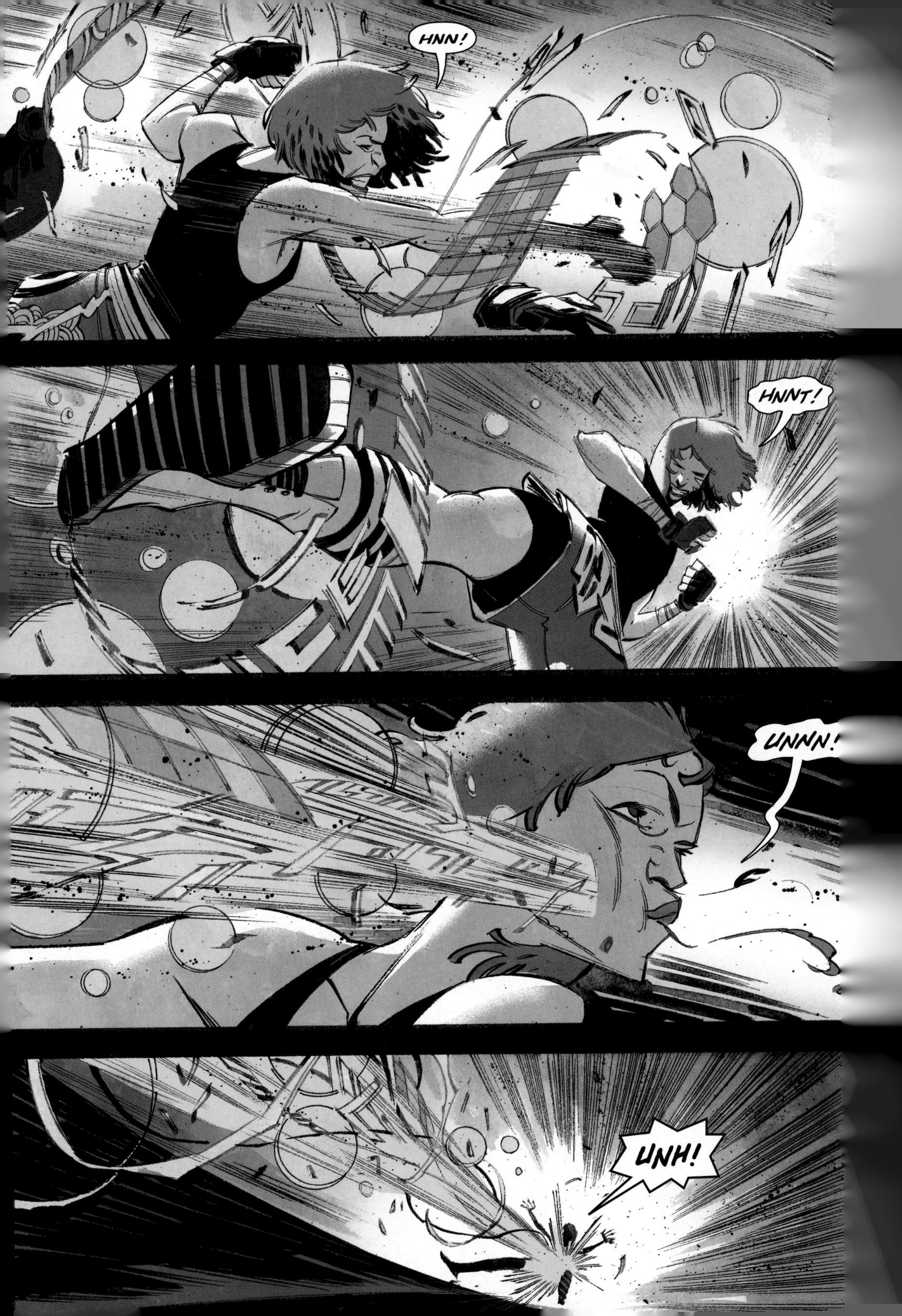
HNN!
HNNT!
UNNN!
UNH!

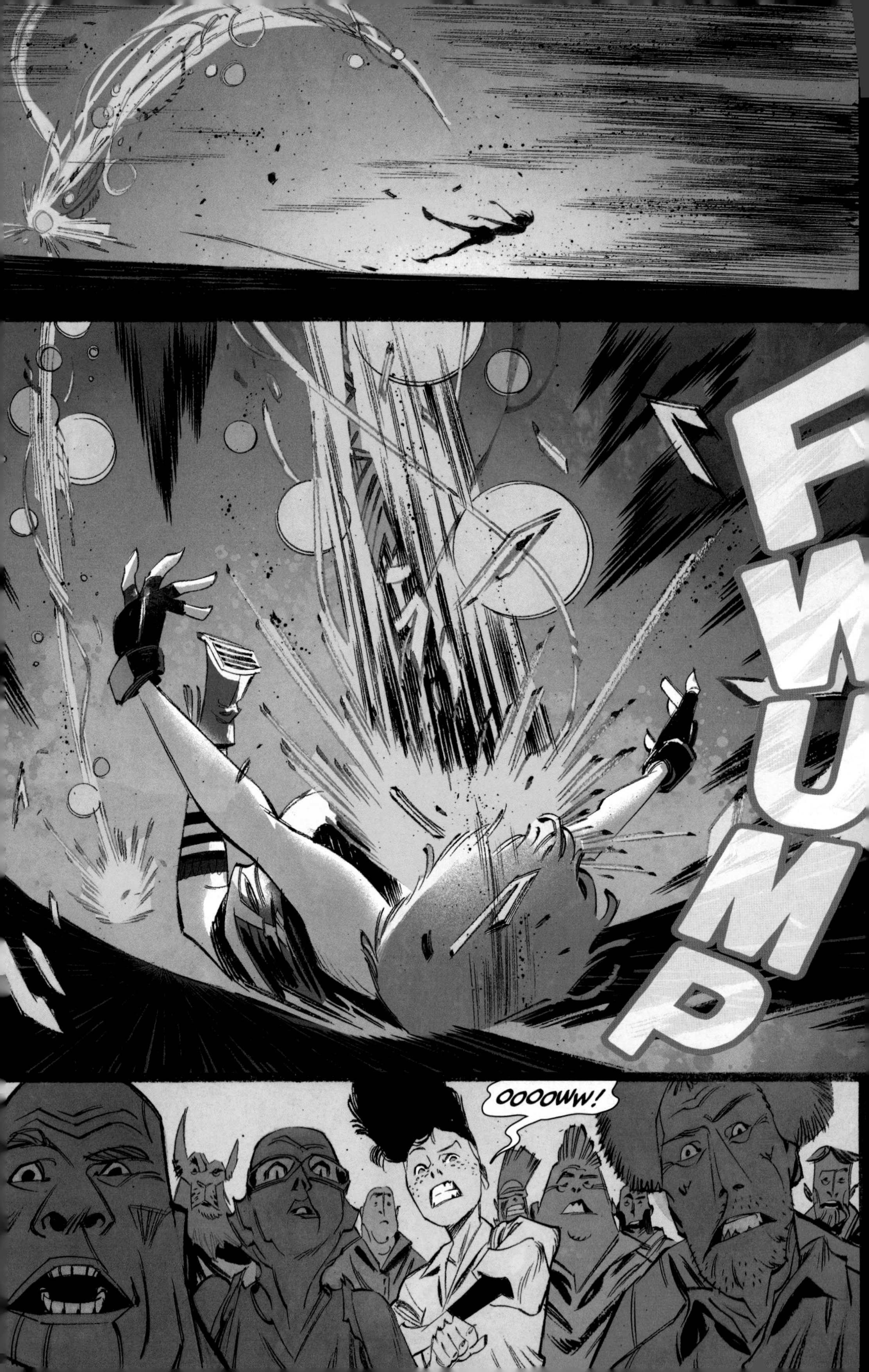
FWUMP
OOOOWW!

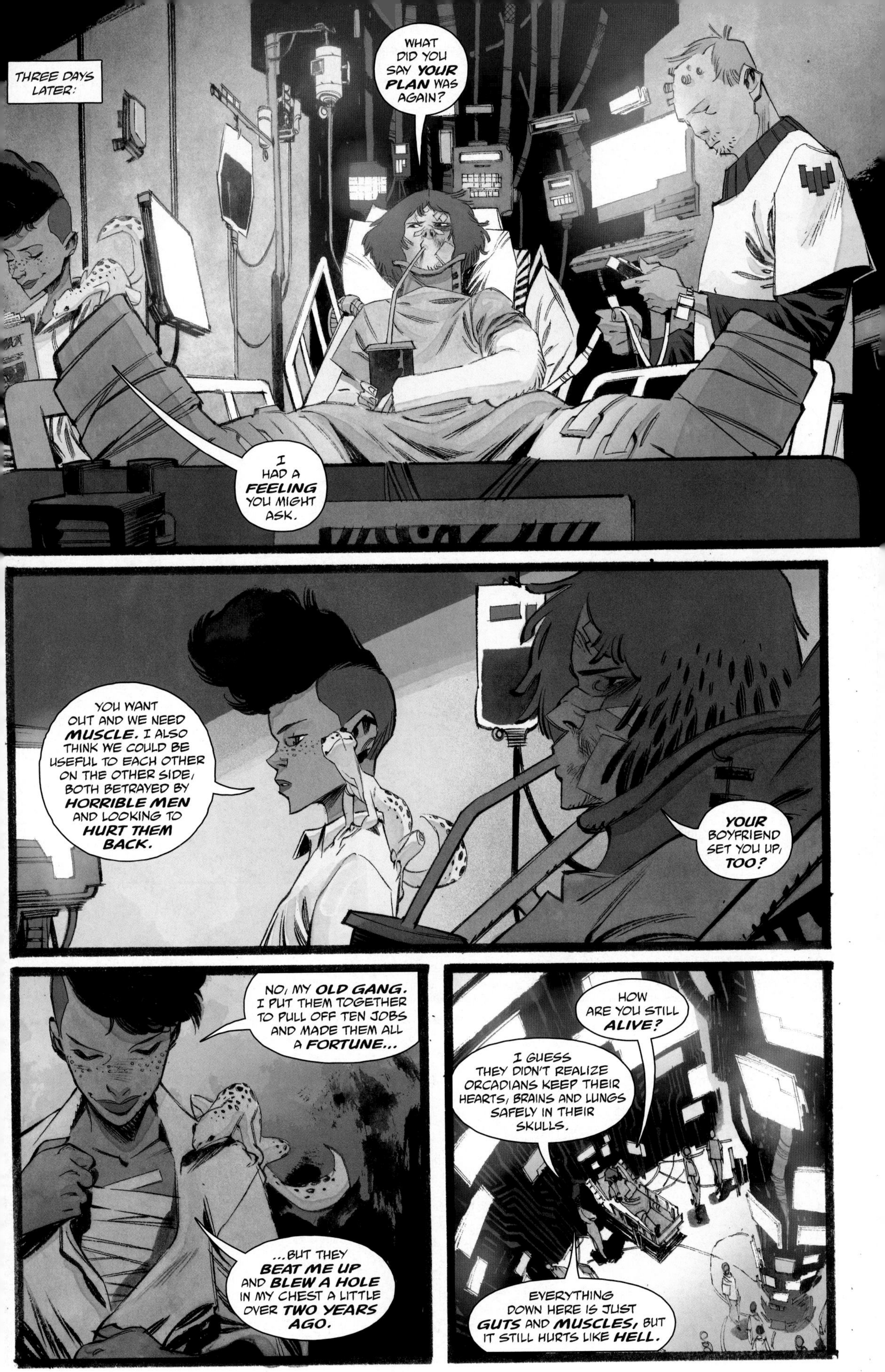
THREE DAYS LATER:
WHAT DID YOU SAY YOUR PLAN WAS AGAIN?
I HAD A FEELING YOU MIGHT ASK.
YOU WANT OUT AND WE NEED MUSCLE. I ALSO THINK WE COULD BE USEFUL TO EACH OTHER ON THE OTHER SIDE; BOTH BETRAYED BY HORRIBLE MEN AND LOOKING TO HURT THEM BACK.
YOUR BOYFRIEND SET YOU UP, TOO?
NO, MY OLD GANG. I PUT THEM TOGETHER TO PULL OFF TEN JOBS AND MADE THEM ALL A FORTUNE...
...BUT THEY BEAT ME UP AND BLEW A HOLE IN MY CHEST A LITTLE OVER TWO YEARS AGO.
HOW ARE YOU STILL ALIVE?
I GUESS THEY DIDN'T REALIZE ORCADIANS KEEP THEIR HEARTS, BRAINS AND LUNGS SAFELY IN THEIR SKULLS.
EVERYTHING DOWN HERE IS JUST GUTS AND MUSCLES, BUT IT STILL HURTS LIKE HELL.

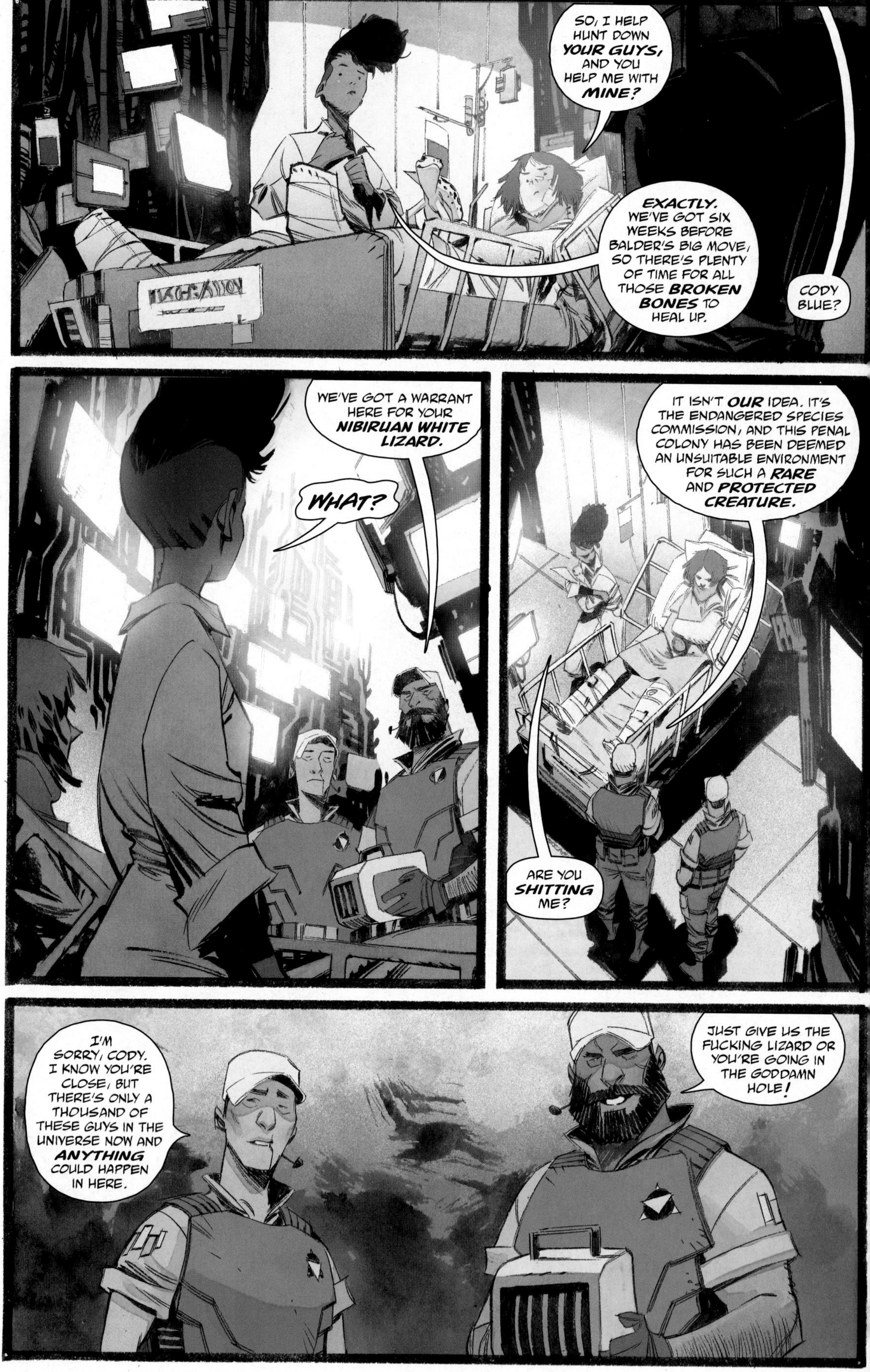
SO, I HELP HUNT DOWN **YOUR GUYS,** AND YOU HELP ME WITH **MINE?**
EXACTLY. WE'VE GOT SIX WEEKS BEFORE BALDER'S BIG MOVE, SO THERE'S PLENTY OF TIME FOR ALL THOSE **BROKEN BONES** TO HEAL UP.
CODY BLUE?
WE'VE GOT A WARRANT HERE FOR YOUR **NIBIRUAN WHITE LIZARD.**
WHAT?
IT ISN'T **OUR** IDEA. IT'S THE ENDANGERED SPECIES COMMISSION, AND THIS PENAL COLONY HAS BEEN DEEMED AN UNSUITABLE ENVIRONMENT FOR SUCH A **RARE** AND **PROTECTED CREATURE.**
ARE YOU **SHITTING** ME?
I'M SORRY, CODY. I KNOW YOU'RE CLOSE, BUT THERE'S ONLY A THOUSAND OF THESE GUYS IN THE UNIVERSE NOW AND **ANYTHING** COULD HAPPEN IN HERE.
JUST GIVE US THE FUCKING LIZARD OR YOU'RE GOING IN THE GODDAMN HOLE!

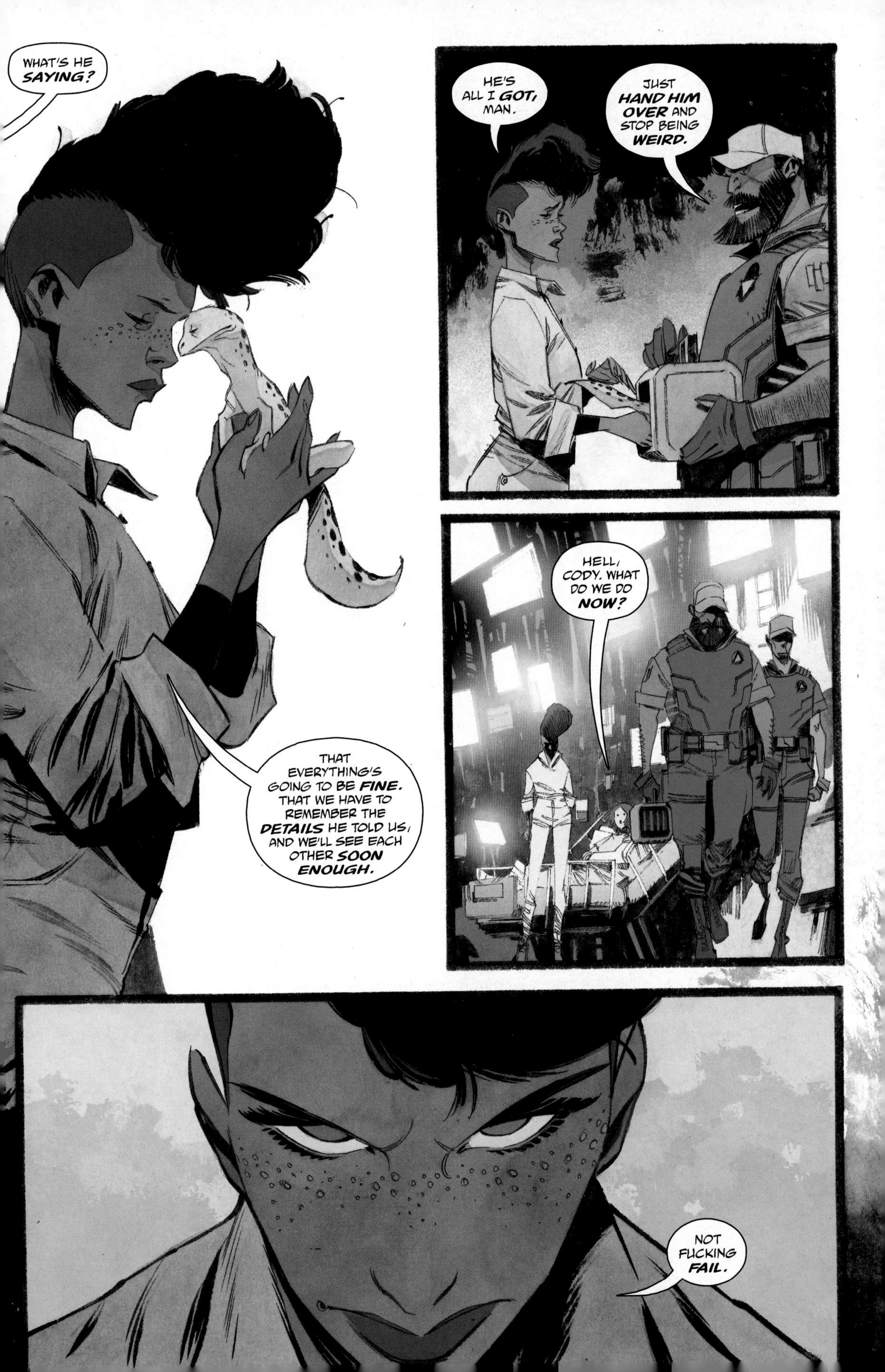
WHAT'S HE SAYING?
HE'S ALL I GOT, MAN.
JUST HAND HIM OVER AND STOP BEING WEIRD.
HELL, CODY. WHAT DO WE DO NOW?
THAT EVERYTHING'S GOING TO BE FINE. THAT WE HAVE TO REMEMBER THE DETAILS HE TOLD US, AND WE'LL SEE EACH OTHER SOON ENOUGH.
NOT FUCKING FAIL.

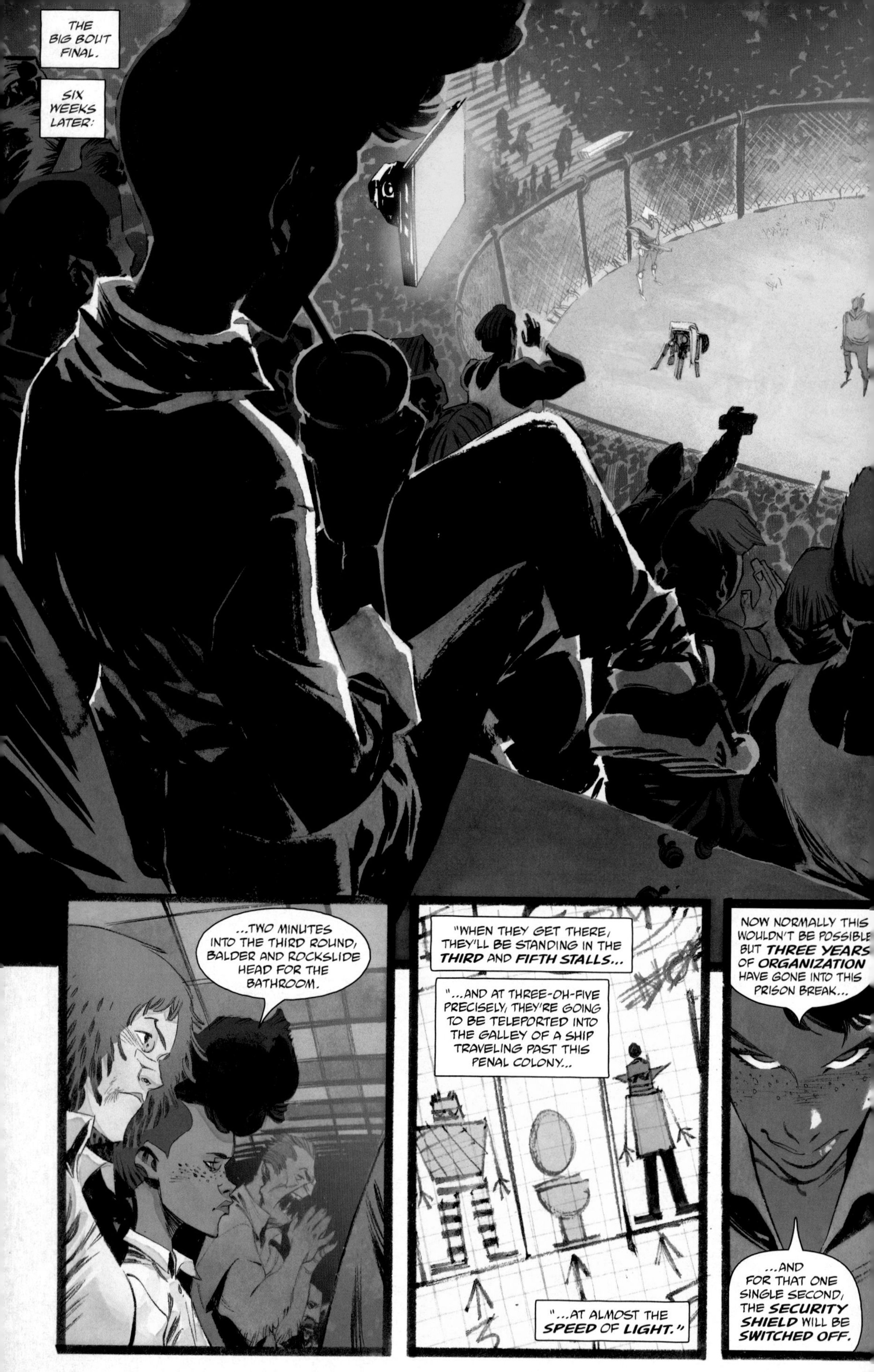
THE BIG BOUT FINAL.
SIX WEEKS LATER:
...TWO MINUTES INTO THE THIRD ROUND, BALDER AND ROCKSLIDE HEAD FOR THE BATHROOM.
"WHEN THEY GET THERE, THEY'LL BE STANDING IN THE THIRD AND FIFTH STALLS...
"...AND AT THREE-OH-FIVE PRECISELY, THEY'RE GOING TO BE TELEPORTED INTO THE GALLEY OF A SHIP TRAVELING PAST THIS PENAL COLONY...
"...AT ALMOST THE SPEED OF LIGHT."
NOW NORMALLY THIS WOULDN'T BE POSSIBLE BUT THREE YEARS OF ORGANIZATION HAVE GONE INTO THIS PRISON BREAK...
...AND FOR THAT ONE SINGLE SECOND, THE SECURITY SHIELD WILL BE SWITCHED OFF.

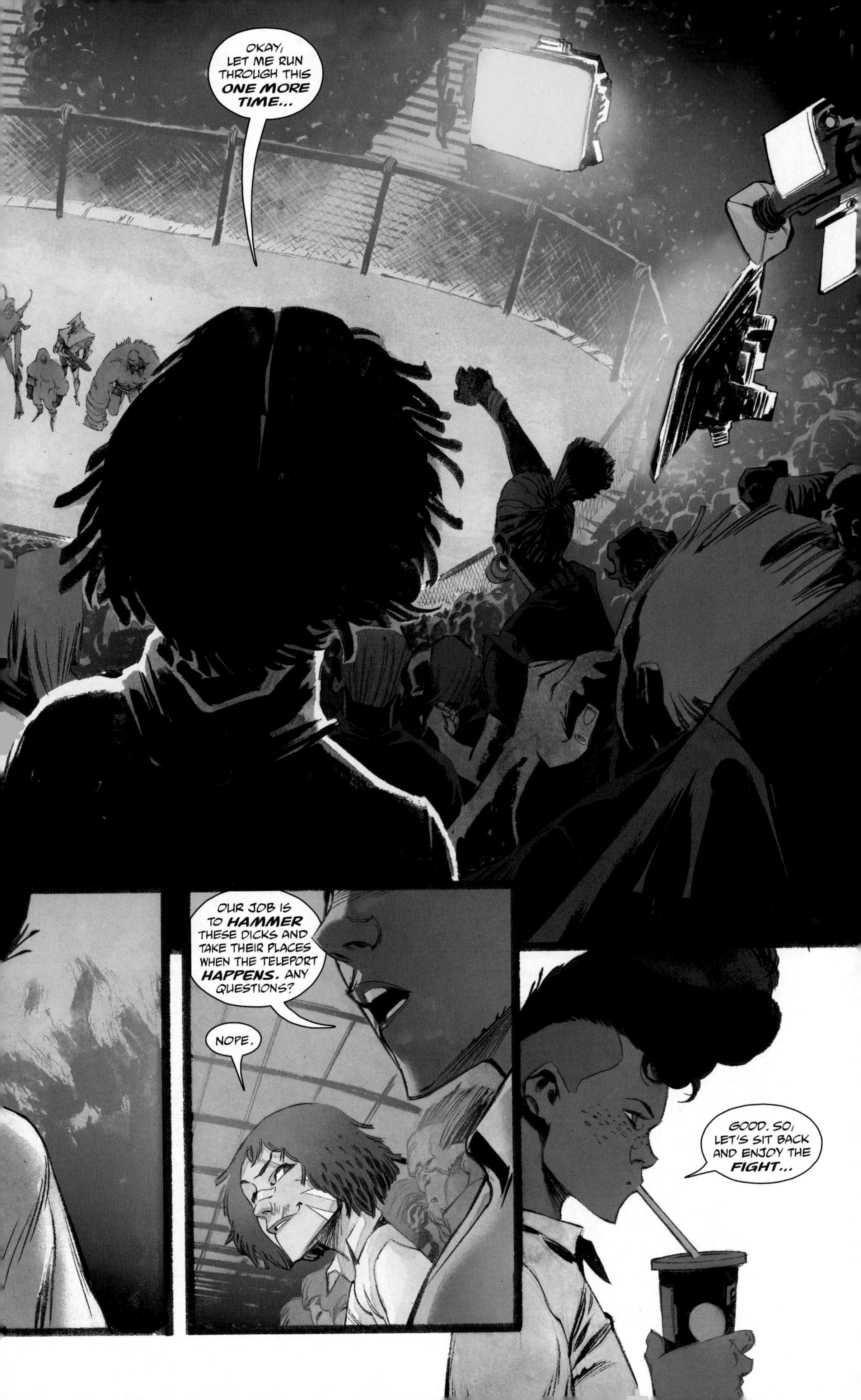
OKAY, LET ME RUN THROUGH THIS ONE MORE TIME...
OUR JOB IS TO HAMMER THESE DICKS AND TAKE THEIR PLACES WHEN THE TELEPORT HAPPENS. ANY QUESTIONS?
NOPE.
GOOD. SO, LET'S SIT BACK AND ENJOY THE FIGHT...

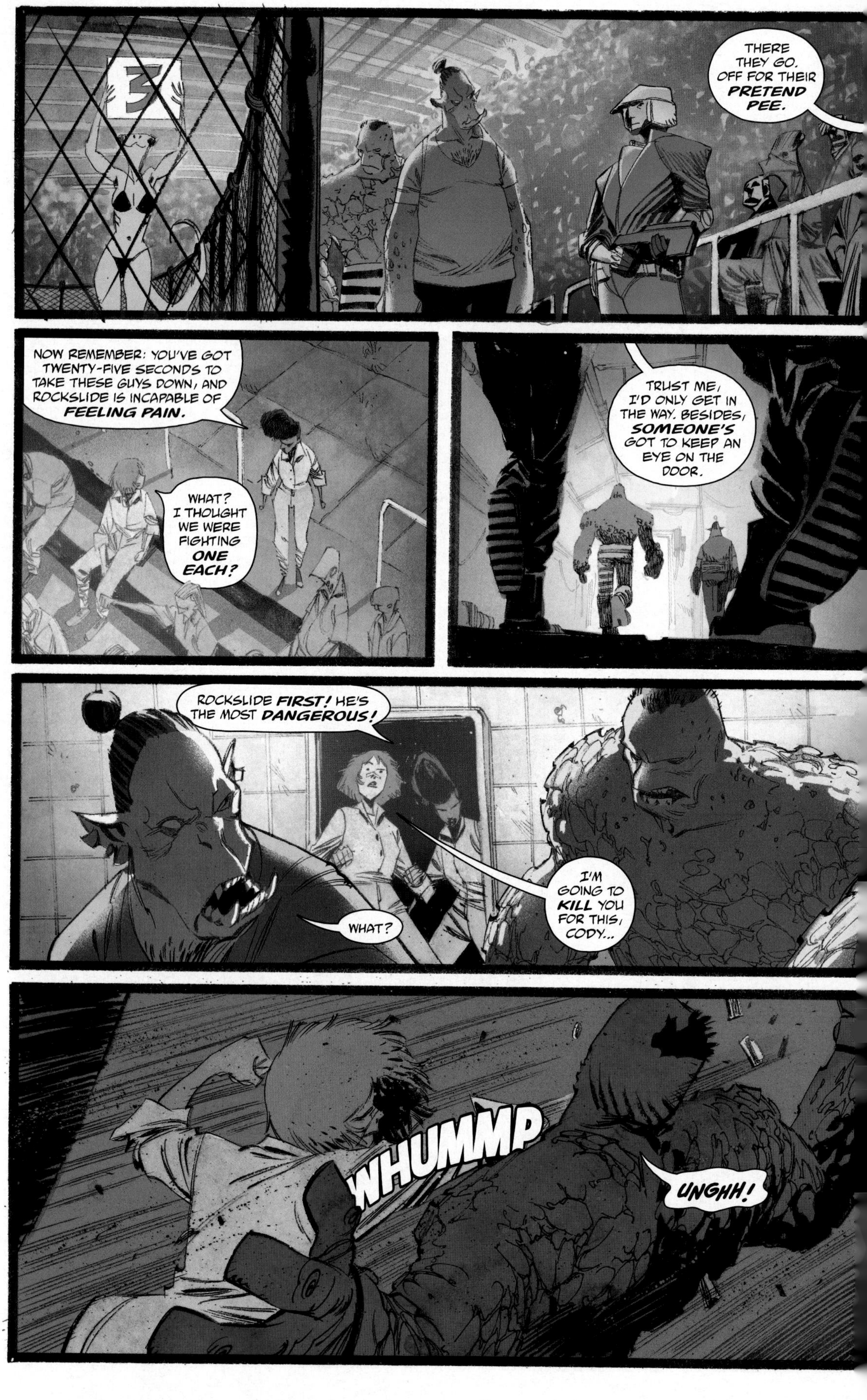
THERE THEY GO. OFF FOR THEIR PRETEND PEE.
NOW REMEMBER: YOU'VE GOT TWENTY-FIVE SECONDS TO TAKE THESE GUYS DOWN, AND ROCKSLIDE IS INCAPABLE OF FEELING PAIN.
WHAT? I THOUGHT WE WERE FIGHTING ONE EACH?
TRUST ME, I'D ONLY GET IN THE WAY. BESIDES, SOMEONE'S GOT TO KEEP AN EYE ON THE DOOR.
ROCKSLIDE FIRST! HE'S THE MOST DANGEROUS!
WHAT?
I'M GOING TO KILL YOU FOR THIS, CODY...
WHUMMP
UNGHH!

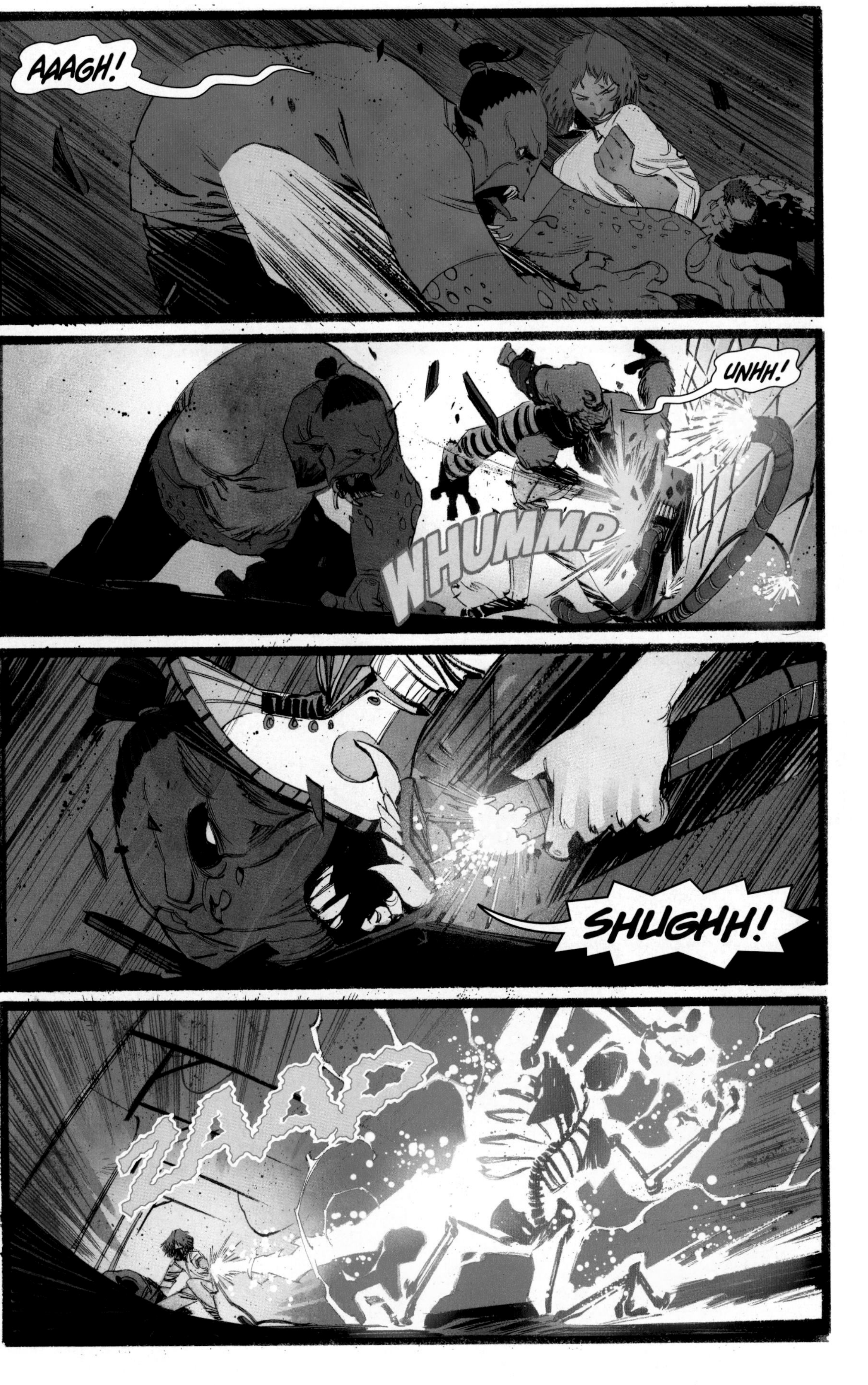
AAAGH!
UNHH!
WHUMMP
SHUGHH!
ZAAP

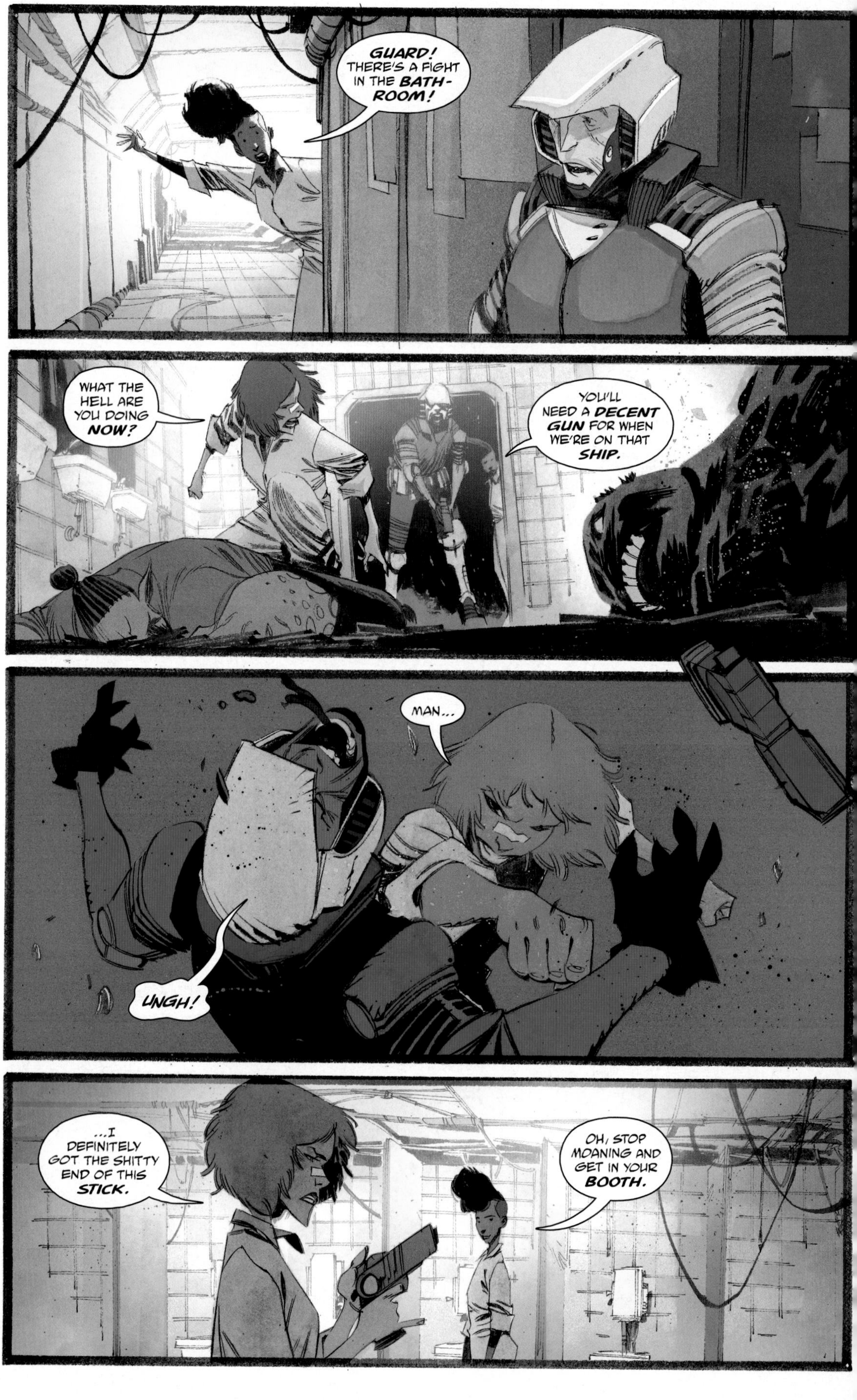
GUARD! THERE'S A FIGHT IN THE BATH-ROOM!
WHAT THE HELL ARE YOU DOING NOW?
YOU'LL NEED A DECENT GUN FOR WHEN WE'RE ON THAT SHIP.
MAN...
UNGH!
...I DEFINITELY GOT THE SHITTY END OF THIS STICK.
OH, STOP MOANING AND GET IN YOUR BOOTH.

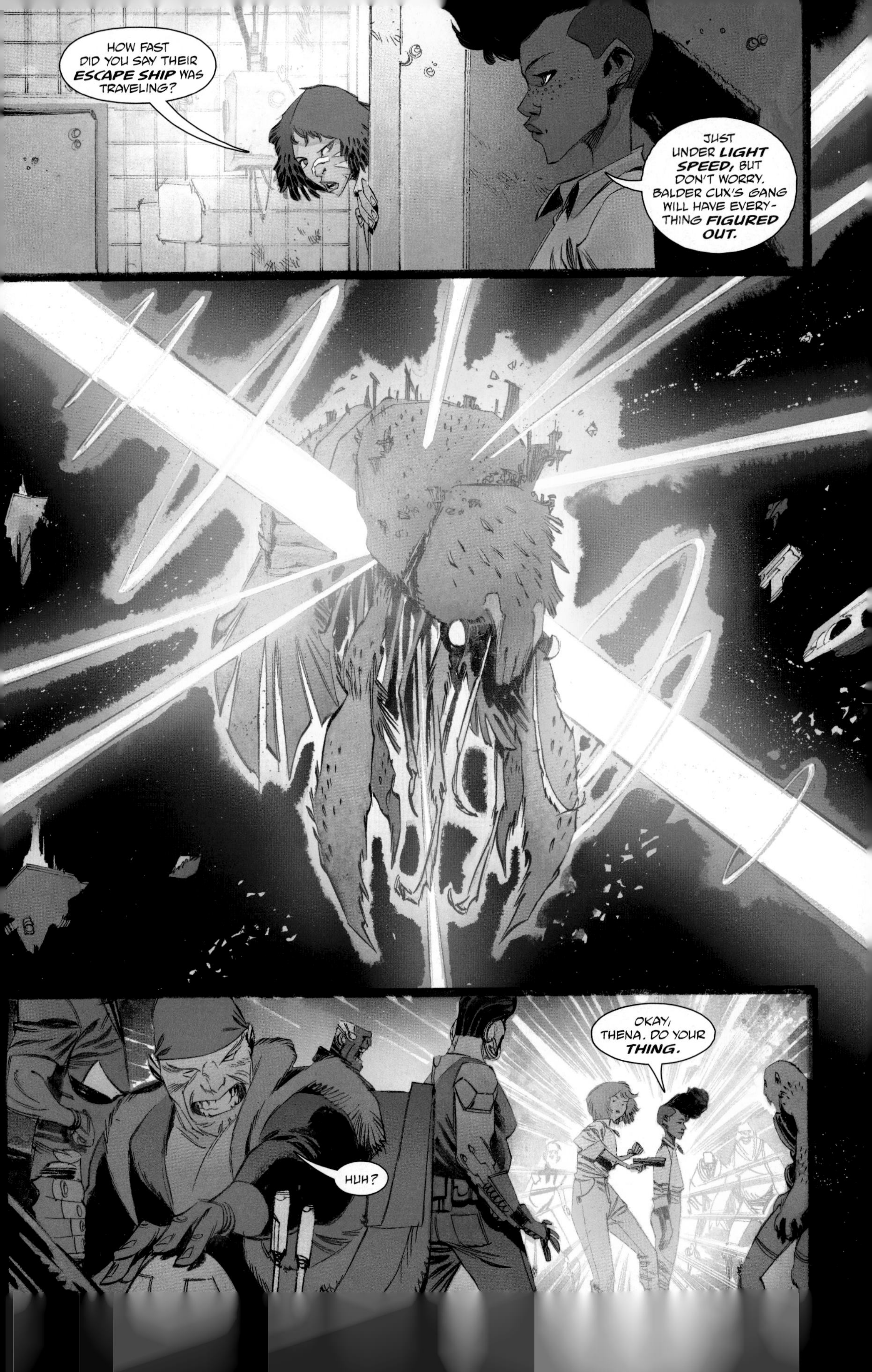
HOW FAST DID YOU SAY THEIR ESCAPE SHIP WAS TRAVELING?
JUST UNDER LIGHT SPEED, BUT DON'T WORRY. BALDER CUX'S GANG WILL HAVE EVERY-THING FIGURED OUT.
OKAY, THENA. DO YOUR THING.
HUH?

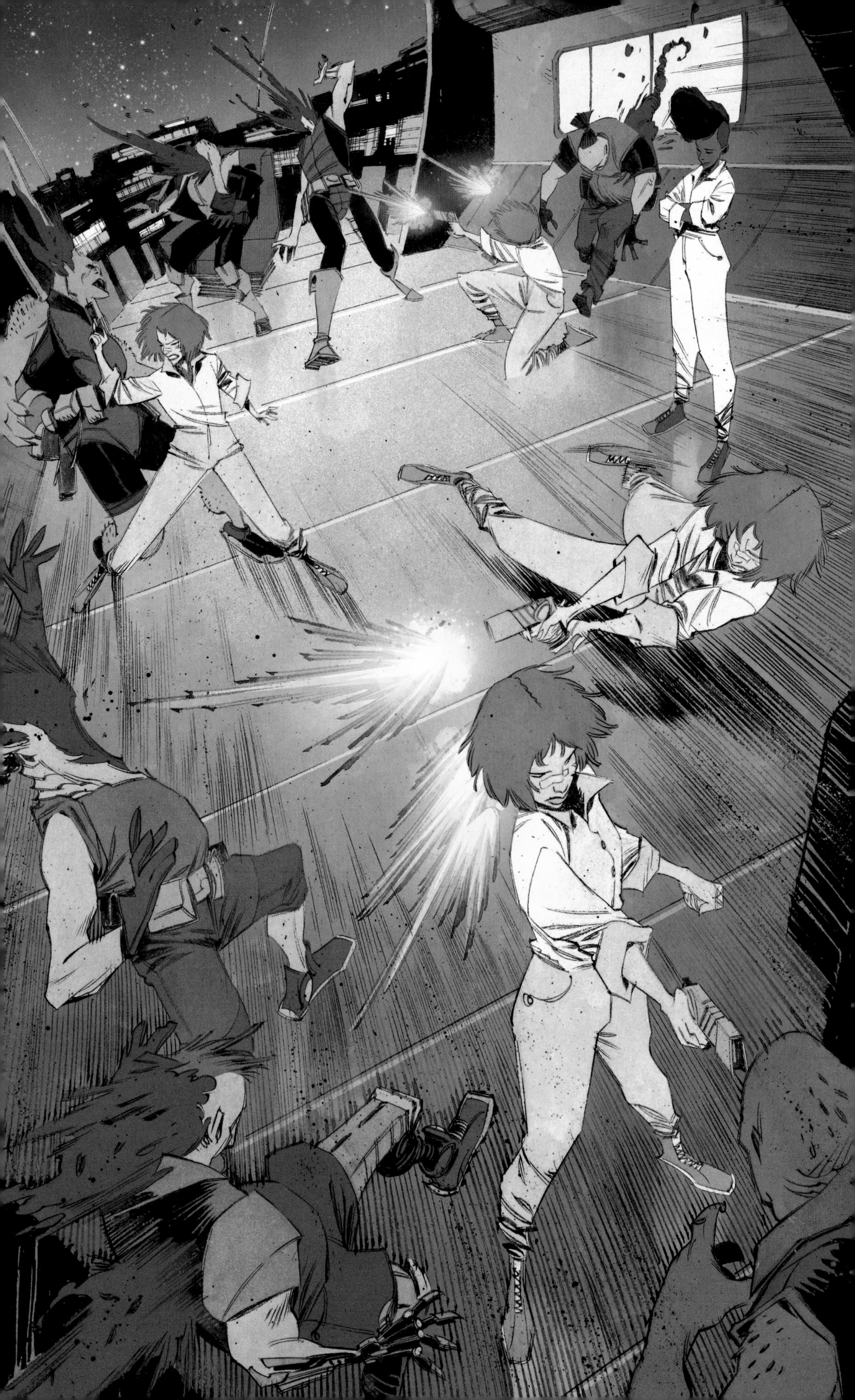

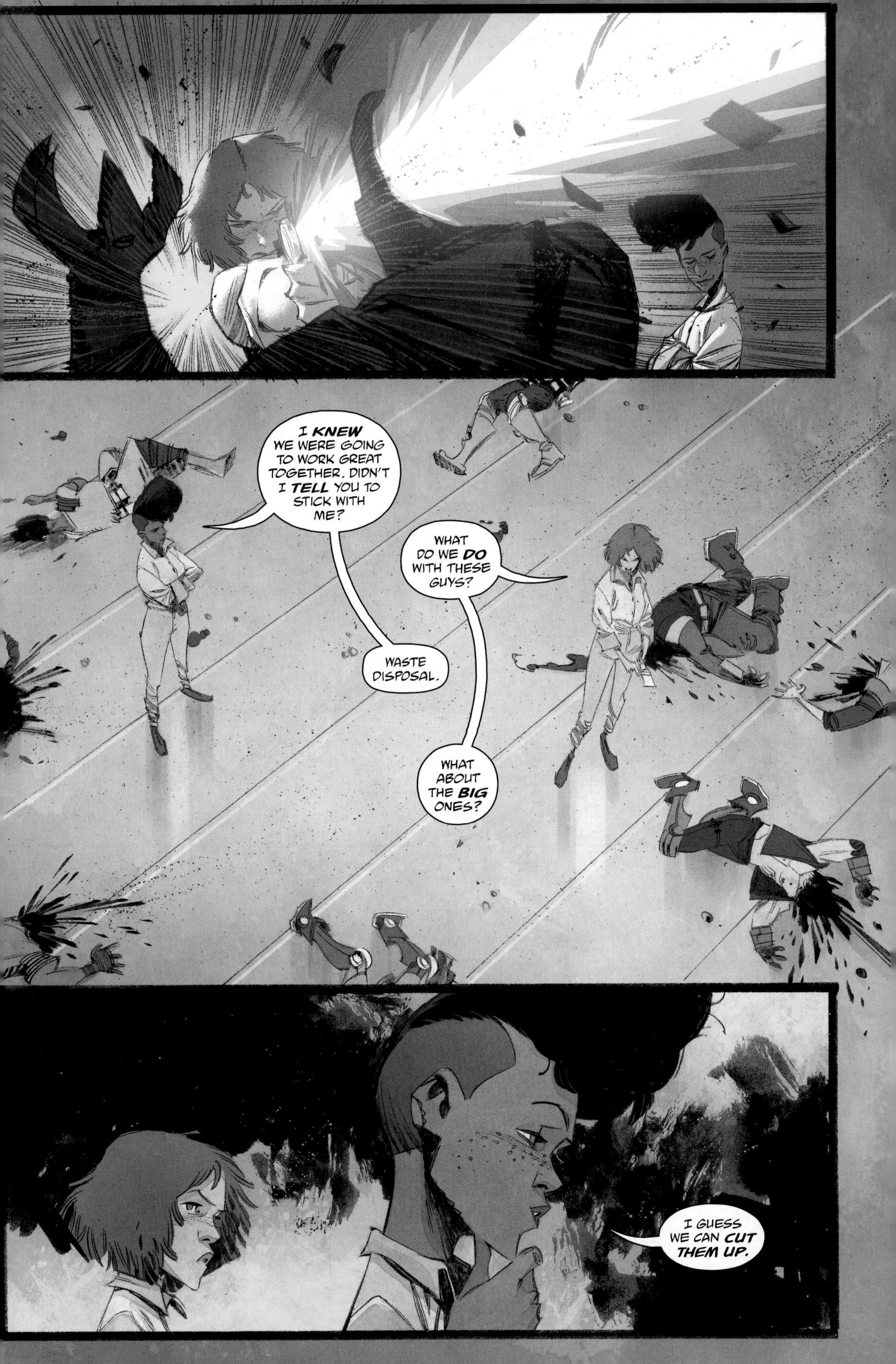
I KNEW WE WERE GOING TO WORK GREAT TOGETHER. DIDN'T I TELL YOU TO STICK WITH ME?
WHAT DO WE DO WITH THESE GUYS?
WASTE DISPOSAL.
WHAT ABOUT THE BIG ONES?
I GUESS WE CAN CUT THEM UP.

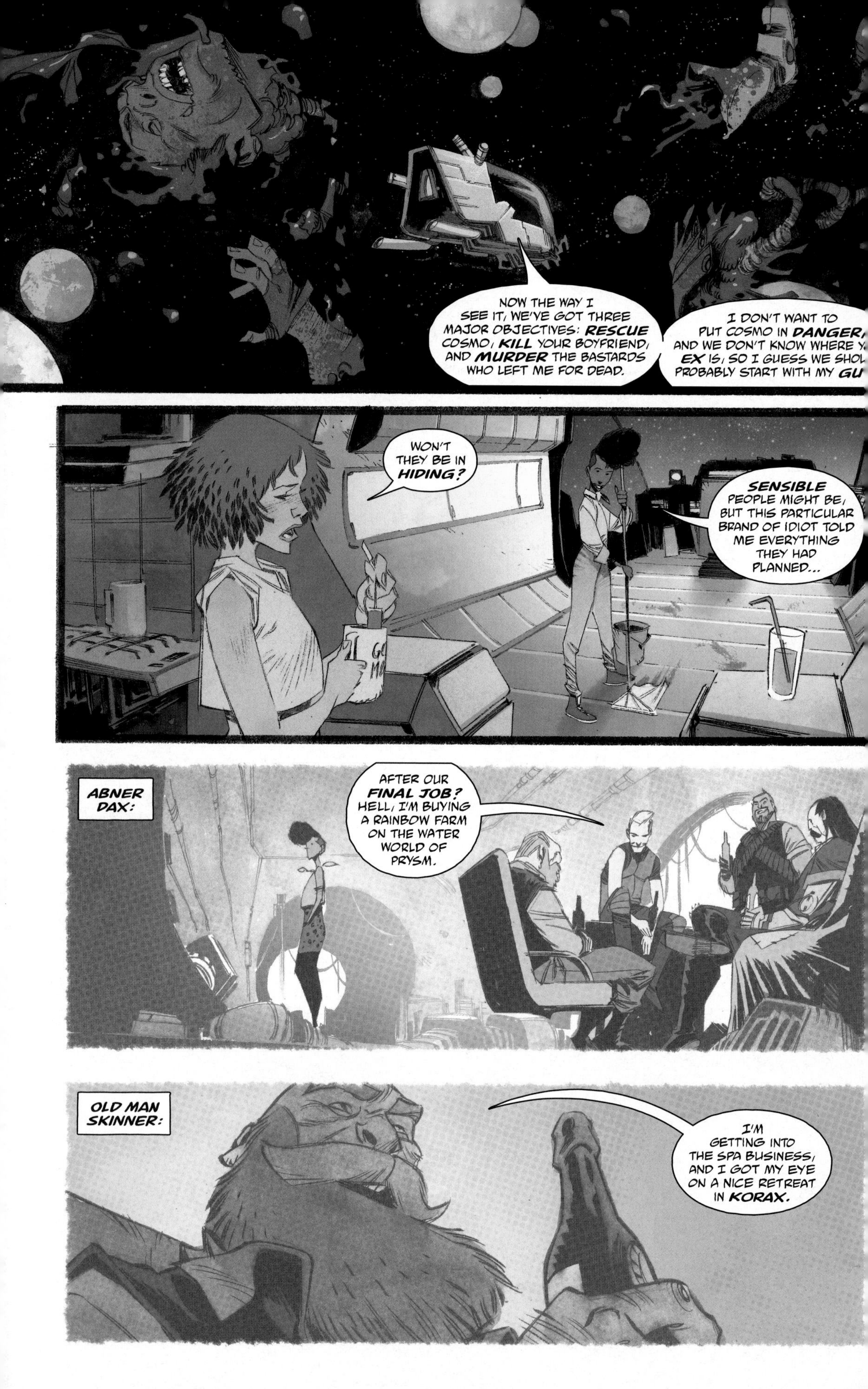
NOW THE WAY I SEE IT, WE'VE GOT THREE MAJOR OBJECTIVES: RESCUE COSMO, KILL YOUR BOYFRIEND, AND MURDER THE BASTARDS WHO LEFT ME FOR DEAD.
I DON'T WANT TO PUT COSMO IN DANGER, AND WE DON'T KNOW WHERE Y EX IS, SO I GUESS WE SHOL PROBABLY START WITH MY GU
WON'T THEY BE IN HIDING?
SENSIBLE PEOPLE MIGHT BE, BUT THIS PARTICULAR BRAND OF IDIOT TOLD ME EVERYTHING THEY HAD PLANNED...
ABNER DAX:
AFTER OUR FINAL JOB? HELL, I'M BUYING A RAINBOW FARM ON THE WATER WORLD OF PRYSM.
OLD MAN SKINNER:
I'M GETTING INTO THE SPA BUSINESS, AND I GOT MY EYE ON A NICE RETREAT IN KORAX.

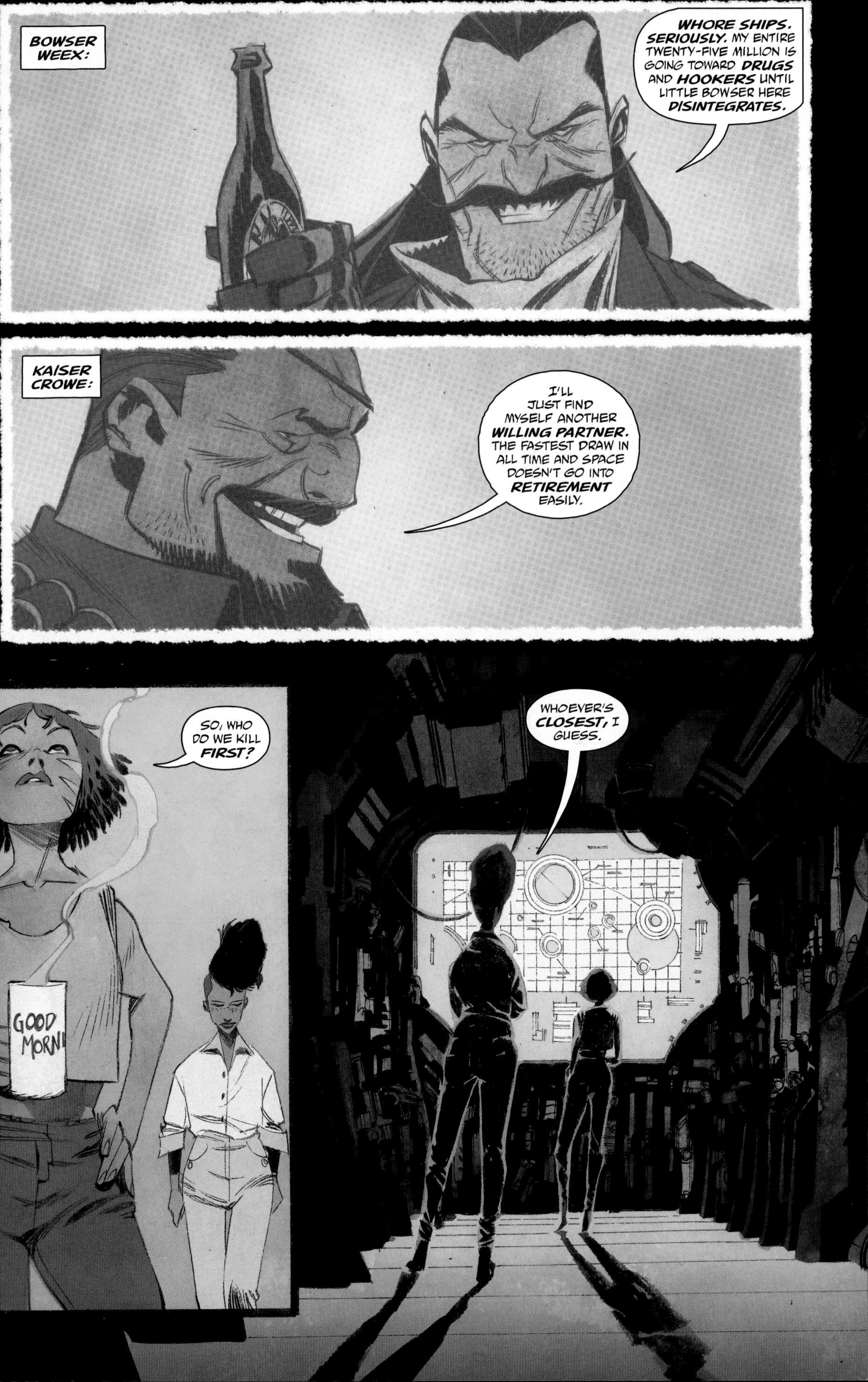
BOWSER WEEX:
WHORE SHIPS. SERIOUSLY. MY ENTIRE TWENTY-FIVE MILLION IS GOING TOWARD DRUGS AND HOOKERS UNTIL LITTLE BOWSER HERE DISINTEGRATES.
KAISER CROWE:
I'LL JUST FIND MYSELF ANOTHER WILLING PARTNER. THE FASTEST DRAW IN ALL TIME AND SPACE DOESN'T GO INTO RETIREMENT EASILY.
SO, WHO DO WE KILL FIRST?
WHOEVER'S CLOSEST, I GUESS.
GOOD MORNI

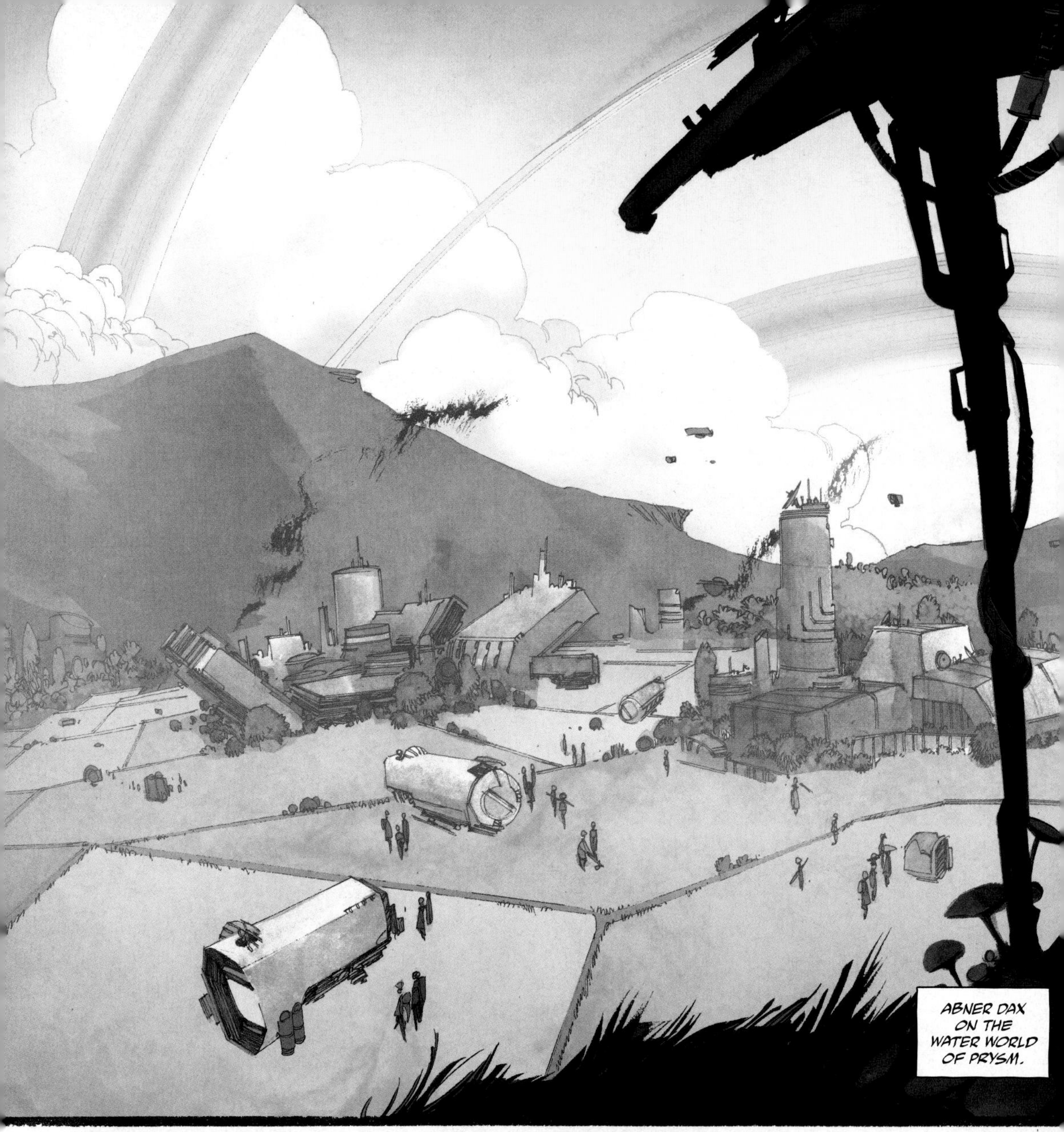
ABNER DAX ON THE WATER WORLD OF PRYSM.

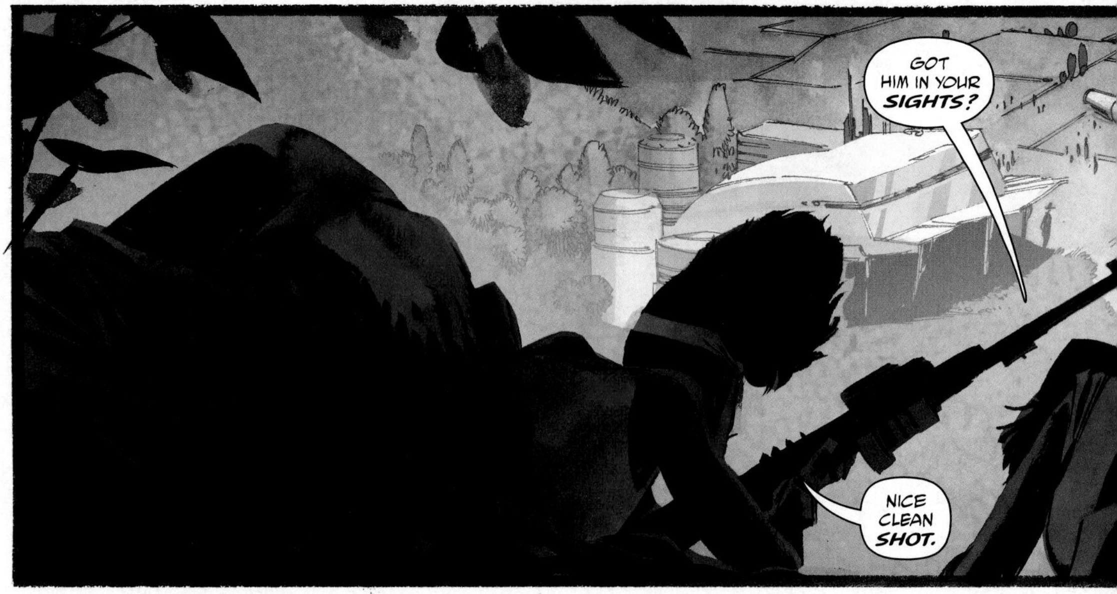
GOT HIM IN YOUR SIGHTS?
NICE CLEAN SHOT.

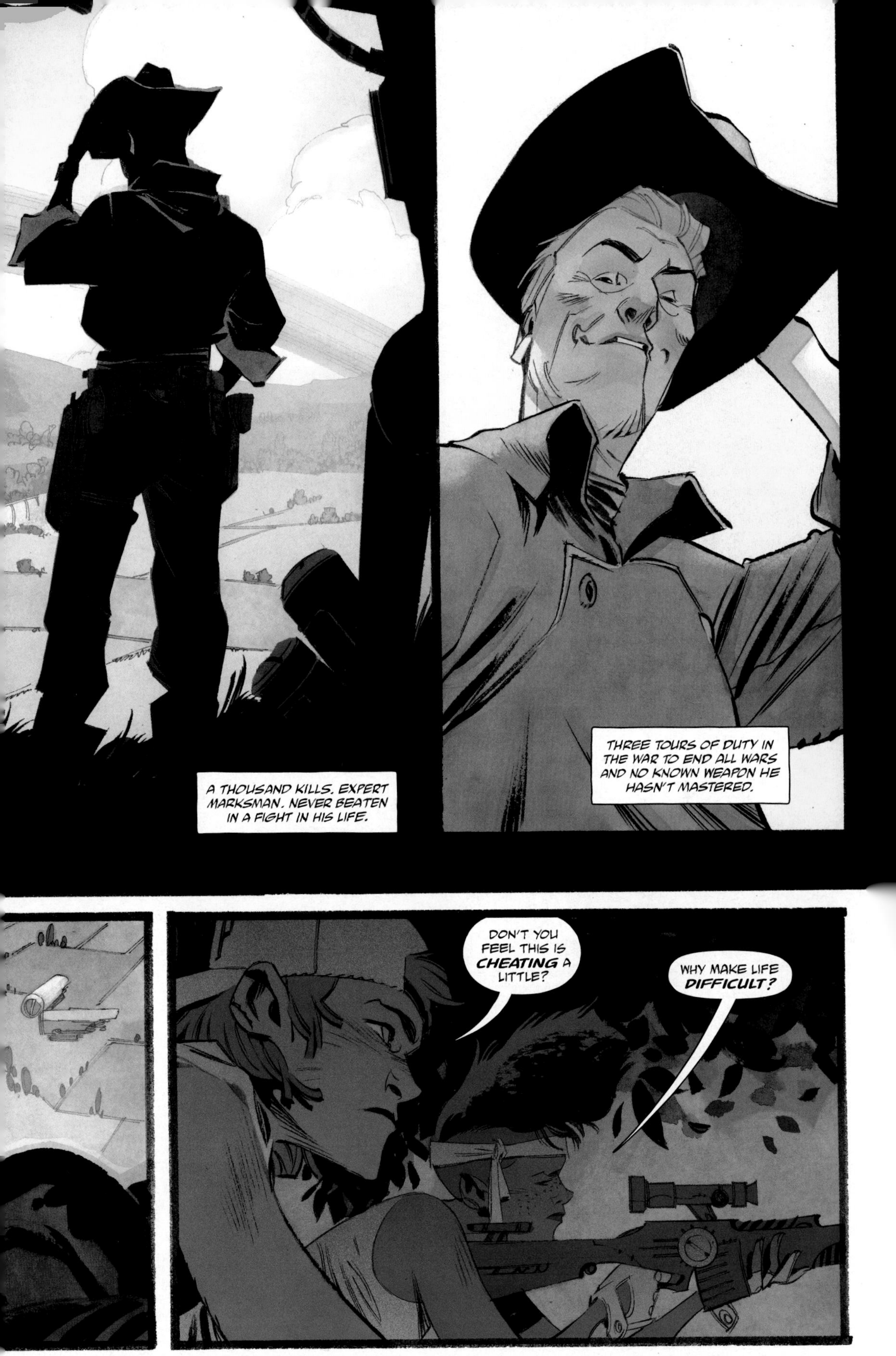
A THOUSAND KILLS. EXPERT MARKSMAN. NEVER BEATEN IN A FIGHT IN HIS LIFE.
THREE TOURS OF DUTY IN THE WAR TO END ALL WARS AND NO KNOWN WEAPON HE HASN'T MASTERED.
DON'T YOU FEEL THIS IS **CHEATING** A LITTLE?
WHY MAKE LIFE **DIFFICULT?**

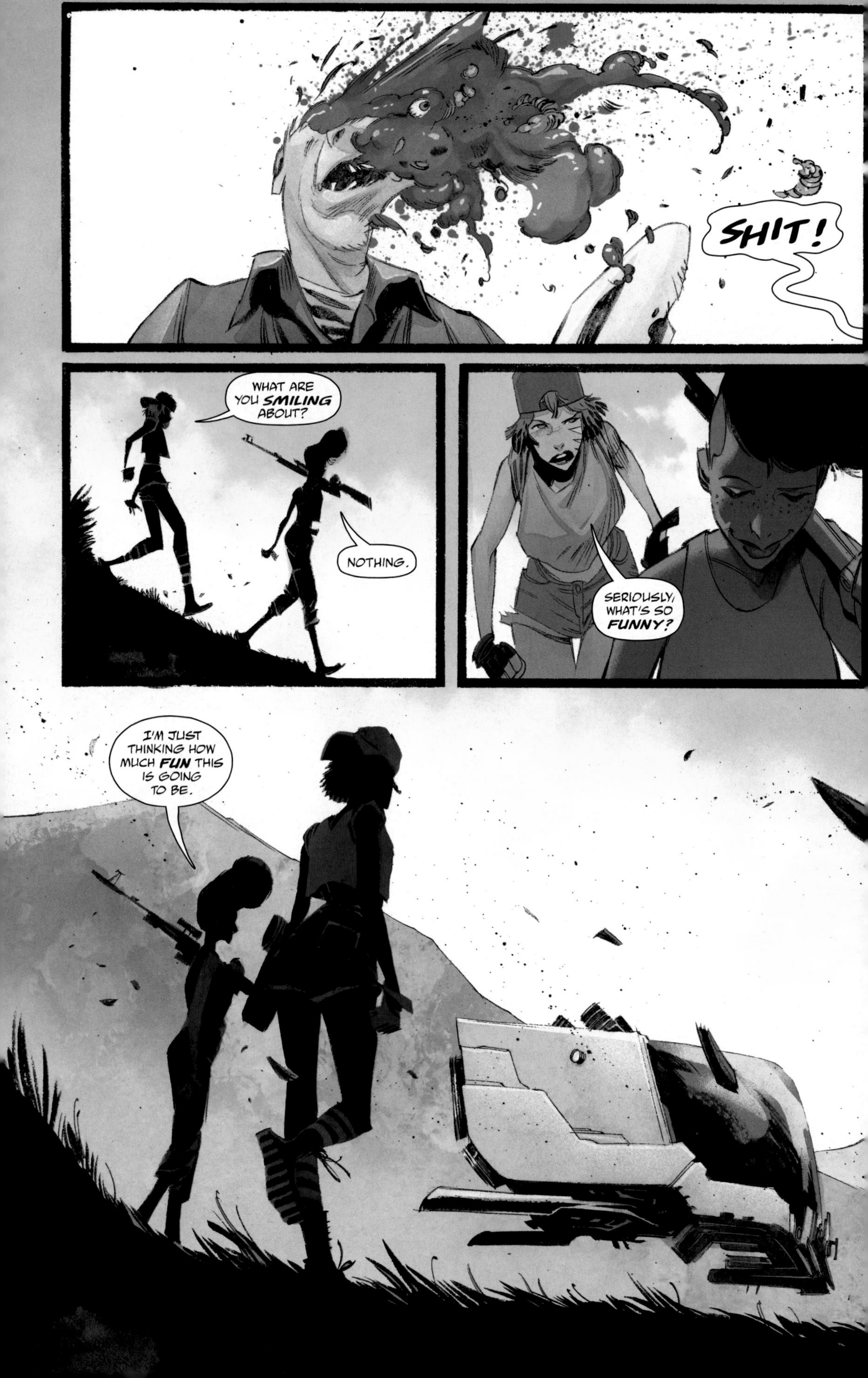
SHIT!
WHAT ARE YOU SMILING ABOUT?
NOTHING.
SERIOUSLY, WHAT'S SO FUNNY?
I'M JUST THINKING HOW MUCH FUN THIS IS GOING TO BE.

Three

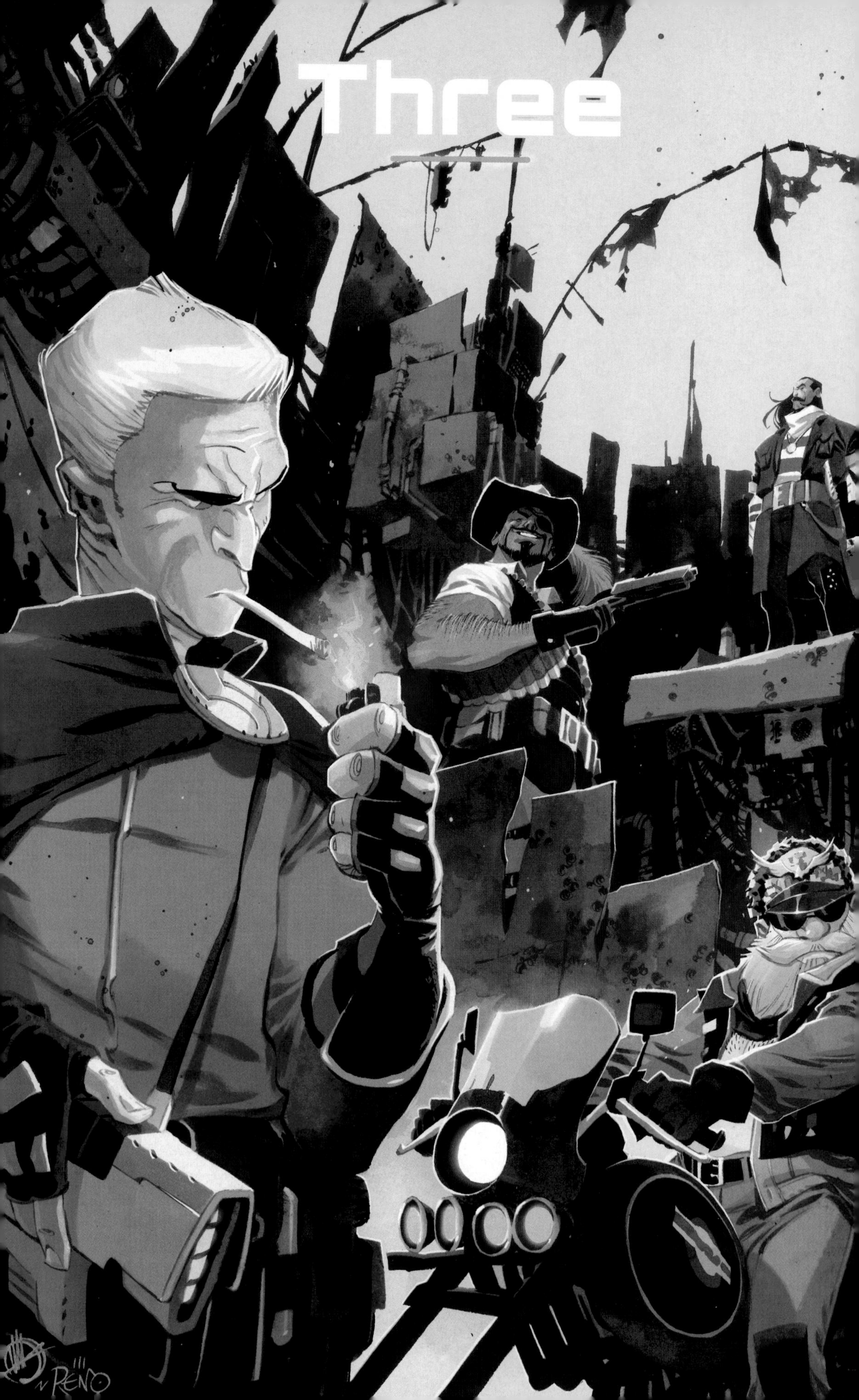

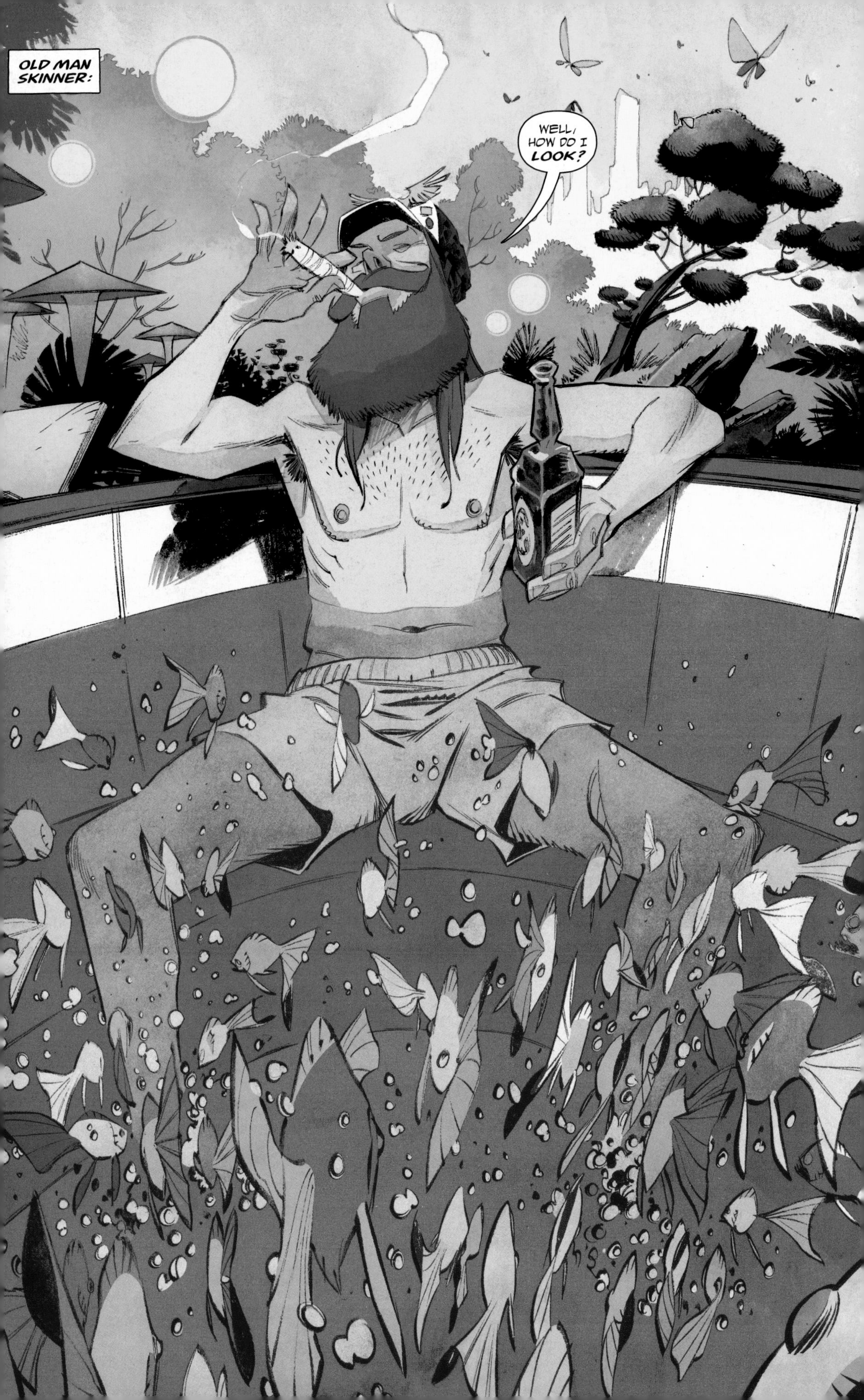
OLD MAN SKINNER:
WELL, HOW DO I LOOK?

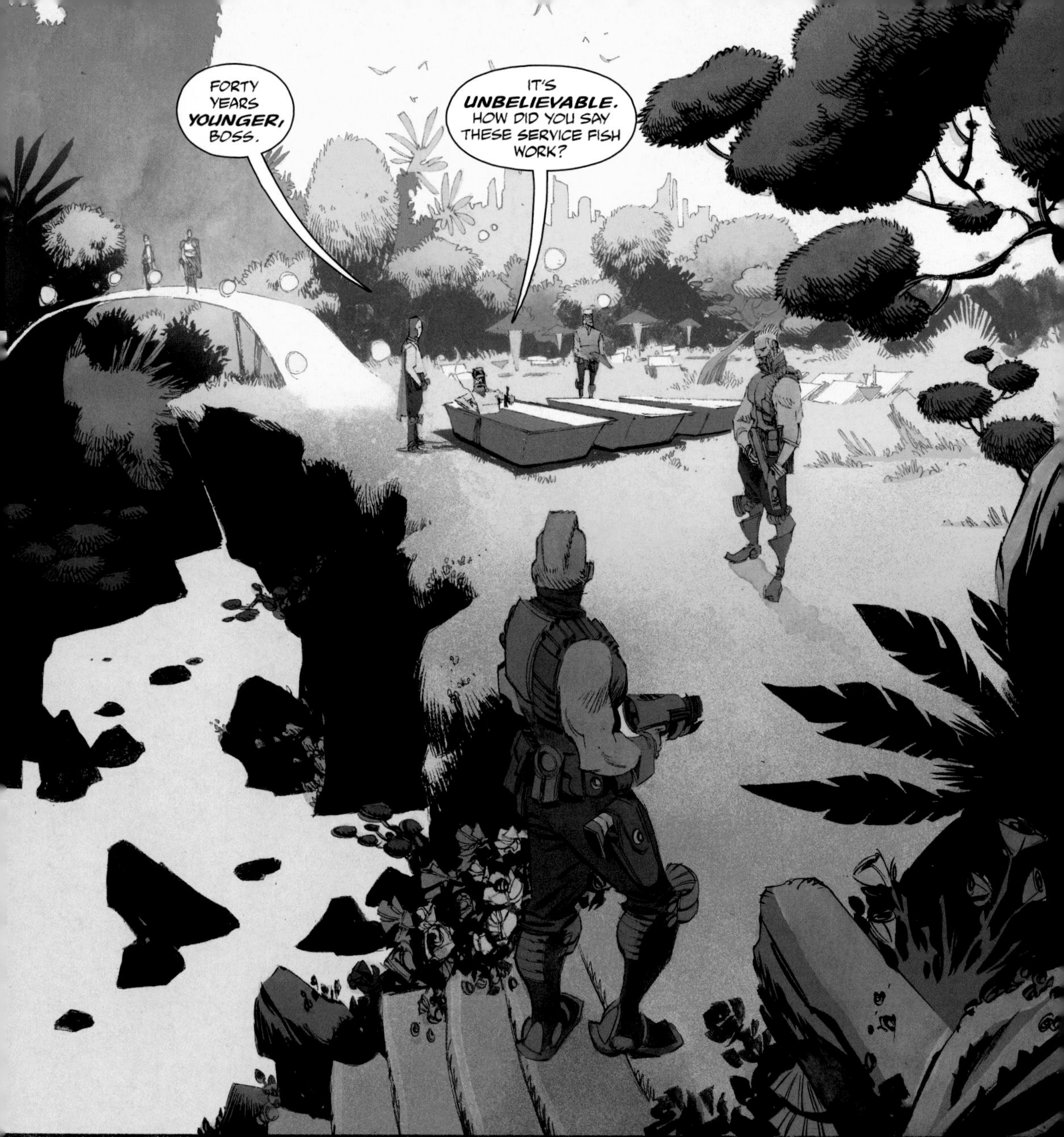
FORTY YEARS YOUNGER, BOSS.
IT'S UNBELIEVABLE. HOW DID YOU SAY THESE SERVICE FISH WORK?

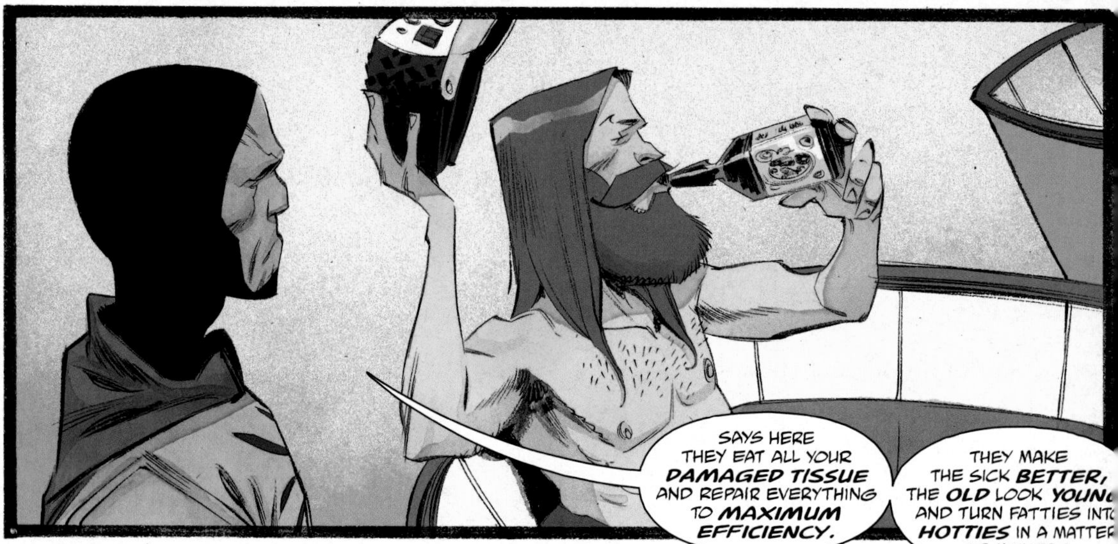
SAYS HERE THEY EAT ALL YOUR DAMAGED TISSUE AND REPAIR EVERYTHING TO MAXIMUM EFFICIENCY.
THEY MAKE THE SICK BETTER, THE OLD LOOK YOUN AND TURN FATTIES INT HOTTIES IN A MATTE OF MINUTES.

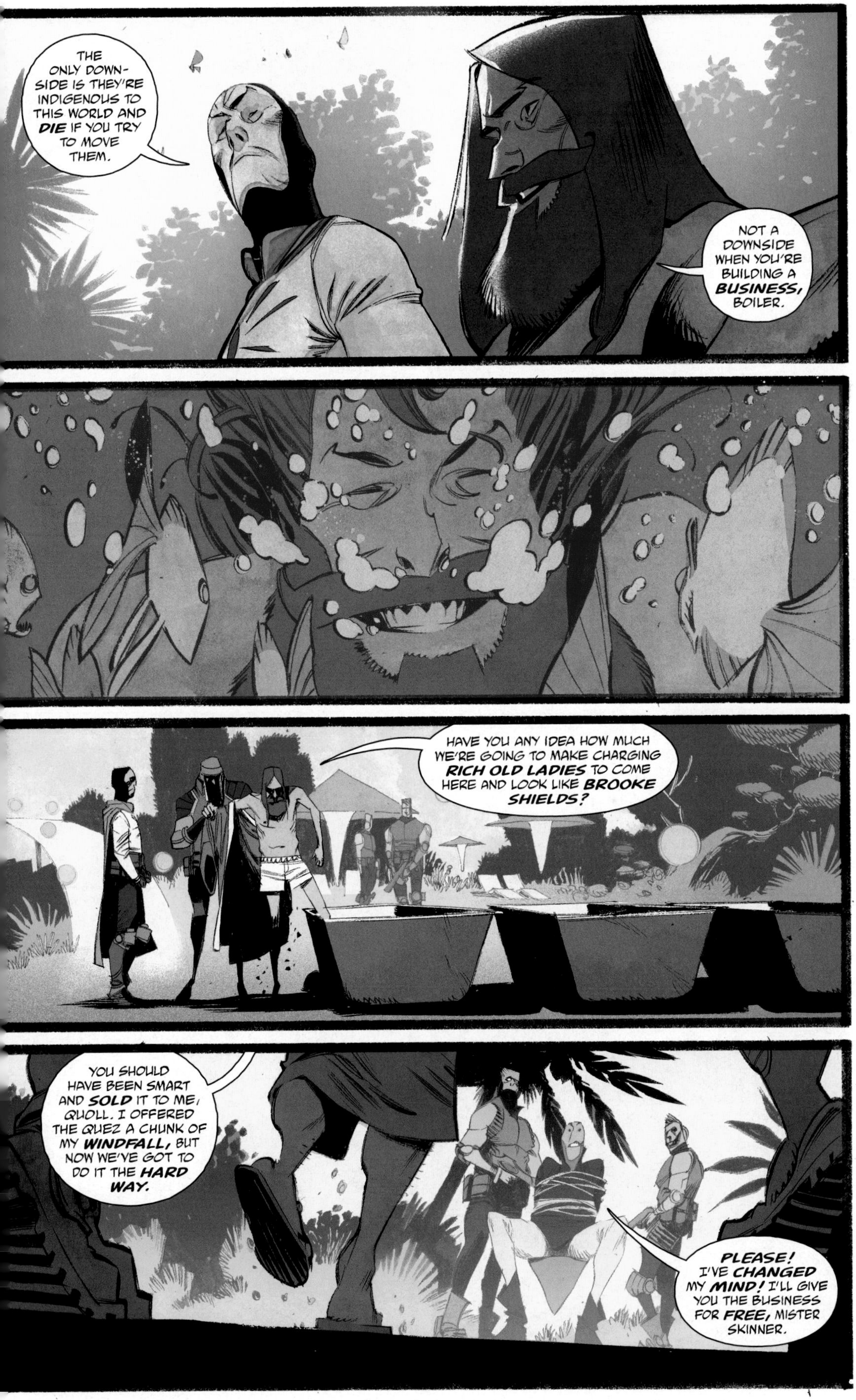
THE ONLY DOWN-SIDE IS THEY'RE INDIGENOUS TO THIS WORLD AND DIE IF YOU TRY TO MOVE THEM.
NOT A DOWNSIDE WHEN YOU'RE BUILDING A BUSINESS, BOILER.
HAVE YOU ANY IDEA HOW MUCH WE'RE GOING TO MAKE CHARGING RICH OLD LADIES TO COME HERE AND LOOK LIKE BROOKE SHIELDS?
YOU SHOULD HAVE BEEN SMART AND SOLD IT TO ME, QUOLL. I OFFERED THE QUEZ A CHUNK OF MY WINDFALL, BUT NOW WE'VE GOT TO DO IT THE HARD WAY.
PLEASE! I'VE CHANGED MY MIND! I'LL GIVE YOU THE BUSINESS FOR FREE, MISTER SKINNER.

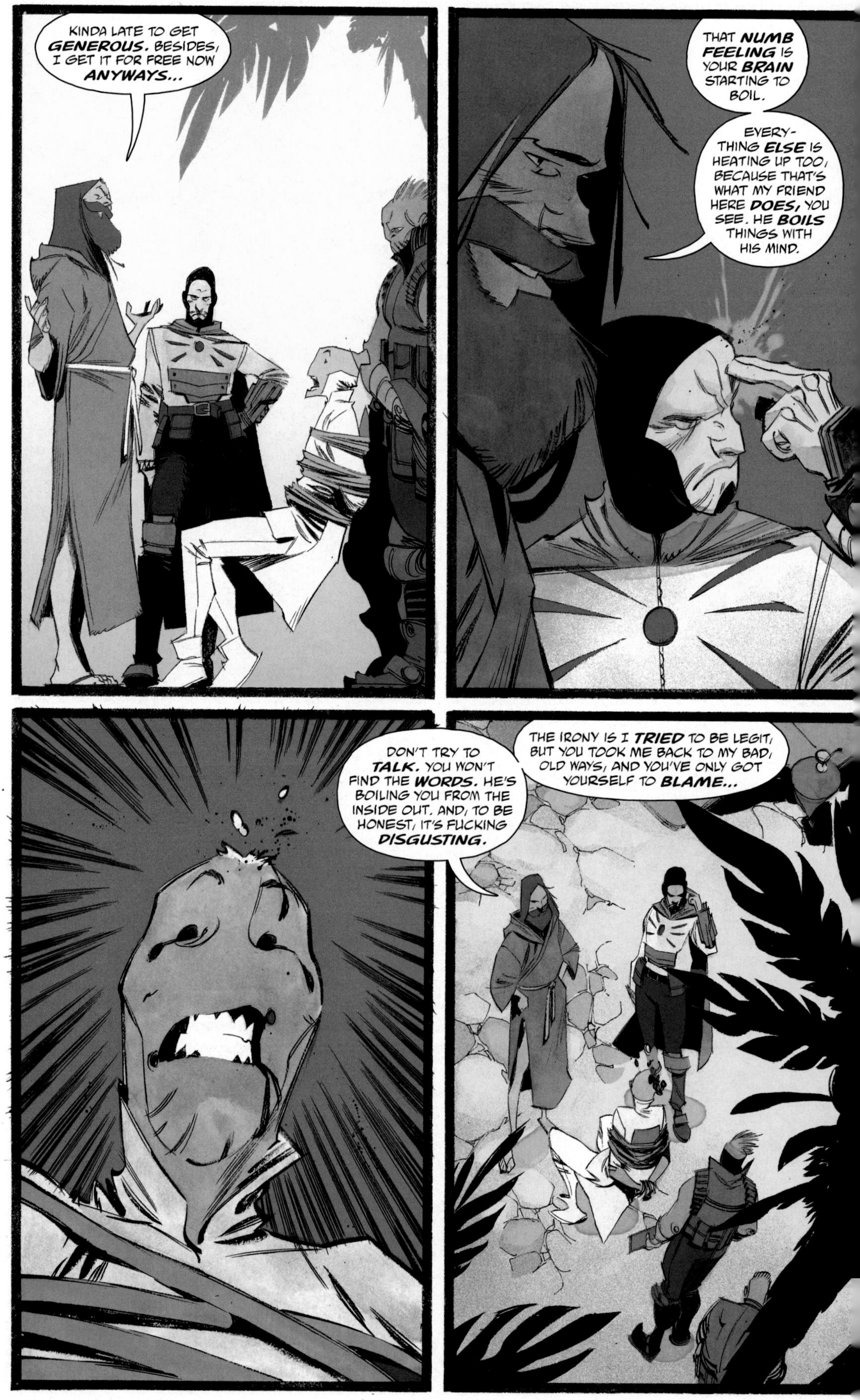
KINDA LATE TO GET **GENEROUS.** BESIDES, I GET IT FOR FREE NOW **ANYWAYS...**
THAT **NUMB FEELING** IS YOUR **BRAIN** STARTING TO BOIL.
EVERY-THING **ELSE** IS HEATING UP TOO, BECAUSE THAT'S WHAT MY FRIEND HERE **DOES,** YOU SEE. HE **BOILS** THINGS WITH HIS MIND.
DON'T TRY TO **TALK.** YOU WON'T FIND THE **WORDS.** HE'S BOILING YOU FROM THE INSIDE OUT. AND, TO BE HONEST, IT'S FUCKING **DISGUSTING.**
THE IRONY IS I **TRIED** TO BE LEGIT, BUT YOU TOOK ME BACK TO MY BAD, OLD WAYS, AND YOU'VE ONLY GOT YOURSELF TO **BLAME...**

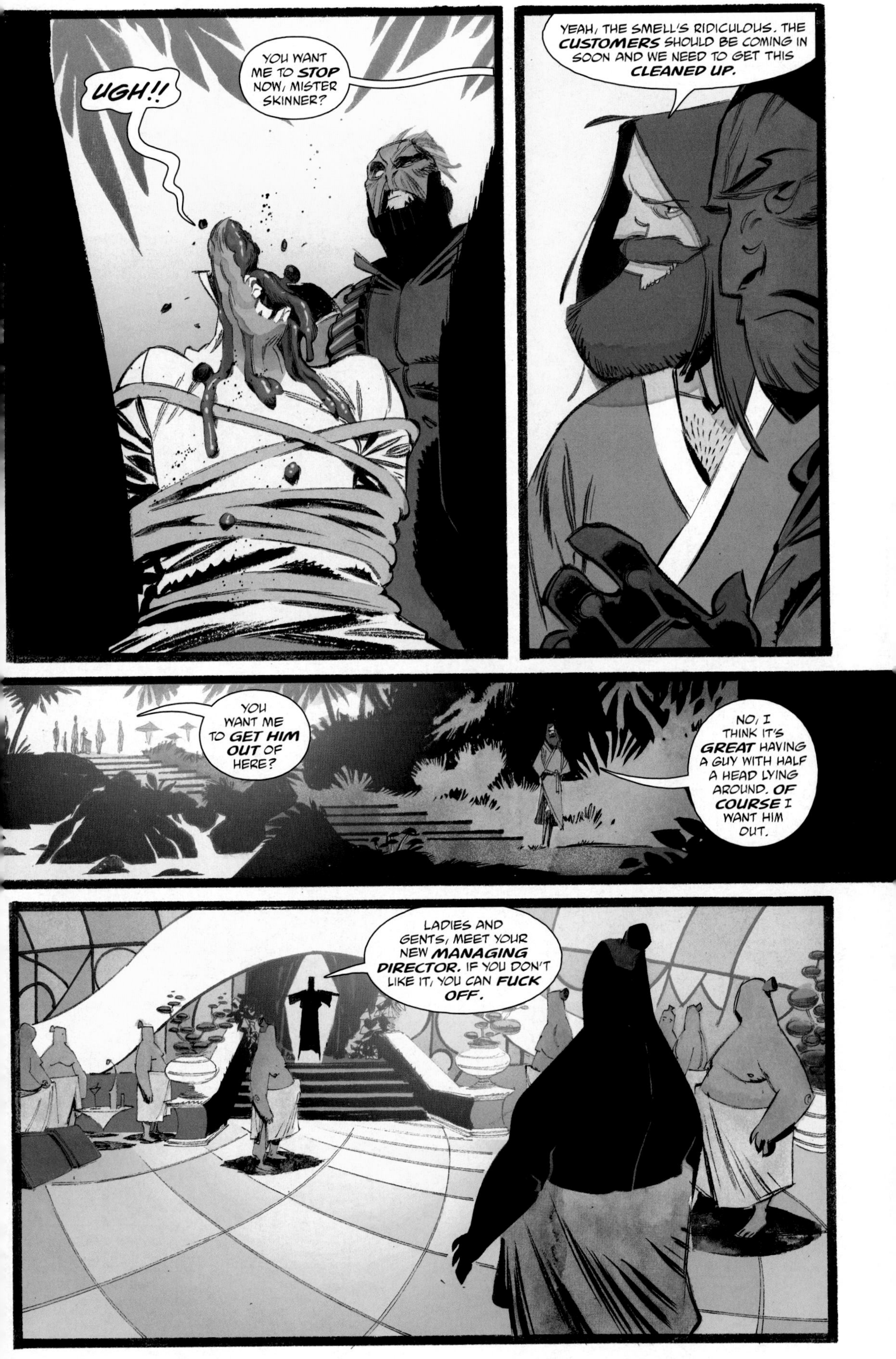
YOU WANT ME TO STOP NOW, MISTER SKINNER?
UGH!!
YEAH, THE SMELL'S RIDICULOUS. THE CUSTOMERS SHOULD BE COMING IN SOON AND WE NEED TO GET THIS CLEANED UP.
YOU WANT ME TO GET HIM OUT OF HERE?
NO, I THINK IT'S GREAT HAVING A GUY WITH HALF A HEAD LYING AROUND. OF COURSE I WANT HIM OUT.
LADIES AND GENTS, MEET YOUR NEW MANAGING DIRECTOR. IF YOU DON'T LIKE IT, YOU CAN FUCK OFF.

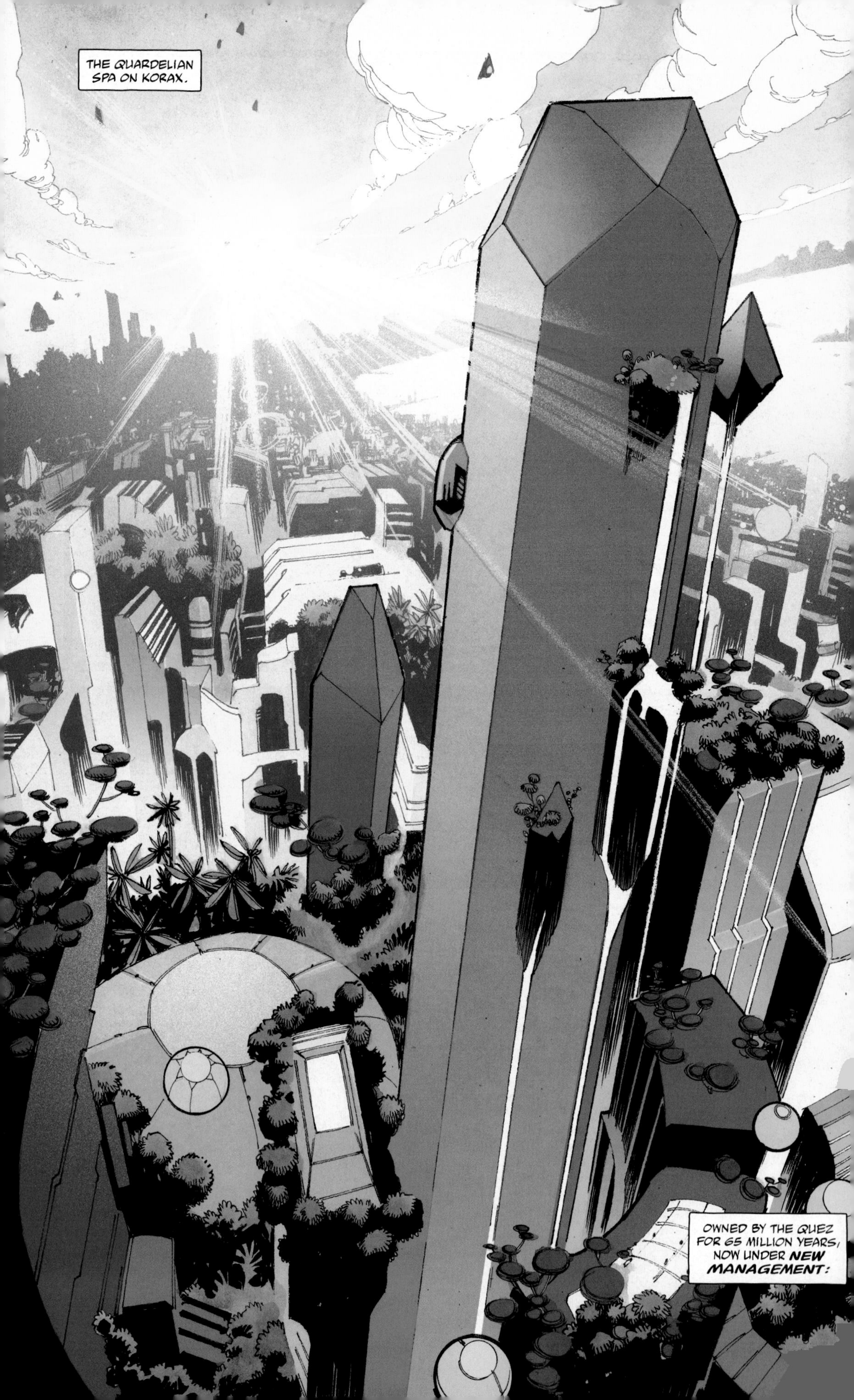
THE QUARDELIAN SPA ON KORAX.
OWNED BY THE QUEZ FOR 65 MILLION YEARS, NOW UNDER **NEW MANAGEMENT**:

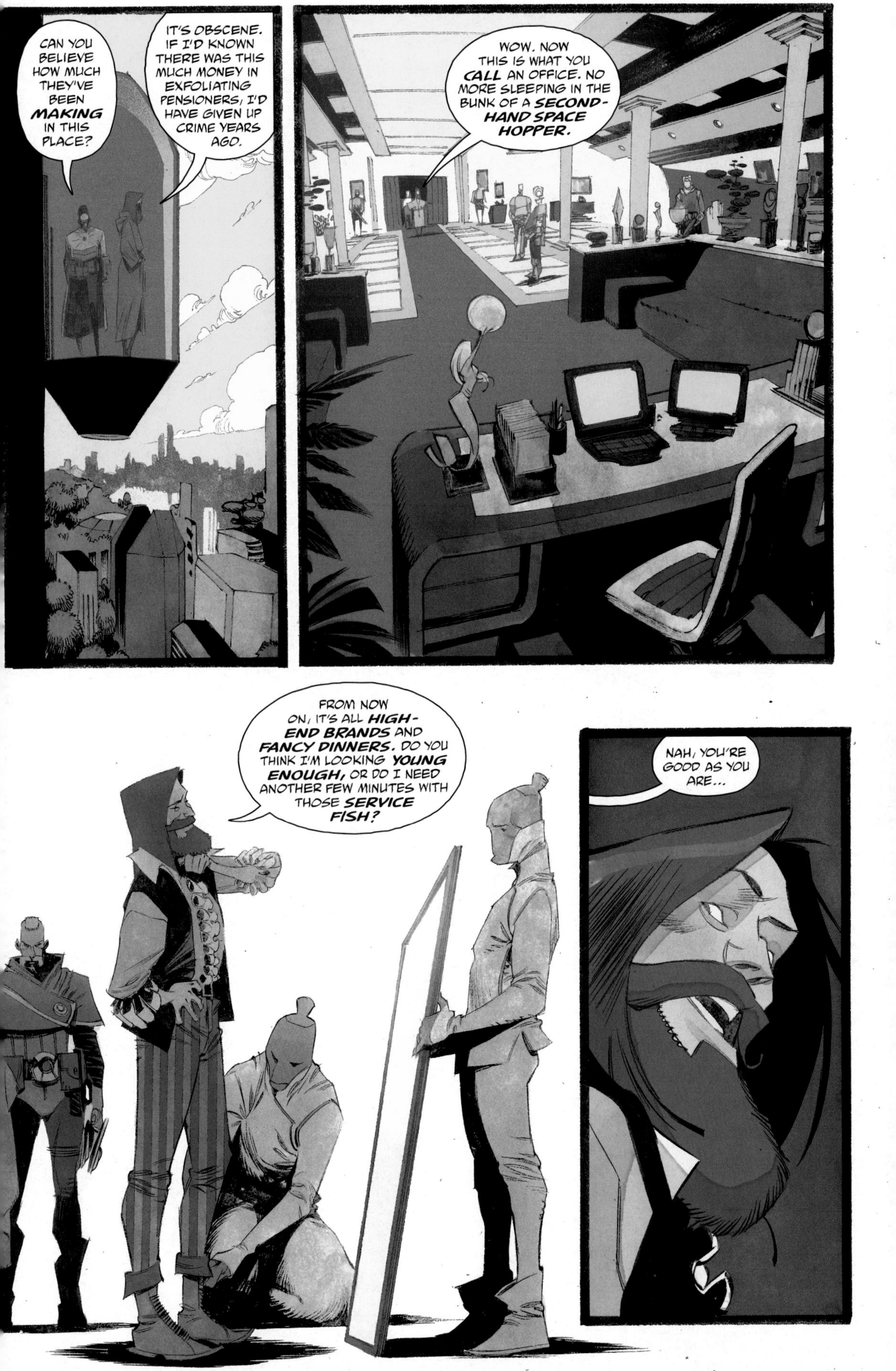
CAN YOU BELIEVE HOW MUCH THEY'VE BEEN **MAKING** IN THIS PLACE?
IT'S OBSCENE. IF I'D KNOWN THERE WAS THIS MUCH MONEY IN EXFOLIATING PENSIONERS, I'D HAVE GIVEN UP CRIME YEARS AGO.
WOW. NOW THIS IS WHAT YOU **CALL** AN OFFICE. NO MORE SLEEPING IN THE BUNK OF A **SECOND-HAND SPACE HOPPER.**
FROM NOW ON, IT'S ALL **HIGH-END BRANDS** AND **FANCY DINNERS.** DO YOU THINK I'M LOOKING **YOUNG ENOUGH,** OR DO I NEED ANOTHER FEW MINUTES WITH THOSE **SERVICE FISH?**
NAH, YOU'RE GOOD AS YOU ARE...

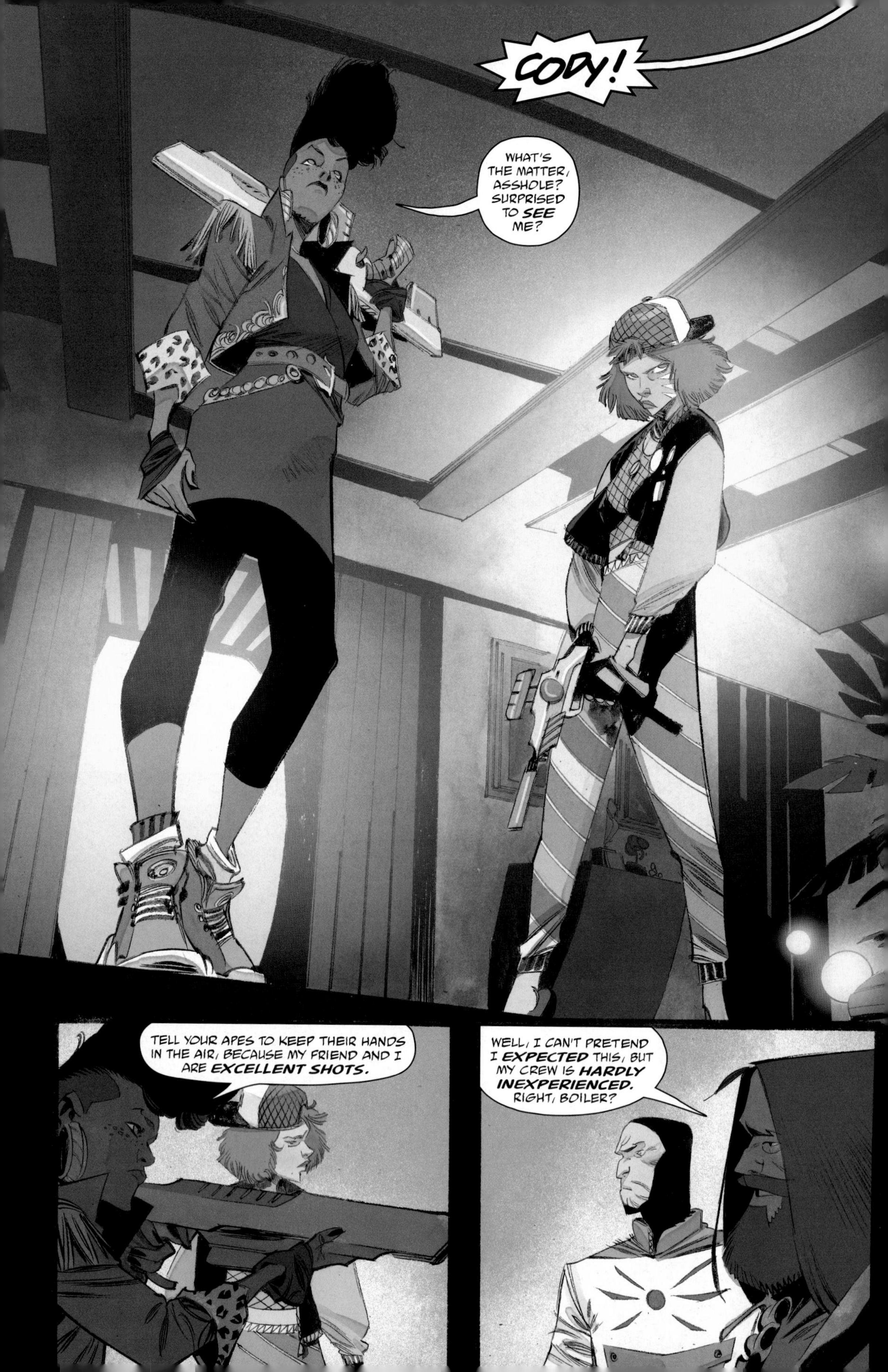
CODY!
WHAT'S THE MATTER, ASSHOLE? SURPRISED TO SEE ME?
TELL YOUR APES TO KEEP THEIR HANDS IN THE AIR, BECAUSE MY FRIEND AND I ARE EXCELLENT SHOTS.
WELL, I CAN'T PRETEND I EXPECTED THIS, BUT MY CREW IS HARDLY INEXPERIENCED. RIGHT, BOILER?

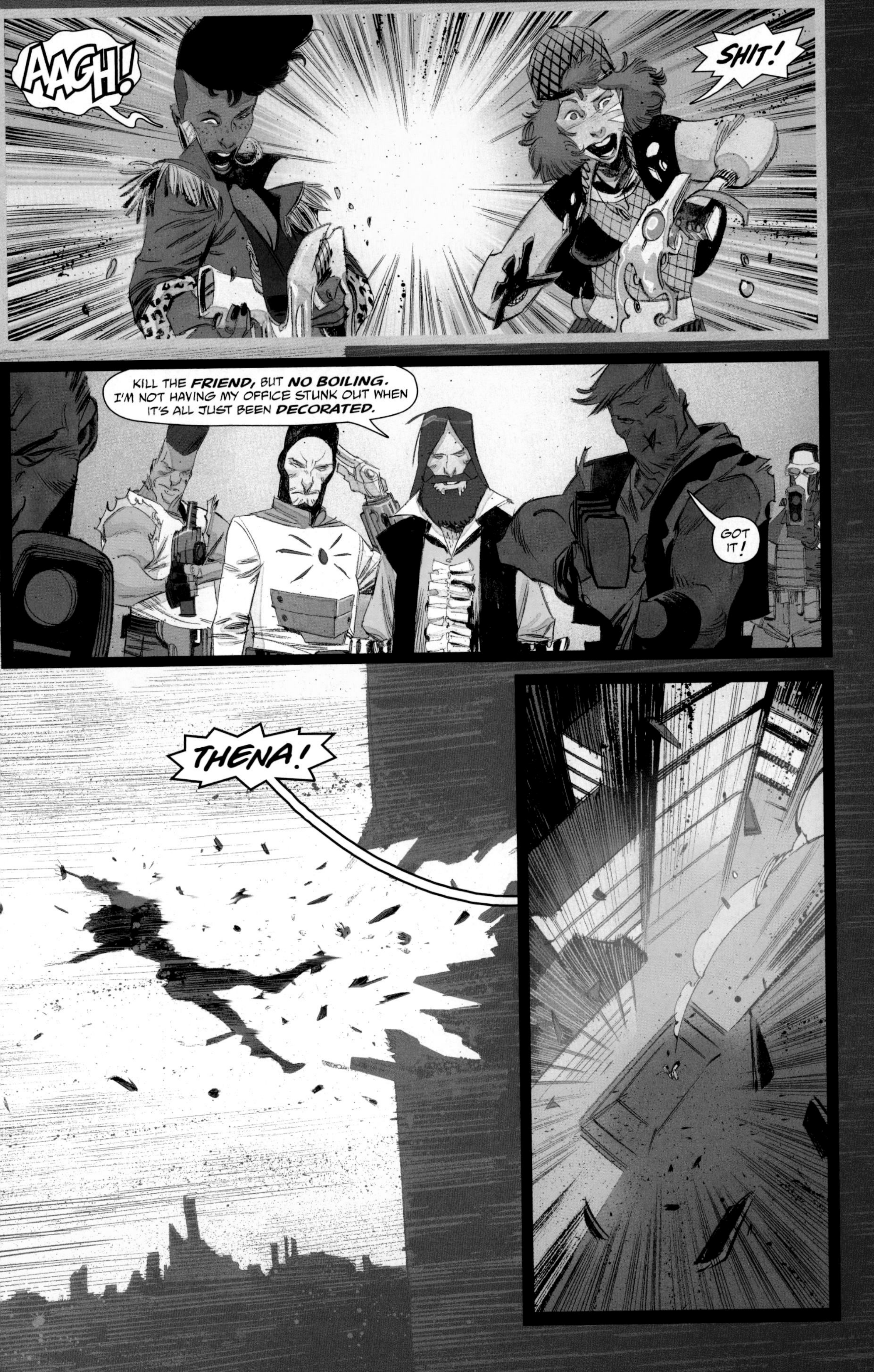
AAGH!
SHIT!
KILL THE FRIEND, BUT NO BOILING. I'M NOT HAVING MY OFFICE STUNK OUT WHEN IT'S ALL JUST BEEN DECORATED.
GOT IT!
THENA!

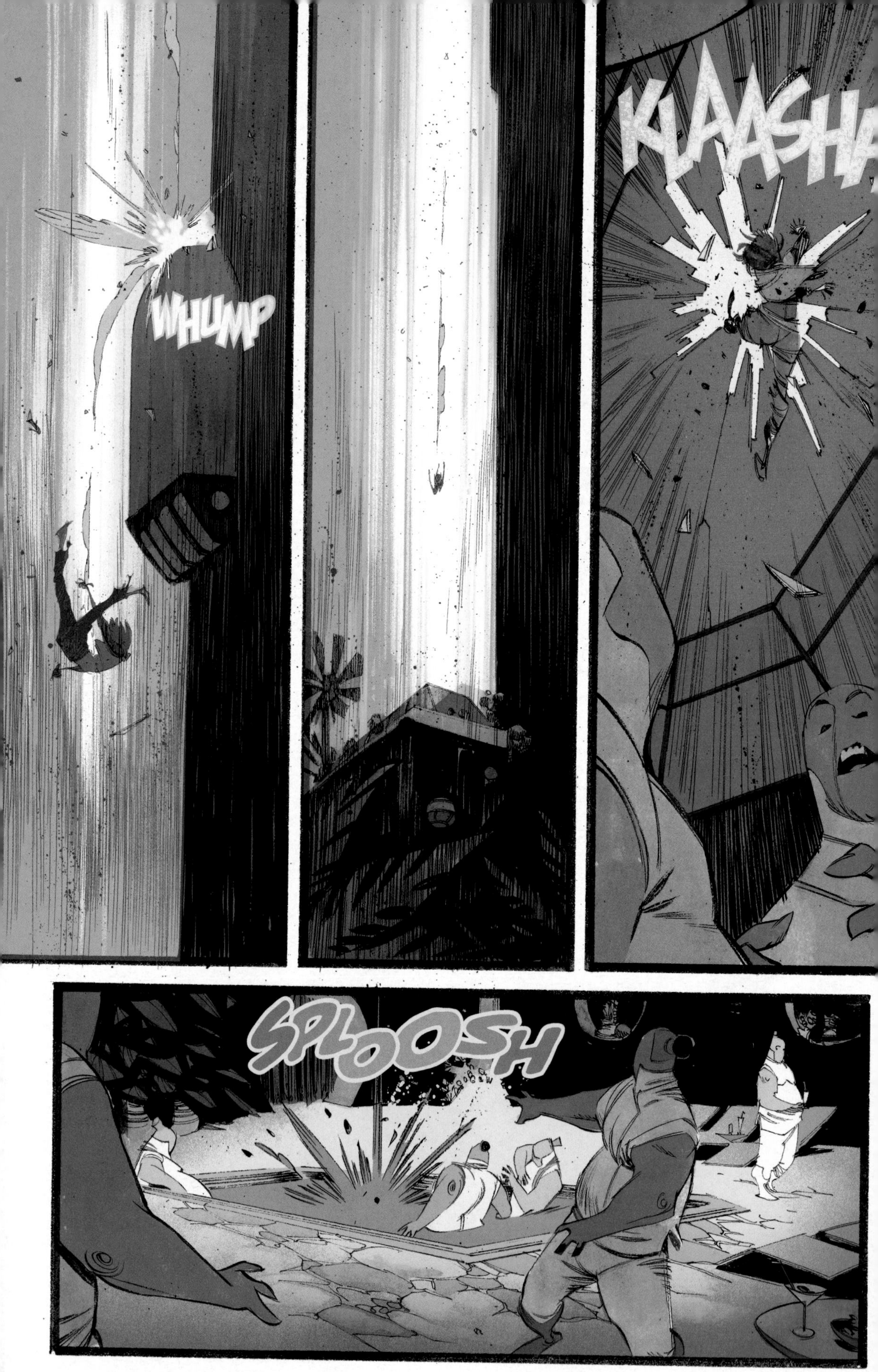
WHUMP
KLAASHA
SPLOOSH

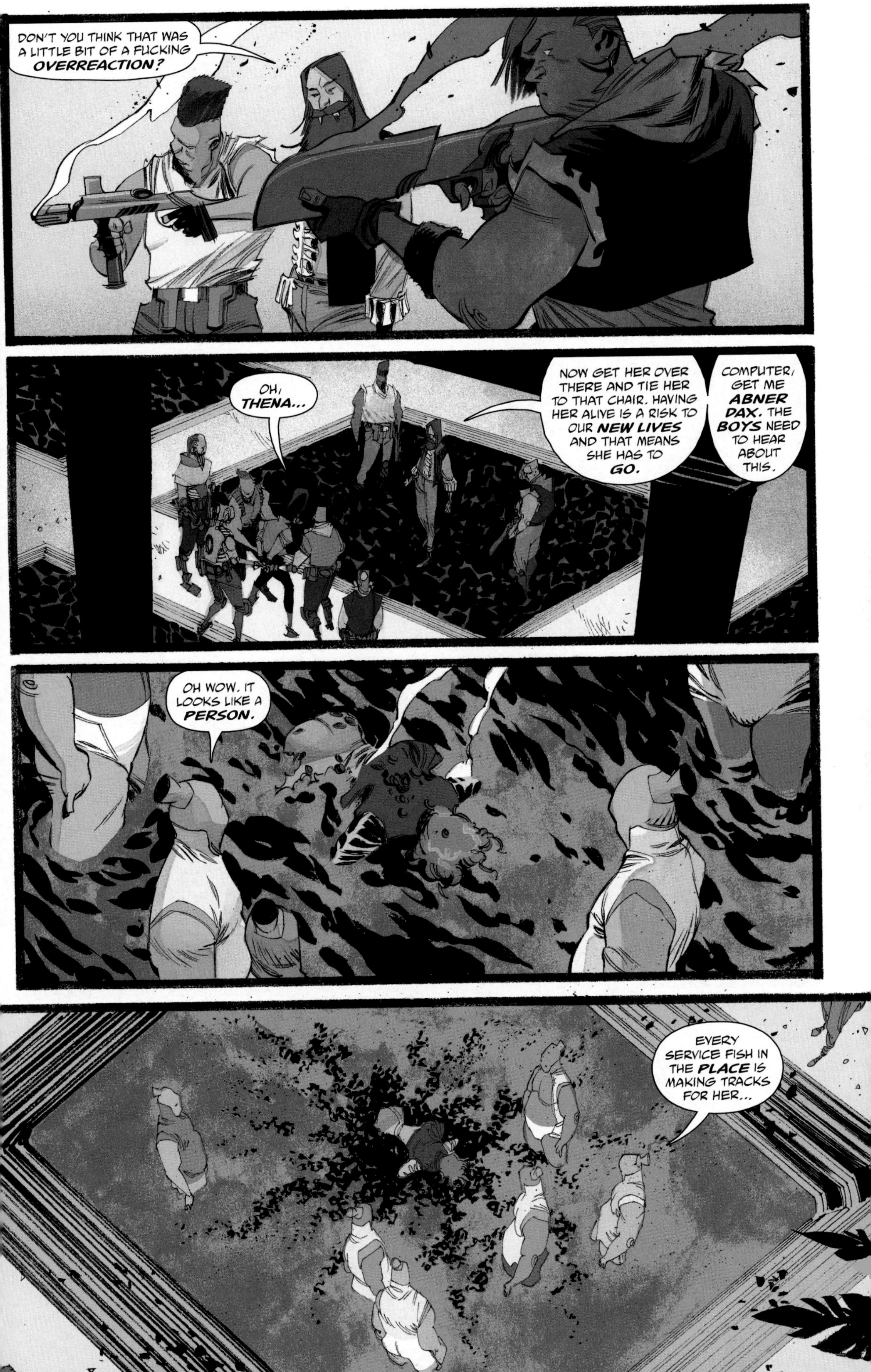
DON'T YOU THINK THAT WAS A LITTLE BIT OF A FUCKING OVERREACTION?
OH, THENA...
NOW GET HER OVER THERE AND TIE HER TO THAT CHAIR. HAVING HER ALIVE IS A RISK TO OUR NEW LIVES AND THAT MEANS SHE HAS TO GO.
COMPUTER, GET ME ABNER DAX. THE BOYS NEED TO HEAR ABOUT THIS.
OH WOW. IT LOOKS LIKE A PERSON.
EVERY SERVICE FISH IN THE PLACE IS MAKING TRACKS FOR HER...

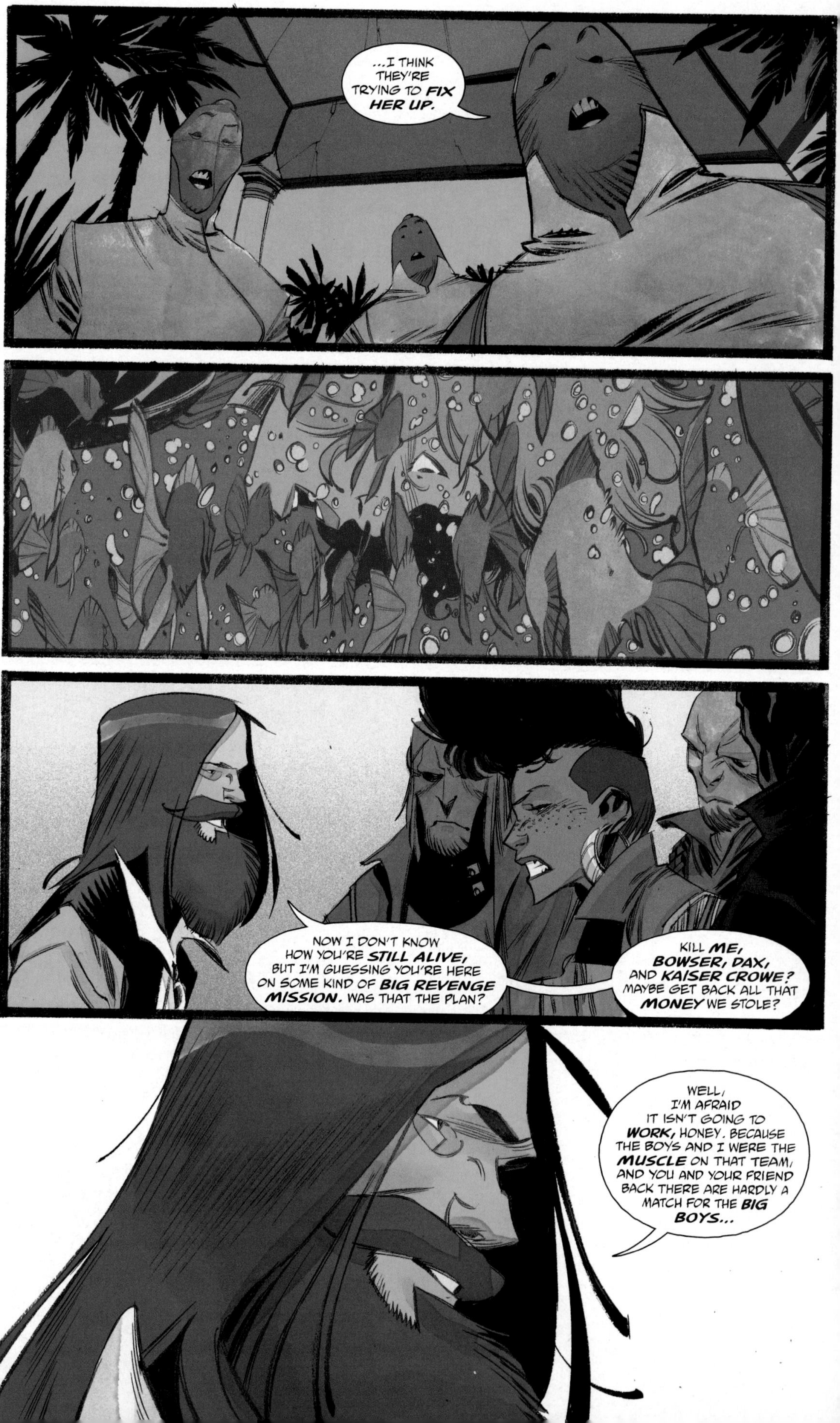
...I THINK THEY'RE TRYING TO FIX HER UP.
NOW I DON'T KNOW HOW YOU'RE STILL ALIVE, BUT I'M GUESSING YOU'RE HERE ON SOME KIND OF BIG REVENGE MISSION. WAS THAT THE PLAN?
KILL ME, BOWSER, DAX, AND KAISER CROWE? MAYBE GET BACK ALL THAT MONEY WE STOLE?
WELL, I'M AFRAID IT ISN'T GOING TO WORK, HONEY. BECAUSE THE BOYS AND I WERE THE MUSCLE ON THAT TEAM, AND YOU AND YOUR FRIEND BACK THERE ARE HARDLY A MATCH FOR THE BIG BOYS...

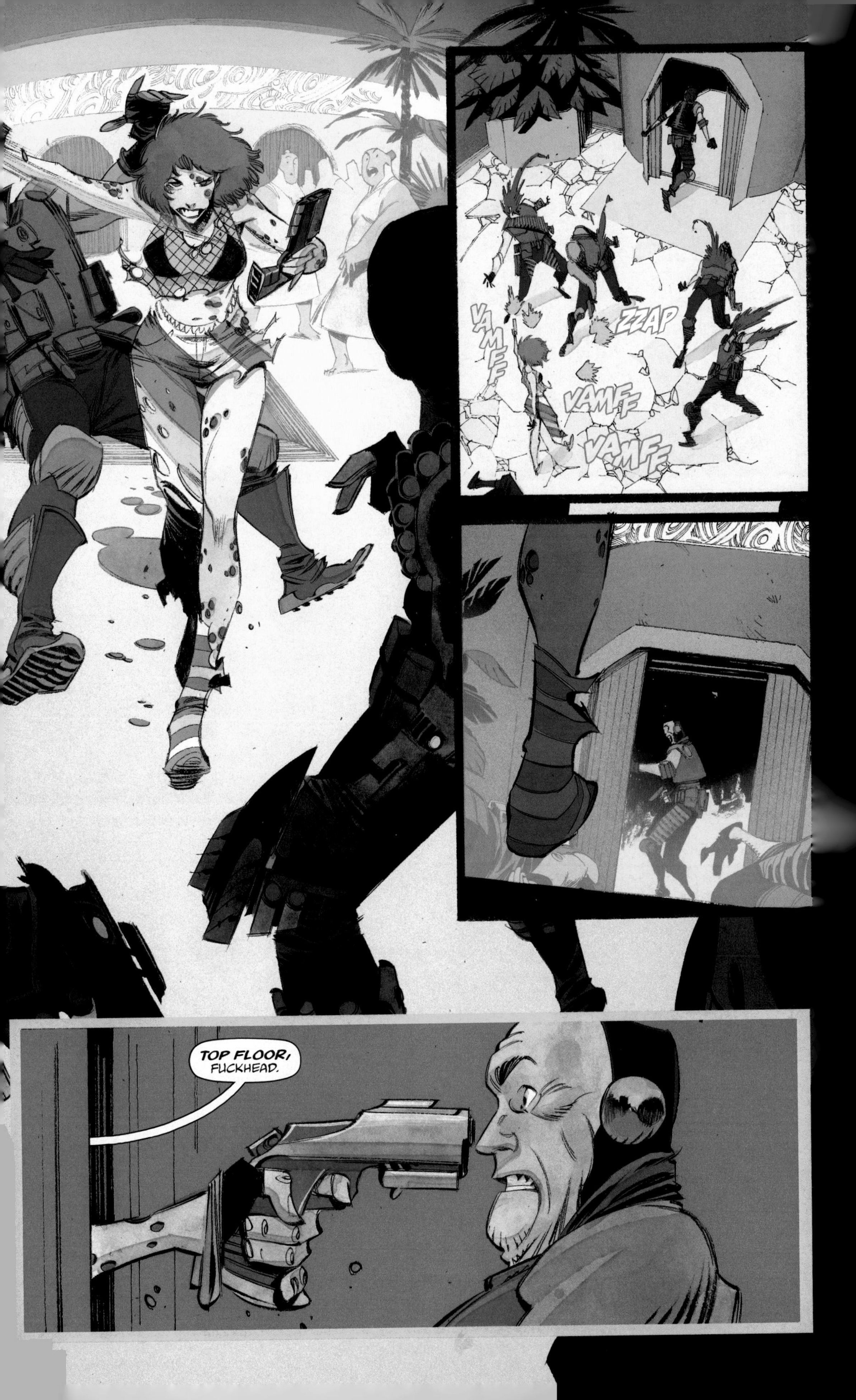
VAMFF
ZZAP
VAMFF
VAMFF
TOP FLOOR,
FUCKHEAD.

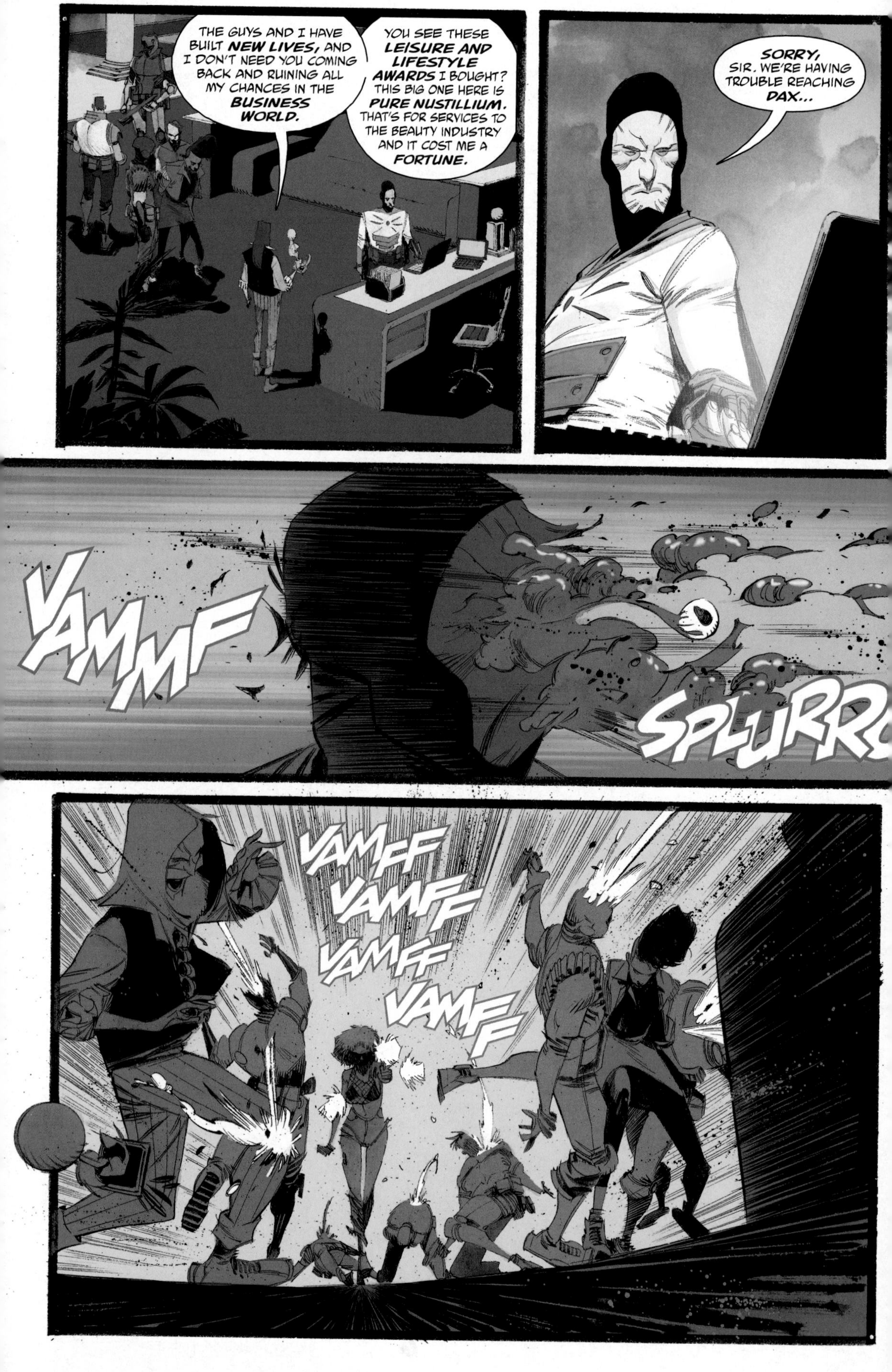
THE GUYS AND I HAVE BUILT NEW LIVES, AND I DON'T NEED YOU COMING BACK AND RUINING ALL MY CHANCES IN THE BUSINESS WORLD.
YOU SEE THESE LEISURE AND LIFESTYLE AWARDS I BOUGHT? THIS BIG ONE HERE IS PURE NUSTILLIUM. THAT'S FOR SERVICES TO THE BEAUTY INDUSTRY AND IT COST ME A FORTUNE.
SORRY, SIR. WE'RE HAVING TROUBLE REACHING DAX...
VAMMF
SPLURRG
VAMFF
VAMFF
VAMFF
VAMFF

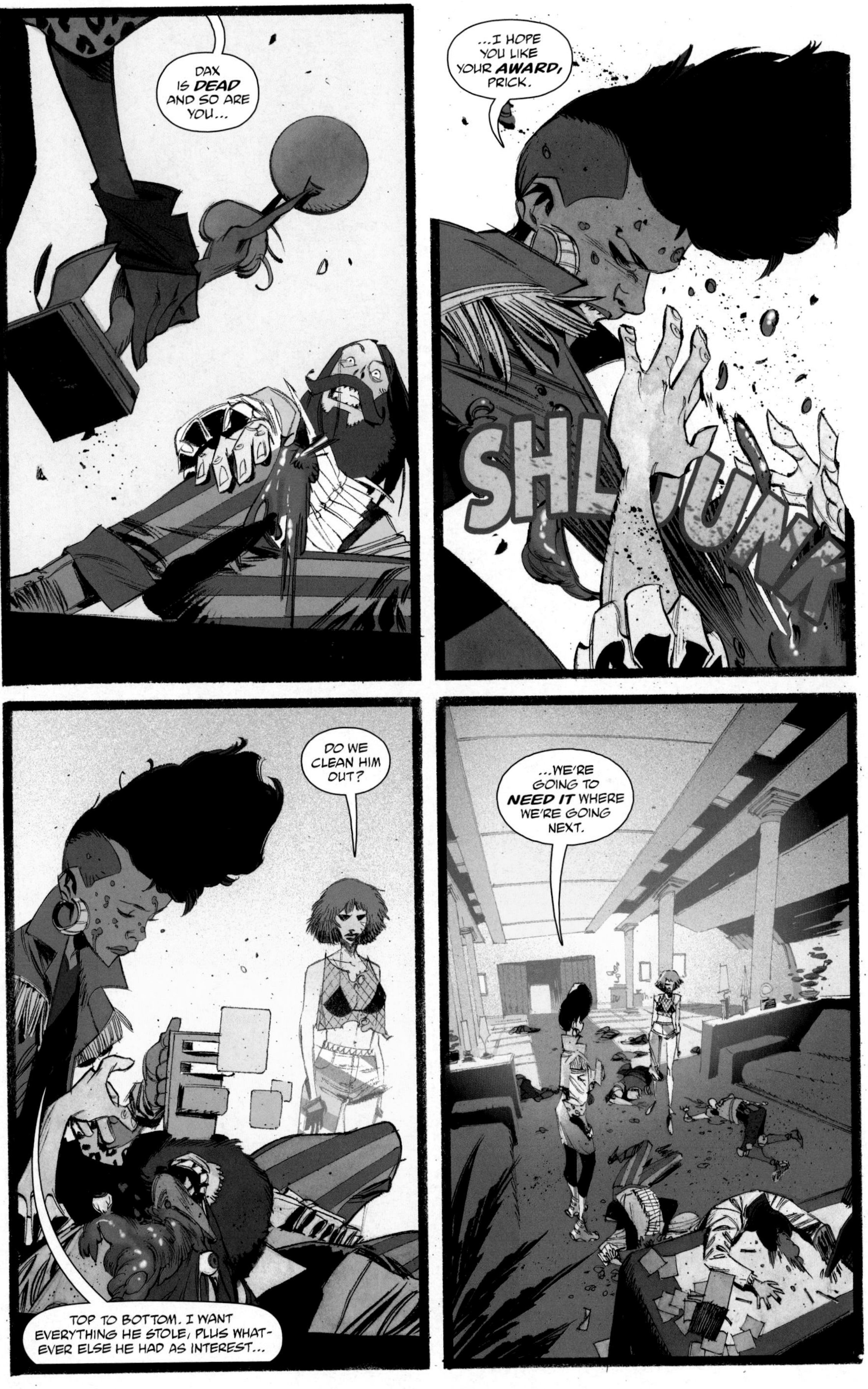
DAX IS DEAD AND SO ARE YOU...
...I HOPE YOU LIKE YOUR AWARD, PRICK.
SHLUNK
DO WE CLEAN HIM OUT?
TOP TO BOTTOM. I WANT EVERYTHING HE STOLE, PLUS WHAT-EVER ELSE HE HAD AS INTEREST...
...WE'RE GOING TO NEED IT WHERE WE'RE GOING NEXT.

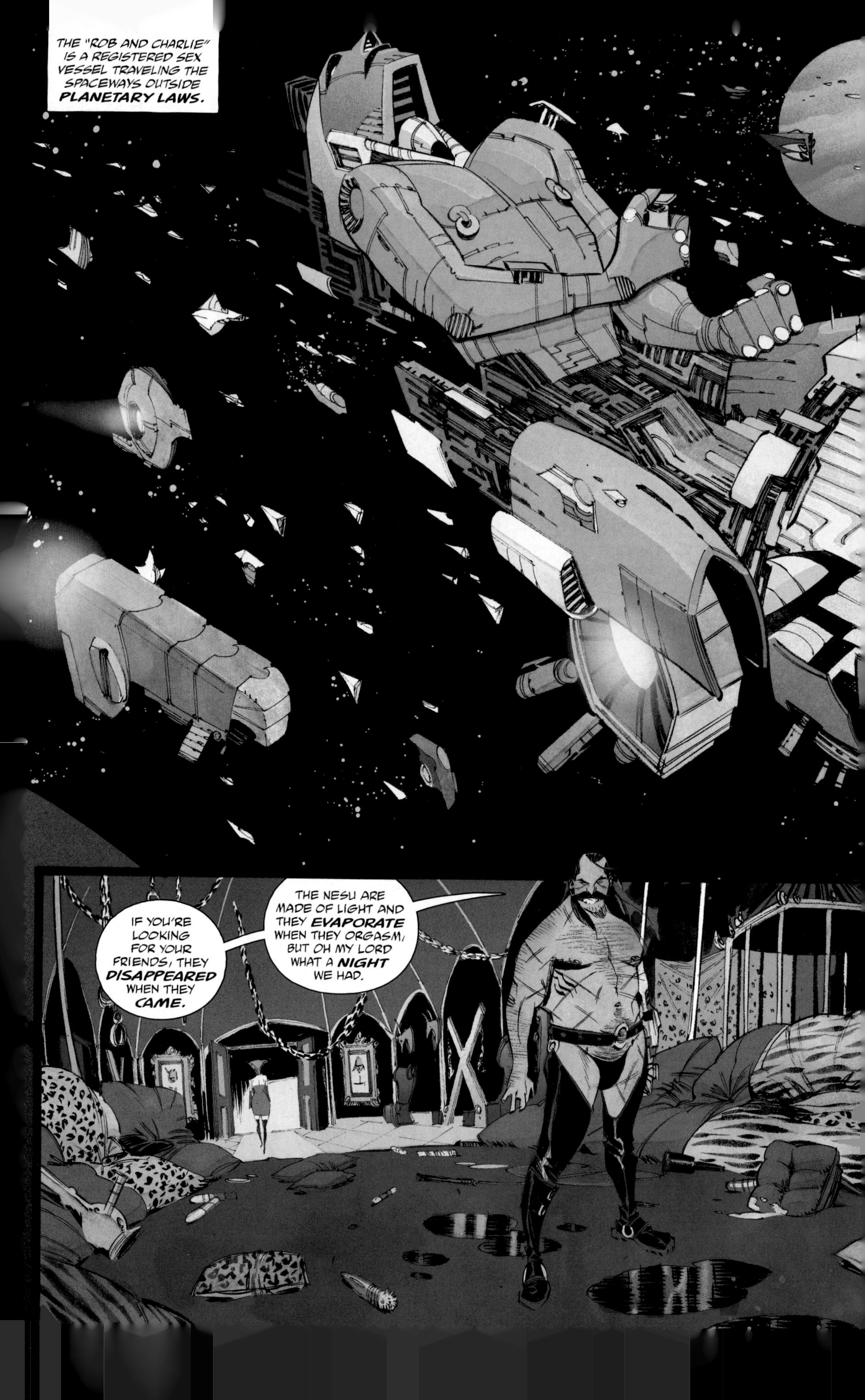
THE "ROB AND CHARLIE" IS A REGISTERED SEX VESSEL TRAVELING THE SPACEWAYS OUTSIDE PLANETARY LAWS.
IF YOU'RE LOOKING FOR YOUR FRIENDS, THEY DISAPPEARED WHEN THEY CAME.
THE NESU ARE MADE OF LIGHT AND THEY EVAPORATE WHEN THEY ORGASM, BUT OH MY LORD WHAT A NIGHT WE HAD.

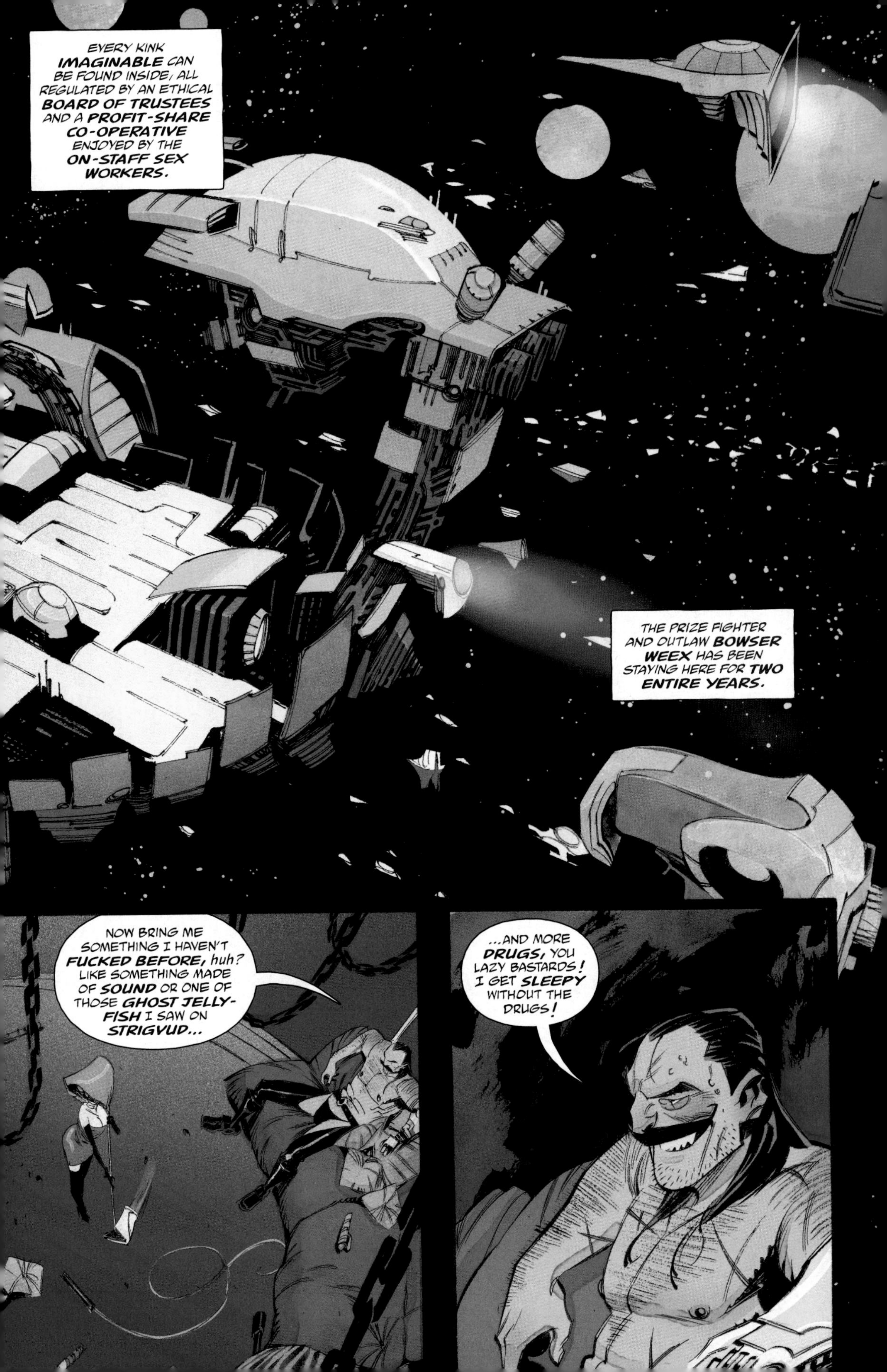
EVERY KINK IMAGINABLE CAN BE FOUND INSIDE, ALL REGULATED BY AN ETHICAL BOARD OF TRUSTEES AND A PROFIT-SHARE CO-OPERATIVE ENJOYED BY THE ON-STAFF SEX WORKERS.
THE PRIZE FIGHTER AND OUTLAW BOWSER WEEX HAS BEEN STAYING HERE FOR TWO ENTIRE YEARS.
NOW BRING ME SOMETHING I HAVEN'T FUCKED BEFORE, huh? LIKE SOMETHING MADE OF SOUND OR ONE OF THOSE GHOST JELLY-FISH I SAW ON STRIGVUD...
...AND MORE DRUGS, YOU LAZY BASTARDS! I GET SLEEPY WITHOUT THE DRUGS!

FROM WHAT I'M HEARING, HE'S BURNED THROUGH HALF HIS LOOT *ALREADY.*

WHATEVER HE'S NOT SPENDING ON *PROSTITUTES* HE'S BEEN BLOWING ON *NARCOTICS* ON THE *VIP* LEVEL SINCE THE DAY HE *CHECKED IN.*

HE WAS *ALWAYS* A CREEP, BUT MONEY JUST EXAGGERATES WHO YOU *REALLY ARE,* AND NOW HE'S GONE *FULL THROTTLE.*

THE SEX WORKERS *HATE* HIM, BUT THEY CAN'T KICK HIM OUT AS LONG AS HE'S PAYING AND NOT BREAKING ANY *RULES.*

SO, WHAT'S T PLAN

BOOK A ROOM NEXT TO HIM. FORCE OUR WAY IN.

BOWSER WEEX IS A *FORMER WRESTLER,* SO WE NEED TO ATTACK WHEN HE'S REALLY *FUCKED UP.*

PARDON ME, MISS.

MY NAME IS CLEMENCY HOOTKINS. I WONDERED IF I MIGHT INTEREST YOU IN GIVING UP YOUR *LIFE* FOR A LARGE AMOUNT OF *MONEY?*

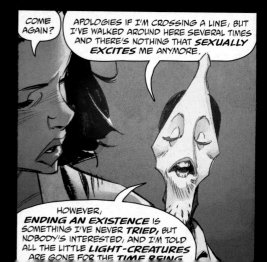

COME AGAIN?

APOLOGIES IF I'M CROSSING A LINE, BUT I'VE WALKED AROUND HERE SEVERAL TIMES AND THERE'S NOTHING THAT *SEXUALLY EXCITES* ME ANYMORE.

HOWEVER, *ENDING AN EXISTENCE* IS SOMETHING I'VE NEVER *TRIED,* BUT I'M TOLD NOBODY'S INTERESTED, AND I'M TOLD ALL THE LITTLE *LIGHT-CREATURES* ARE GONE FOR THE *TIME BEING*

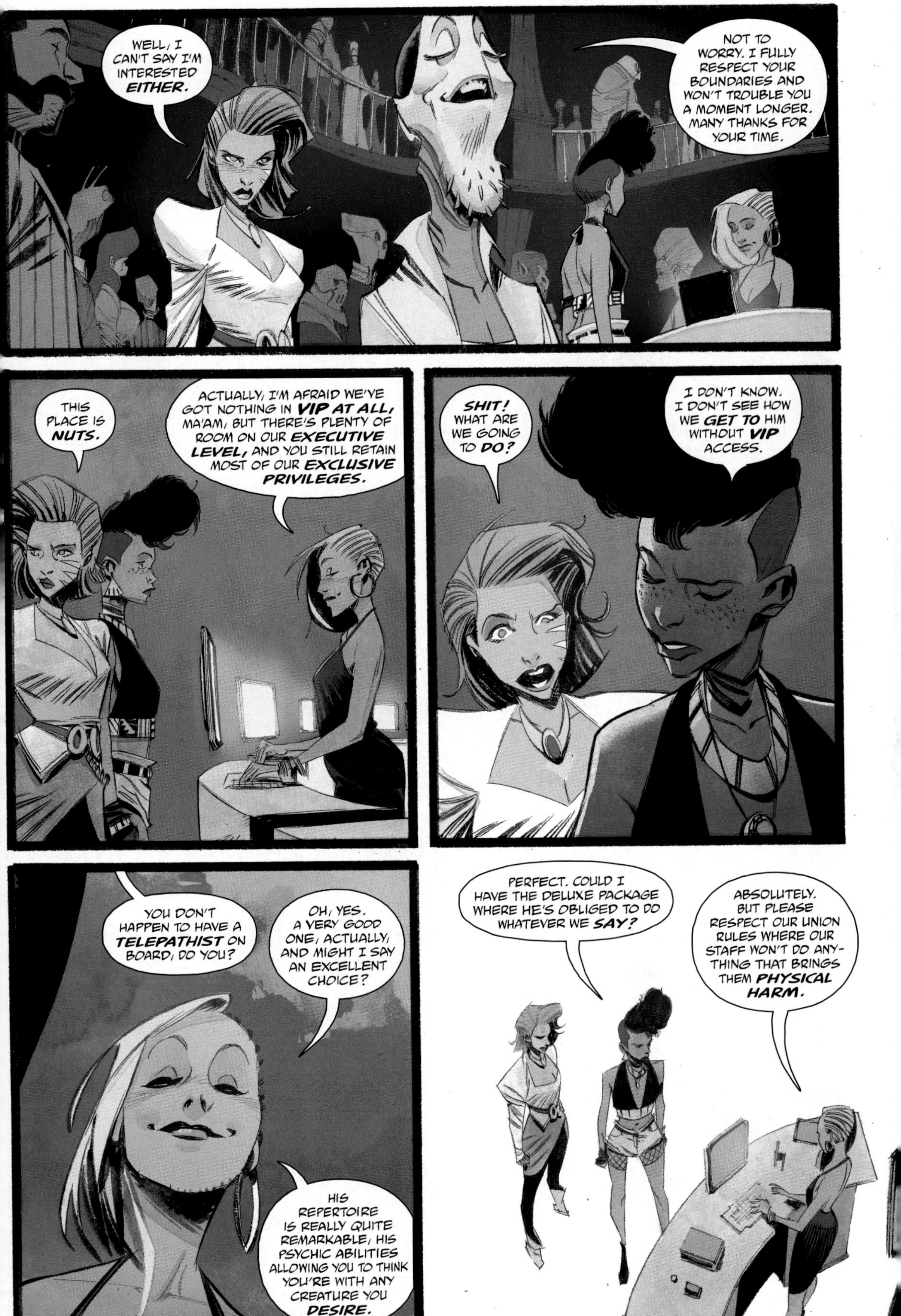
WELL, I CAN'T SAY I'M INTERESTED **EITHER.**
NOT TO WORRY. I FULLY RESPECT YOUR BOUNDARIES AND WON'T TROUBLE YOU A MOMENT LONGER. MANY THANKS FOR YOUR TIME.
THIS PLACE IS **NUTS.**
ACTUALLY, I'M AFRAID WE'VE GOT NOTHING IN **VIP AT ALL,** MA'AM, BUT THERE'S PLENTY OF ROOM ON OUR **EXECUTIVE LEVEL,** AND YOU STILL RETAIN MOST OF OUR **EXCLUSIVE PRIVILEGES.**
SHIT! WHAT ARE WE GOING TO **DO?**
I DON'T KNOW. I DON'T SEE HOW WE **GET TO** HIM WITHOUT **VIP** ACCESS.
YOU DON'T HAPPEN TO HAVE A **TELEPATHIST** ON BOARD, DO YOU?
OH, YES. A VERY GOOD ONE, ACTUALLY, AND MIGHT I SAY AN EXCELLENT CHOICE?
HIS REPERTOIRE IS REALLY QUITE REMARKABLE, HIS PSYCHIC ABILITIES ALLOWING YOU TO THINK YOU'RE WITH ANY CREATURE YOU **DESIRE.**
PERFECT. COULD I HAVE THE DELUXE PACKAGE WHERE HE'S OBLIGED TO DO WHATEVER WE **SAY?**
ABSOLUTELY. BUT PLEASE RESPECT OUR UNION RULES WHERE OUR STAFF WON'T DO ANYTHING THAT BRINGS THEM **PHYSICAL HARM.**

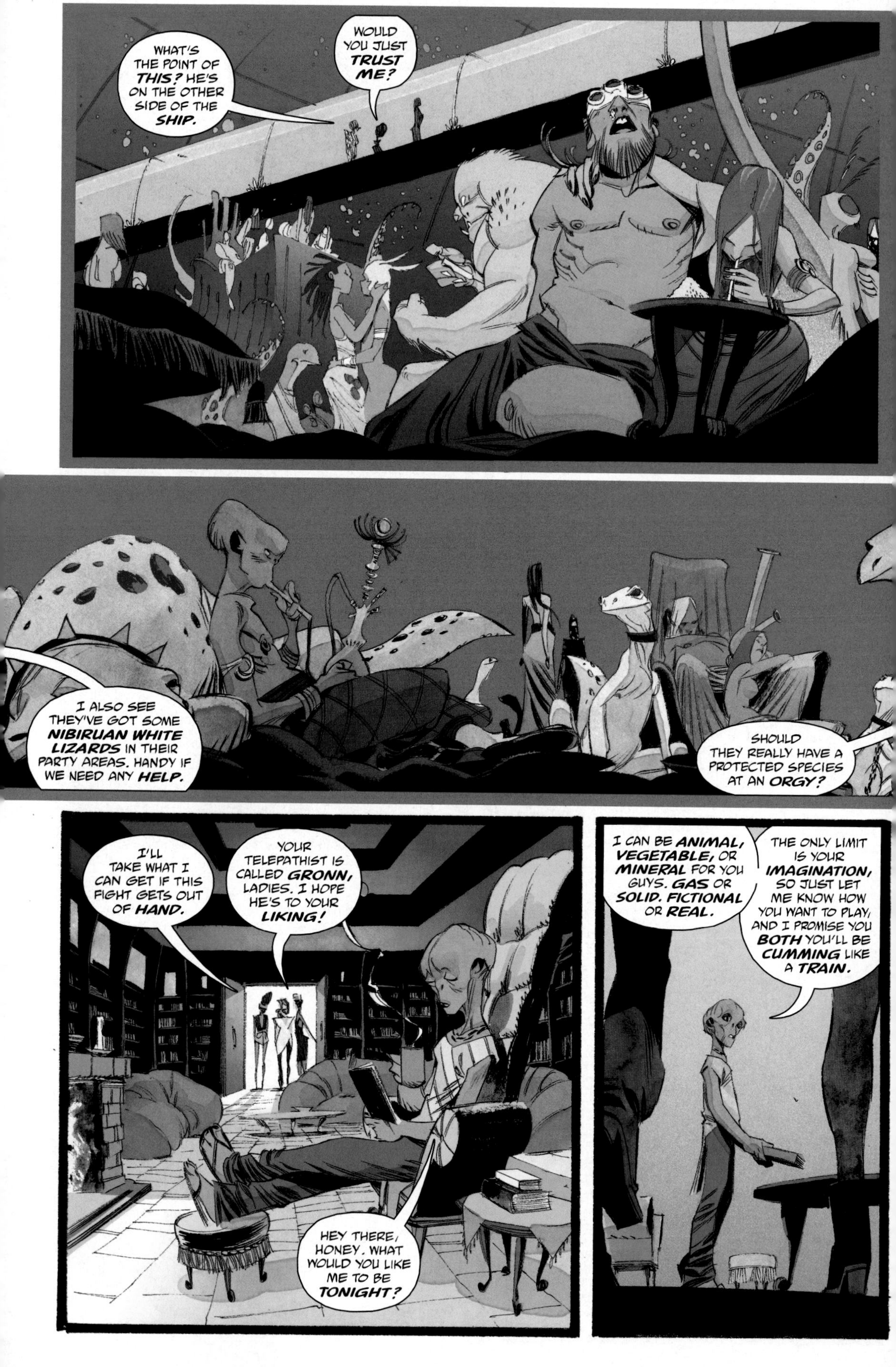
WHAT'S THE POINT OF THIS? HE'S ON THE OTHER SIDE OF THE SHIP.
WOULD YOU JUST TRUST ME?
I ALSO SEE THEY'VE GOT SOME NIBIRUAN WHITE LIZARDS IN THEIR PARTY AREAS. HANDY IF WE NEED ANY HELP.
SHOULD THEY REALLY HAVE A PROTECTED SPECIES AT AN ORGY?
I'LL TAKE WHAT I CAN GET IF THIS FIGHT GETS OUT OF HAND.
YOUR TELEPATHIST IS CALLED GRONN, LADIES. I HOPE HE'S TO YOUR LIKING!
HEY THERE, HONEY. WHAT WOULD YOU LIKE ME TO BE TONIGHT?
I CAN BE ANIMAL, VEGETABLE, OR MINERAL FOR YOU GUYS. GAS OR SOLID. FICTIONAL OR REAL.
THE ONLY LIMIT IS YOUR IMAGINATION, SO JUST LET ME KNOW HOW YOU WANT TO PLAY, AND I PROMISE YOU BOTH YOU'LL BE CUMMING LIKE A TRAIN.

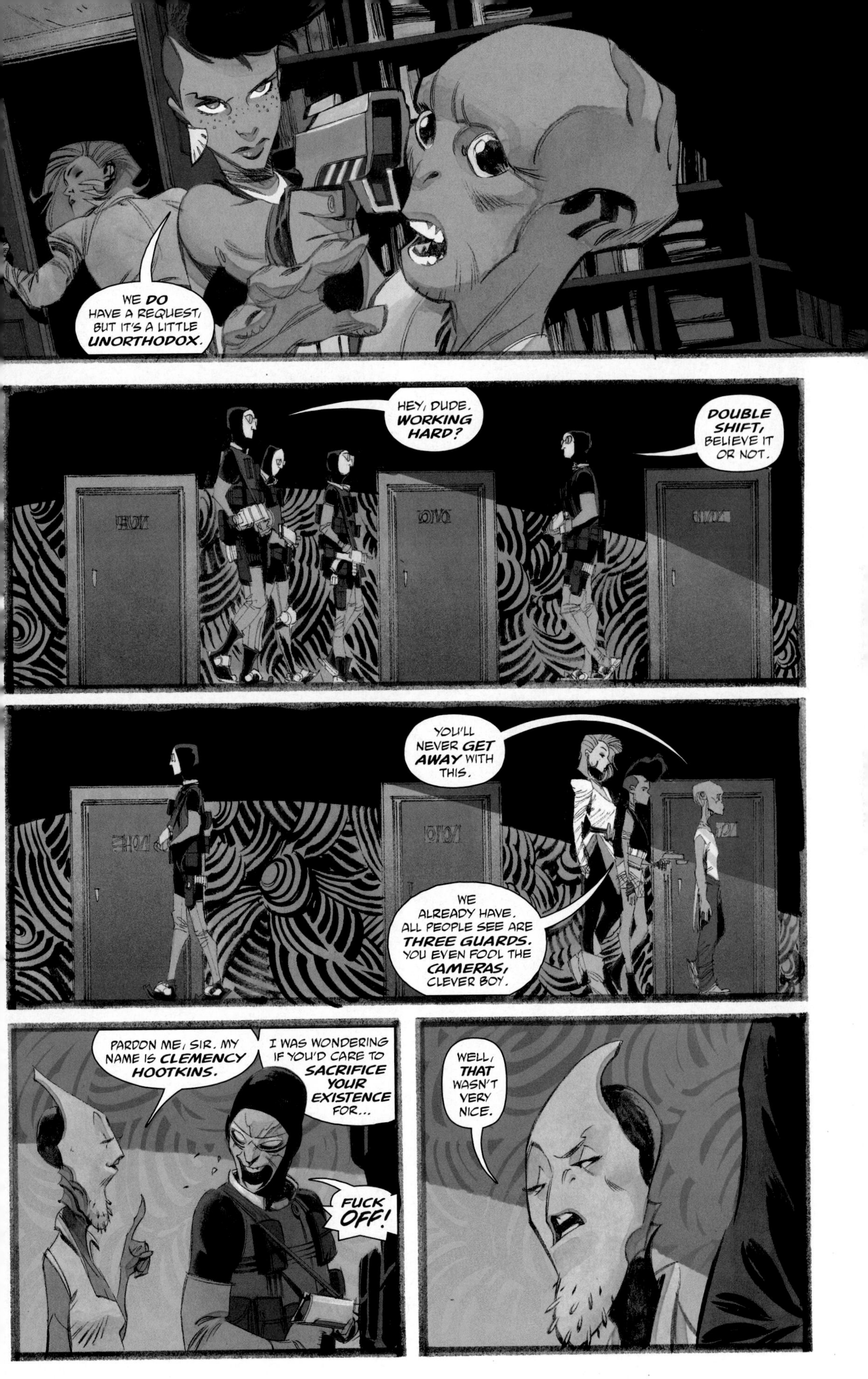
WE DO HAVE A REQUEST, BUT IT'S A LITTLE UNORTHODOX.
HEY, DUDE. WORKING HARD?
DOUBLE SHIFT, BELIEVE IT OR NOT.
YOU'LL NEVER GET AWAY WITH THIS.
WE ALREADY HAVE. ALL PEOPLE SEE ARE THREE GUARDS. YOU EVEN FOOL THE CAMERAS, CLEVER BOY.
PARDON ME, SIR. MY NAME IS CLEMENCY HOOTKINS.
I WAS WONDERING IF YOU'D CARE TO SACRIFICE YOUR EXISTENCE FOR...
FUCK OFF!
WELL, THAT WASN'T VERY NICE.

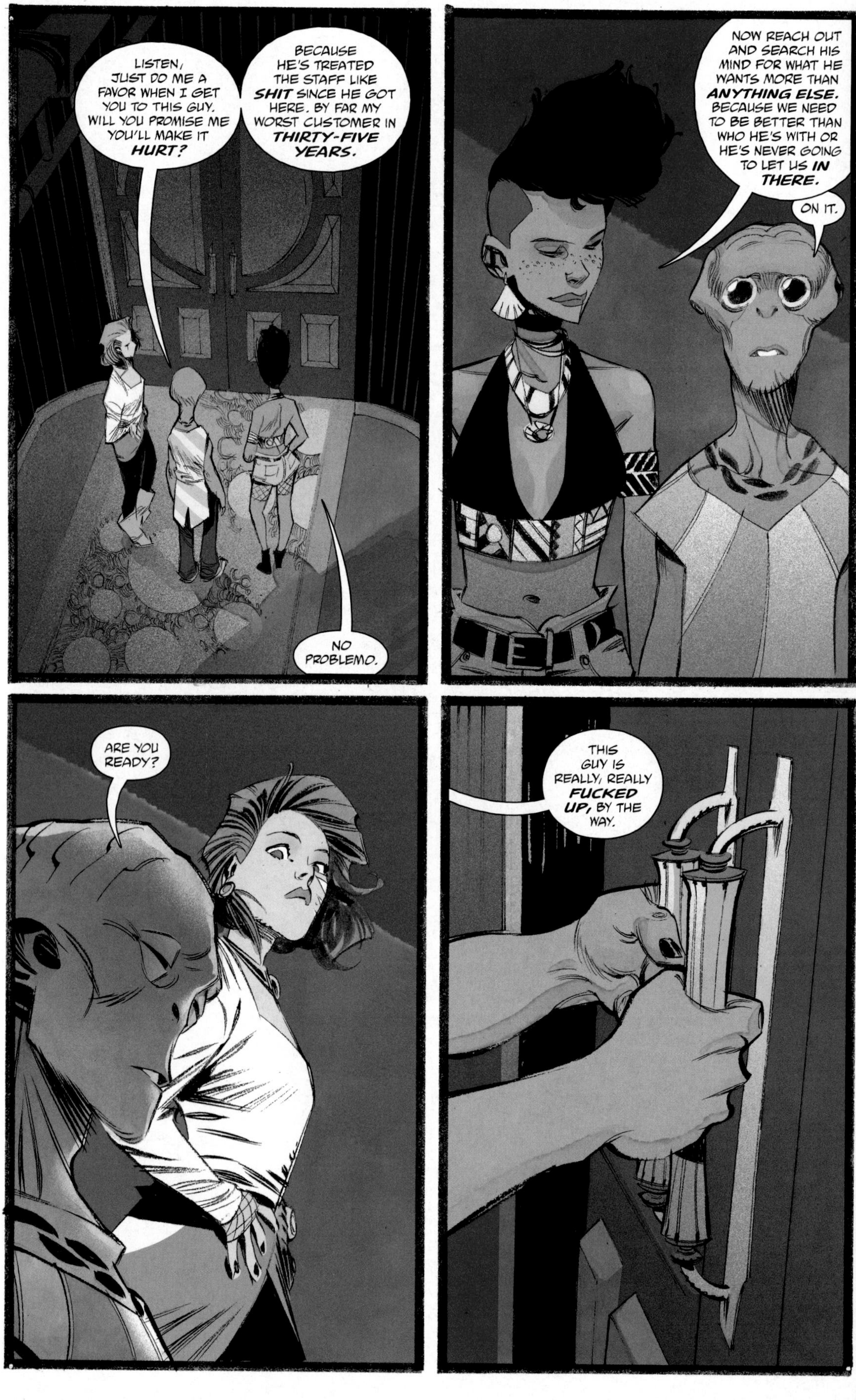
LISTEN, JUST DO ME A FAVOR WHEN I GET YOU TO THIS GUY. WILL YOU PROMISE ME YOU'LL MAKE IT HURT?
BECAUSE HE'S TREATED THE STAFF LIKE SHIT SINCE HE GOT HERE. BY FAR MY WORST CUSTOMER IN THIRTY-FIVE YEARS.
NO PROBLEMO.
NOW REACH OUT AND SEARCH HIS MIND FOR WHAT HE WANTS MORE THAN ANYTHING ELSE. BECAUSE WE NEED TO BE BETTER THAN WHO HE'S WITH OR HE'S NEVER GOING TO LET US IN THERE.
ON IT.
ARE YOU READY?
THIS GUY IS REALLY, REALLY FUCKED UP, BY THE WAY.

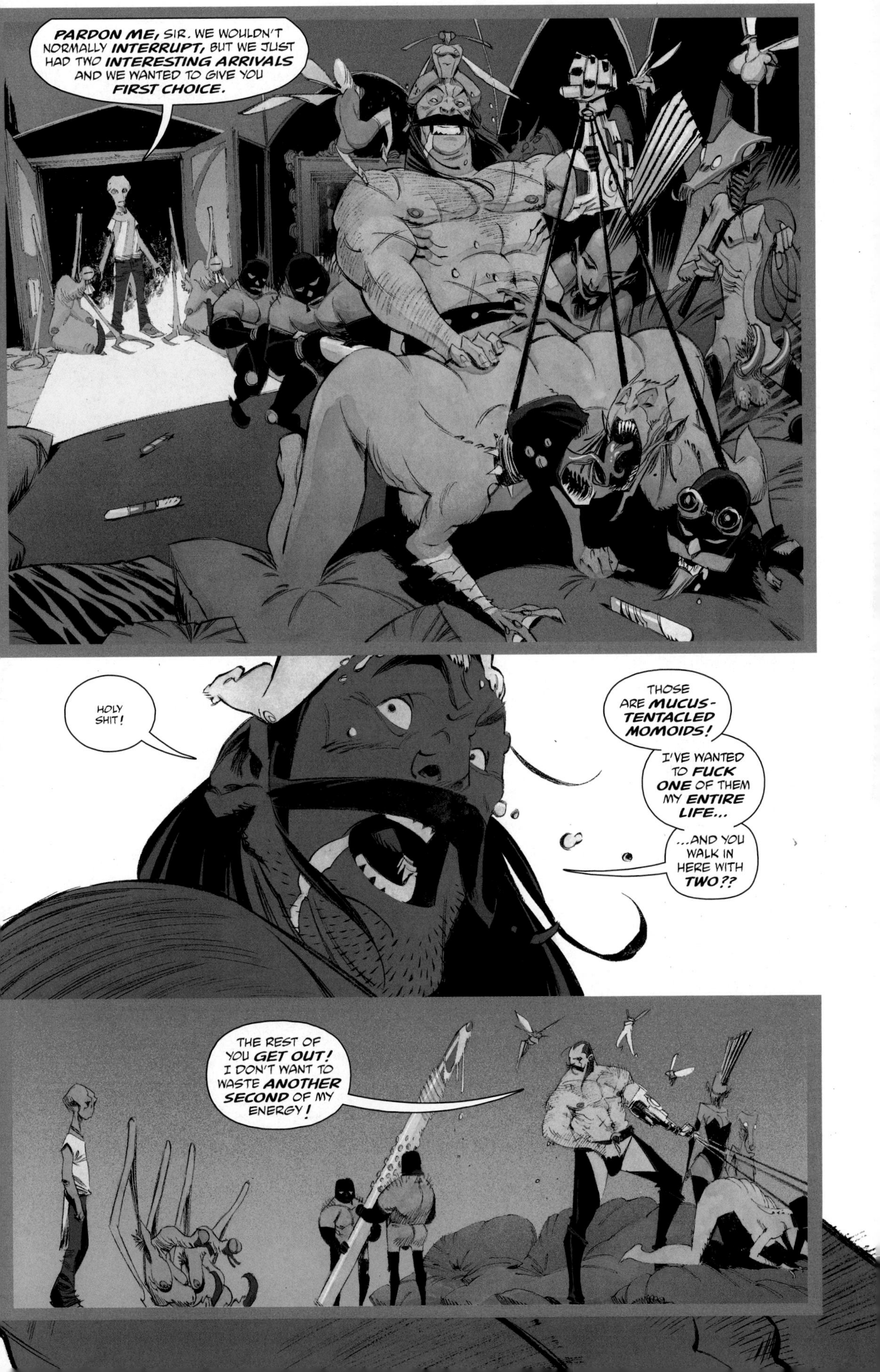
PARDON ME, SIR. WE WOULDN'T NORMALLY INTERRUPT, BUT WE JUST HAD TWO INTERESTING ARRIVALS AND WE WANTED TO GIVE YOU FIRST CHOICE.
HOLY SHIT!
THOSE ARE MUCUS-TENTACLED MOMOIDS!
I'VE WANTED TO FUCK ONE OF THEM MY ENTIRE LIFE...
...AND YOU WALK IN HERE WITH TWO??
THE REST OF YOU GET OUT! I DON'T WANT TO WASTE ANOTHER SECOND OF MY ENERGY!

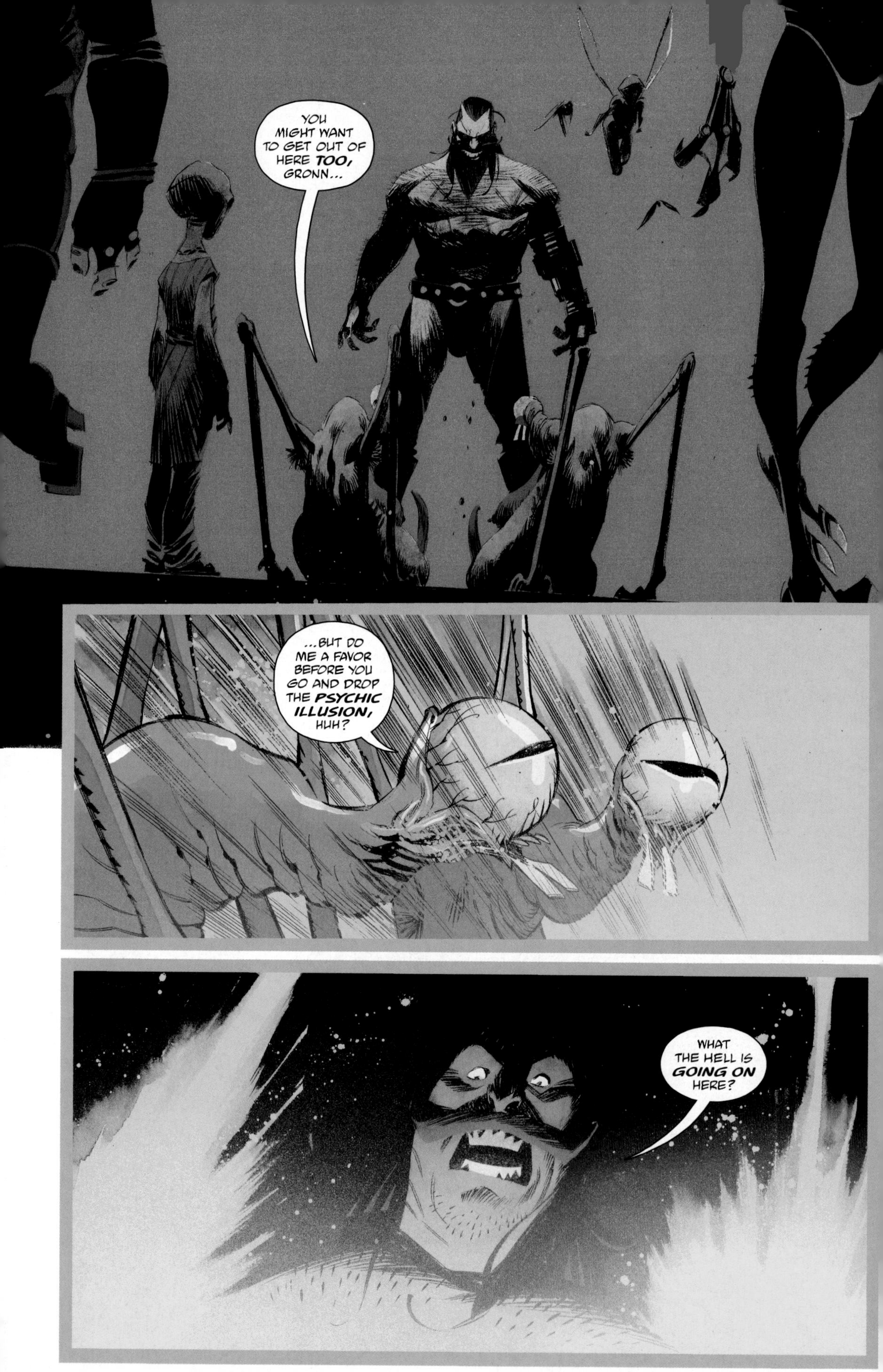
YOU MIGHT WANT TO GET OUT OF HERE **TOO,** GRONN...
...BUT DO ME A FAVOR BEFORE YOU GO AND DROP THE **PSYCHIC ILLUSION,** HUH?
WHAT THE HELL IS **GOING ON** HERE?

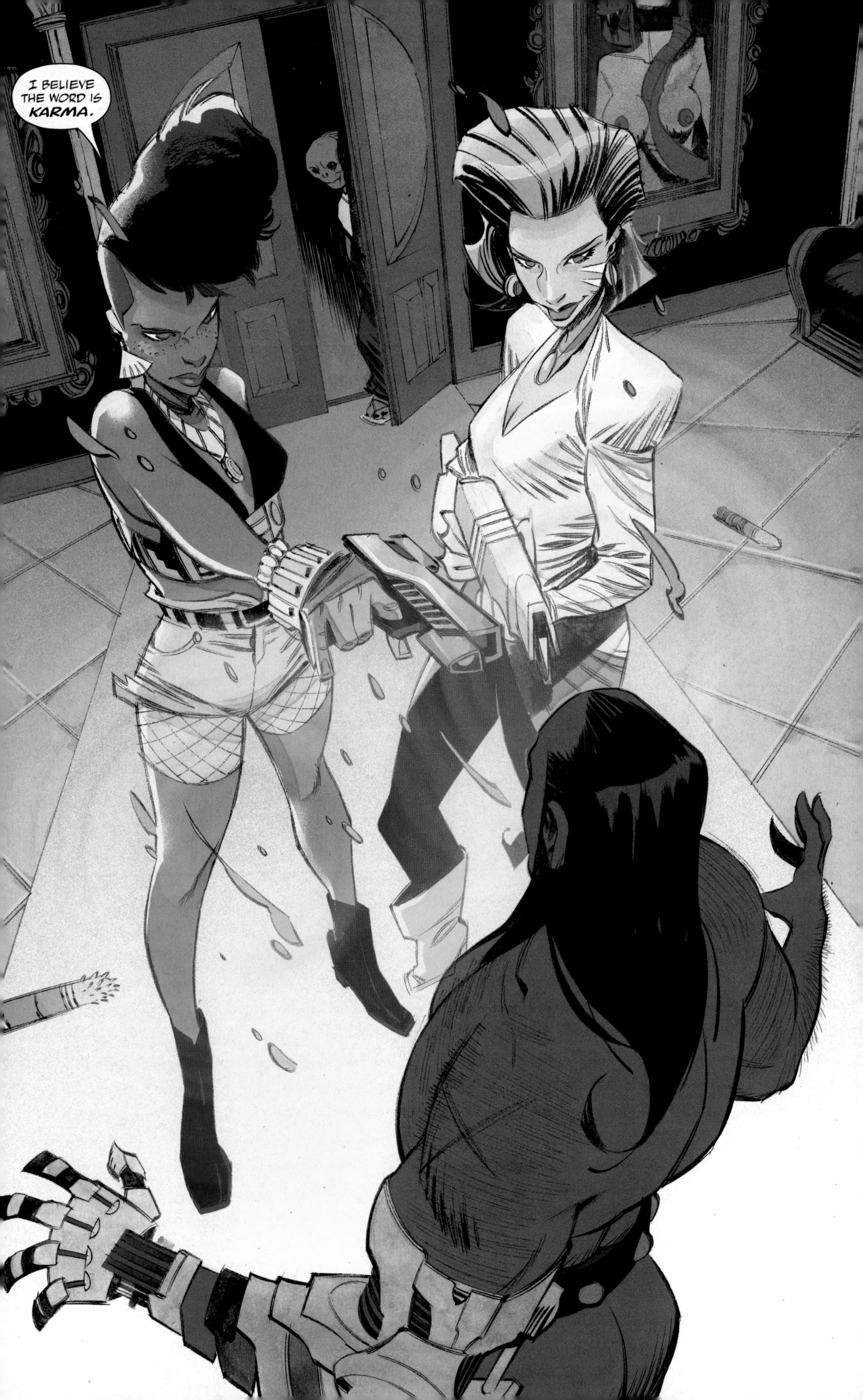
I BELIEVE THE WORD IS KARMA.

Four

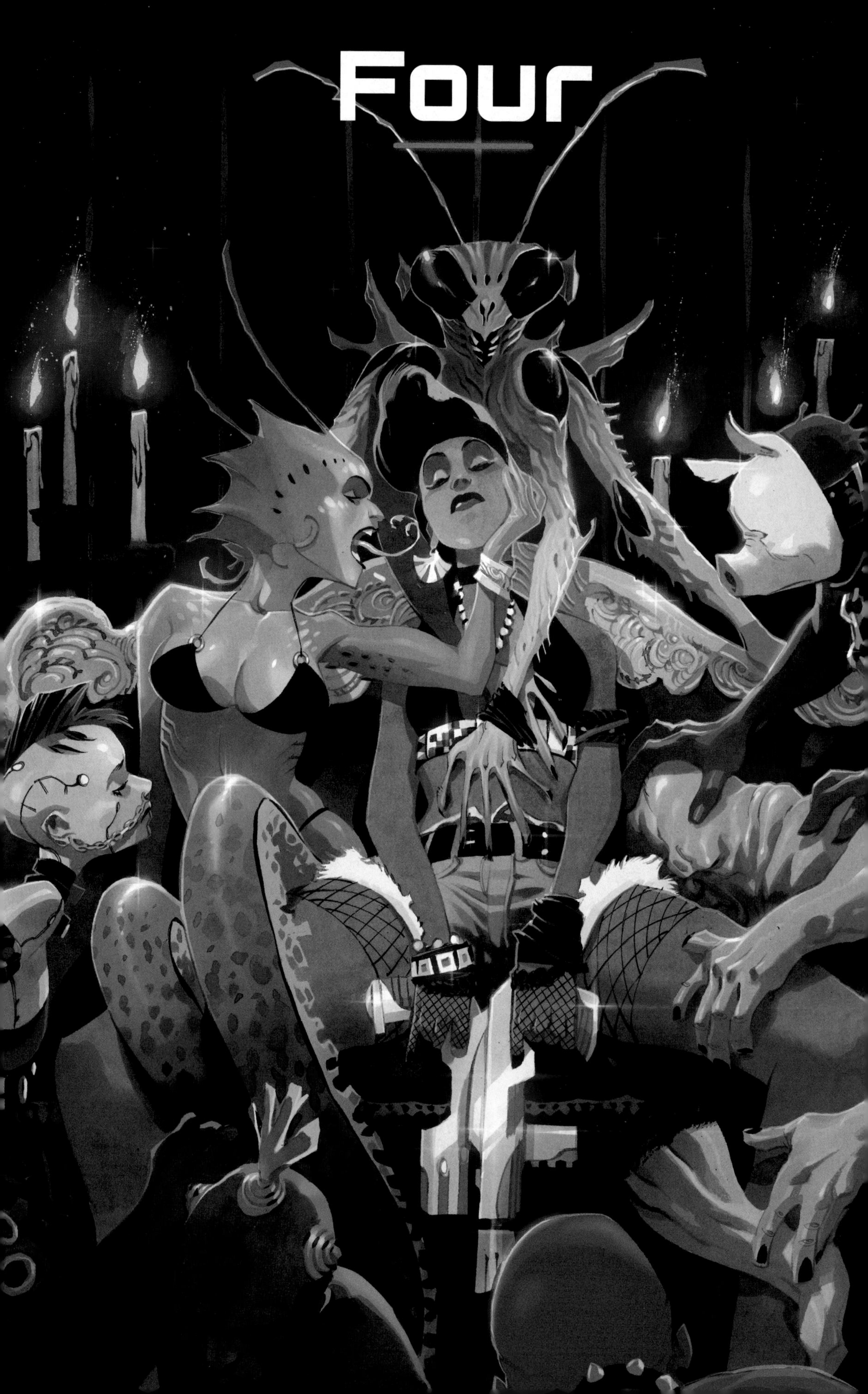

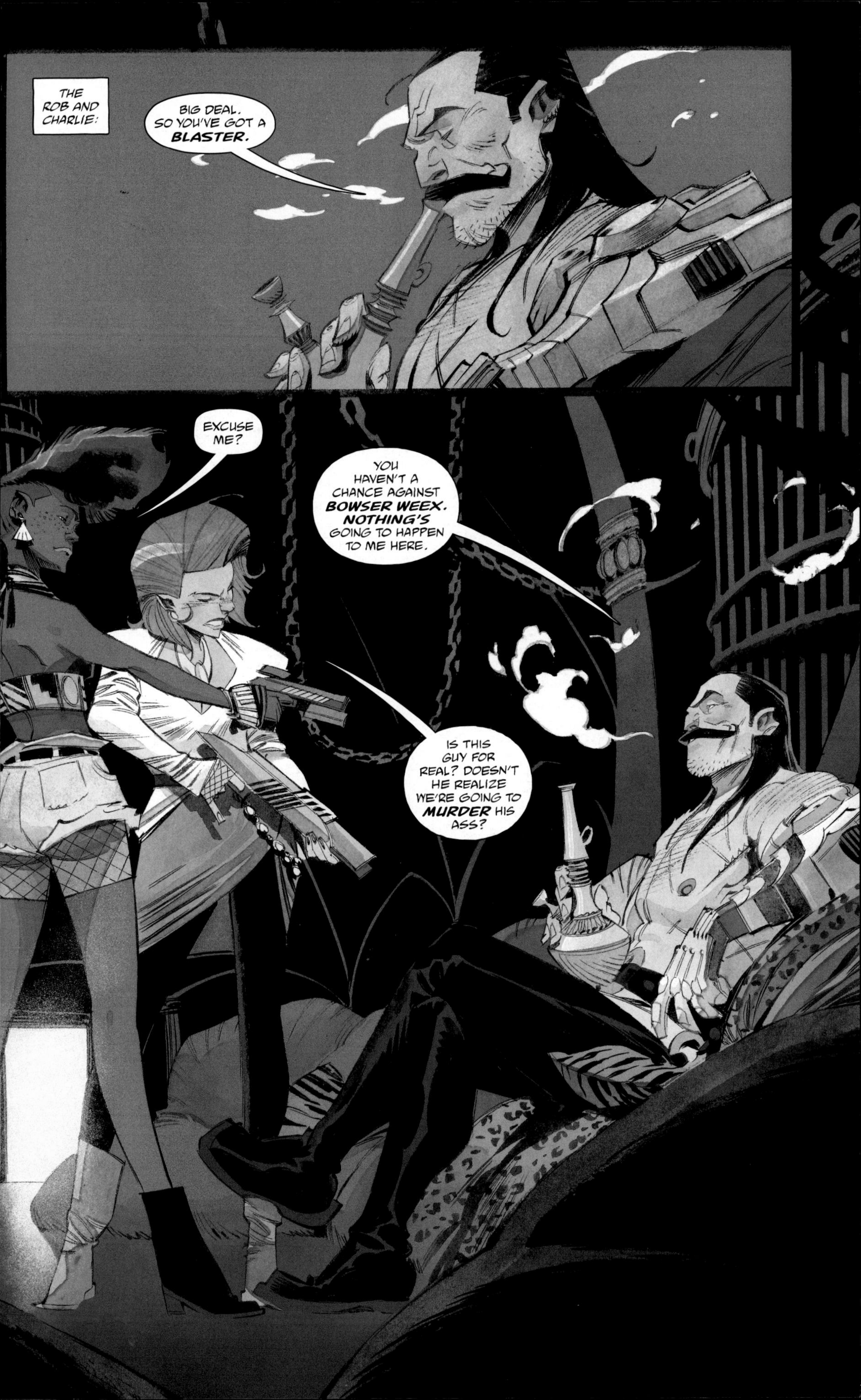
THE ROB AND CHARLIE:
BIG DEAL. SO YOU'VE GOT A BLASTER.
EXCUSE ME?
YOU HAVEN'T A CHANCE AGAINST BOWSER WEEX. NOTHING'S GOING TO HAPPEN TO ME HERE.
IS THIS GUY FOR REAL? DOESN'T HE REALIZE WE'RE GOING TO MURDER HIS ASS?

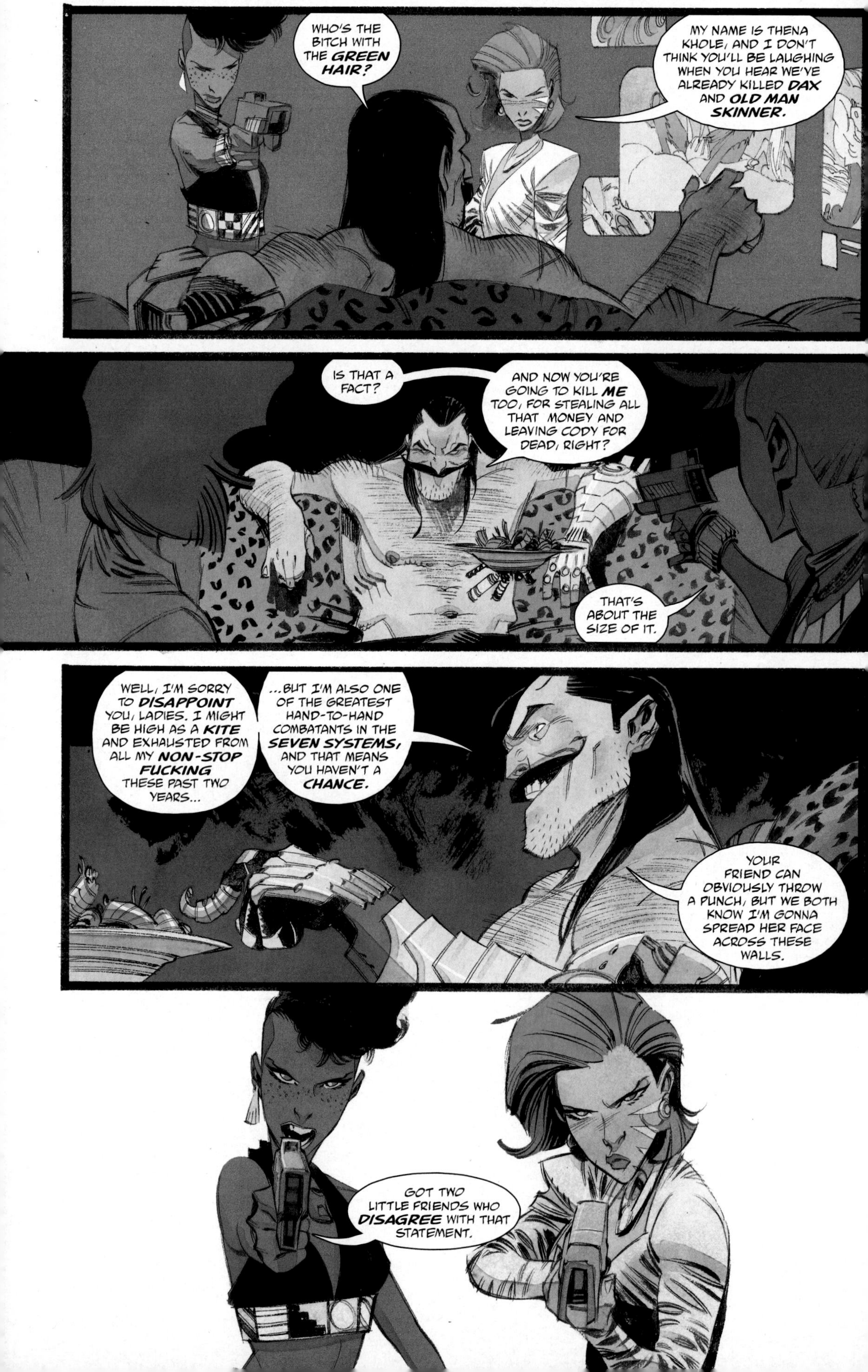
WHO'S THE BITCH WITH THE GREEN HAIR?
MY NAME IS THENA KHOLE, AND I DON'T THINK YOU'LL BE LAUGHING WHEN YOU HEAR WE'VE ALREADY KILLED DAX AND OLD MAN SKINNER.
IS THAT A FACT?
AND NOW YOU'RE GOING TO KILL ME TOO, FOR STEALING ALL THAT MONEY AND LEAVING CODY FOR DEAD, RIGHT?
THAT'S ABOUT THE SIZE OF IT.
WELL, I'M SORRY TO DISAPPOINT YOU, LADIES. I MIGHT BE HIGH AS A KITE AND EXHAUSTED FROM ALL MY NON-STOP FUCKING THESE PAST TWO YEARS...
...BUT I'M ALSO ONE OF THE GREATEST HAND-TO-HAND COMBATANTS IN THE SEVEN SYSTEMS, AND THAT MEANS YOU HAVEN'T A CHANCE.
YOUR FRIEND CAN OBVIOUSLY THROW A PUNCH, BUT WE BOTH KNOW I'M GONNA SPREAD HER FACE ACROSS THESE WALLS.
GOT TWO LITTLE FRIENDS WHO DISAGREE WITH THAT STATEMENT.

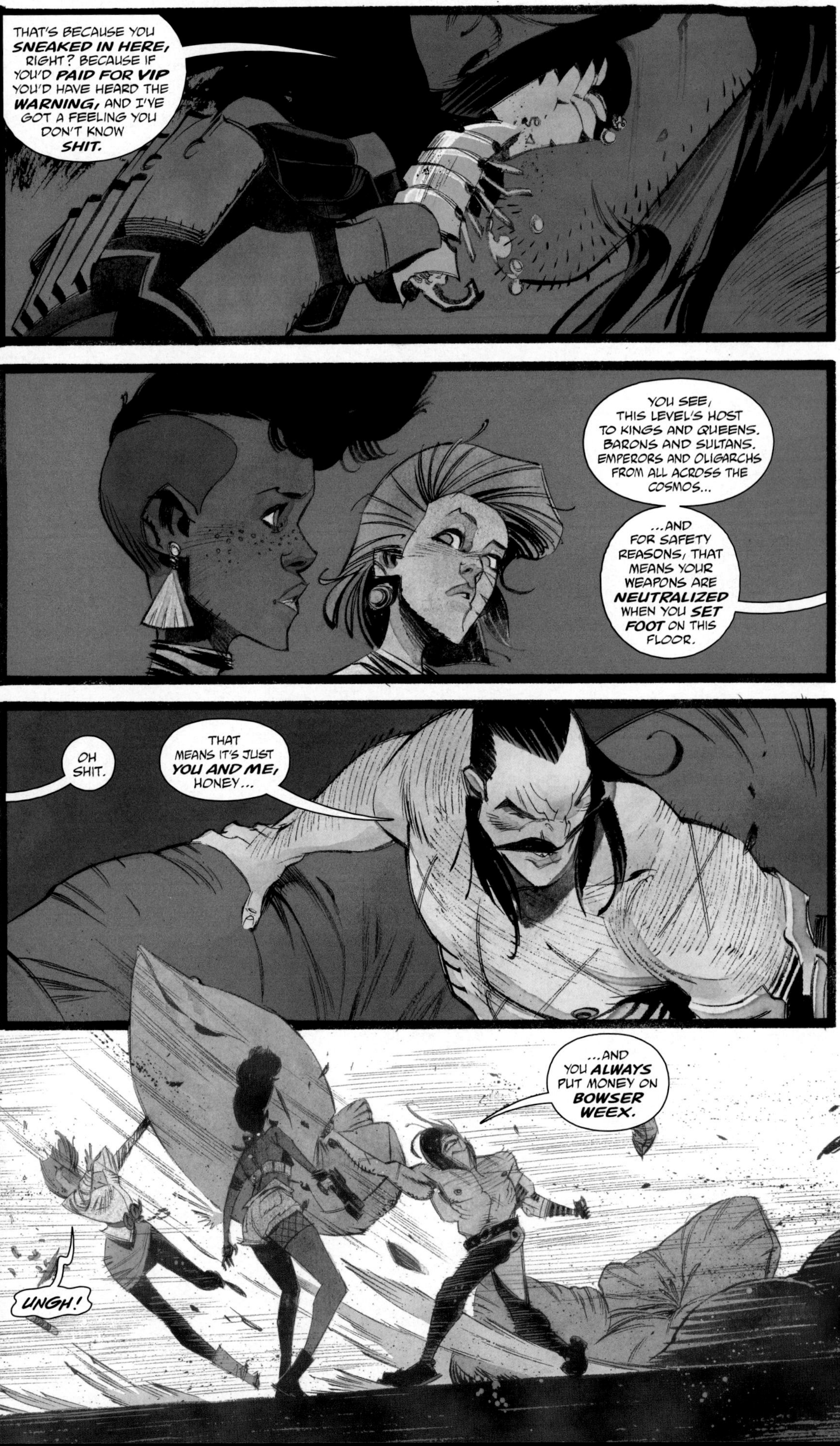

THAT'S BECAUSE YOU SNEAKED IN HERE, RIGHT? BECAUSE IF YOU'D PAID FOR VIP YOU'D HAVE HEARD THE WARNING, AND I'VE GOT A FEELING YOU DON'T KNOW SHIT.
YOU SEE, THIS LEVEL'S HOST TO KINGS AND QUEENS. BARONS AND SULTANS. EMPERORS AND OLIGARCHS FROM ALL ACROSS THE COSMOS...
...AND FOR SAFETY REASONS, THAT MEANS YOUR WEAPONS ARE NEUTRALIZED WHEN YOU SET FOOT ON THIS FLOOR.
OH SHIT.
THAT MEANS IT'S JUST YOU AND ME, HONEY...
...AND YOU ALWAYS PUT MONEY ON BOWSER WEEX.
UNGH!

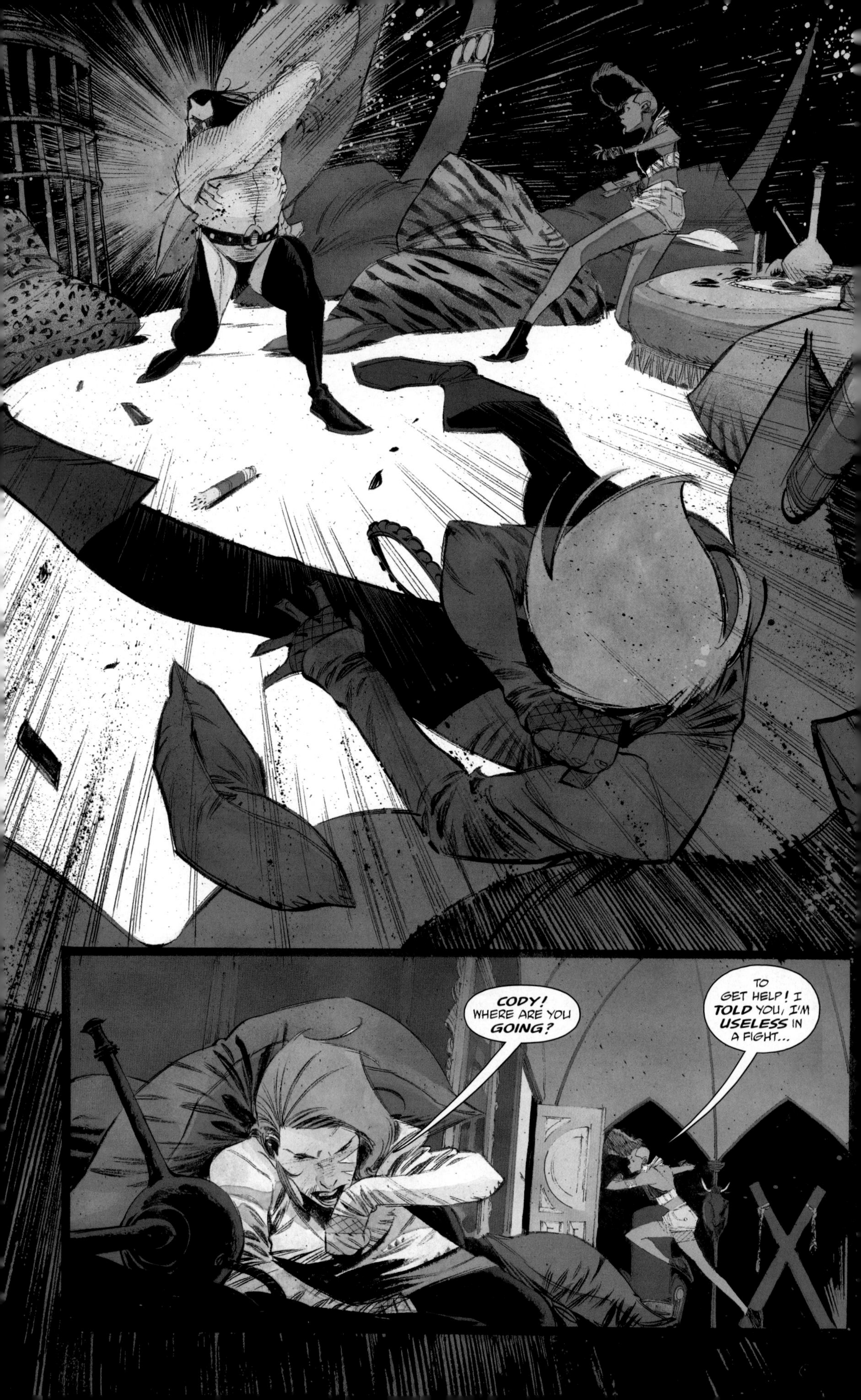
CODY! WHERE ARE YOU GOING?
TO GET HELP! I TOLD YOU, I'M USELESS IN A FIGHT...

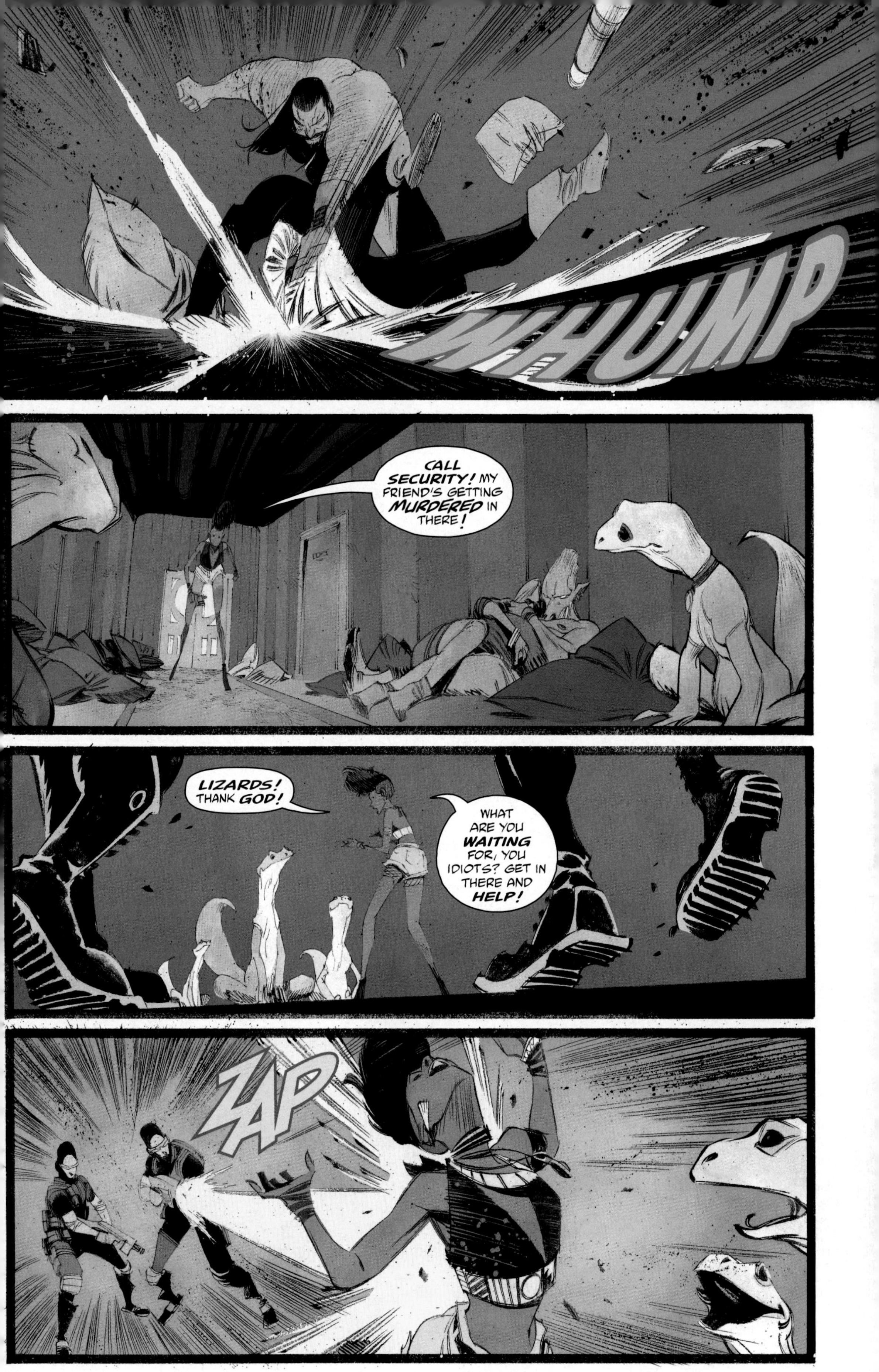
WHUMP
CALL SECURITY! MY FRIEND'S GETTING MURDERED IN THERE!
LIZARDS! THANK GOD!
WHAT ARE YOU WAITING FOR, YOU IDIOTS? GET IN THERE AND HELP!
ZAP

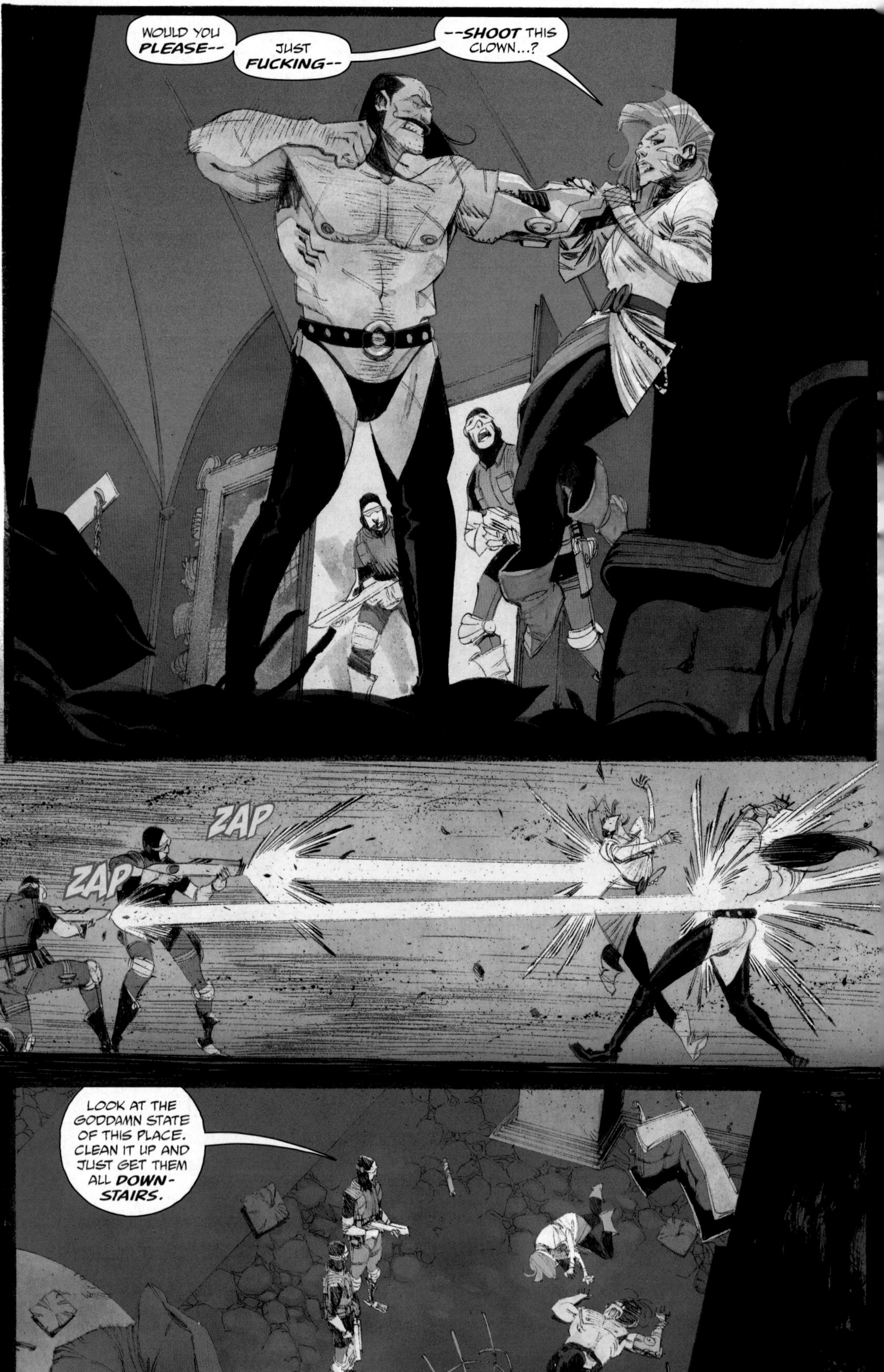
WOULD YOU PLEASE--
JUST FUCKING--
--SHOOT THIS CLOWN...?
ZAP
ZAP
LOOK AT THE GODDAMN STATE OF THIS PLACE. CLEAN IT UP AND JUST GET THEM ALL DOWN-STAIRS.

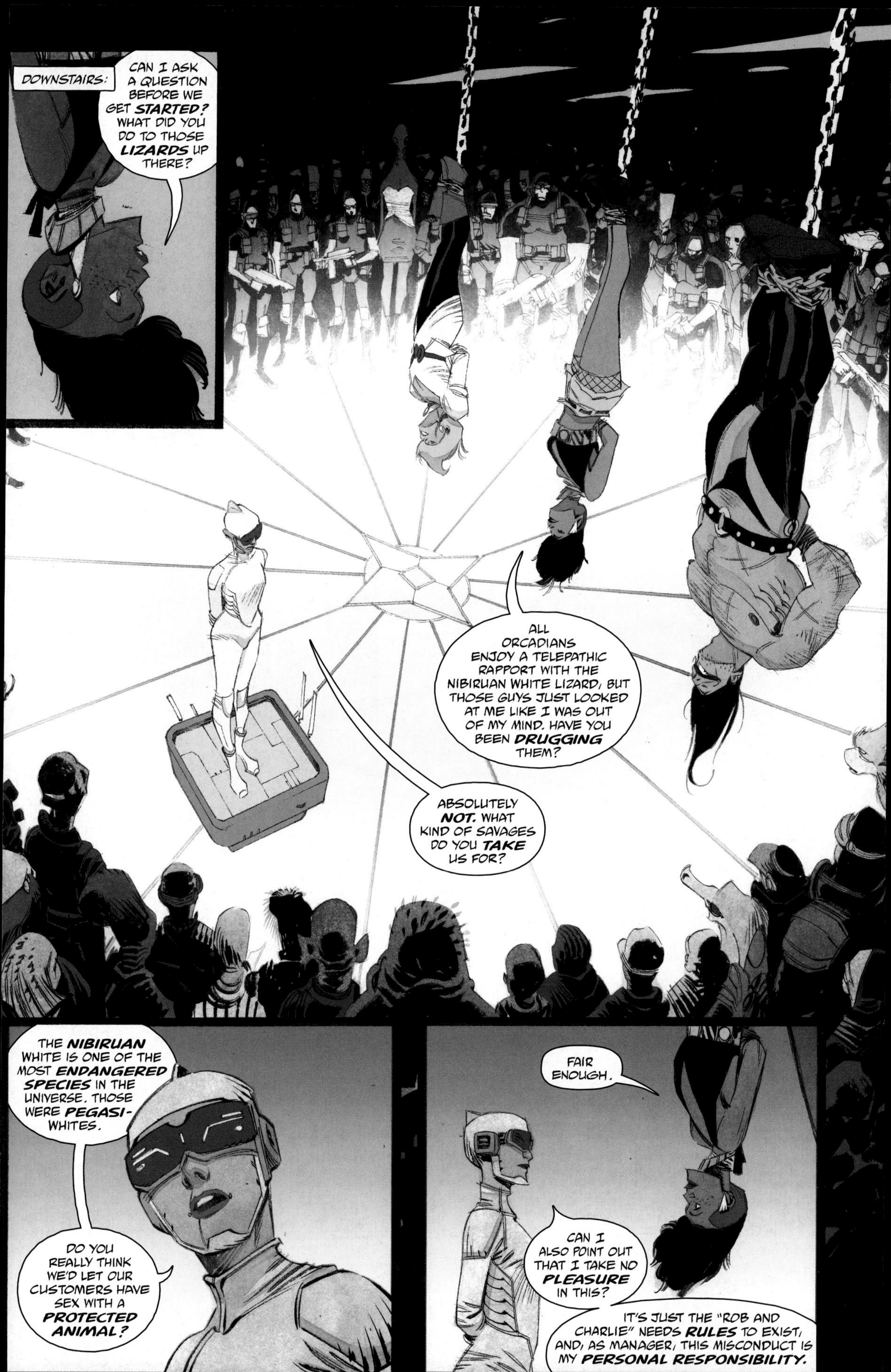
DOWNSTAIRS:
CAN I ASK A QUESTION BEFORE WE GET STARTED? WHAT DID YOU DO TO THOSE LIZARDS UP THERE?
ALL ORCADIANS ENJOY A TELEPATHIC RAPPORT WITH THE NIBIRUAN WHITE LIZARD, BUT THOSE GUYS JUST LOOKED AT ME LIKE I WAS OUT OF MY MIND. HAVE YOU BEEN DRUGGING THEM?
ABSOLUTELY NOT. WHAT KIND OF SAVAGES DO YOU TAKE US FOR?
THE NIBIRUAN WHITE IS ONE OF THE MOST ENDANGERED SPECIES IN THE UNIVERSE. THOSE WERE PEGASI-WHITES.
DO YOU REALLY THINK WE'D LET OUR CUSTOMERS HAVE SEX WITH A PROTECTED ANIMAL?
FAIR ENOUGH.
CAN I ALSO POINT OUT THAT I TAKE NO PLEASURE IN THIS?
IT'S JUST THE "ROB AND CHARLIE" NEEDS RULES TO EXIST, AND, AS MANAGER, THIS MISCONDUCT IS MY PERSONAL RESPONSIBILITY.

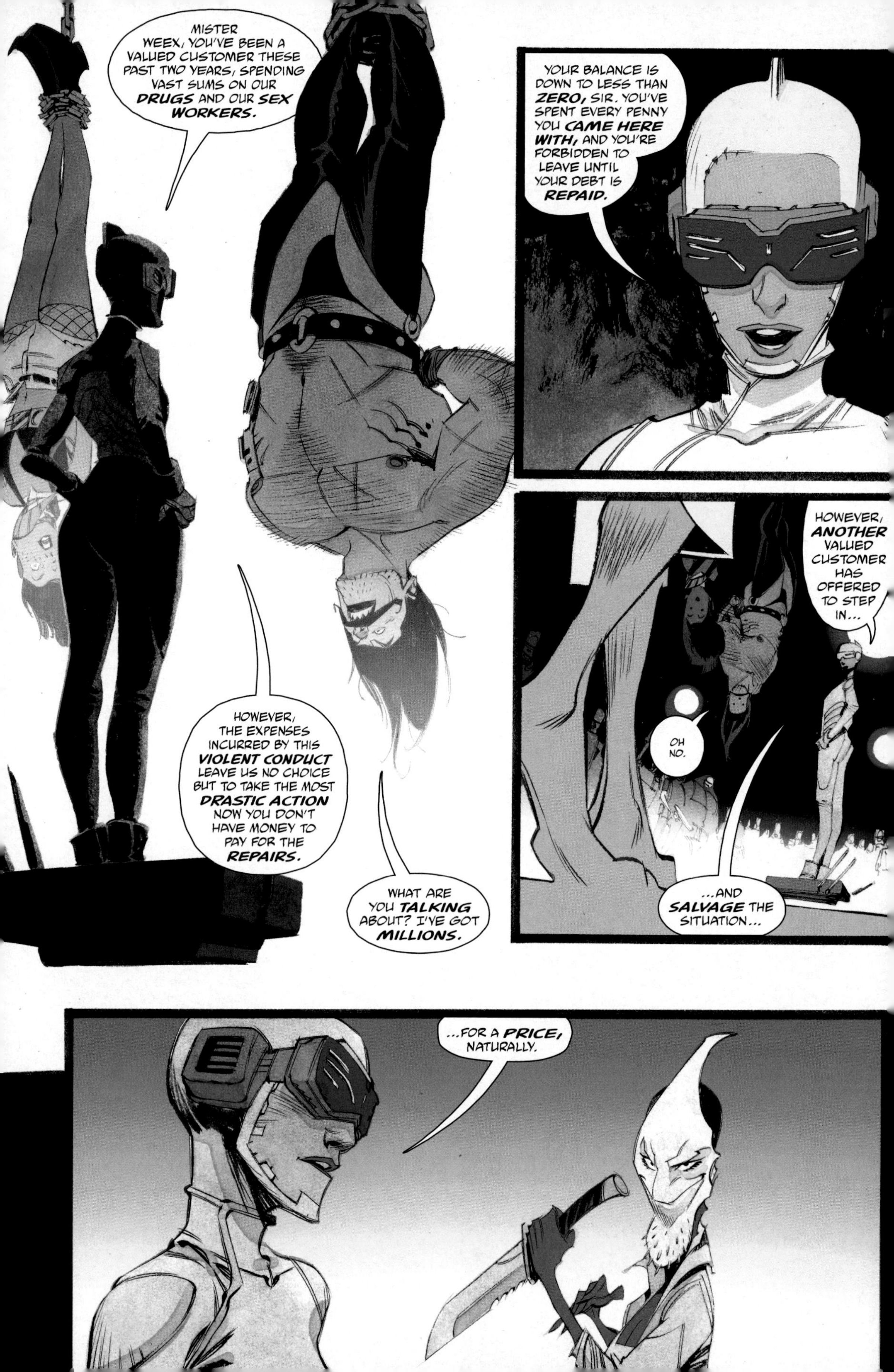
MISTER WEEX, YOU'VE BEEN A VALUED CUSTOMER THESE PAST TWO YEARS, SPENDING VAST SUMS ON OUR DRUGS AND OUR SEX WORKERS.
YOUR BALANCE IS DOWN TO LESS THAN ZERO, SIR. YOU'VE SPENT EVERY PENNY YOU CAME HERE WITH, AND YOU'RE FORBIDDEN TO LEAVE UNTIL YOUR DEBT IS REPAID.
HOWEVER, THE EXPENSES INCURRED BY THIS VIOLENT CONDUCT LEAVE US NO CHOICE BUT TO TAKE THE MOST DRASTIC ACTION NOW YOU DON'T HAVE MONEY TO PAY FOR THE REPAIRS.
WHAT ARE YOU TALKING ABOUT? I'VE GOT MILLIONS.
HOWEVER, ANOTHER VALUED CUSTOMER HAS OFFERED TO STEP IN...
OH NO.
...AND SALVAGE THE SITUATION...
...FOR A PRICE, NATURALLY.

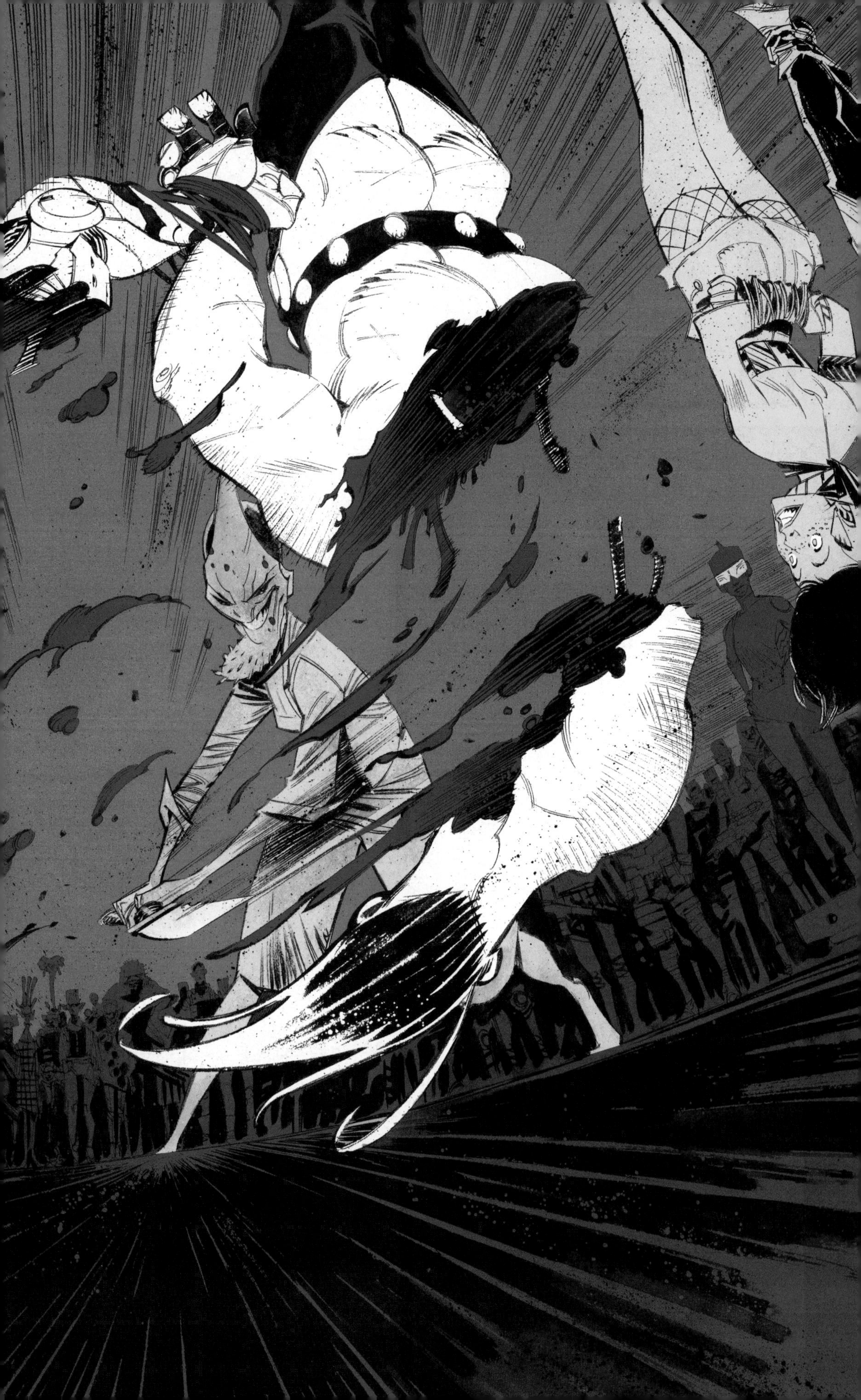

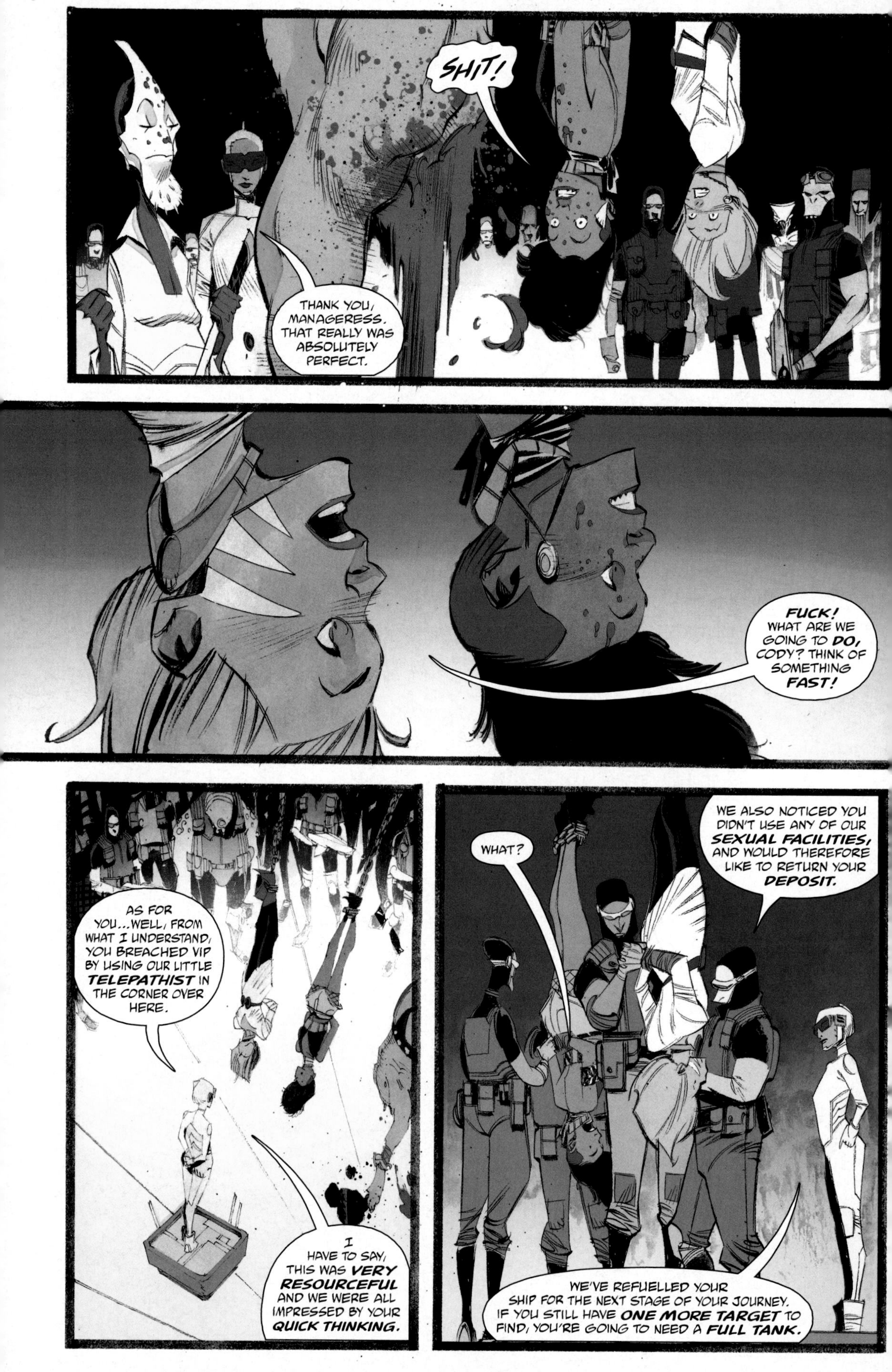
SHIT!
THANK YOU, MANAGERESS. THAT REALLY WAS ABSOLUTELY PERFECT.
FUCK! WHAT ARE WE GOING TO DO, CODY? THINK OF SOMETHING FAST!
AS FOR YOU...WELL, FROM WHAT I UNDERSTAND, YOU BREACHED VIP BY USING OUR LITTLE TELEPATHIST IN THE CORNER OVER HERE.
I HAVE TO SAY, THIS WAS VERY RESOURCEFUL AND WE WERE ALL IMPRESSED BY YOUR QUICK THINKING.
WHAT?
WE ALSO NOTICED YOU DIDN'T USE ANY OF OUR SEXUAL FACILITIES, AND WOULD THEREFORE LIKE TO RETURN YOUR DEPOSIT.
WE'VE REFUELLED YOUR SHIP FOR THE NEXT STAGE OF YOUR JOURNEY. IF YOU STILL HAVE ONE MORE TARGET TO FIND, YOU'RE GOING TO NEED A FULL TANK.

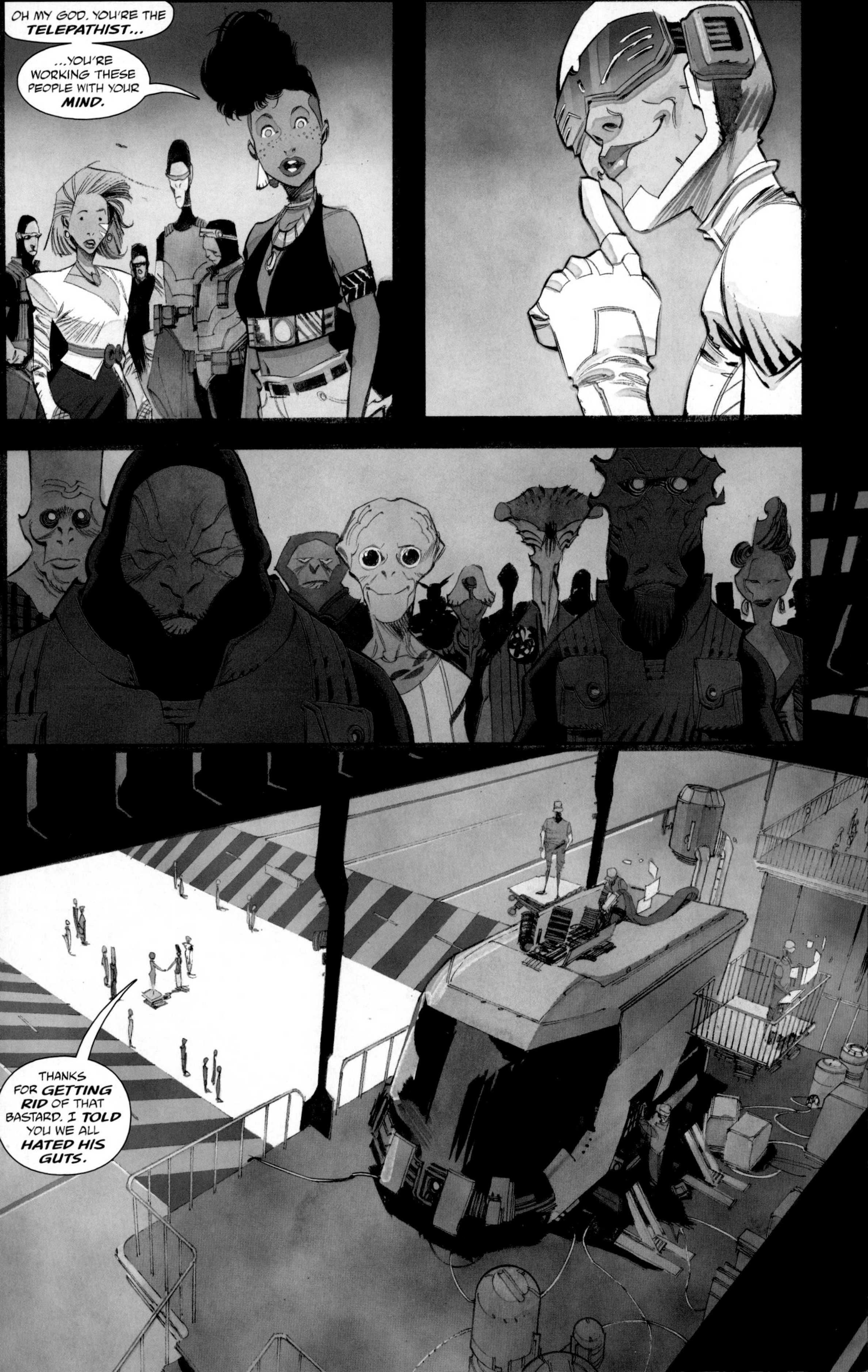
OH MY GOD. YOU'RE THE TELEPATHIST...
...YOU'RE WORKING THESE PEOPLE WITH YOUR MIND.
THANKS FOR GETTING RID OF THAT BASTARD. I TOLD YOU WE ALL HATED HIS GUTS.

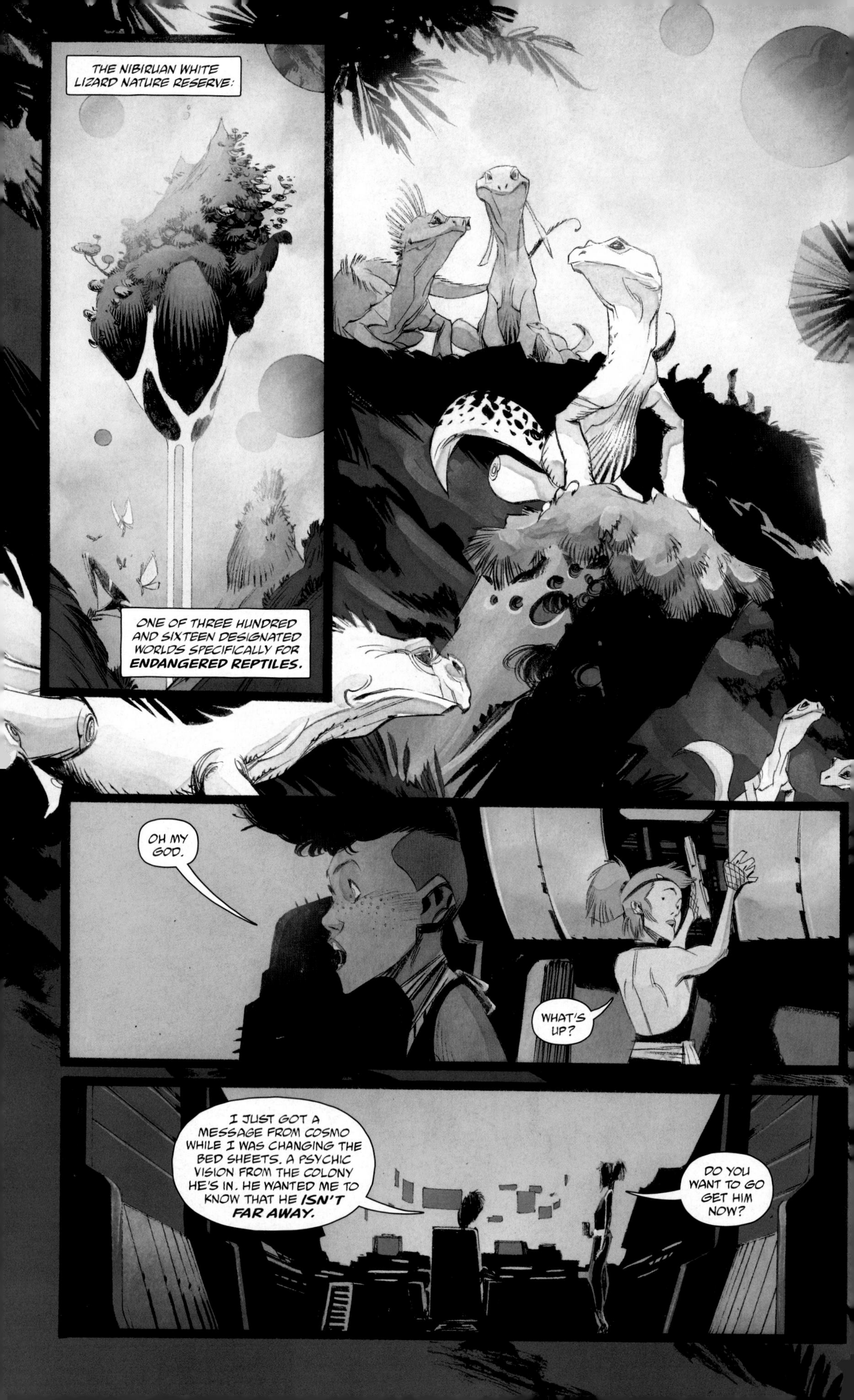
THE NIBIRUAN WHITE LIZARD NATURE RESERVE:
ONE OF THREE HUNDRED AND SIXTEEN DESIGNATED WORLDS SPECIFICALLY FOR **ENDANGERED REPTILES.**
OH MY GOD.
WHAT'S UP?
I JUST GOT A MESSAGE FROM COSMO WHILE I WAS CHANGING THE BED SHEETS. A PSYCHIC VISION FROM THE COLONY HE'S IN. HE WANTED ME TO KNOW THAT HE **ISN'T FAR AWAY.**
DO YOU WANT TO GO GET HIM NOW?

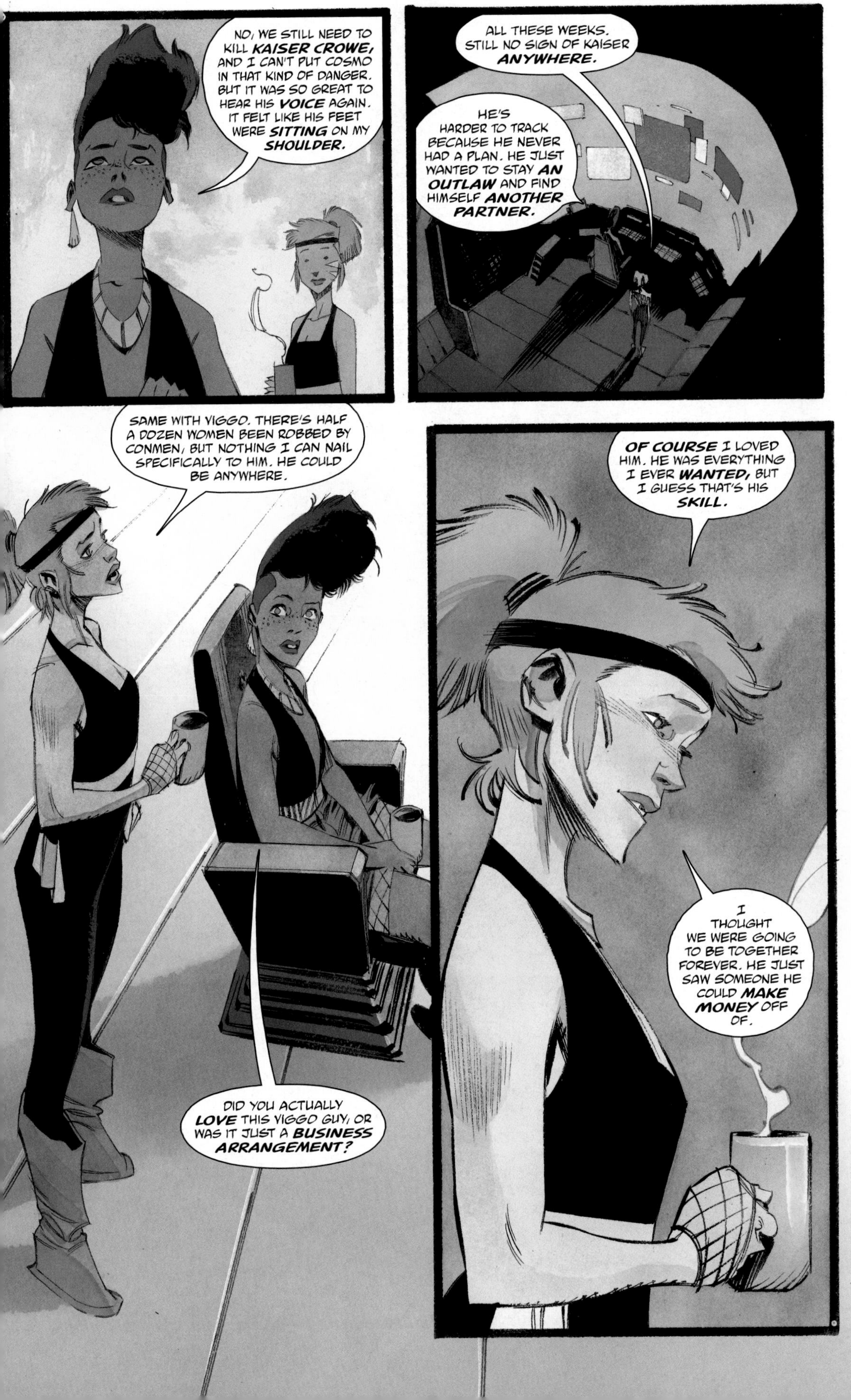

NO, WE STILL NEED TO KILL KAISER CROWE, AND I CAN'T PUT COSMO IN THAT KIND OF DANGER. BUT IT WAS SO GREAT TO HEAR HIS VOICE AGAIN. IT FELT LIKE HIS FEET WERE SITTING ON MY SHOULDER.
ALL THESE WEEKS. STILL NO SIGN OF KAISER ANYWHERE.
HE'S HARDER TO TRACK BECAUSE HE NEVER HAD A PLAN. HE JUST WANTED TO STAY AN OUTLAW AND FIND HIMSELF ANOTHER PARTNER.
SAME WITH VIGGO. THERE'S HALF A DOZEN WOMEN BEEN ROBBED BY CONMEN, BUT NOTHING I CAN NAIL SPECIFICALLY TO HIM. HE COULD BE ANYWHERE.
DID YOU ACTUALLY LOVE THIS VIGGO GUY, OR WAS IT JUST A BUSINESS ARRANGEMENT?
OF COURSE I LOVED HIM. HE WAS EVERYTHING I EVER WANTED, BUT I GUESS THAT'S HIS SKILL.
I THOUGHT WE WERE GOING TO BE TOGETHER FOREVER. HE JUST SAW SOMEONE HE COULD MAKE MONEY OFF OF.

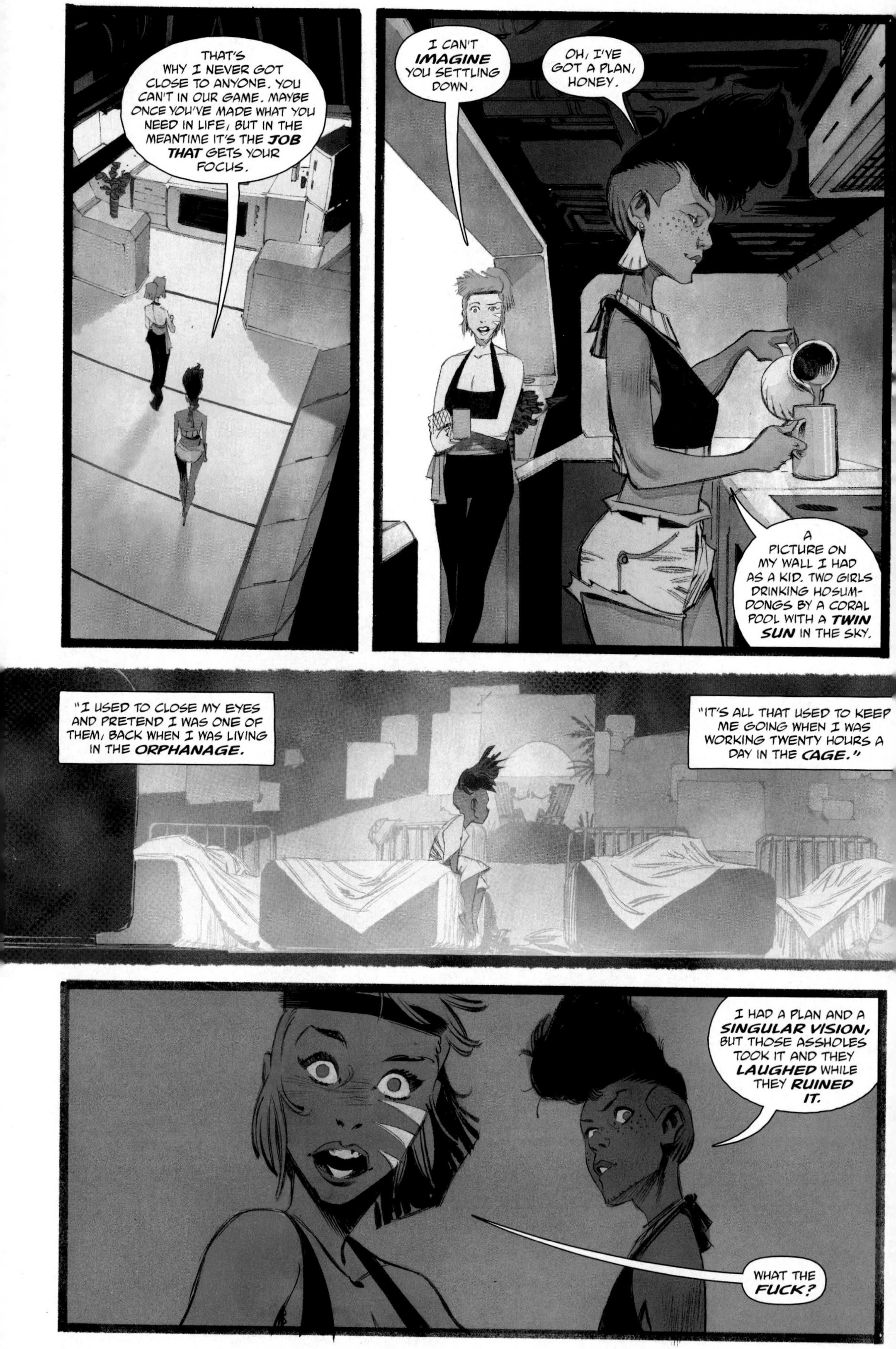
THAT'S WHY I NEVER GOT CLOSE TO ANYONE. YOU CAN'T IN OUR GAME. MAYBE ONCE YOU'VE MADE WHAT YOU NEED IN LIFE, BUT IN THE MEANTIME IT'S THE JOB THAT GETS YOUR FOCUS.
I CAN'T IMAGINE YOU SETTLING DOWN.
OH, I'VE GOT A PLAN, HONEY.
A PICTURE ON MY WALL I HAD AS A KID. TWO GIRLS DRINKING HOSUM-DONGS BY A CORAL POOL WITH A TWIN SUN IN THE SKY.
"I USED TO CLOSE MY EYES AND PRETEND I WAS ONE OF THEM, BACK WHEN I WAS LIVING IN THE ORPHANAGE.
"IT'S ALL THAT USED TO KEEP ME GOING WHEN I WAS WORKING TWENTY HOURS A DAY IN THE CAGE."
I HAD A PLAN AND A SINGULAR VISION, BUT THOSE ASSHOLES TOOK IT AND THEY LAUGHED WHILE THEY RUINED IT.
WHAT THE FUCK?

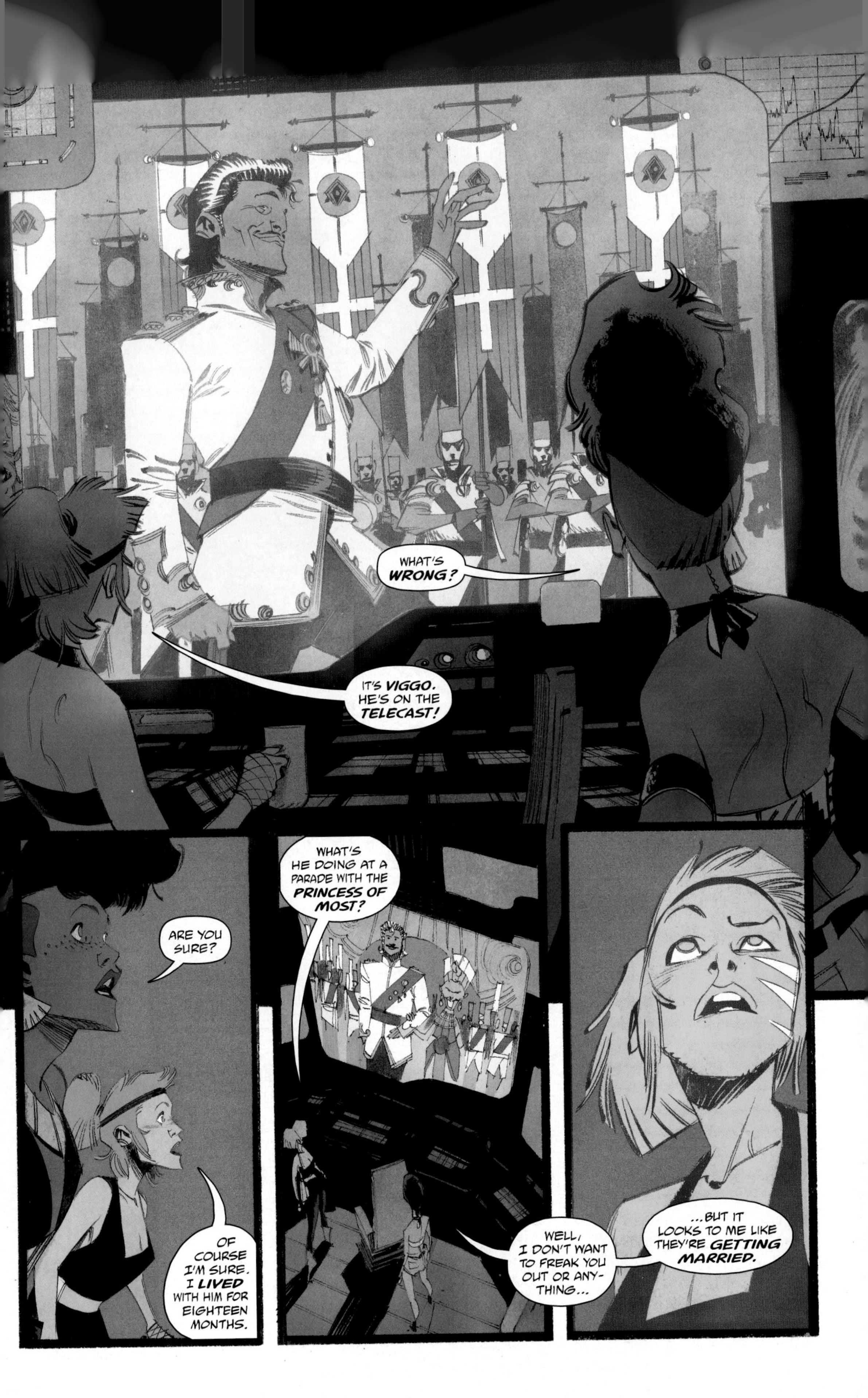
WHAT'S WRONG?
IT'S VIGGO. HE'S ON THE TELECAST!
ARE YOU SURE?
OF COURSE I'M SURE. I LIVED WITH HIM FOR EIGHTEEN MONTHS.
WHAT'S HE DOING AT A PARADE WITH THE PRINCESS OF MOST?
WELL, I DON'T WANT TO FREAK YOU OUT OR ANY-THING...
...BUT IT LOOKS TO ME LIKE THEY'RE GETTING MARRIED.

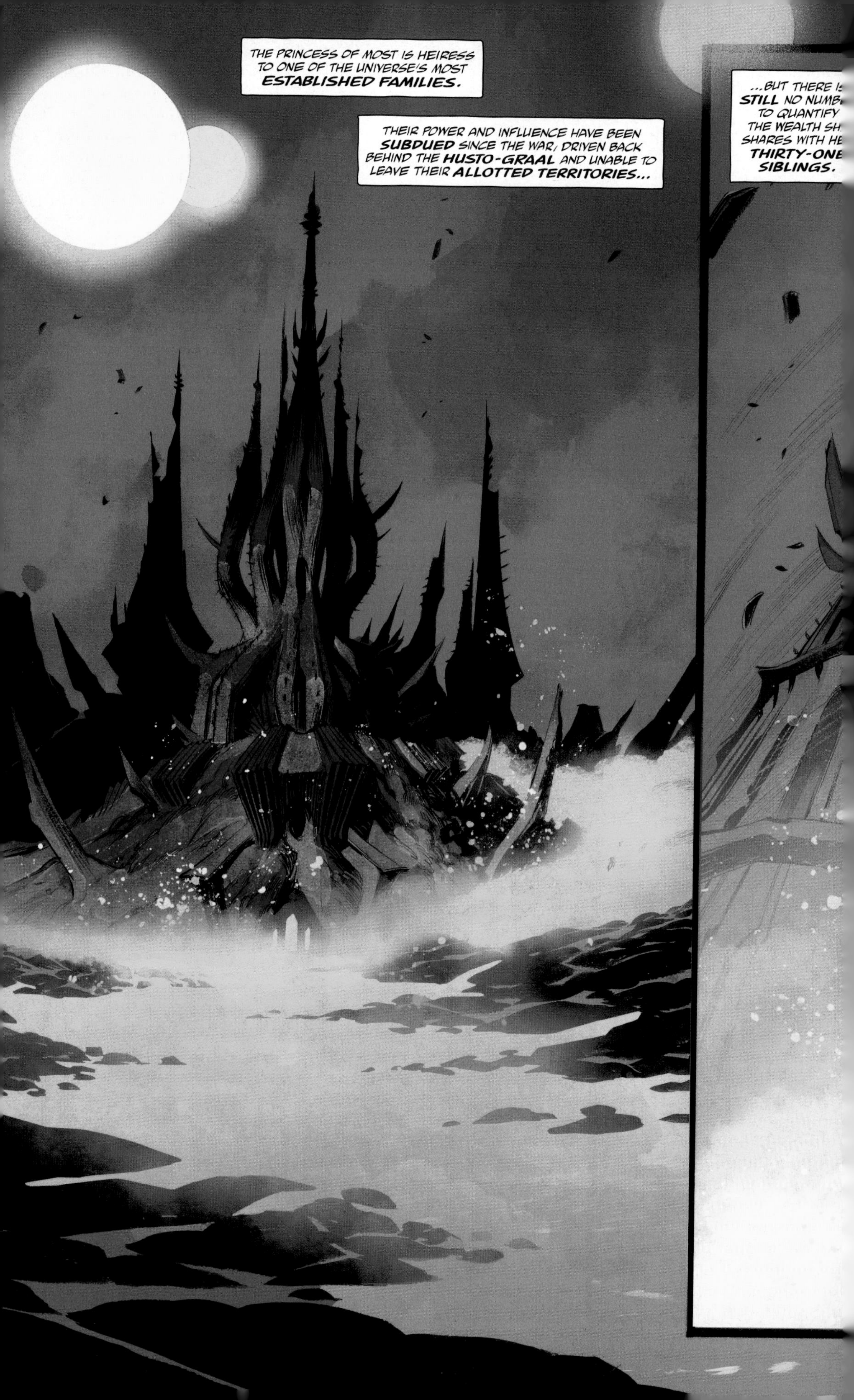

THE PRINCESS OF MOST IS HEIRESS TO ONE OF THE UNIVERSE'S MOST ESTABLISHED FAMILIES.
THEIR POWER AND INFLUENCE HAVE BEEN SUBDUED SINCE THE WAR, DRIVEN BACK BEHIND THE HUSTO-GRAAL AND UNABLE TO LEAVE THEIR ALLOTTED TERRITORIES...
...BUT THERE IS STILL NO NUMB TO QUANTIFY THE WEALTH SH SHARES WITH HE THIRTY-ONE SIBLINGS.

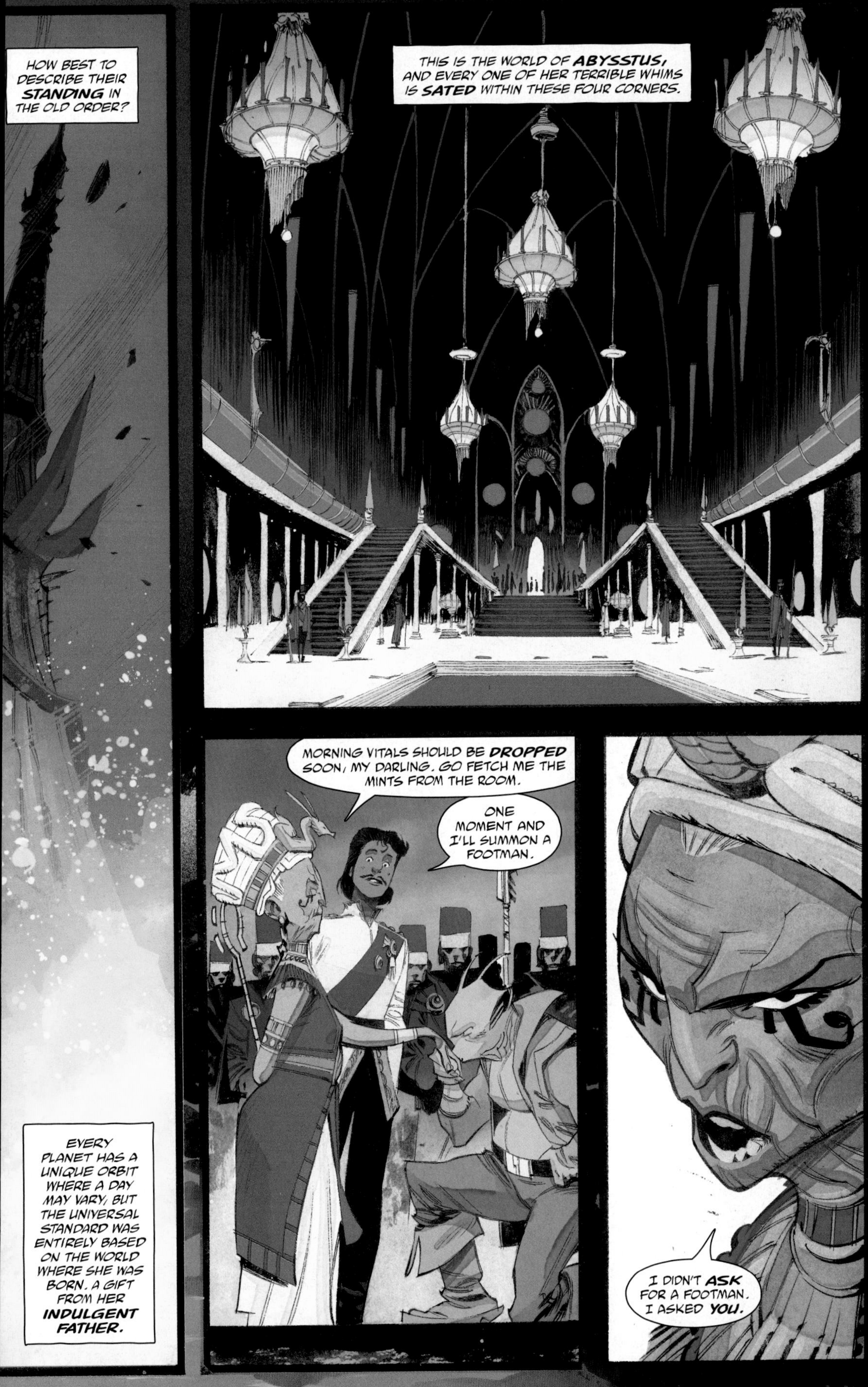

HOW BEST TO DESCRIBE THEIR STANDING IN THE OLD ORDER?
THIS IS THE WORLD OF ABYSSTUS, AND EVERY ONE OF HER TERRIBLE WHIMS IS SATED WITHIN THESE FOUR CORNERS.
EVERY PLANET HAS A UNIQUE ORBIT WHERE A DAY MAY VARY, BUT THE UNIVERSAL STANDARD WAS ENTIRELY BASED ON THE WORLD WHERE SHE WAS BORN. A GIFT FROM HER INDULGENT FATHER.
MORNING VITALS SHOULD BE DROPPED SOON, MY DARLING. GO FETCH ME THE MINTS FROM THE ROOM.
ONE MOMENT AND I'LL SUMMON A FOOTMAN.
I DIDN'T ASK FOR A FOOTMAN. I ASKED YOU.

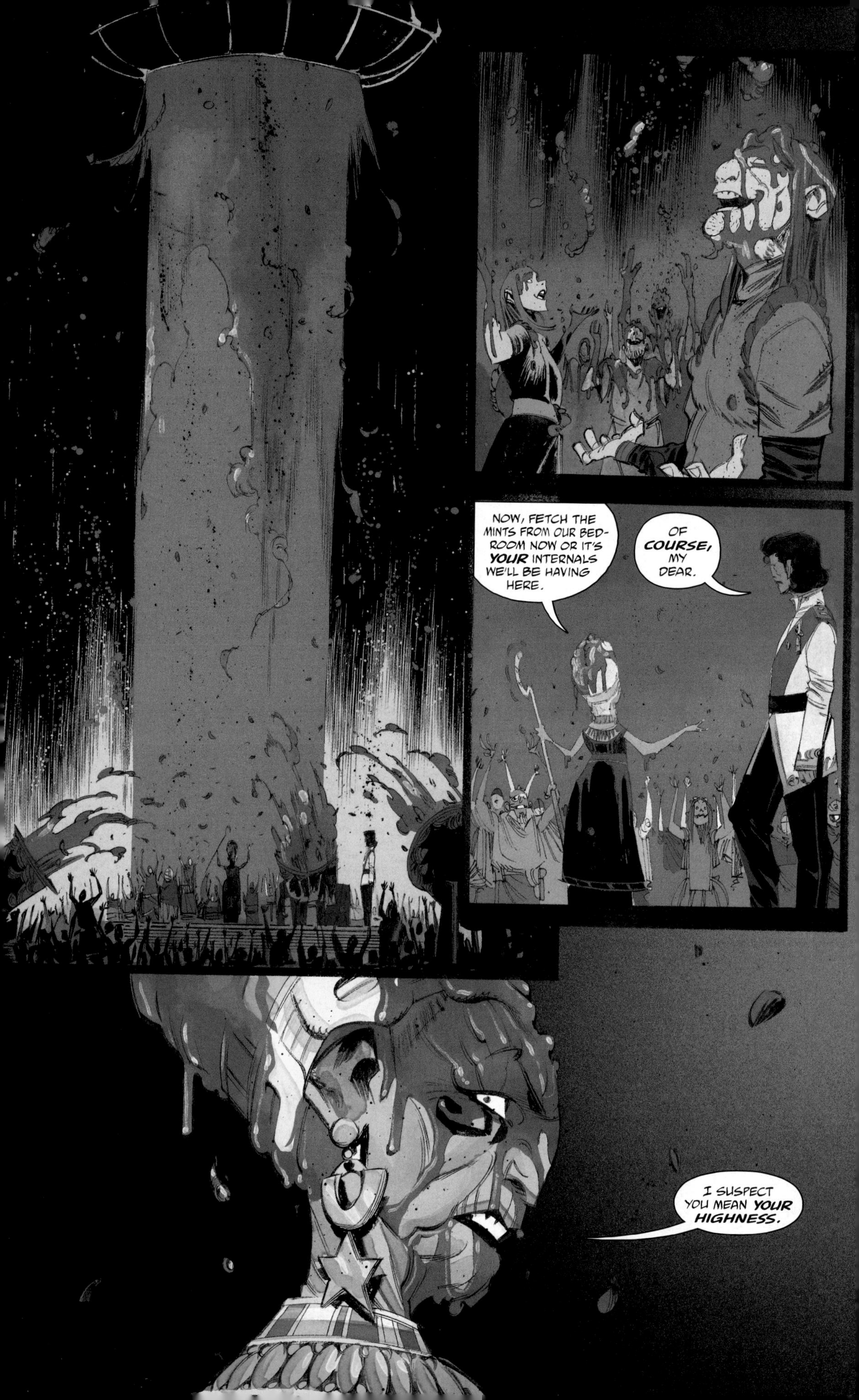
NOW, FETCH THE MINTS FROM OUR BED-ROOM NOW OR IT'S YOUR INTERNALS WE'LL BE HAVING HERE.
OF COURSE, MY DEAR.
I SUSPECT YOU MEAN YOUR HIGHNESS.

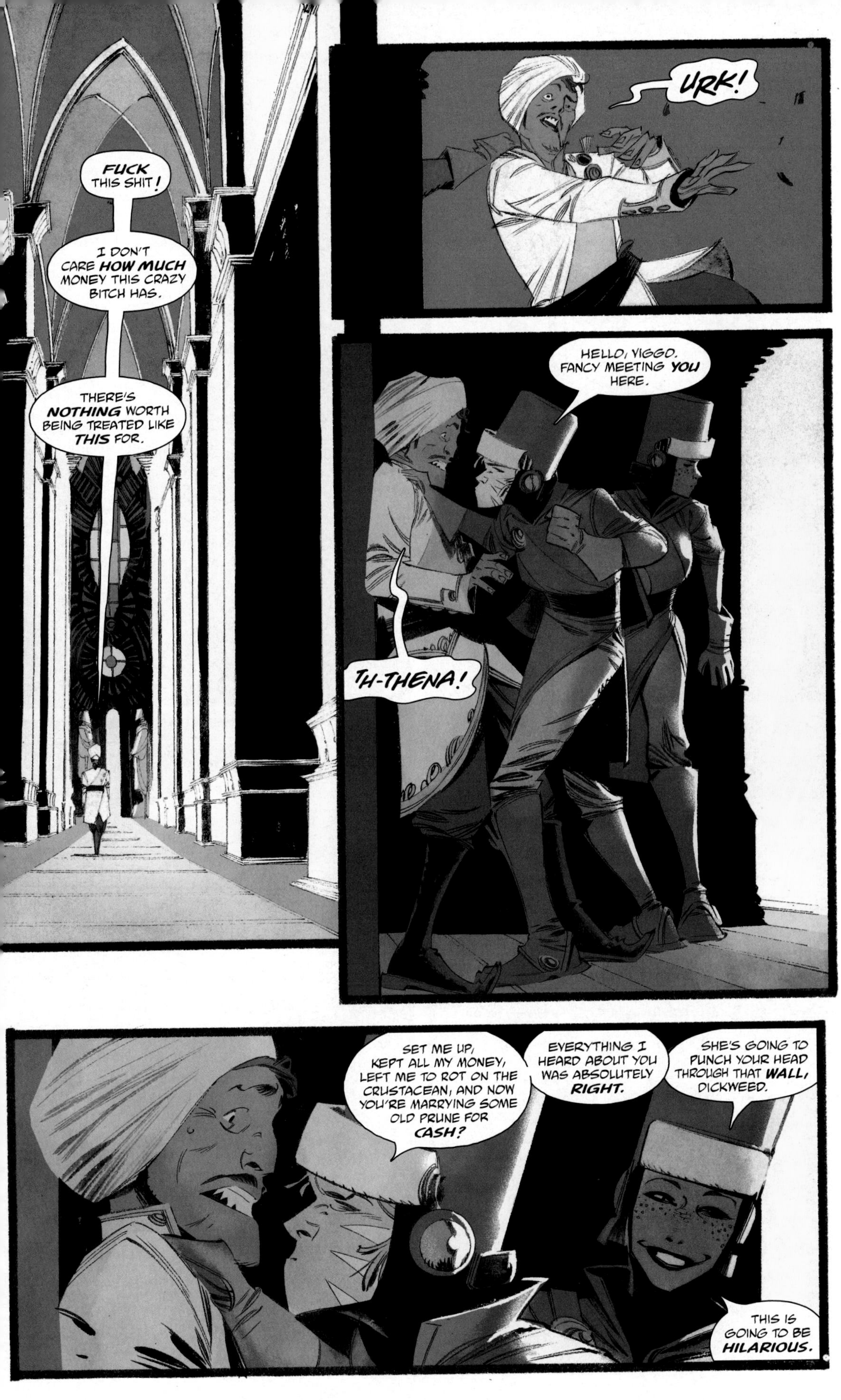
FUCK THIS SHIT!
I DON'T CARE HOW MUCH MONEY THIS CRAZY BITCH HAS.
THERE'S NOTHING WORTH BEING TREATED LIKE THIS FOR.
URK!
HELLO, VIGGO. FANCY MEETING YOU HERE.
TH-THENA!
SET ME UP, KEPT ALL MY MONEY, LEFT ME TO ROT ON THE CRUSTACEAN, AND NOW YOU'RE MARRYING SOME OLD PRUNE FOR CASH?
EVERYTHING I HEARD ABOUT YOU WAS ABSOLUTELY RIGHT.
SHE'S GOING TO PUNCH YOUR HEAD THROUGH THAT WALL, DICKWEED.
THIS IS GOING TO BE HILARIOUS.

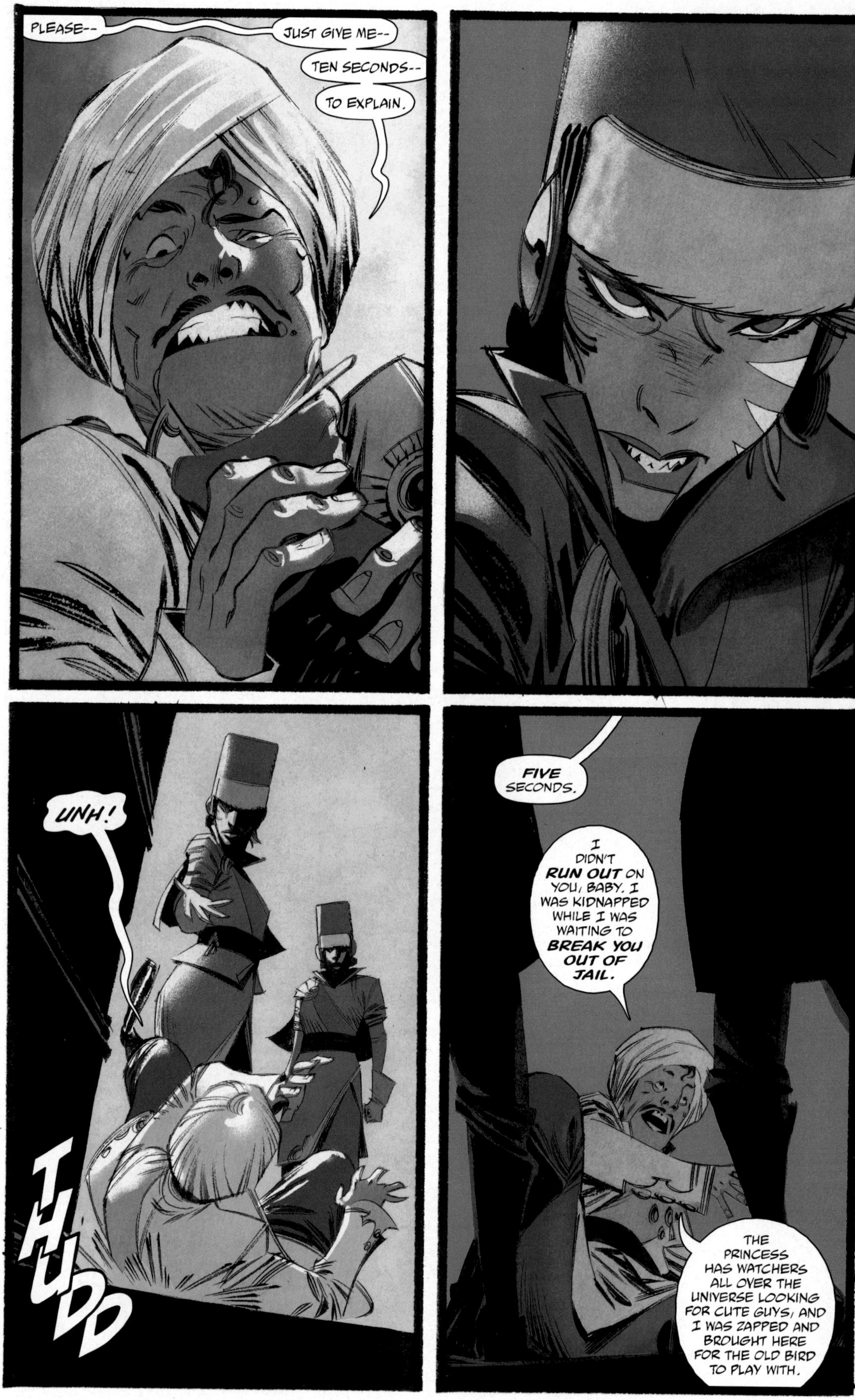
PLEASE--
JUST GIVE ME--
TEN SECONDS--
TO EXPLAIN.
UNH!
THUDD
FIVE SECONDS.
I DIDN'T RUN OUT ON YOU, BABY. I WAS KIDNAPPED WHILE I WAS WAITING TO BREAK YOU OUT OF JAIL.
THE PRINCESS HAS WATCHERS ALL OVER THE UNIVERSE LOOKING FOR CUTE GUYS, AND I WAS ZAPPED AND BROUGHT HERE FOR THE OLD BIRD TO PLAY WITH.

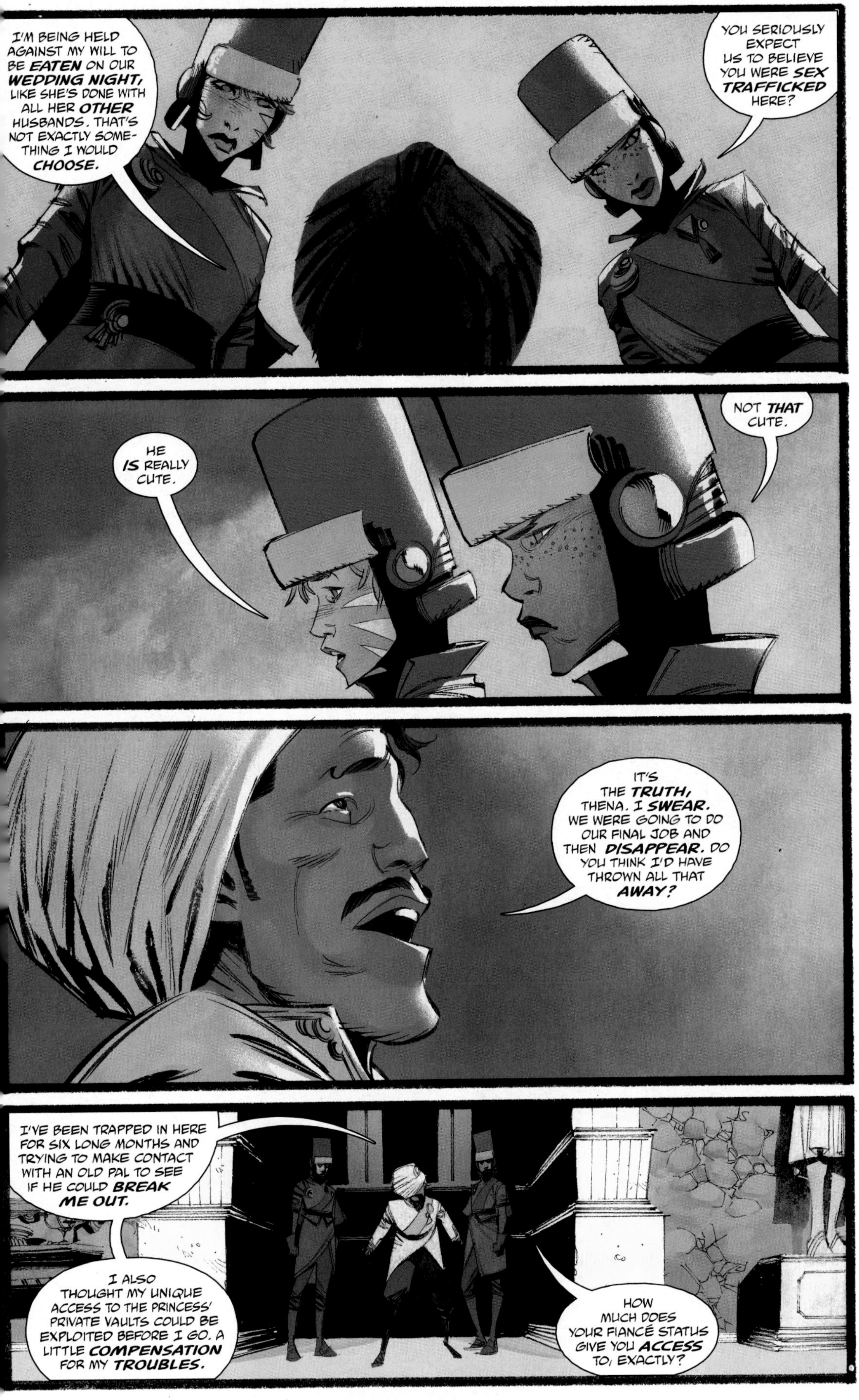
I'M BEING HELD AGAINST MY WILL TO BE EATEN ON OUR WEDDING NIGHT, LIKE SHE'S DONE WITH ALL HER OTHER HUSBANDS. THAT'S NOT EXACTLY SOME-THING I WOULD CHOOSE.
YOU SERIOUSLY EXPECT US TO BELIEVE YOU WERE SEX TRAFFICKED HERE?
HE IS REALLY CUTE.
NOT THAT CUTE.
IT'S THE TRUTH, THENA. I SWEAR. WE WERE GOING TO DO OUR FINAL JOB AND THEN DISAPPEAR. DO YOU THINK I'D HAVE THROWN ALL THAT AWAY?
I'VE BEEN TRAPPED IN HERE FOR SIX LONG MONTHS AND TRYING TO MAKE CONTACT WITH AN OLD PAL TO SEE IF HE COULD BREAK ME OUT.
I ALSO THOUGHT MY UNIQUE ACCESS TO THE PRINCESS' PRIVATE VAULTS COULD BE EXPLOITED BEFORE I GO. A LITTLE COMPENSATION FOR MY TROUBLES.
HOW MUCH DOES YOUR FIANCÉ STATUS GIVE YOU ACCESS TO, EXACTLY?

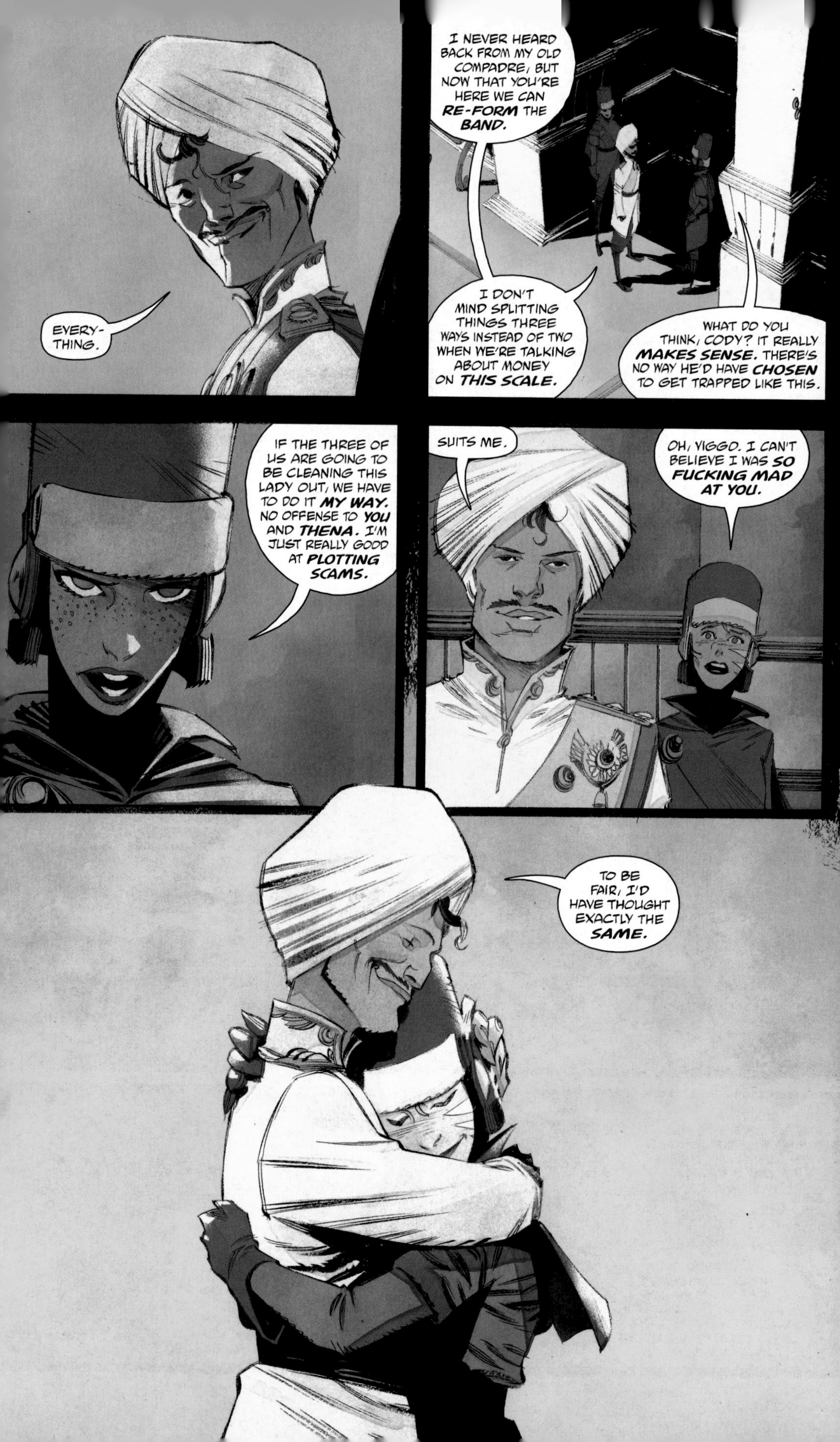
EVERY-THING.
I NEVER HEARD BACK FROM MY OLD COMPADRE, BUT NOW THAT YOU'RE HERE WE CAN RE-FORM THE BAND.
I DON'T MIND SPLITTING THINGS THREE WAYS INSTEAD OF TWO WHEN WE'RE TALKING ABOUT MONEY ON THIS SCALE.
WHAT DO YOU THINK, CODY? IT REALLY MAKES SENSE. THERE'S NO WAY HE'D HAVE CHOSEN TO GET TRAPPED LIKE THIS.
IF THE THREE OF US ARE GOING TO BE CLEANING THIS LADY OUT, WE HAVE TO DO IT MY WAY. NO OFFENSE TO YOU AND THENA. I'M JUST REALLY GOOD AT PLOTTING SCAMS.
SUITS ME.
OH, VIGGO. I CAN'T BELIEVE I WAS SO FUCKING MAD AT YOU.
TO BE FAIR, I'D HAVE THOUGHT EXACTLY THE SAME.

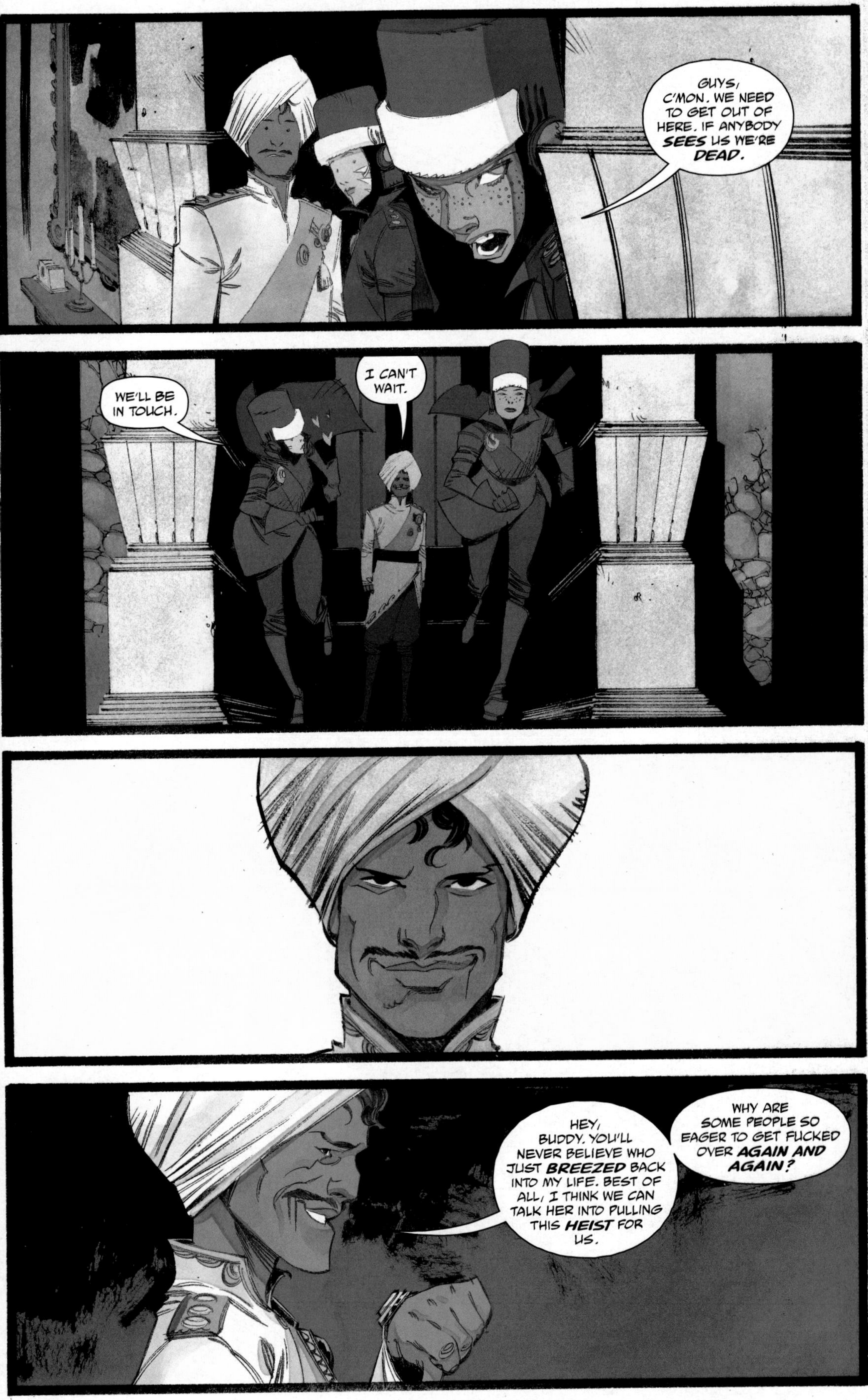
GUYS, C'MON. WE NEED TO GET OUT OF HERE. IF ANYBODY SEES US WE'RE DEAD.
WE'LL BE IN TOUCH.
I CAN'T WAIT.
HEY, BUDDY. YOU'LL NEVER BELIEVE WHO JUST BREEZED BACK INTO MY LIFE. BEST OF ALL, I THINK WE CAN TALK HER INTO PULLING THIS HEIST FOR US.
WHY ARE SOME PEOPLE SO EAGER TO GET FUCKED OVER AGAIN AND AGAIN?

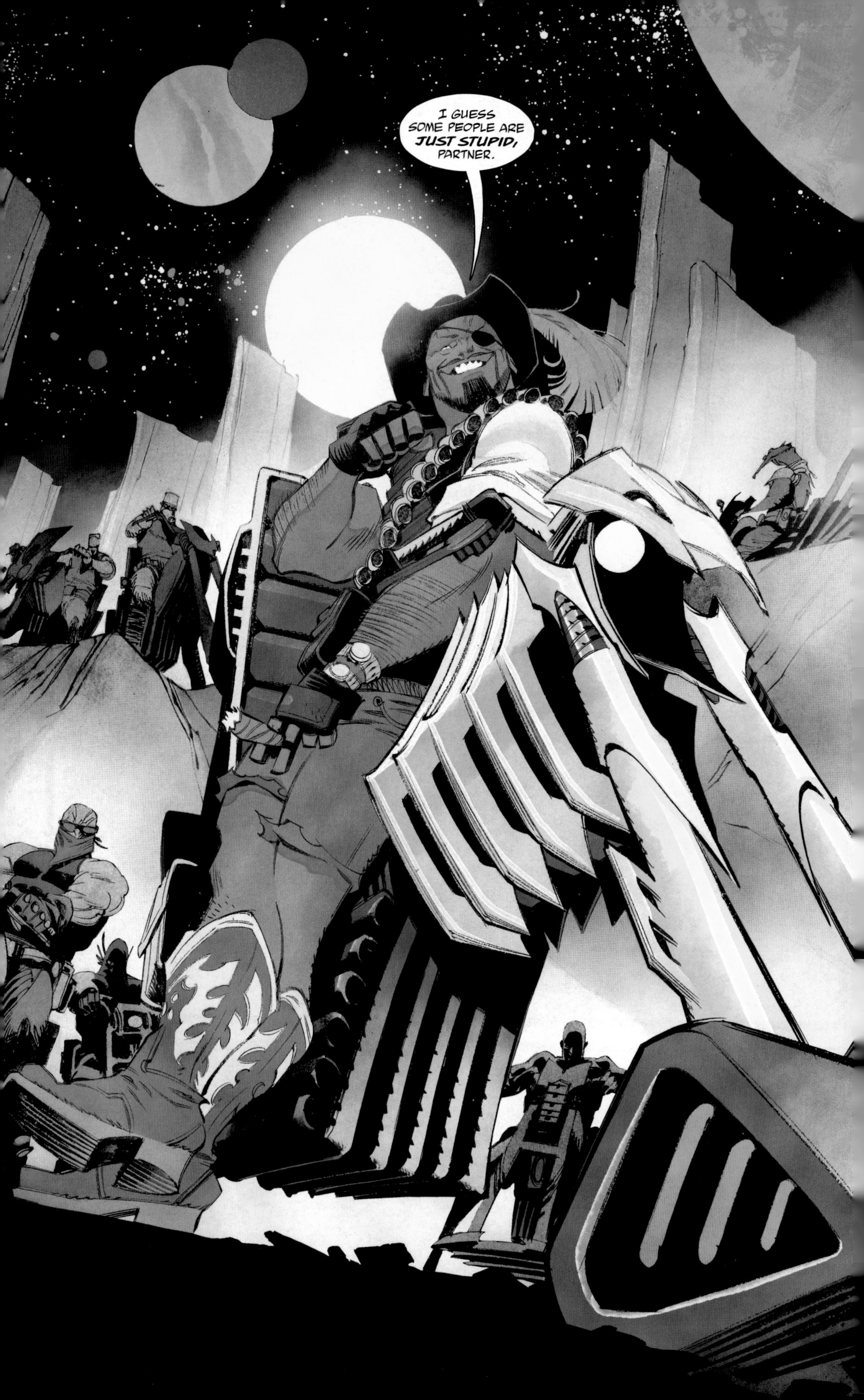
I GUESS SOME PEOPLE ARE ***JUST STUPID,*** PARTNER.

Five

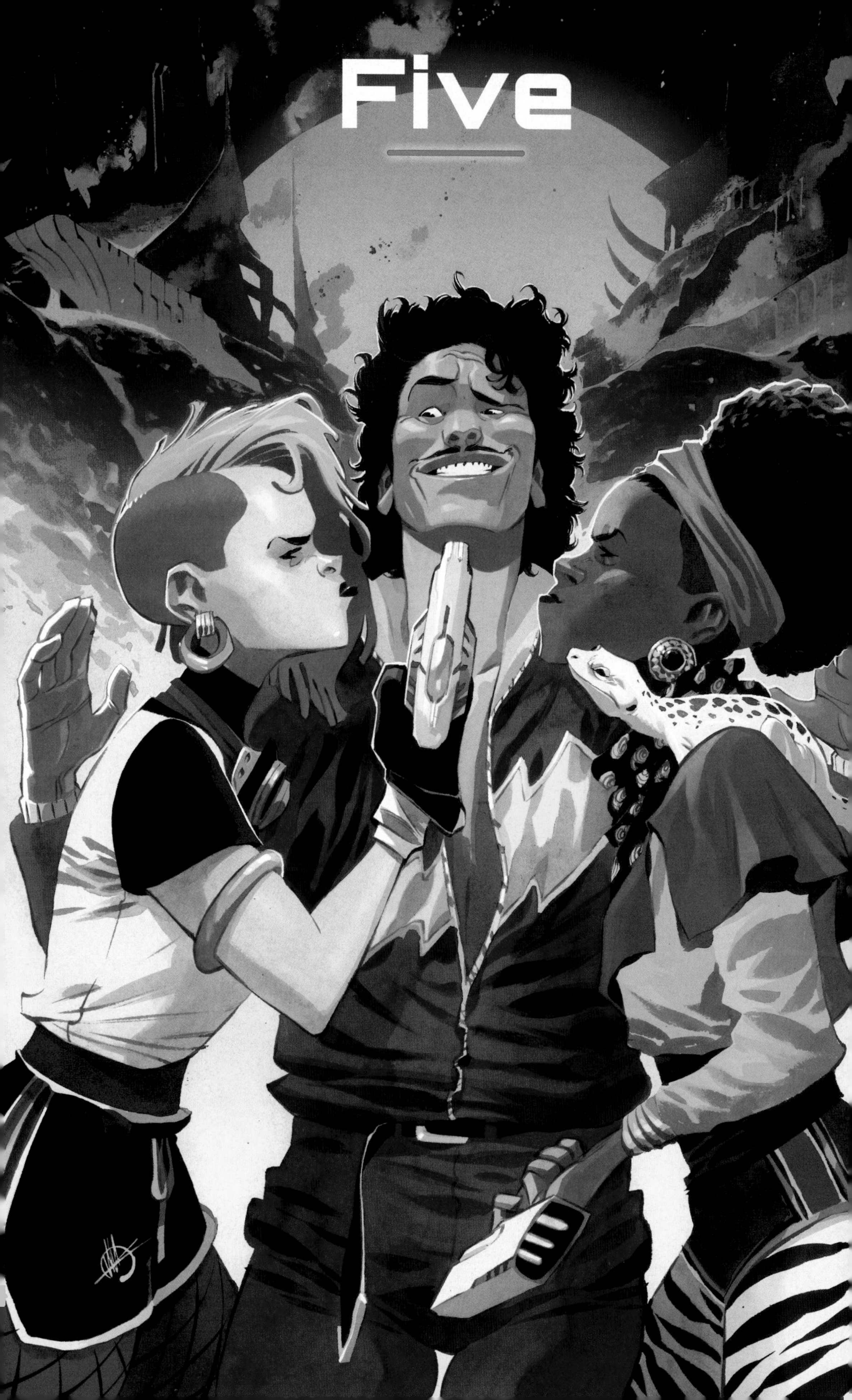

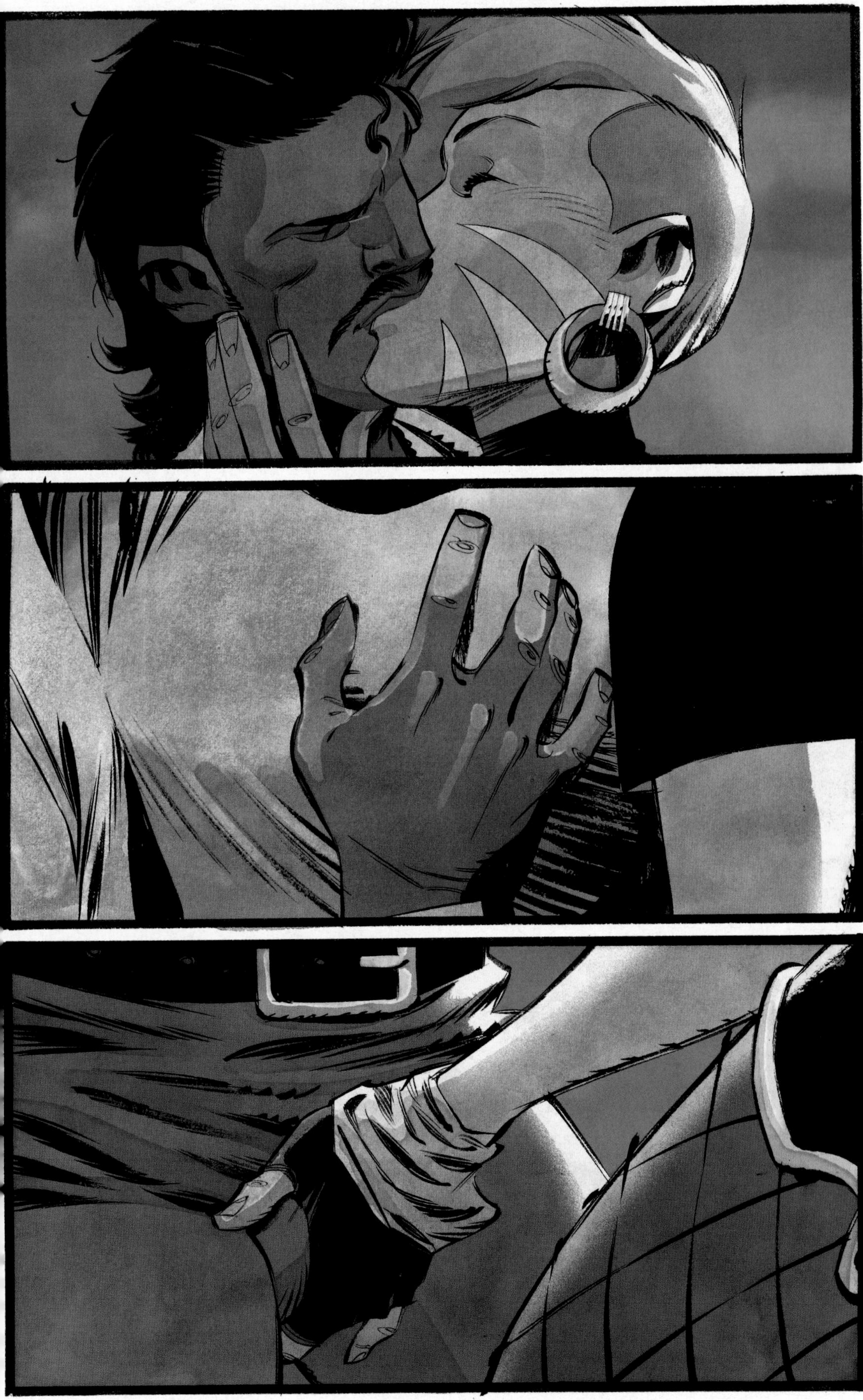

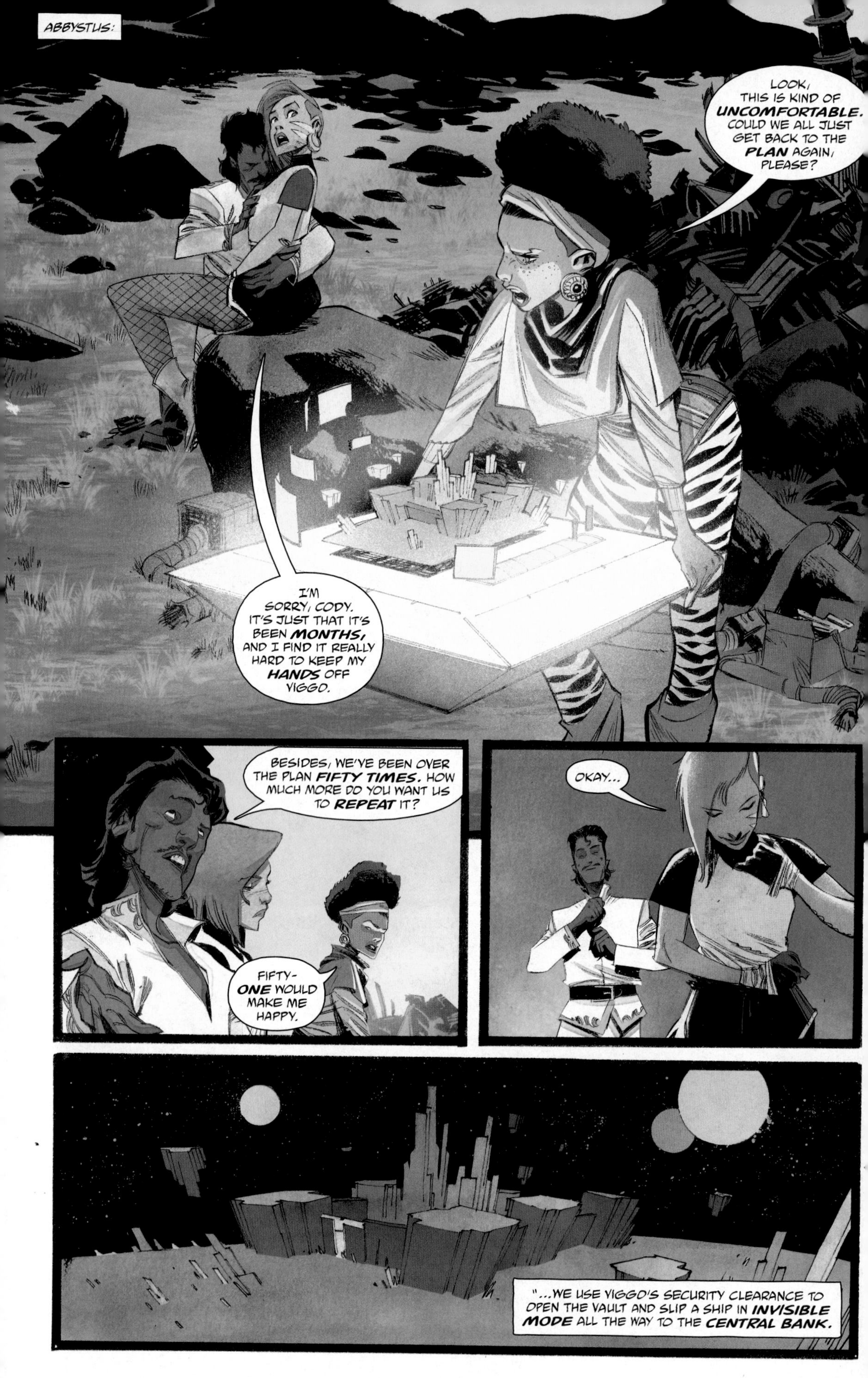
ABBYSTUS:
LOOK, THIS IS KIND OF UNCOMFORTABLE. COULD WE ALL JUST GET BACK TO THE PLAN AGAIN, PLEASE?
I'M SORRY, CODY. IT'S JUST THAT IT'S BEEN MONTHS, AND I FIND IT REALLY HARD TO KEEP MY HANDS OFF VIGGO.
BESIDES, WE'VE BEEN OVER THE PLAN FIFTY TIMES. HOW MUCH MORE DO YOU WANT US TO REPEAT IT?
FIFTY-ONE WOULD MAKE ME HAPPY.
OKAY...
"...WE USE VIGGO'S SECURITY CLEARANCE TO OPEN THE VAULT AND SLIP A SHIP IN INVISIBLE MODE ALL THE WAY TO THE CENTRAL BANK.

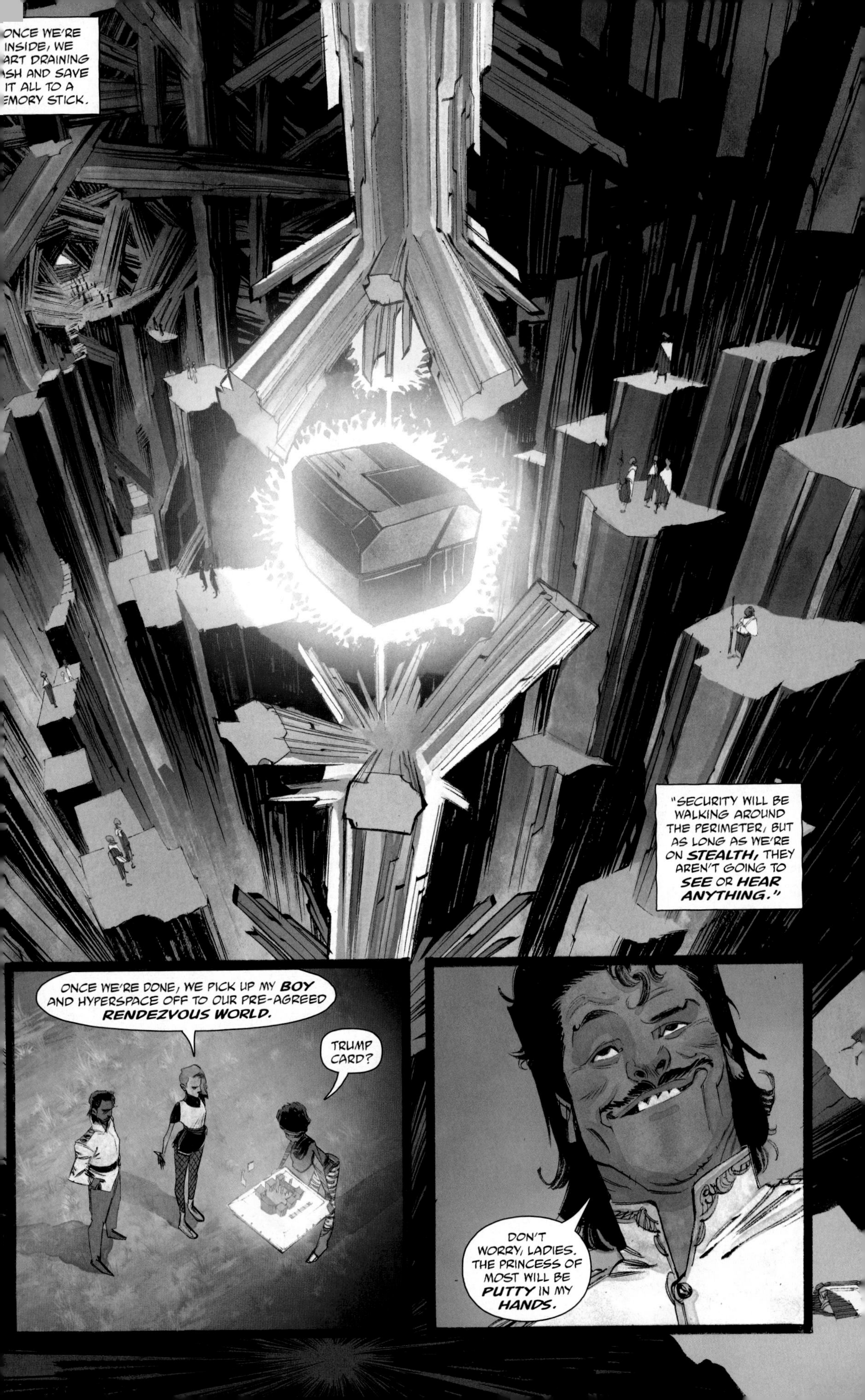
ONCE WE'RE INSIDE, WE ART DRAINING ASH AND SAVE IT ALL TO A EMORY STICK.
"SECURITY WILL BE WALKING AROUND THE PERIMETER, BUT AS LONG AS WE'RE ON STEALTH, THEY AREN'T GOING TO SEE OR HEAR ANYTHING."
ONCE WE'RE DONE, WE PICK UP MY BOY AND HYPERSPACE OFF TO OUR PRE-AGREED RENDEZVOUS WORLD.
TRUMP CARD?
DON'T WORRY, LADIES. THE PRINCESS OF MOST WILL BE PUTTY IN MY HANDS.

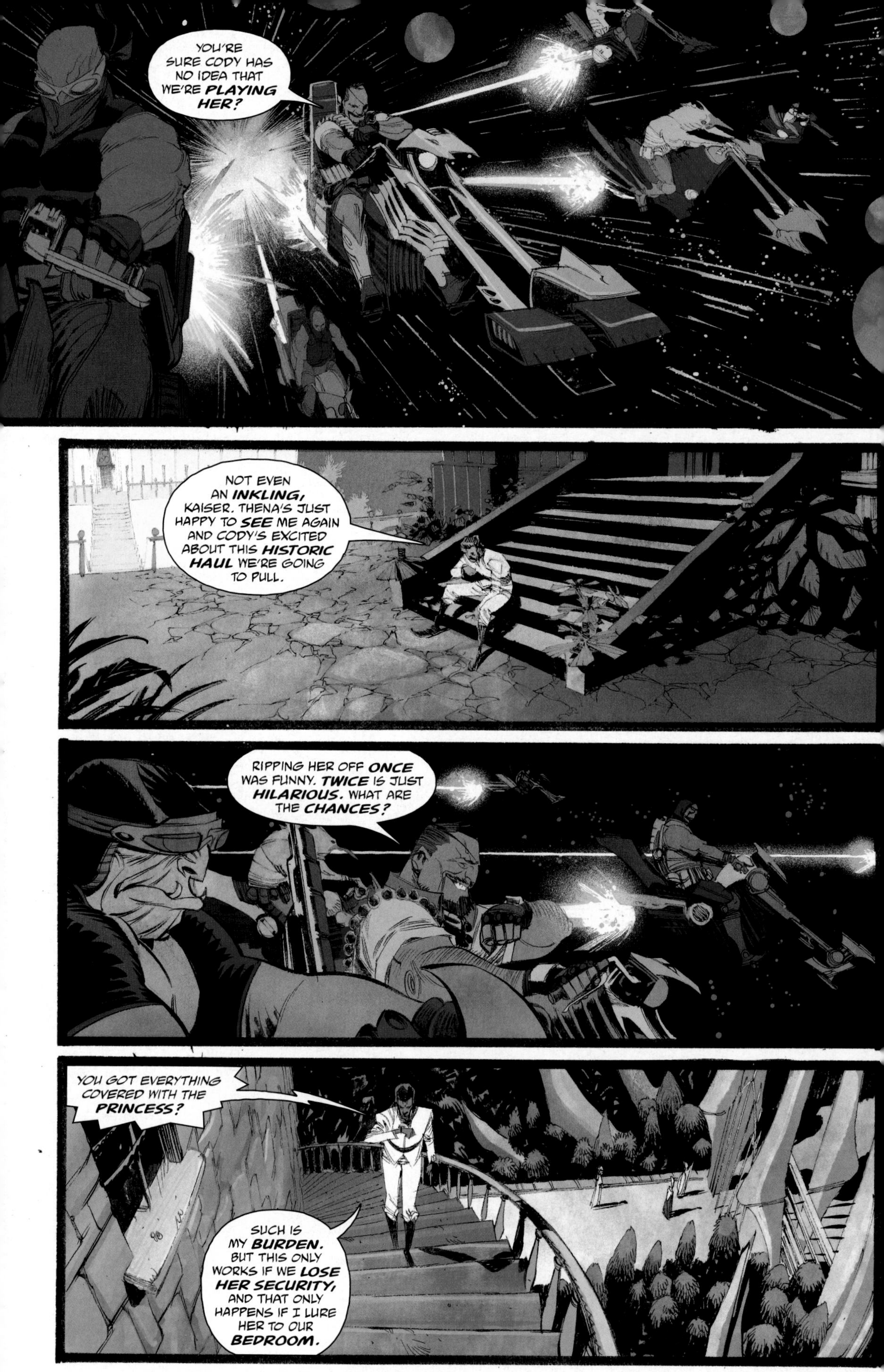
YOU'RE SURE CODY HAS NO IDEA THAT WE'RE PLAYING HER?
NOT EVEN AN INKLING, KAISER. THENA'S JUST HAPPY TO SEE ME AGAIN AND CODY'S EXCITED ABOUT THIS HISTORIC HAUL WE'RE GOING TO PULL.
RIPPING HER OFF ONCE WAS FUNNY. TWICE IS JUST HILARIOUS. WHAT ARE THE CHANCES?
YOU GOT EVERYTHING COVERED WITH THE PRINCESS?
SUCH IS MY BURDEN. BUT THIS ONLY WORKS IF WE LOSE HER SECURITY, AND THAT ONLY HAPPENS IF I LURE HER TO OUR BEDROOM.

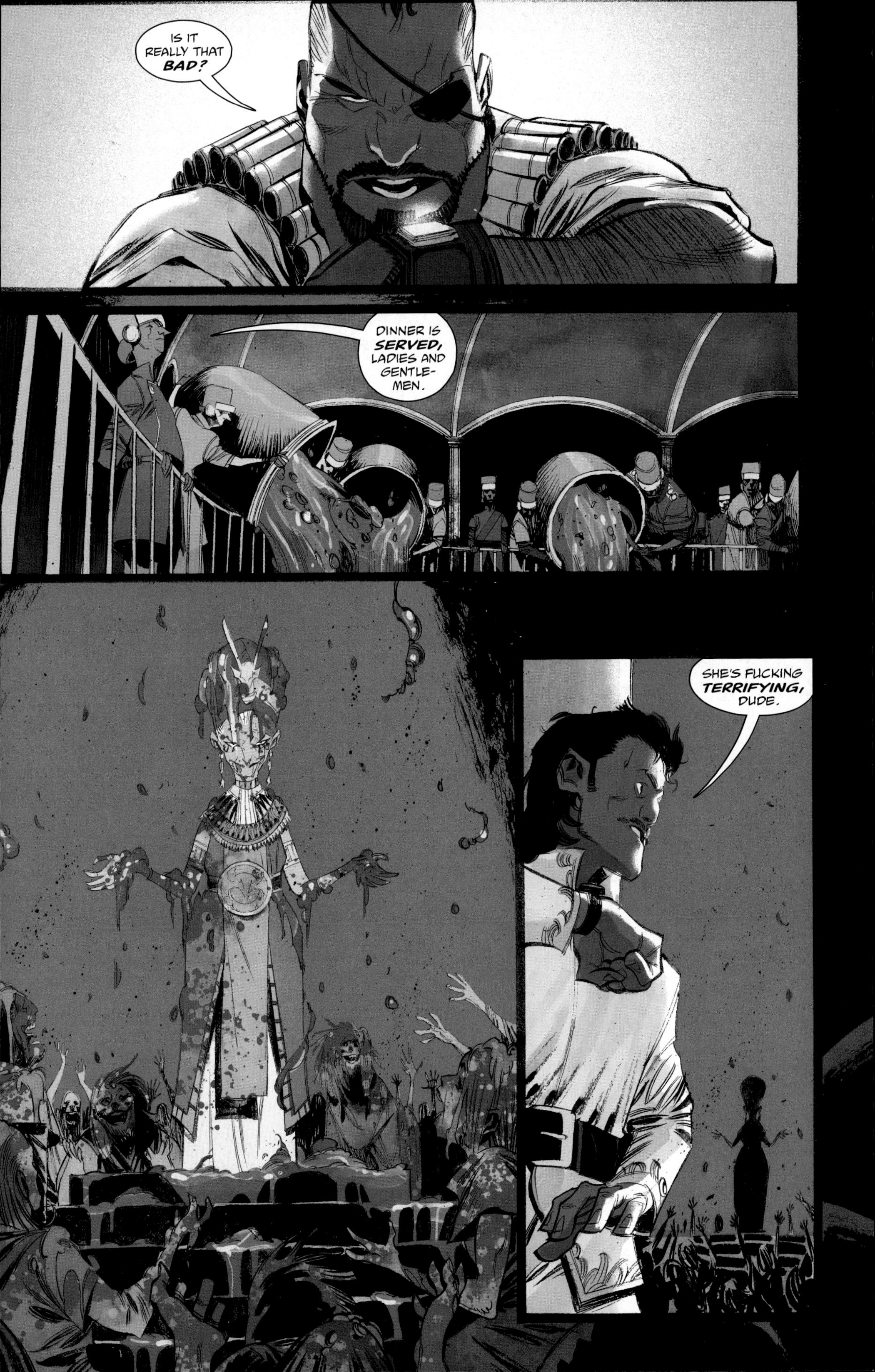
IS IT REALLY THAT BAD?
DINNER IS SERVED, LADIES AND GENTLE-MEN.
SHE'S FUCKING TERRIFYING, DUDE.

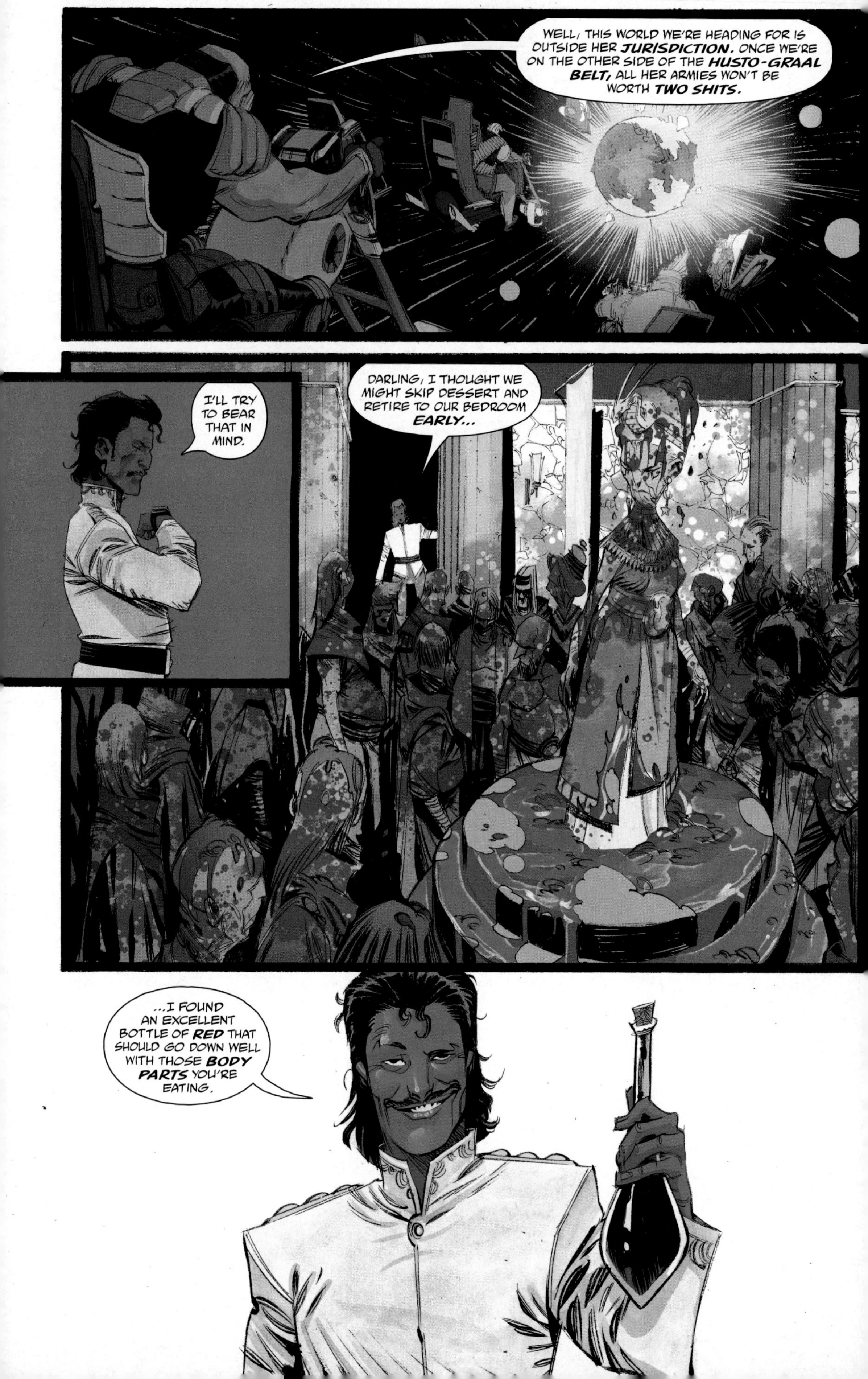
WELL, THIS WORLD WE'RE HEADING FOR IS OUTSIDE HER JURISDICTION. ONCE WE'RE ON THE OTHER SIDE OF THE HUSTO-GRAAL BELT, ALL HER ARMIES WON'T BE WORTH TWO SHITS.
I'LL TRY TO BEAR THAT IN MIND.
DARLING, I THOUGHT WE MIGHT SKIP DESSERT AND RETIRE TO OUR BEDROOM EARLY...
...I FOUND AN EXCELLENT BOTTLE OF RED THAT SHOULD GO DOWN WELL WITH THOSE BODY PARTS YOU'RE EATING.

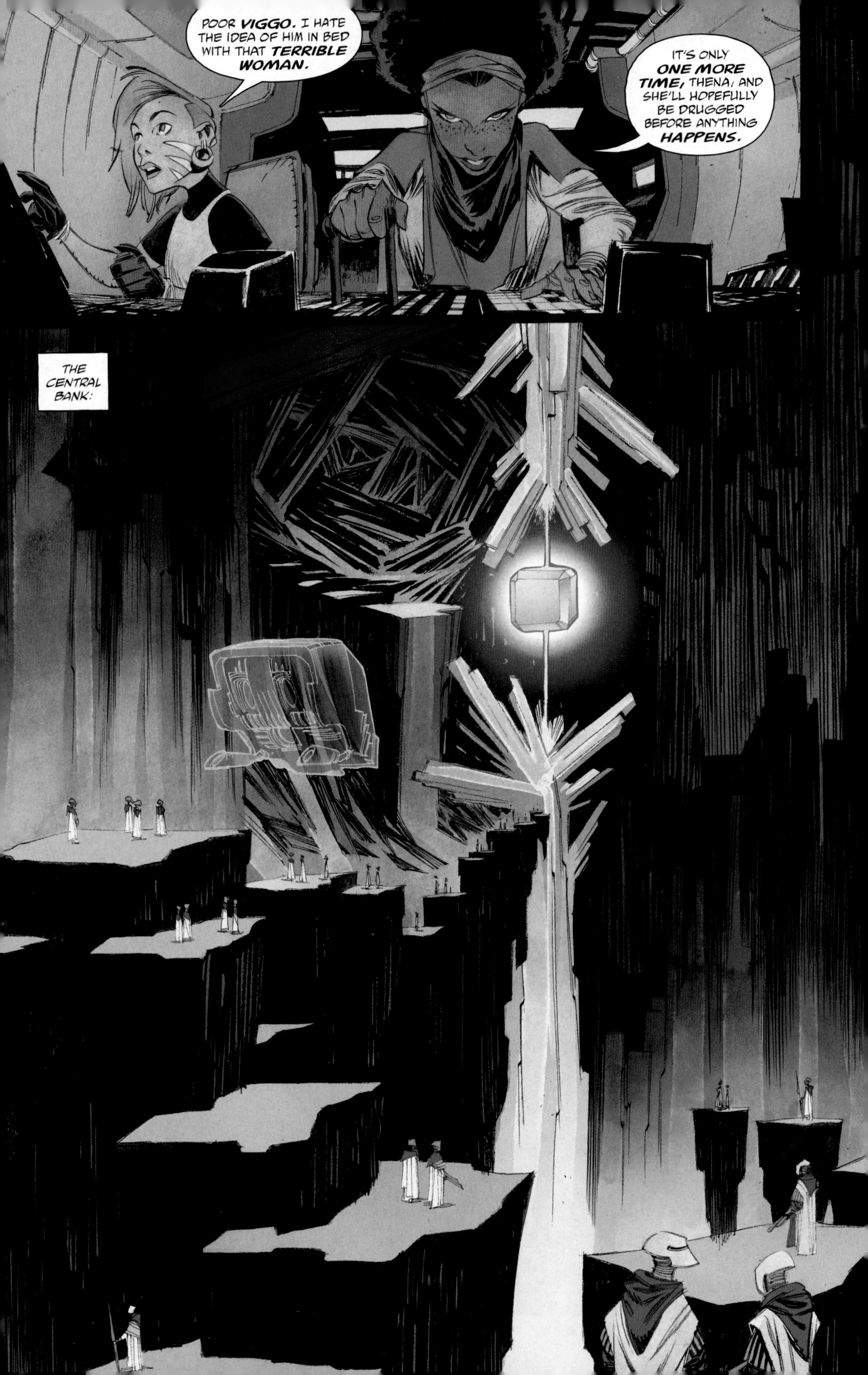
POOR VIGGO. I HATE THE IDEA OF HIM IN BED WITH THAT TERRIBLE WOMAN.
IT'S ONLY ONE MORE TIME, THENA, AND SHE'LL HOPEFULLY BE DRUGGED BEFORE ANYTHING HAPPENS.
THE CENTRAL BANK:

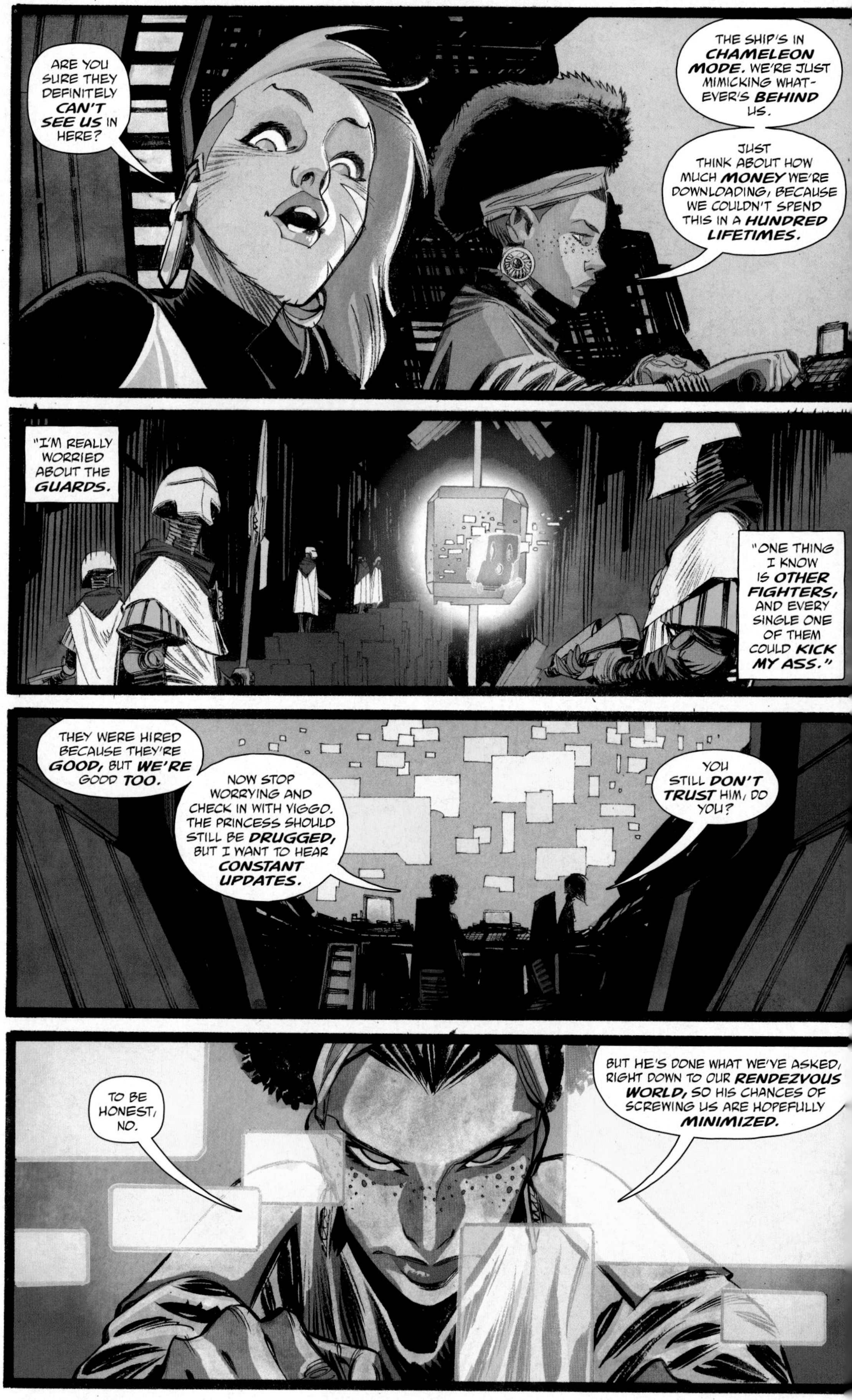
ARE YOU SURE THEY DEFINITELY CAN'T SEE US IN HERE?
THE SHIP'S IN CHAMELEON MODE. WE'RE JUST MIMICKING WHAT-EVER'S BEHIND US.
JUST THINK ABOUT HOW MUCH MONEY WE'RE DOWNLOADING, BECAUSE WE COULDN'T SPEND THIS IN A HUNDRED LIFETIMES.
"I'M REALLY WORRIED ABOUT THE GUARDS.
"ONE THING I KNOW IS OTHER FIGHTERS, AND EVERY SINGLE ONE OF THEM COULD KICK MY ASS."
THEY WERE HIRED BECAUSE THEY'RE GOOD, BUT WE'RE GOOD TOO.
NOW STOP WORRYING AND CHECK IN WITH VIGGO. THE PRINCESS SHOULD STILL BE DRUGGED, BUT I WANT TO HEAR CONSTANT UPDATES.
YOU STILL DON'T TRUST HIM, DO YOU?
TO BE HONEST, NO.
BUT HE'S DONE WHAT WE'VE ASKED, RIGHT DOWN TO OUR RENDEZVOUS WORLD, SO HIS CHANCES OF SCREWING US ARE HOPEFULLY MINIMIZED.

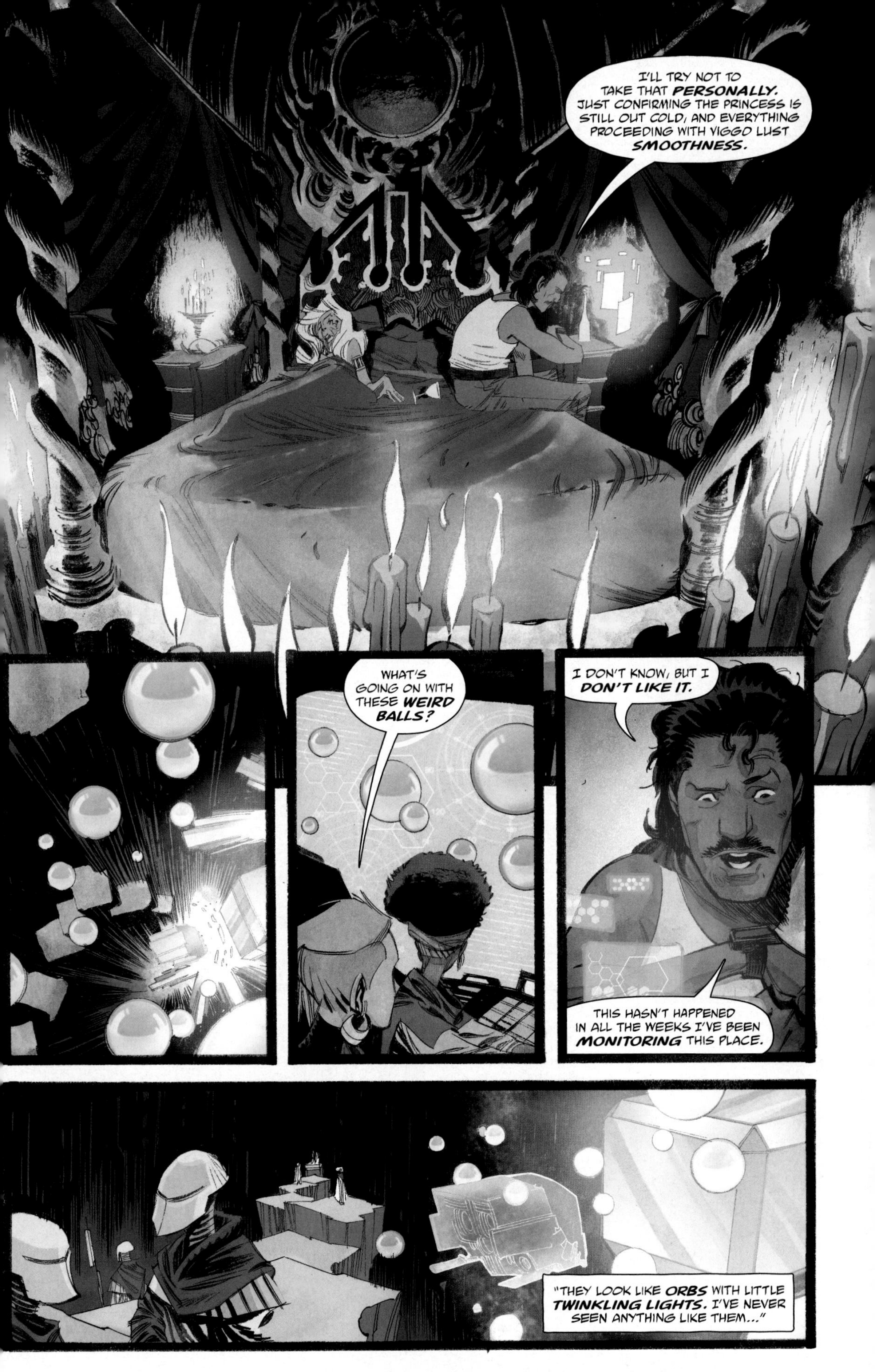
I'LL TRY NOT TO TAKE THAT PERSONALLY. JUST CONFIRMING THE PRINCESS IS STILL OUT COLD, AND EVERYTHING PROCEEDING WITH VIGGO LUST SMOOTHNESS.
WHAT'S GOING ON WITH THESE WEIRD BALLS?
I DON'T KNOW, BUT I DON'T LIKE IT.
THIS HASN'T HAPPENED IN ALL THE WEEKS I'VE BEEN MONITORING THIS PLACE.
"THEY LOOK LIKE ORBS WITH LITTLE TWINKLING LIGHTS. I'VE NEVER SEEN ANYTHING LIKE THEM..."

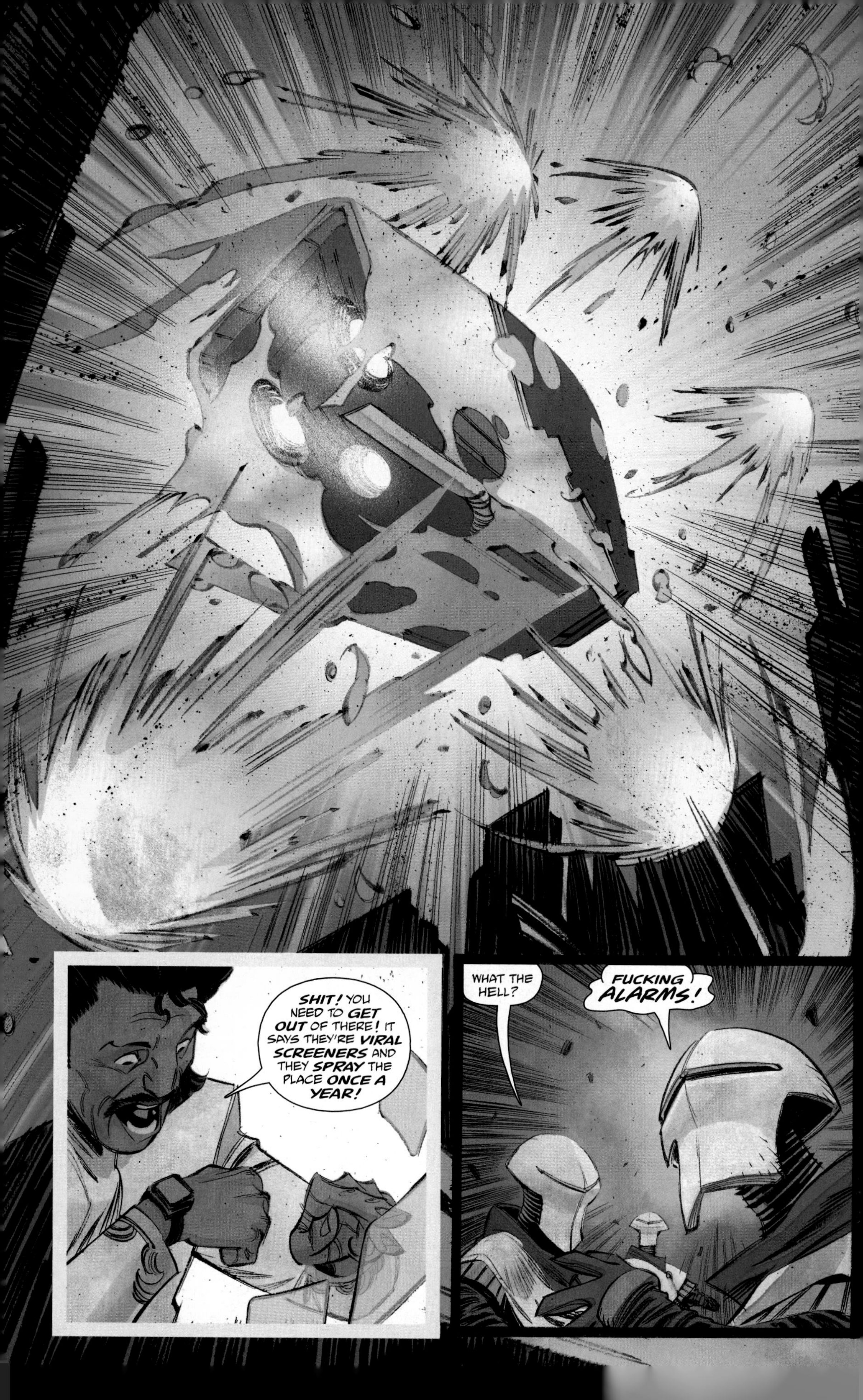
SHIT! YOU NEED TO GET OUT OF THERE! IT SAYS THEY'RE VIRAL SCREENERS AND THEY SPRAY THE PLACE ONCE A YEAR!
WHAT THE HELL?
FUCKING ALARMS!

DON'T EVEN **THINK** ABOUT IT, LADIES AND GENTS. STOP THAT VESSEL FROM LEAVING THE VAULT AND I PROMISE YOU NOW THE PRINCESS **DIES.** DO YOU REALLY WANT THAT ON YOUR RESUME?

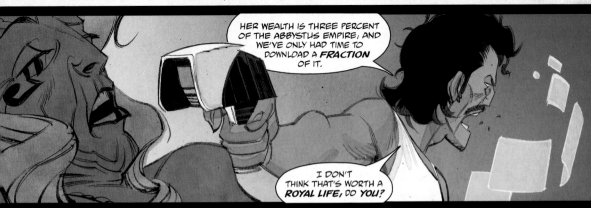

HER WEALTH IS THREE PERCENT OF THE ABBYSTUS EMPIRE, AND WE'VE ONLY HAD TIME TO DOWNLOAD A **FRACTION** OF IT.

I DON'T THINK THAT'S WORTH A **ROYAL LIFE,** DO **YOU?**

I'M NOT **GOING NEAR** THIS.

GOOD BOY.

YOU'RE GOOD TO GO, CODY. YOUR PLAN **WORKED.** NOBODY'S GIVING US ANY GRIEF AT ALL IF THEY THINK IT PUTS THE **PRINCESS** IN DANGER.

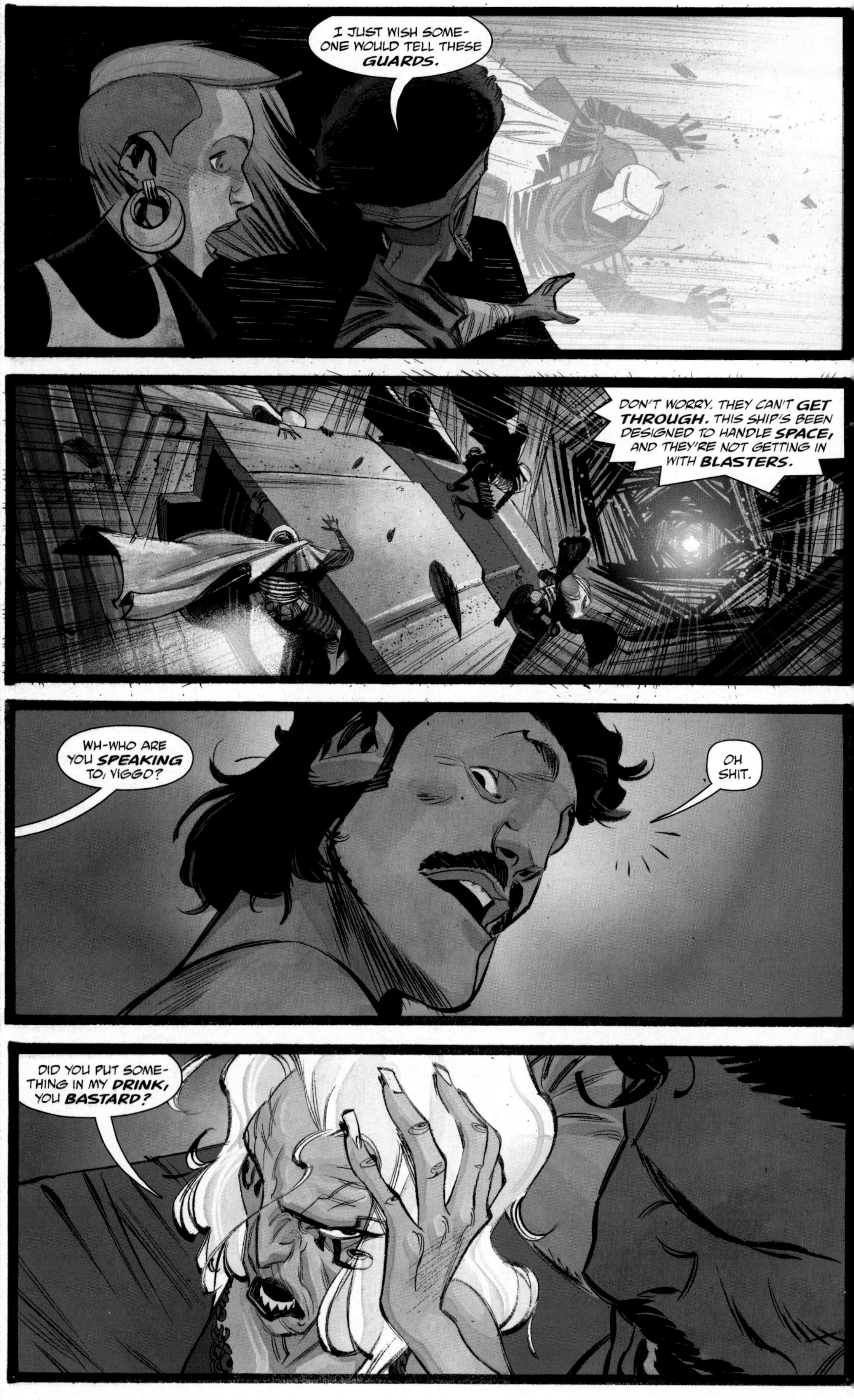
I JUST WISH SOME-ONE WOULD TELL THESE GUARDS.
DON'T WORRY. THEY CAN'T GET THROUGH. THIS SHIP'S BEEN DESIGNED TO HANDLE SPACE, AND THEY'RE NOT GETTING IN WITH BLASTERS.
WH-WHO ARE YOU SPEAKING TO, VIGGO?
OH SHIT.
DID YOU PUT SOME-THING IN MY DRINK, YOU BASTARD?

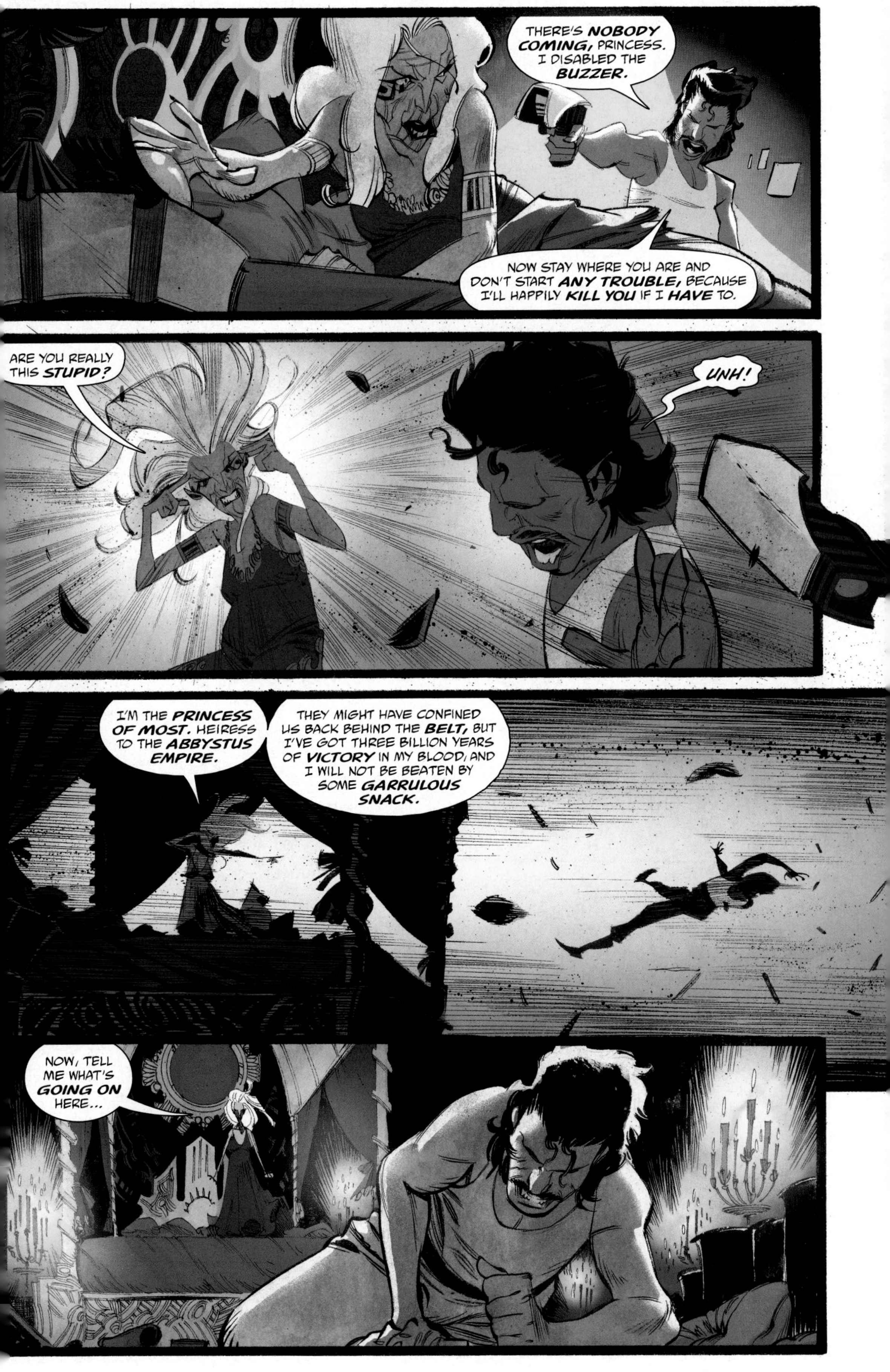
THERE'S NOBODY COMING, PRINCESS. I DISABLED THE BUZZER.
NOW STAY WHERE YOU ARE AND DON'T START ANY TROUBLE, BECAUSE I'LL HAPPILY KILL YOU IF I HAVE TO.
ARE YOU REALLY THIS STUPID?
UNH!
I'M THE PRINCESS OF MOST. HEIRESS TO THE ABBYSTUS EMPIRE.
THEY MIGHT HAVE CONFINED US BACK BEHIND THE BELT, BUT I'VE GOT THREE BILLION YEARS OF VICTORY IN MY BLOOD, AND I WILL NOT BE BEATEN BY SOME GARRULOUS SNACK.
NOW, TELL ME WHAT'S GOING ON HERE...

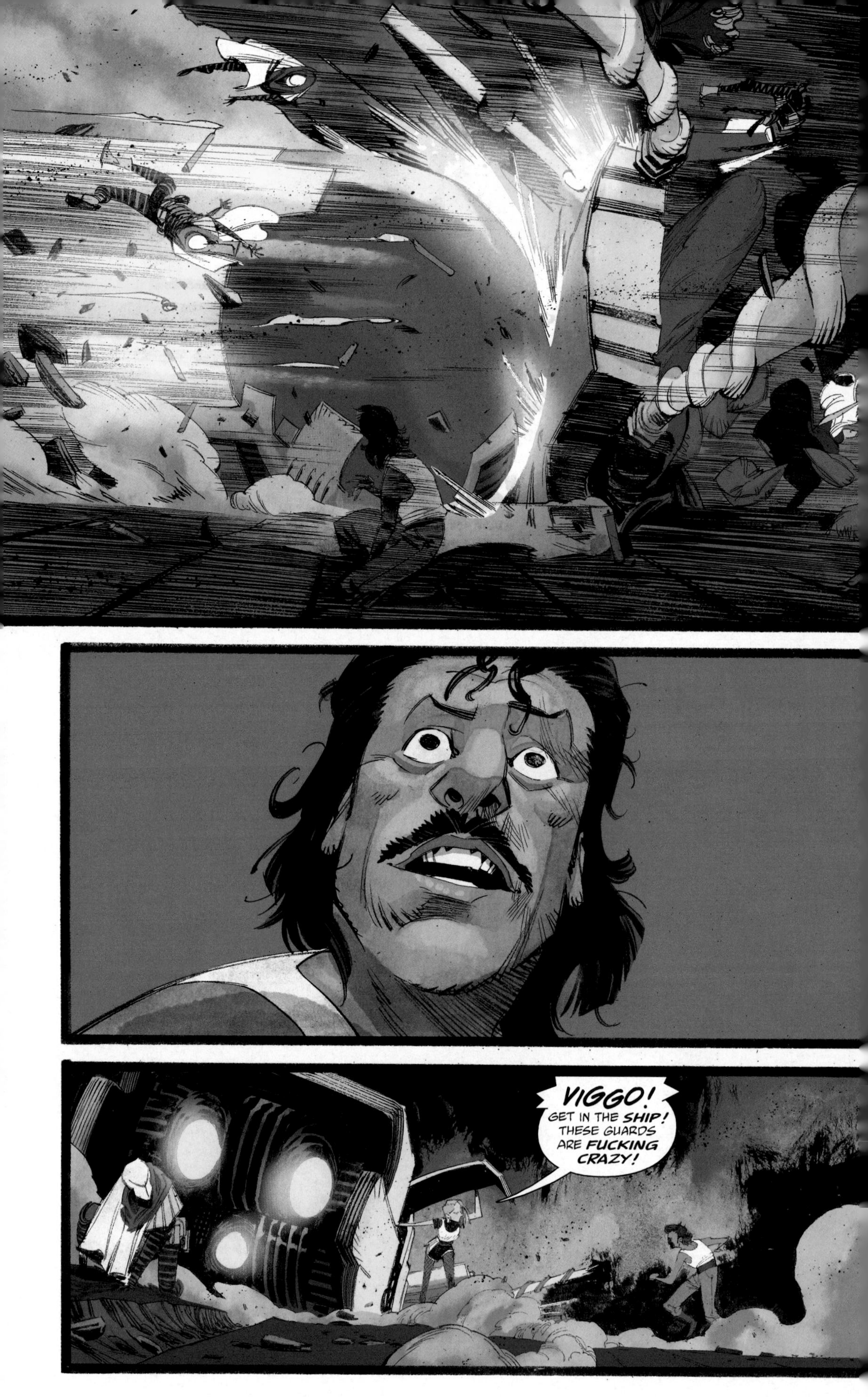
VIGGO! GET IN THE SHIP! THESE GUARDS ARE FUCKING CRAZY!

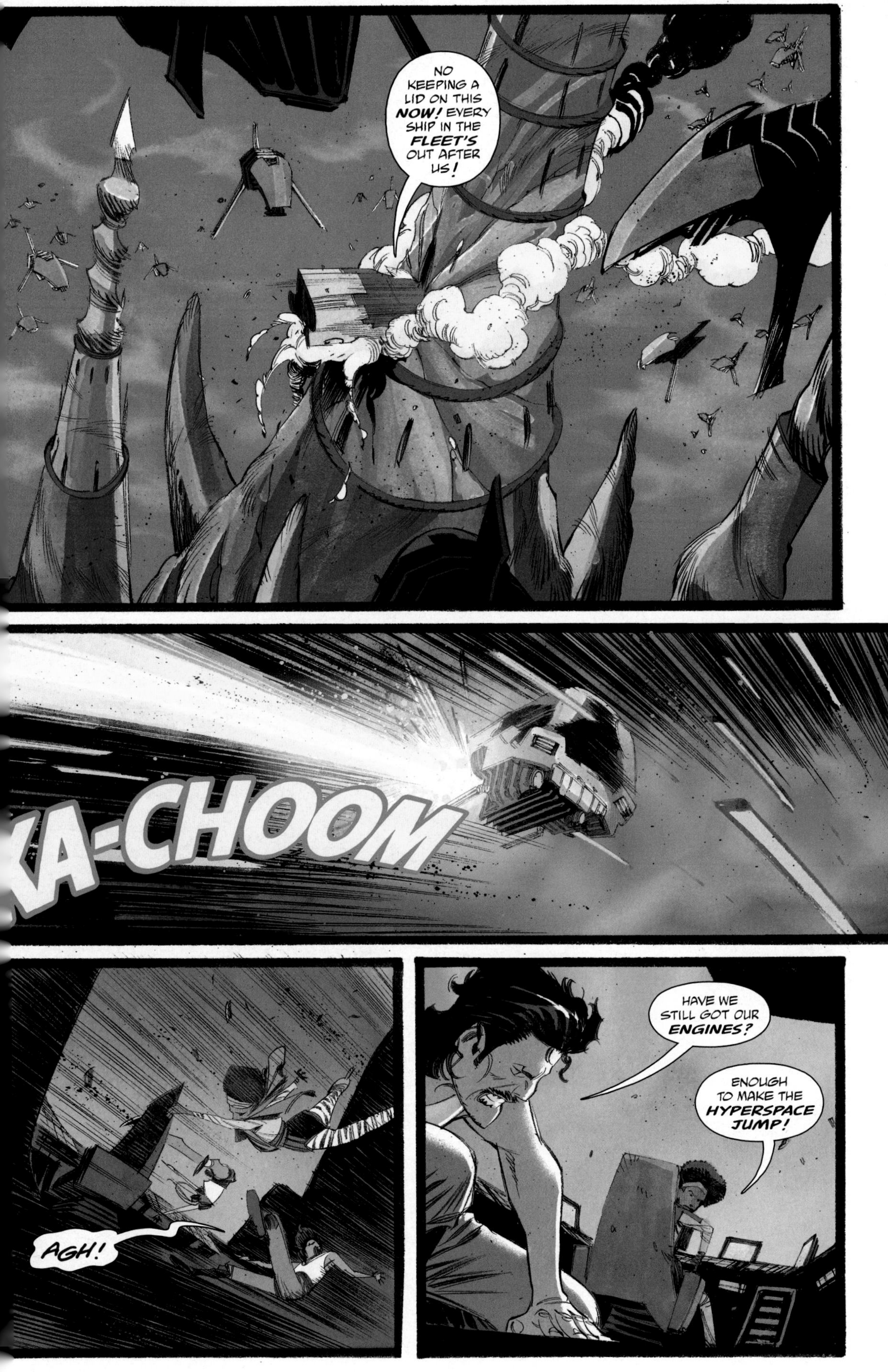
NO KEEPING A LID ON THIS NOW! EVERY SHIP IN THE FLEET'S OUT AFTER US!
KA-CHOOM
AGH!
HAVE WE STILL GOT OUR ENGINES?
ENOUGH TO MAKE THE HYPERSPACE JUMP!

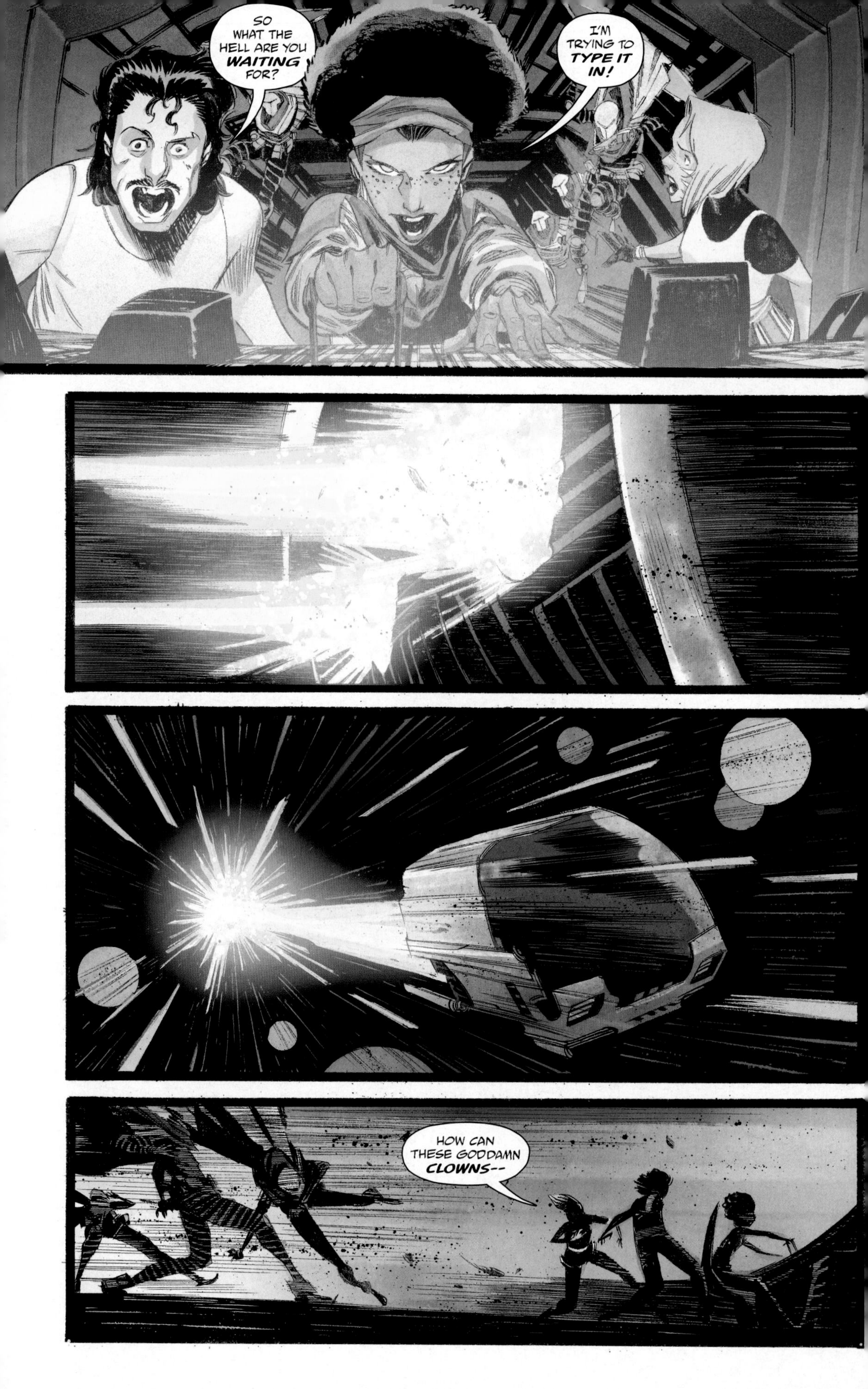
SO WHAT THE HELL ARE YOU WAITING FOR?
I'M TRYING TO TYPE IT IN!
HOW CAN THESE GODDAMN CLOWNS--

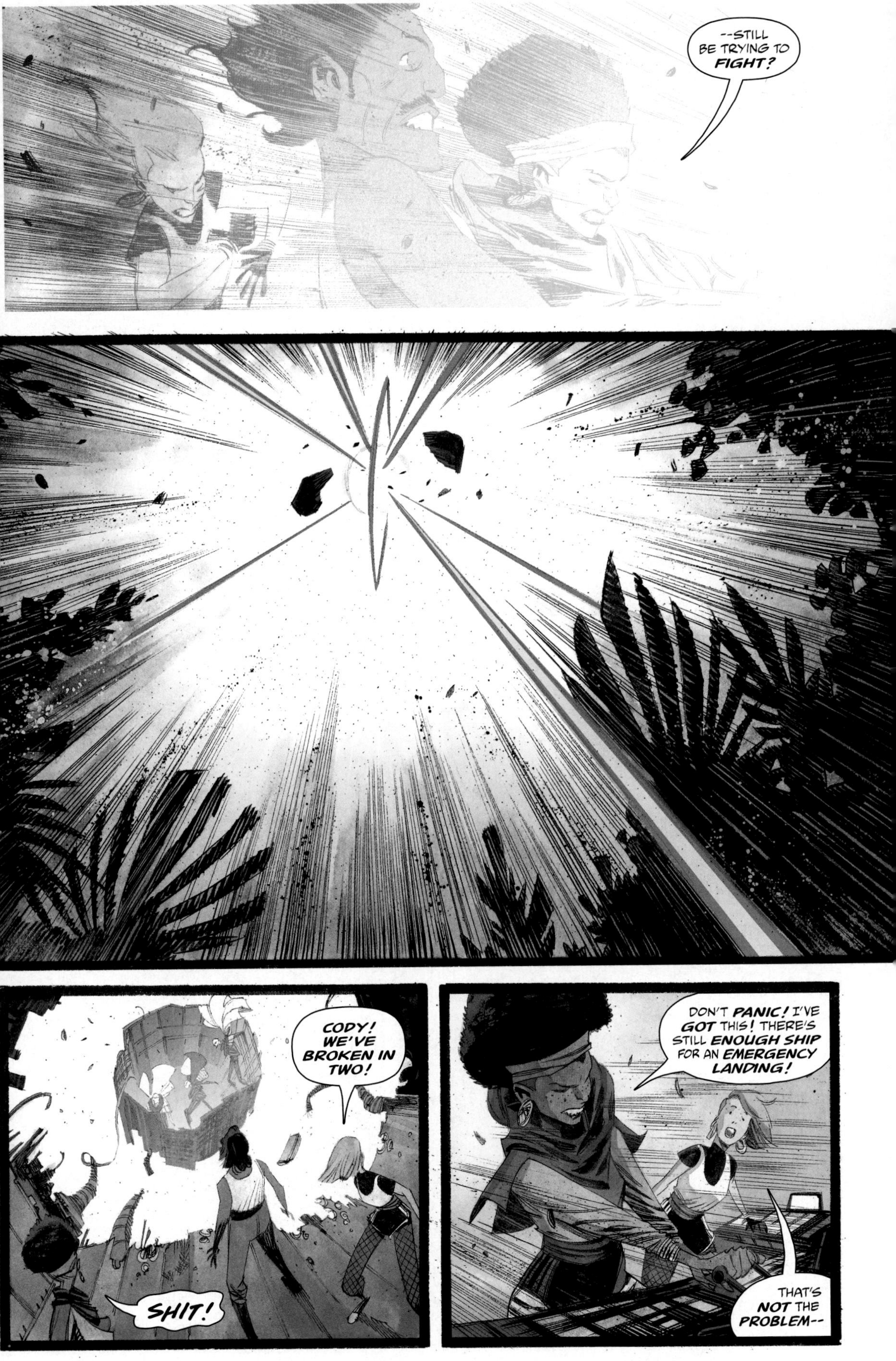
--STILL BE TRYING TO FIGHT?
CODY! WE'VE BROKEN IN TWO!
SHIT!
DON'T PANIC! I'VE GOT THIS! THERE'S STILL ENOUGH SHIP FOR AN EMERGENCY LANDING!
THAT'S NOT THE PROBLEM--

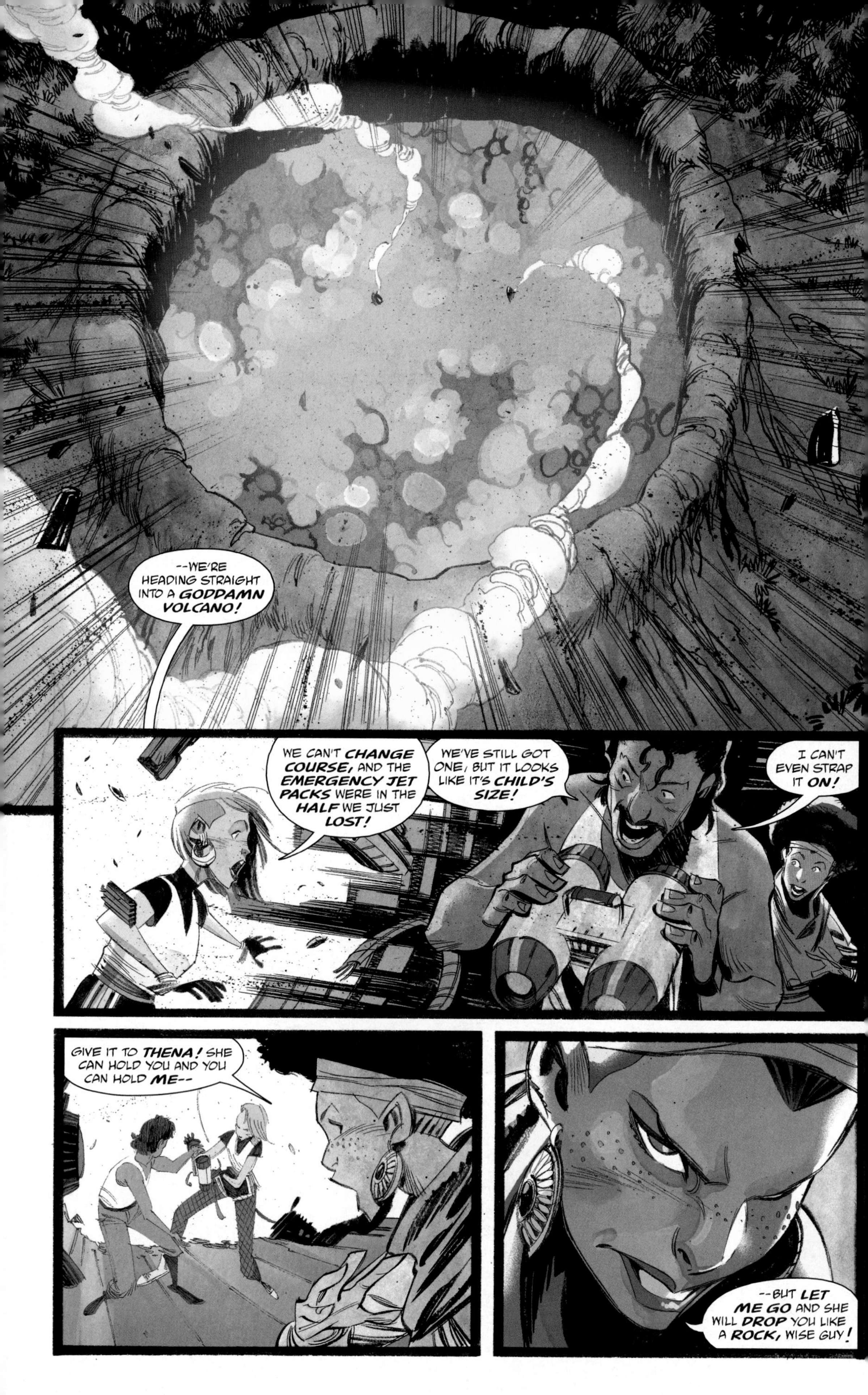
--WE'RE HEADING STRAIGHT INTO A GODDAMN VOLCANO!
WE CAN'T CHANGE COURSE, AND THE EMERGENCY JET PACKS WERE IN THE HALF WE JUST LOST!
WE'VE STILL GOT ONE, BUT IT LOOKS LIKE IT'S CHILD'S SIZE!
I CAN'T EVEN STRAP IT ON!
GIVE IT TO THENA! SHE CAN HOLD YOU AND YOU CAN HOLD ME--
--BUT LET ME GO AND SHE WILL DROP YOU LIKE A ROCK, WISE GUY!

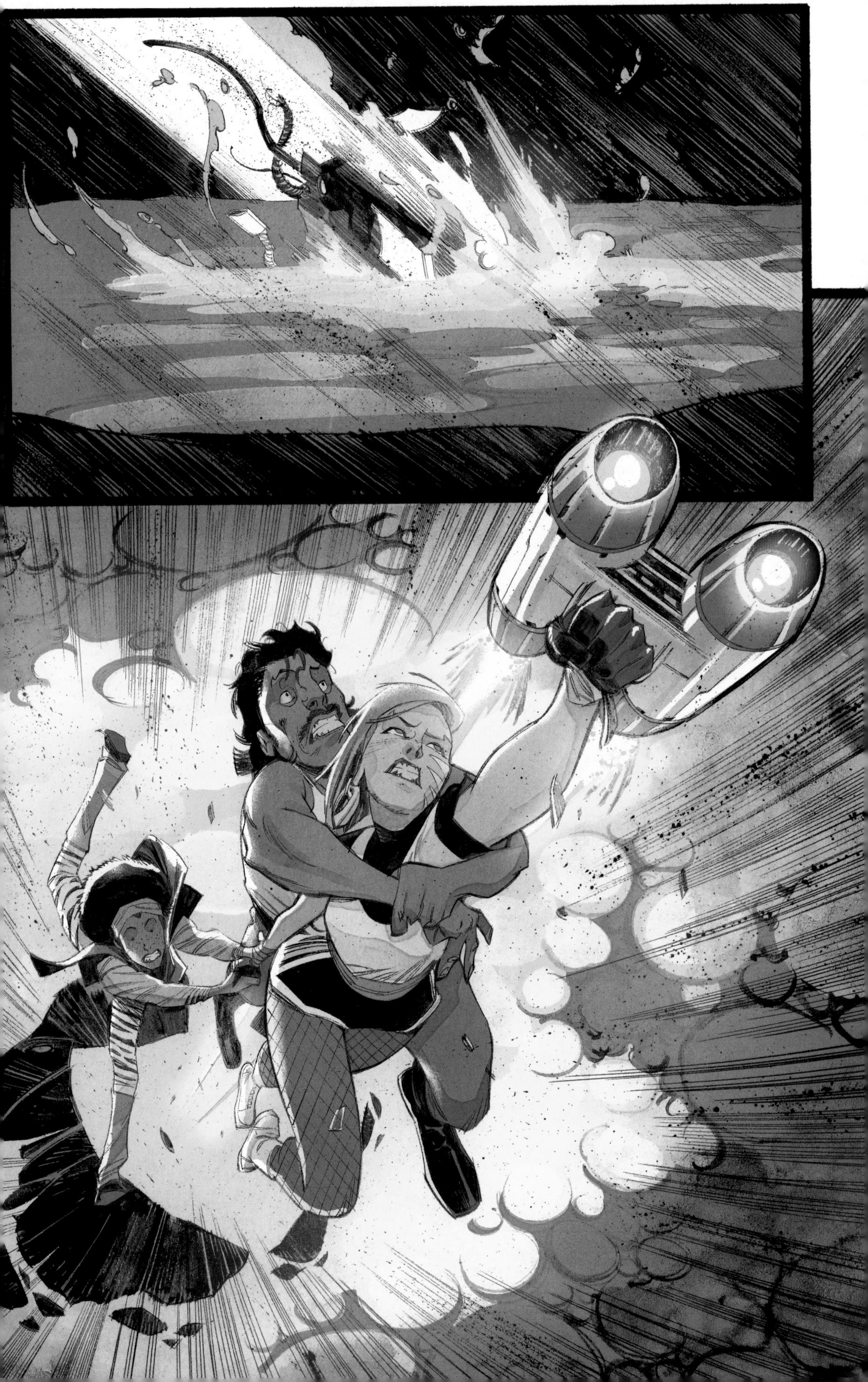

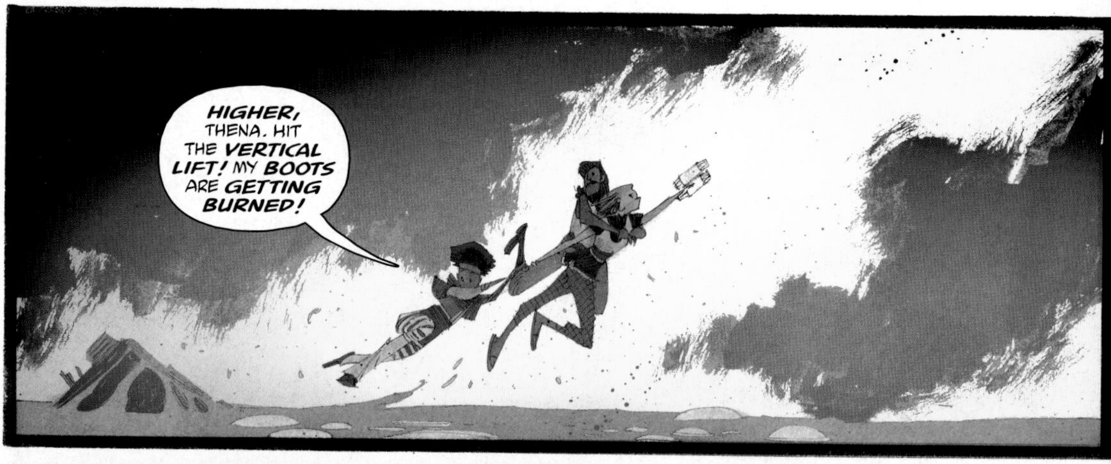
HIGHER, THENA. HIT THE VERTICAL LIFT! MY BOOTS ARE GETTING BURNED!

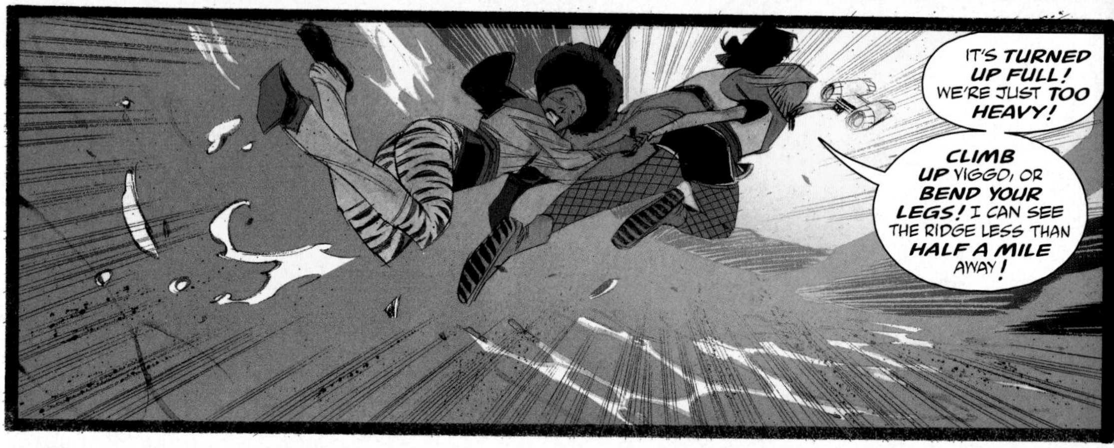
IT'S TURNED UP FULL! WE'RE JUST TOO HEAVY!
CLIMB UP VIGGO, OR BEND YOUR LEGS! I CAN SEE THE RIDGE LESS THAN HALF A MILE AWAY!

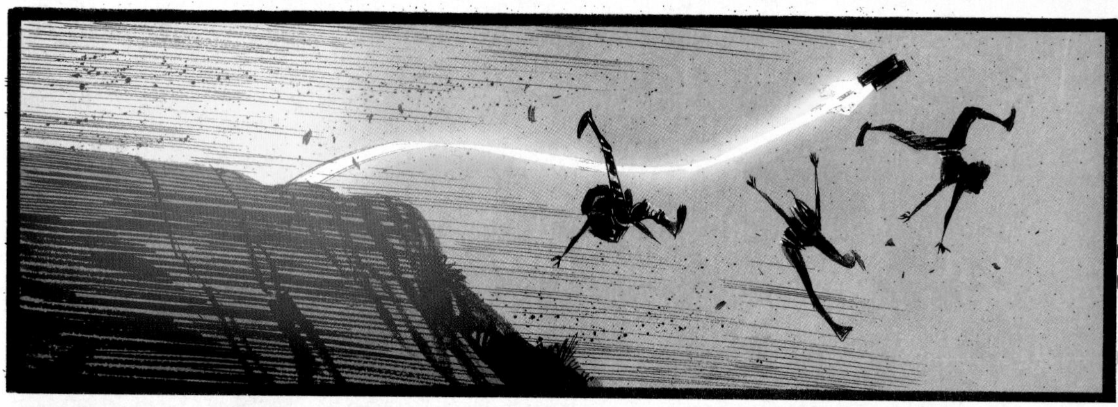

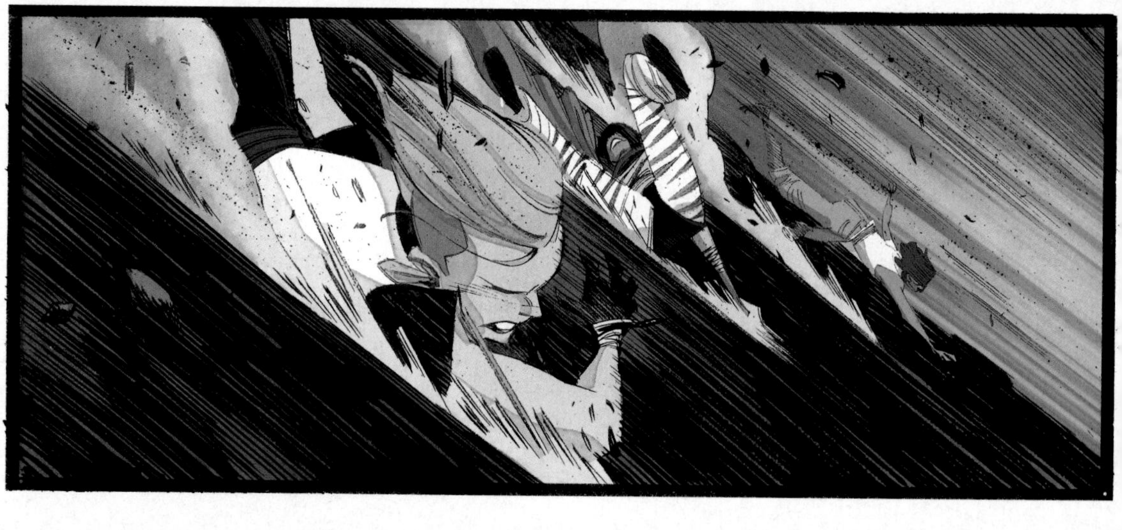

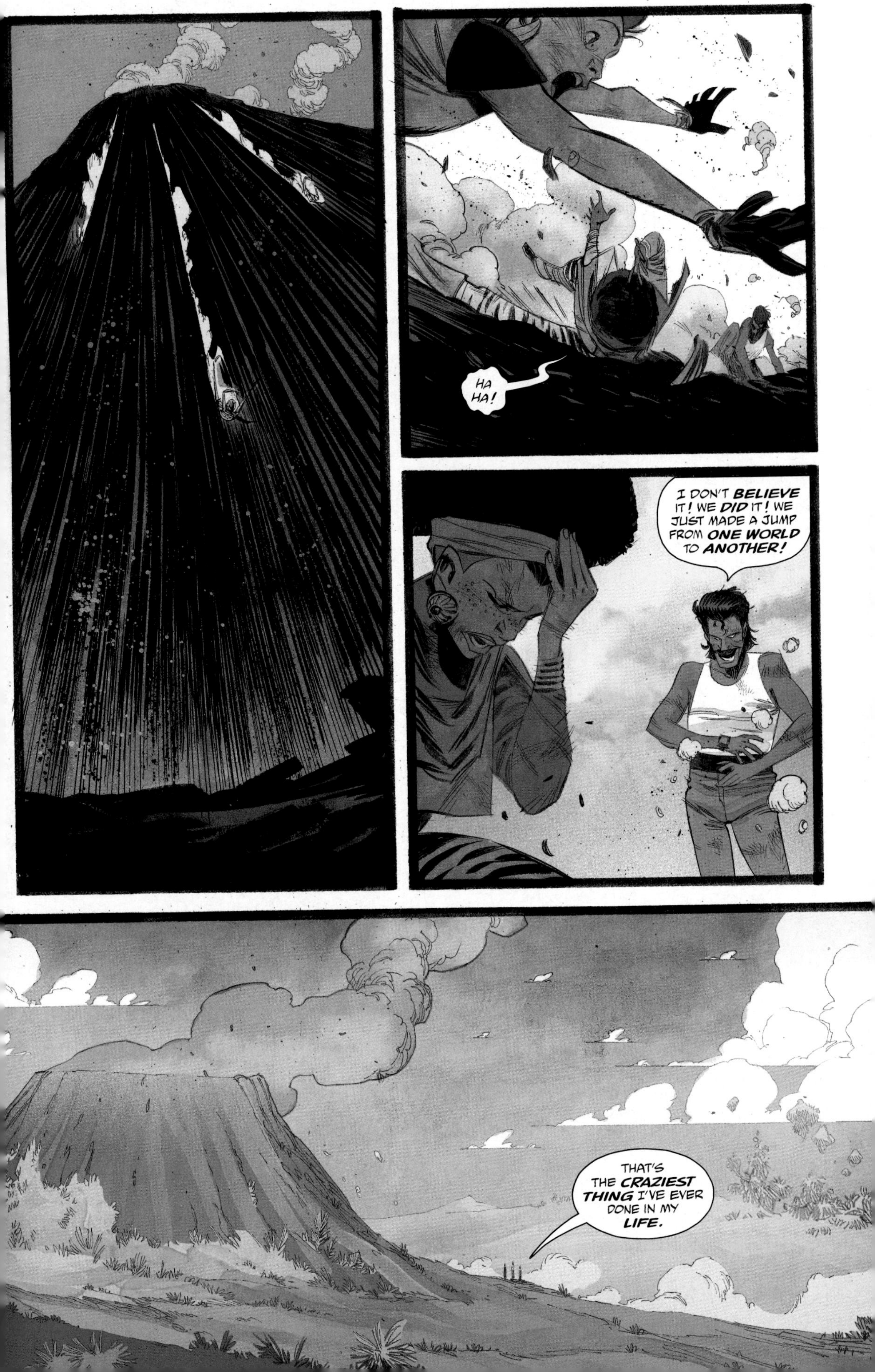
HA HA!
I DON'T BELIEVE IT! WE DID IT! WE JUST MADE A JUMP FROM ONE WORLD TO ANOTHER!
THAT'S THE CRAZIEST THING I'VE EVER DONE IN MY LIFE.

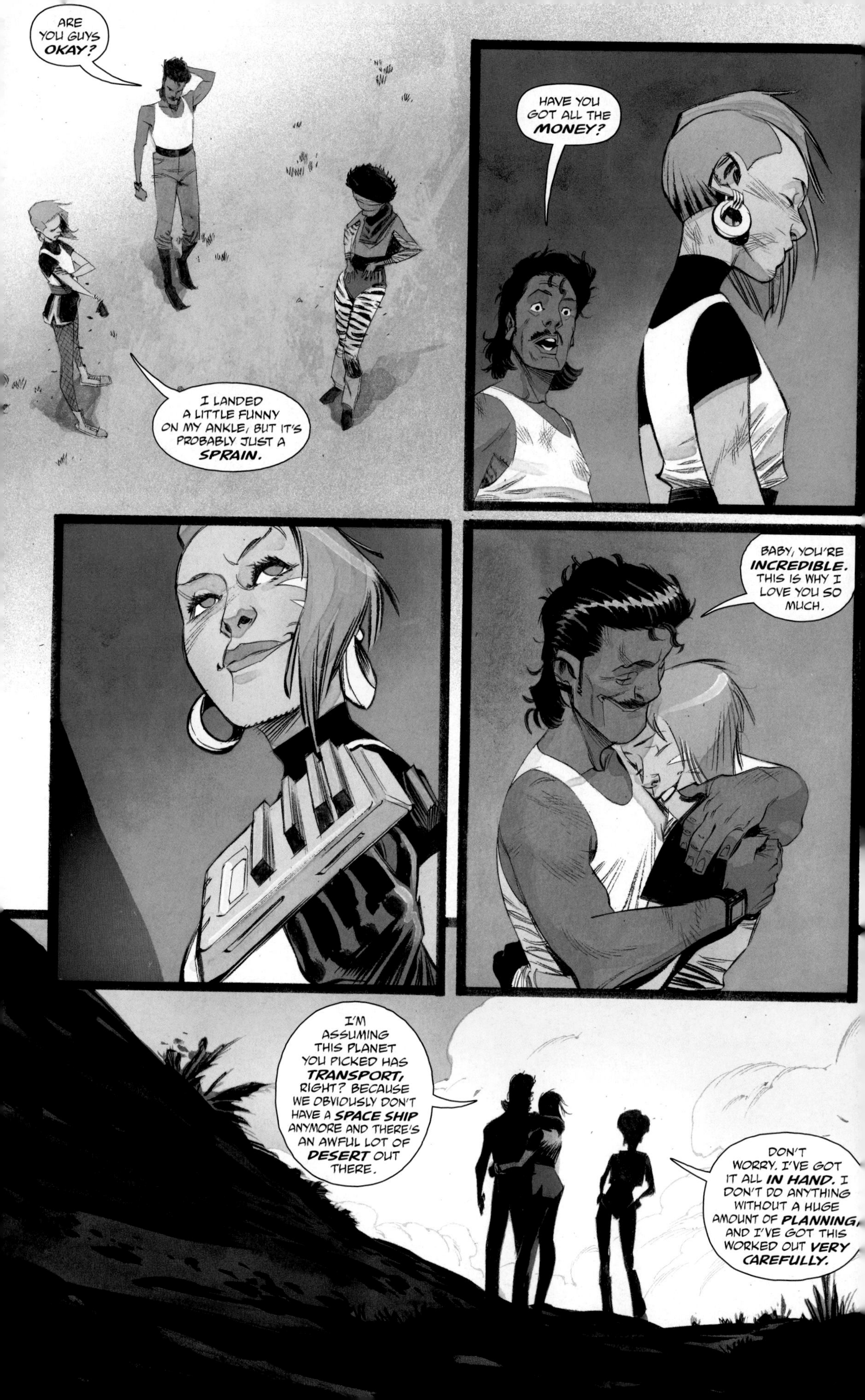
ARE YOU GUYS OKAY?
I LANDED A LITTLE FUNNY ON MY ANKLE, BUT IT'S PROBABLY JUST A SPRAIN.
HAVE YOU GOT ALL THE MONEY?
BABY, YOU'RE INCREDIBLE. THIS IS WHY I LOVE YOU SO MUCH.
I'M ASSUMING THIS PLANET YOU PICKED HAS TRANSPORT, RIGHT? BECAUSE WE OBVIOUSLY DON'T HAVE A SPACE SHIP ANYMORE AND THERE'S AN AWFUL LOT OF DESERT OUT THERE.
DON'T WORRY. I'VE GOT IT ALL IN HAND. I DON'T DO ANYTHING WITHOUT A HUGE AMOUNT OF PLANNING, AND I'VE GOT THIS WORKED OUT VERY CAREFULLY.

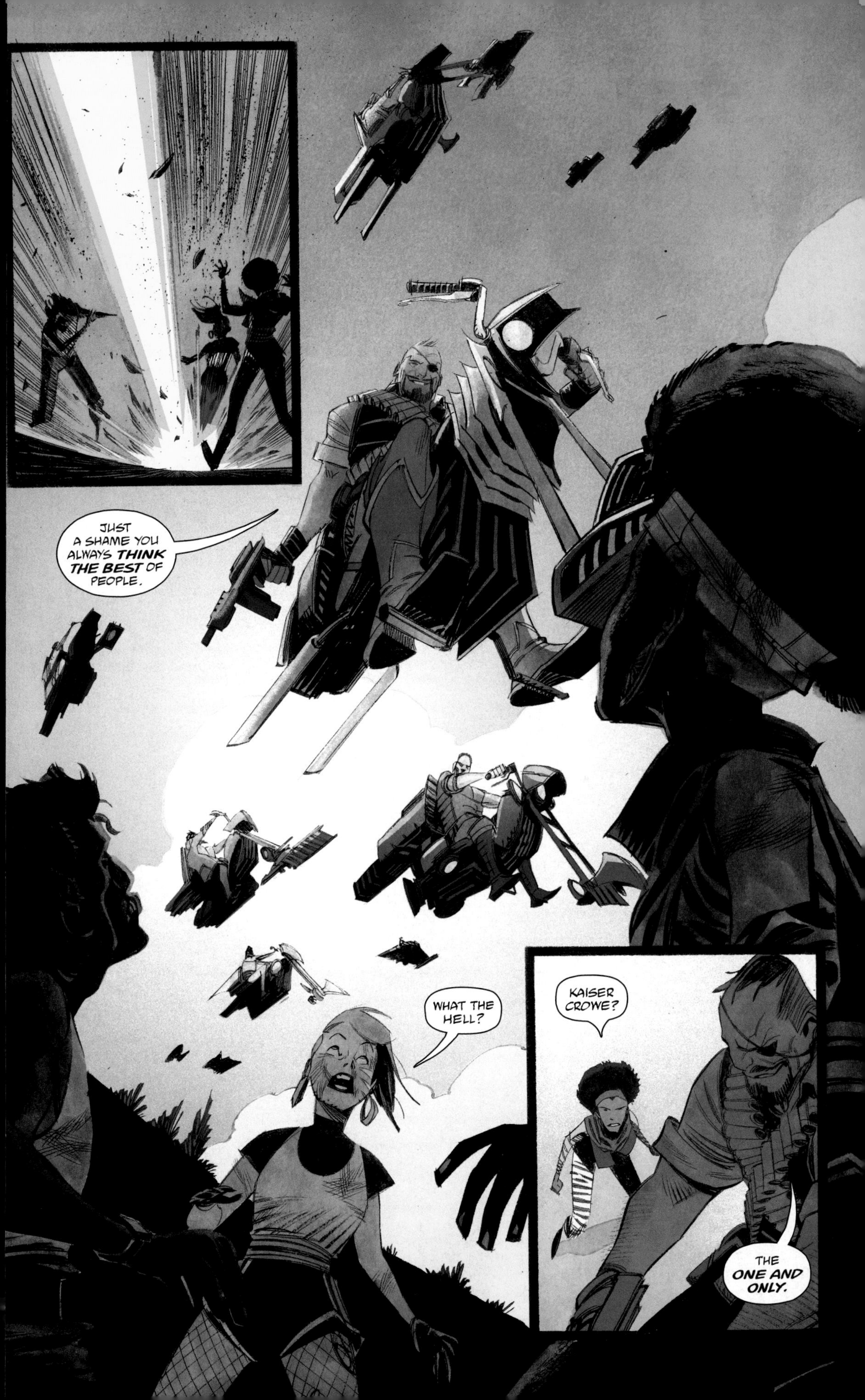
JUST A SHAME YOU ALWAYS THINK THE BEST OF PEOPLE.
WHAT THE HELL?
KAISER CROWE?
THE ONE AND ONLY.

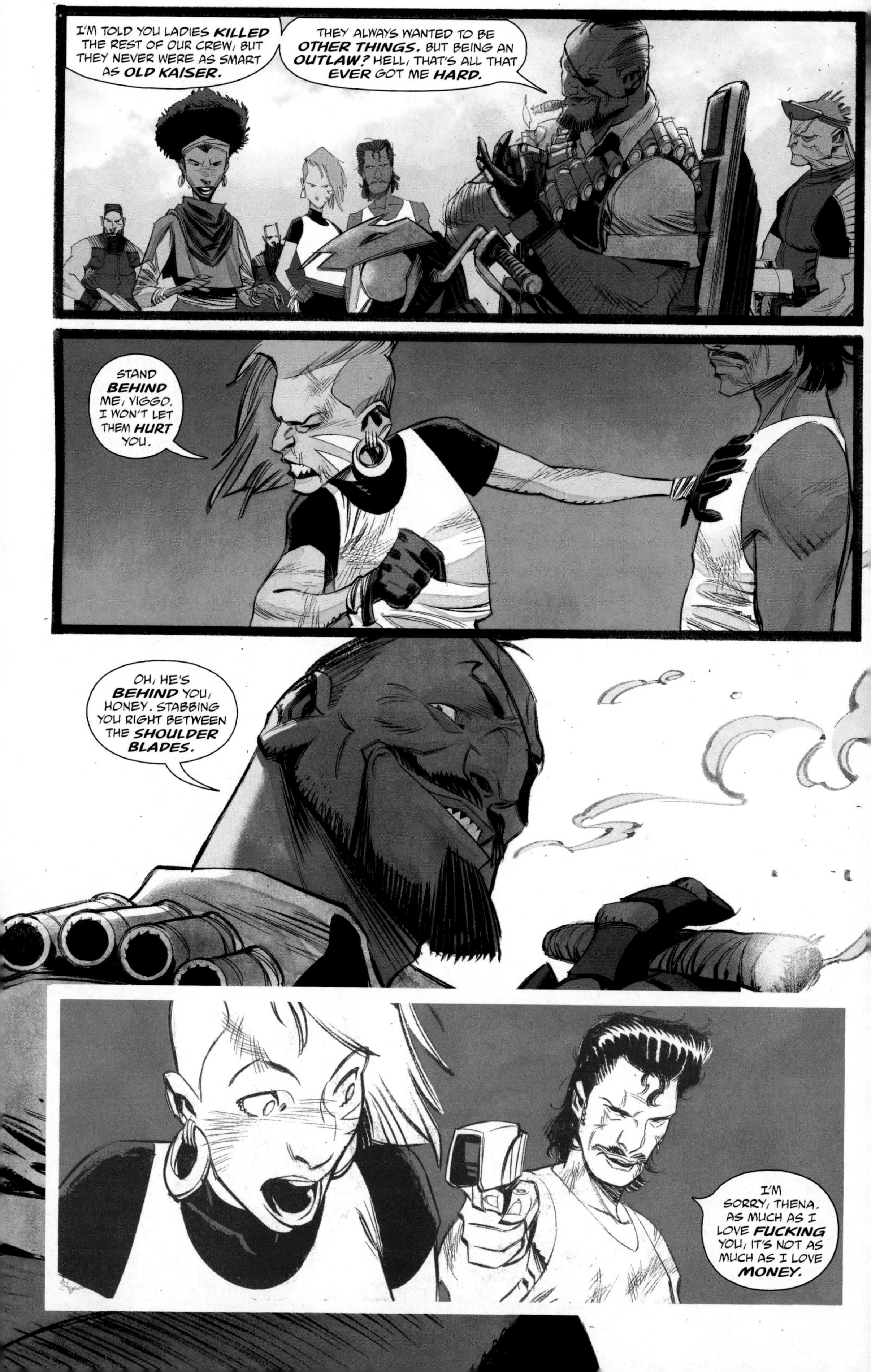
I'M TOLD YOU LADIES KILLED THE REST OF OUR CREW, BUT THEY NEVER WERE AS SMART AS OLD KAISER.
THEY ALWAYS WANTED TO BE OTHER THINGS. BUT BEING AN OUTLAW? HELL, THAT'S ALL THAT EVER GOT ME HARD.
STAND BEHIND ME, VIGGO. I WON'T LET THEM HURT YOU.
OH, HE'S BEHIND YOU, HONEY. STABBING YOU RIGHT BETWEEN THE SHOULDER BLADES.
I'M SORRY, THENA. AS MUCH AS I LOVE FUCKING YOU, IT'S NOT AS MUCH AS I LOVE MONEY.

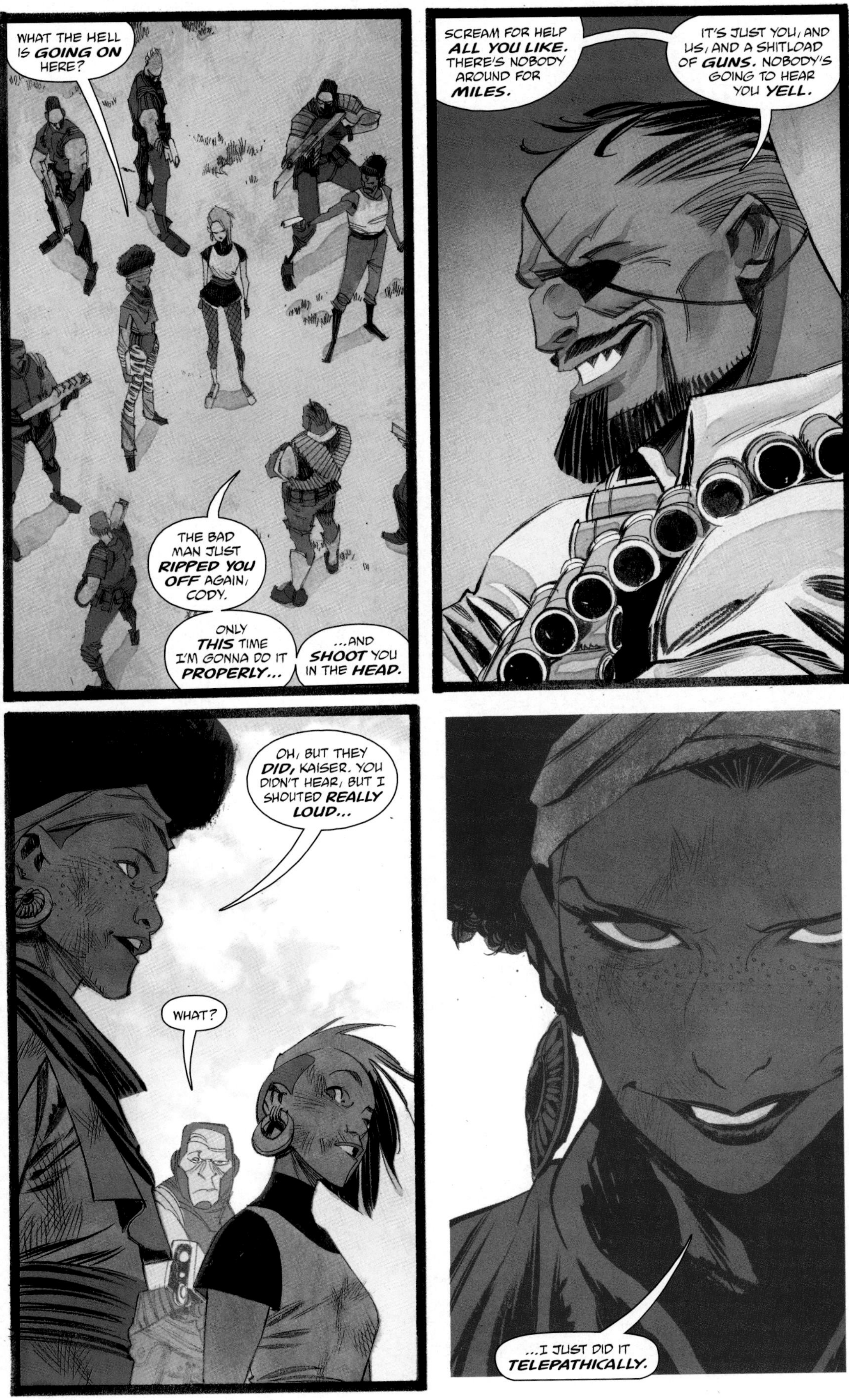
WHAT THE HELL IS GOING ON HERE?
THE BAD MAN JUST RIPPED YOU OFF AGAIN, CODY.
ONLY THIS TIME I'M GONNA DO IT PROPERLY...
...AND SHOOT YOU IN THE HEAD.
SCREAM FOR HELP ALL YOU LIKE. THERE'S NOBODY AROUND FOR MILES.
IT'S JUST YOU, AND US, AND A SHITLOAD OF GUNS. NOBODY'S GOING TO HEAR YOU YELL.
OH, BUT THEY DID, KAISER. YOU DIDN'T HEAR, BUT I SHOUTED REALLY LOUD...
WHAT?
...I JUST DID IT TELEPATHICALLY.

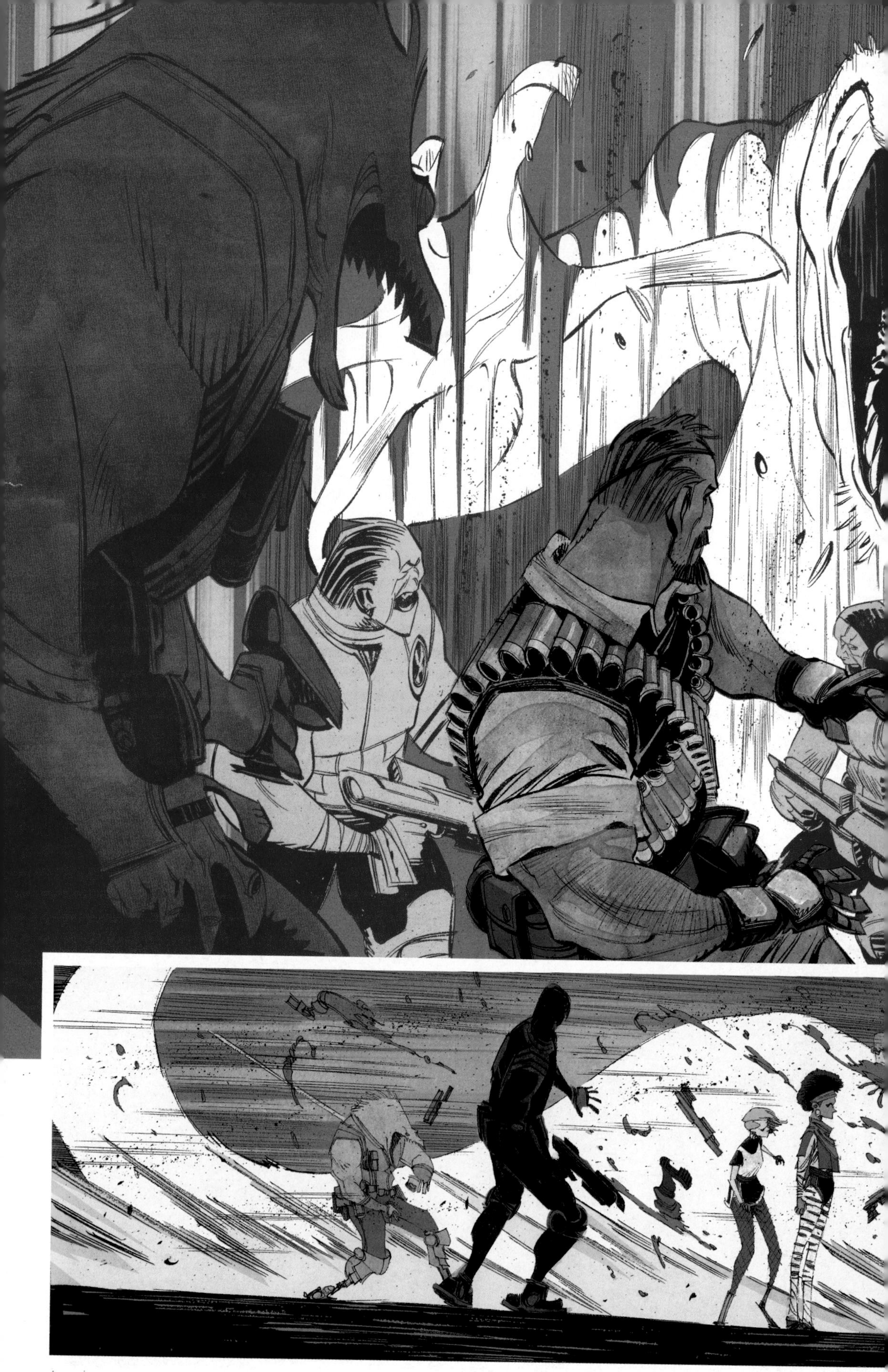

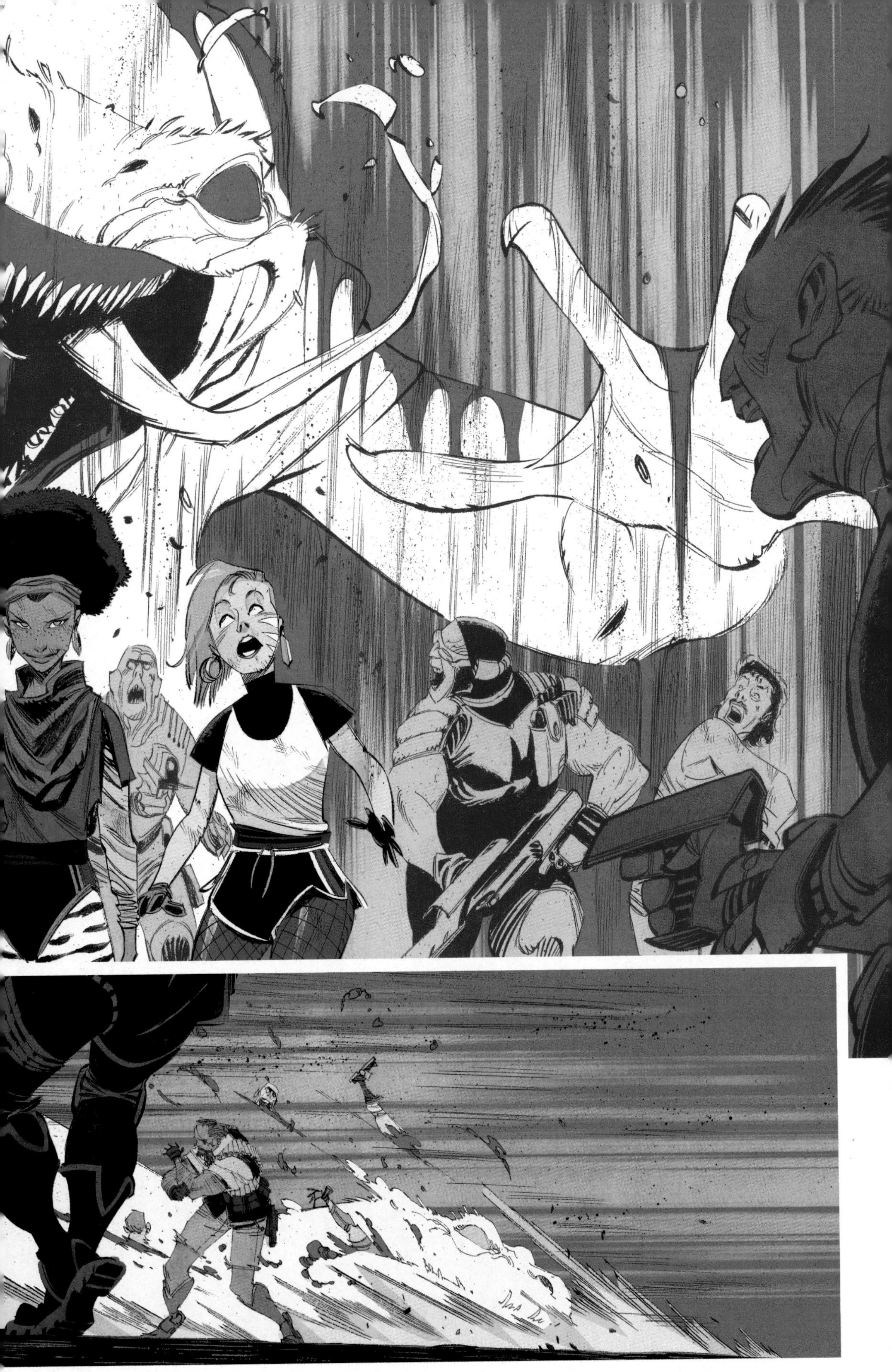

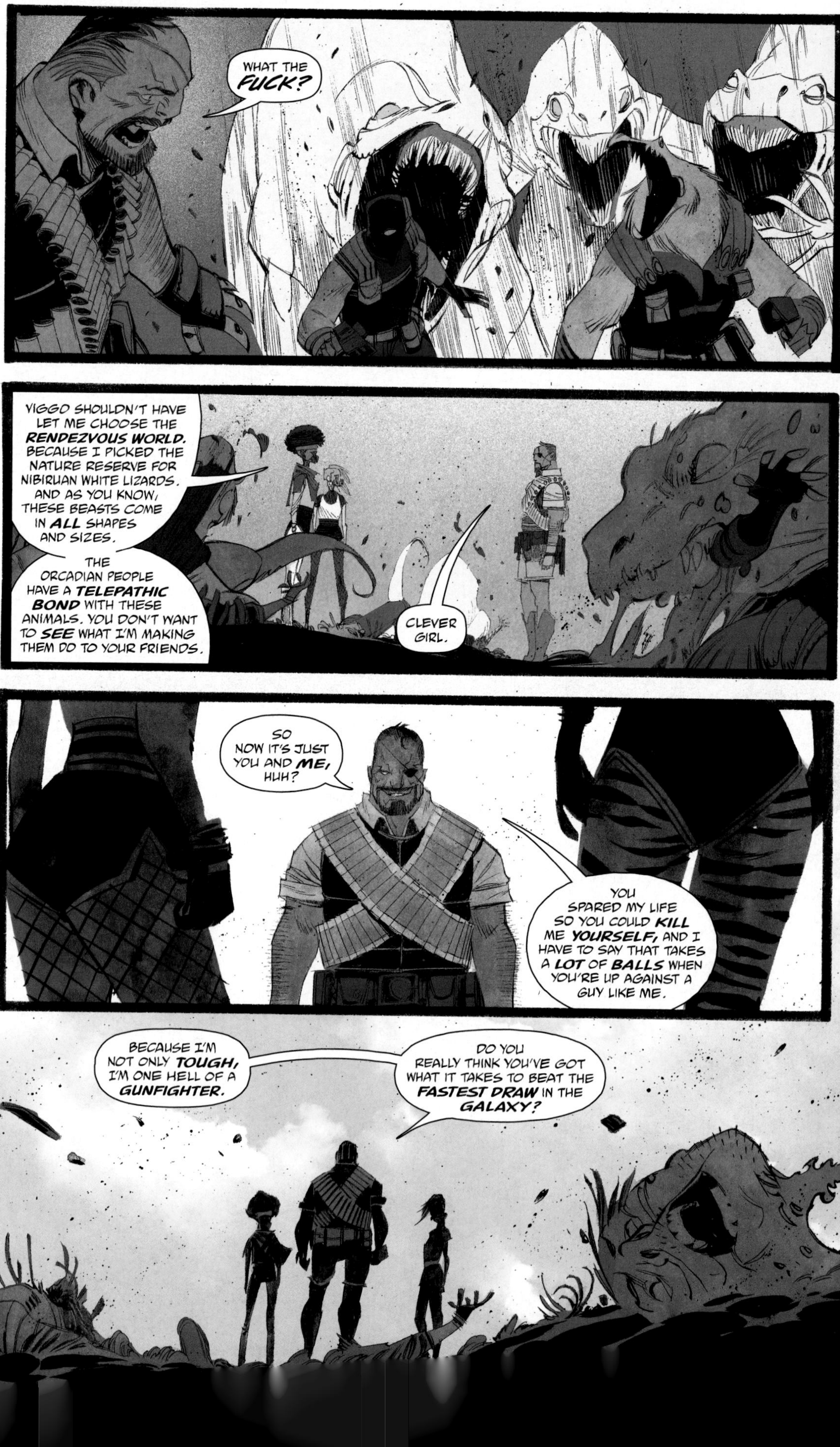
WHAT THE FUCK?
VIGGO SHOULDN'T HAVE LET ME CHOOSE THE RENDEZVOUS WORLD. BECAUSE I PICKED THE NATURE RESERVE FOR NIBIRUAN WHITE LIZARDS. AND AS YOU KNOW, THESE BEASTS COME IN ALL SHAPES AND SIZES.
THE ORCADIAN PEOPLE HAVE A TELEPATHIC BOND WITH THESE ANIMALS. YOU DON'T WANT TO SEE WHAT I'M MAKING THEM DO TO YOUR FRIENDS.
CLEVER GIRL.
SO NOW IT'S JUST YOU AND ME, HUH?
YOU SPARED MY LIFE SO YOU COULD KILL ME YOURSELF, AND I HAVE TO SAY THAT TAKES A LOT OF BALLS WHEN YOU'RE UP AGAINST A GUY LIKE ME.
BECAUSE I'M NOT ONLY TOUGH, I'M ONE HELL OF A GUNFIGHTER.
DO YOU REALLY THINK YOU'VE GOT WHAT IT TAKES TO BEAT THE FASTEST DRAW IN THE GALAXY?

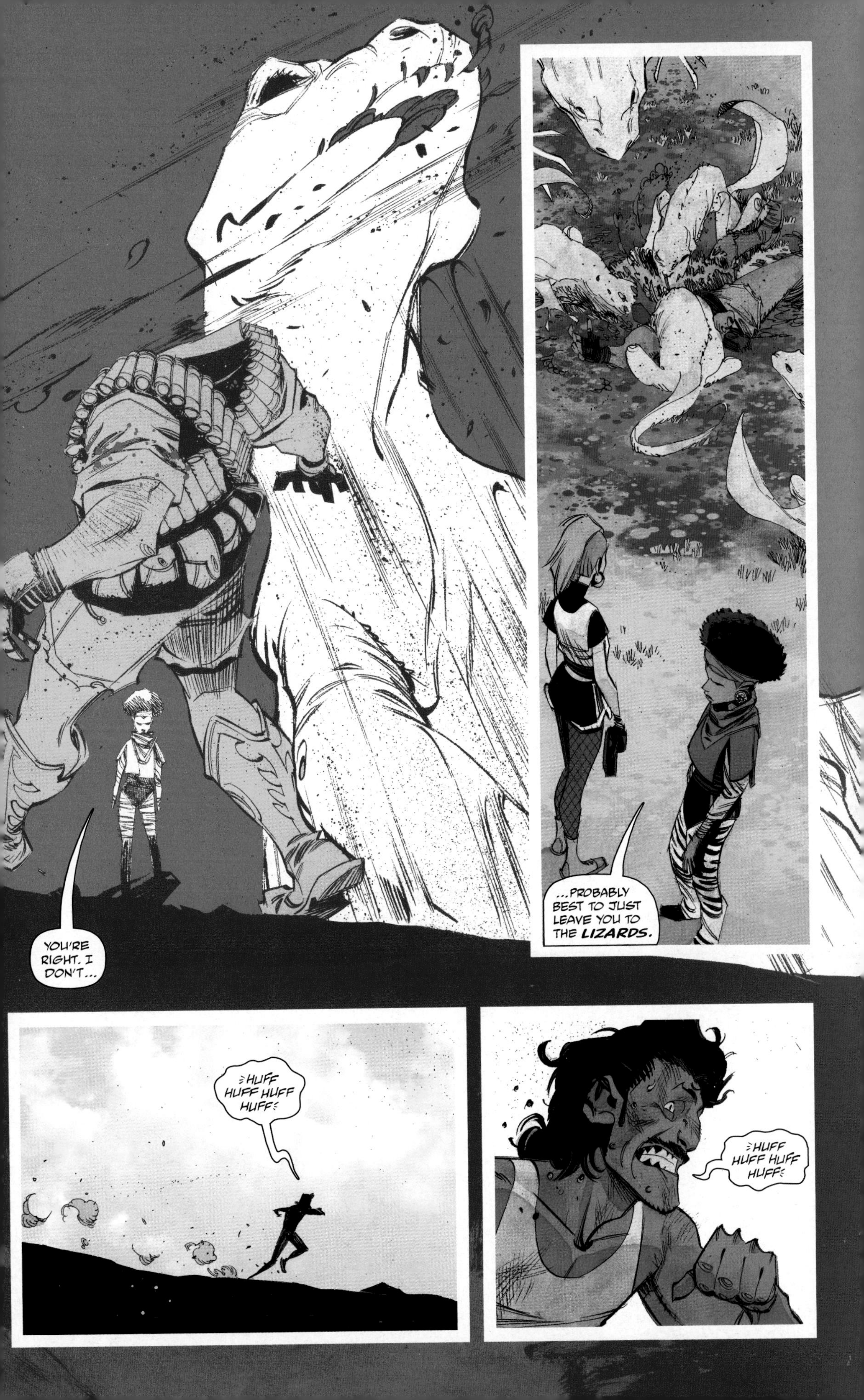
YOU'RE RIGHT. I DON'T...
...PROBABLY BEST TO JUST LEAVE YOU TO THE **LIZARDS.**
HUFF HUFF HUFF HUFF
HUFF HUFF HUFF HUFF

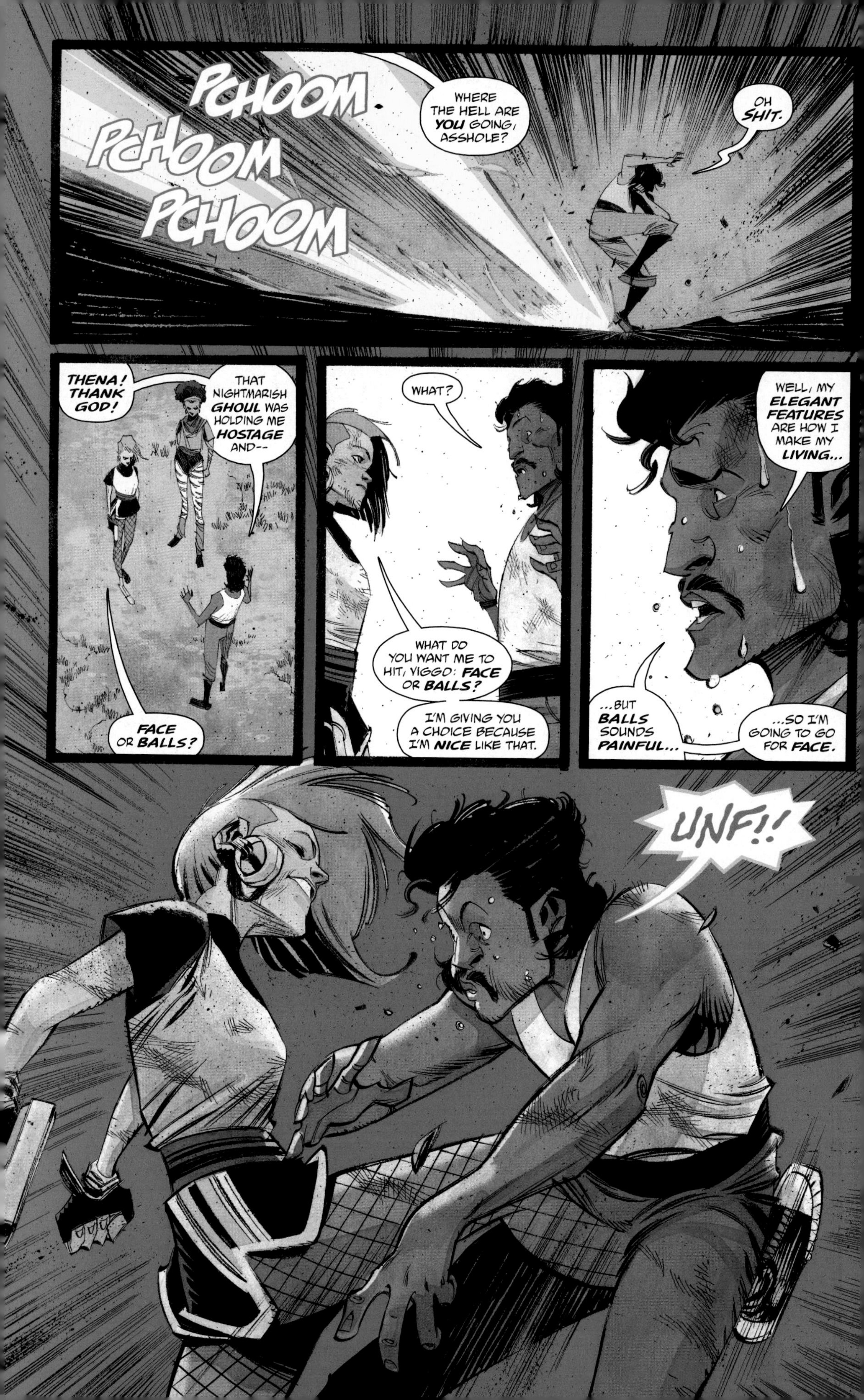
PCHOOM
PCHOOM
PCHOOM
WHERE THE HELL ARE YOU GOING, ASSHOLE?
OH SHIT.
THENA! THANK GOD!
THAT NIGHTMARISH GHOUL WAS HOLDING ME HOSTAGE AND--
FACE OR BALLS?
WHAT?
WHAT DO YOU WANT ME TO HIT, VIGGO: FACE OR BALLS?
I'M GIVING YOU A CHOICE BECAUSE I'M NICE LIKE THAT.
WELL, MY ELEGANT FEATURES ARE HOW I MAKE MY LIVING...
...BUT BALLS SOUNDS PAINFUL...
...SO I'M GOING TO GO FOR FACE.
UNF!!

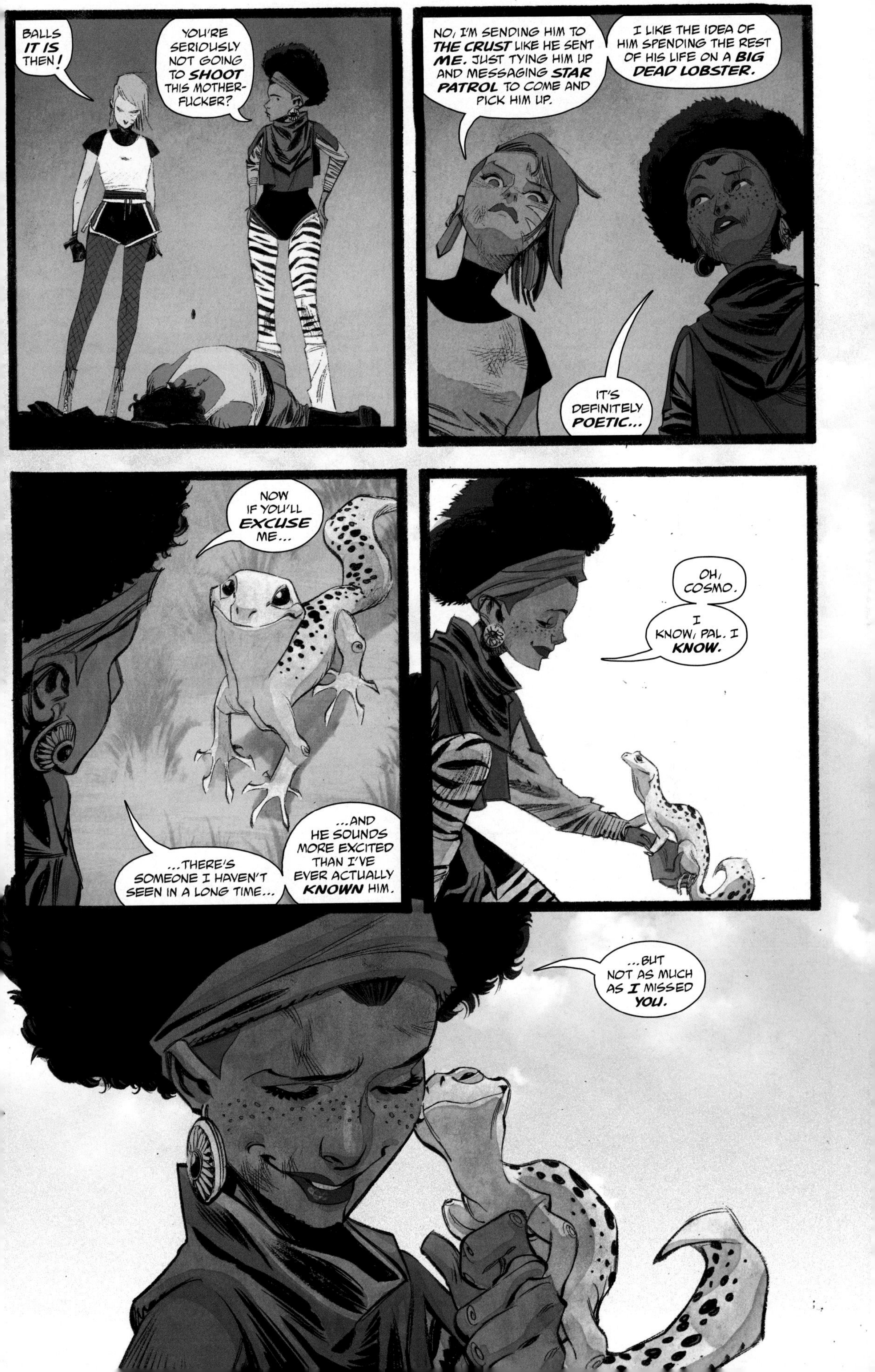
BALLS IT IS THEN!
YOU'RE SERIOUSLY NOT GOING TO SHOOT THIS MOTHER-FUCKER?
NO, I'M SENDING HIM TO THE CRUST LIKE HE SENT ME. JUST TYING HIM UP AND MESSAGING STAR PATROL TO COME AND PICK HIM UP.
I LIKE THE IDEA OF HIM SPENDING THE REST OF HIS LIFE ON A BIG DEAD LOBSTER.
IT'S DEFINITELY POETIC...
NOW IF YOU'LL EXCUSE ME...
...THERE'S SOMEONE I HAVEN'T SEEN IN A LONG TIME...
...AND HE SOUNDS MORE EXCITED THAN I'VE EVER ACTUALLY KNOWN HIM.
OH, COSMO.
I KNOW, PAL. I KNOW.
...BUT NOT AS MUCH AS I MISSED YOU.

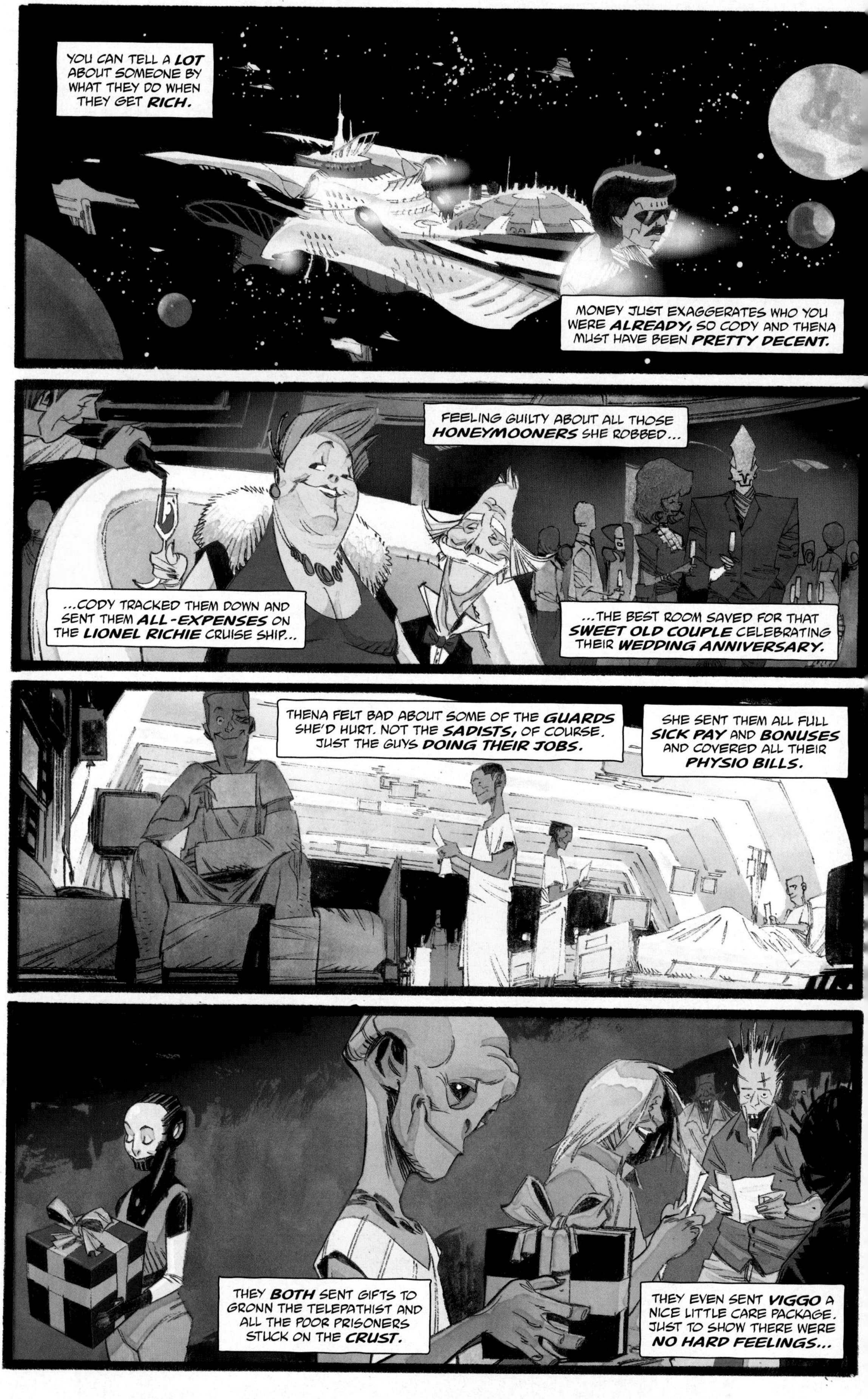
YOU CAN TELL A LOT ABOUT SOMEONE BY WHAT THEY DO WHEN THEY GET RICH.
MONEY JUST EXAGGERATES WHO YOU WERE ALREADY, SO CODY AND THENA MUST HAVE BEEN PRETTY DECENT.
FEELING GUILTY ABOUT ALL THOSE HONEYMOONERS SHE ROBBED...
...CODY TRACKED THEM DOWN AND SENT THEM ALL-EXPENSES ON THE LIONEL RICHIE CRUISE SHIP...
...THE BEST ROOM SAVED FOR THAT SWEET OLD COUPLE CELEBRATING THEIR WEDDING ANNIVERSARY.
THENA FELT BAD ABOUT SOME OF THE GUARDS SHE'D HURT. NOT THE SADISTS, OF COURSE. JUST THE GUYS DOING THEIR JOBS.
SHE SENT THEM ALL FULL SICK PAY AND BONUSES AND COVERED ALL THEIR PHYSIO BILLS.
THEY BOTH SENT GIFTS TO GRONN THE TELEPATHIST AND ALL THE POOR PRISONERS STUCK ON THE CRUST.
THEY EVEN SENT VIGGO A NICE LITTLE CARE PACKAGE. JUST TO SHOW THERE WERE NO HARD FEELINGS...

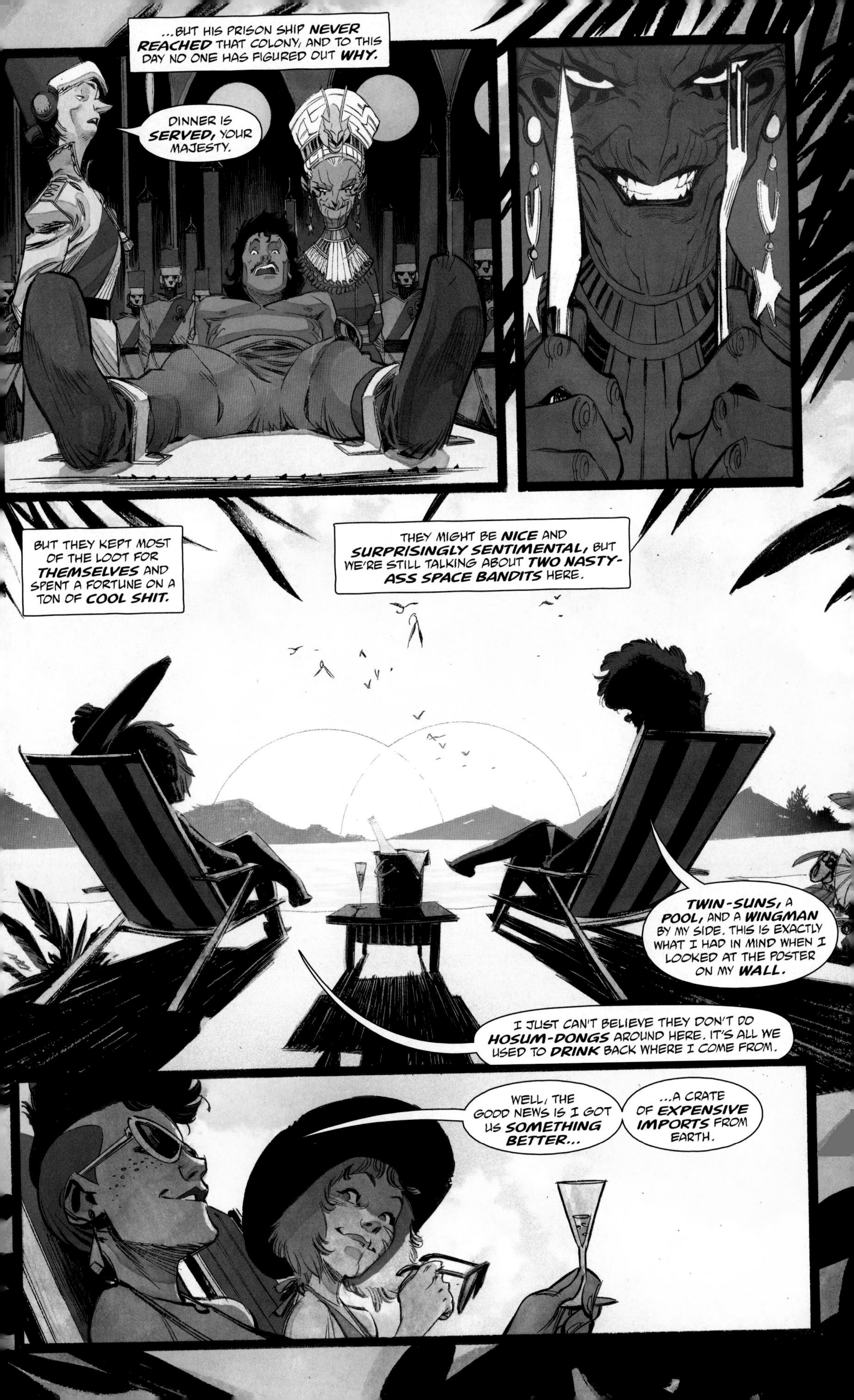
...BUT HIS PRISON SHIP NEVER REACHED THAT COLONY, AND TO THIS DAY NO ONE HAS FIGURED OUT WHY.
DINNER IS SERVED, YOUR MAJESTY.
BUT THEY KEPT MOST OF THE LOOT FOR THEMSELVES AND SPENT A FORTUNE ON A TON OF COOL SHIT.
THEY MIGHT BE NICE AND SURPRISINGLY SENTIMENTAL, BUT WE'RE STILL TALKING ABOUT TWO NASTY-ASS SPACE BANDITS HERE.
TWIN-SUNS, A POOL, AND A WINGMAN BY MY SIDE. THIS IS EXACTLY WHAT I HAD IN MIND WHEN I LOOKED AT THE POSTER ON MY WALL.
I JUST CAN'T BELIEVE THEY DON'T DO HOSUM-DONGS AROUND HERE. IT'S ALL WE USED TO DRINK BACK WHERE I COME FROM.
WELL, THE GOOD NEWS IS I GOT US SOMETHING BETTER...
...A CRATE OF EXPENSIVE IMPORTS FROM EARTH.

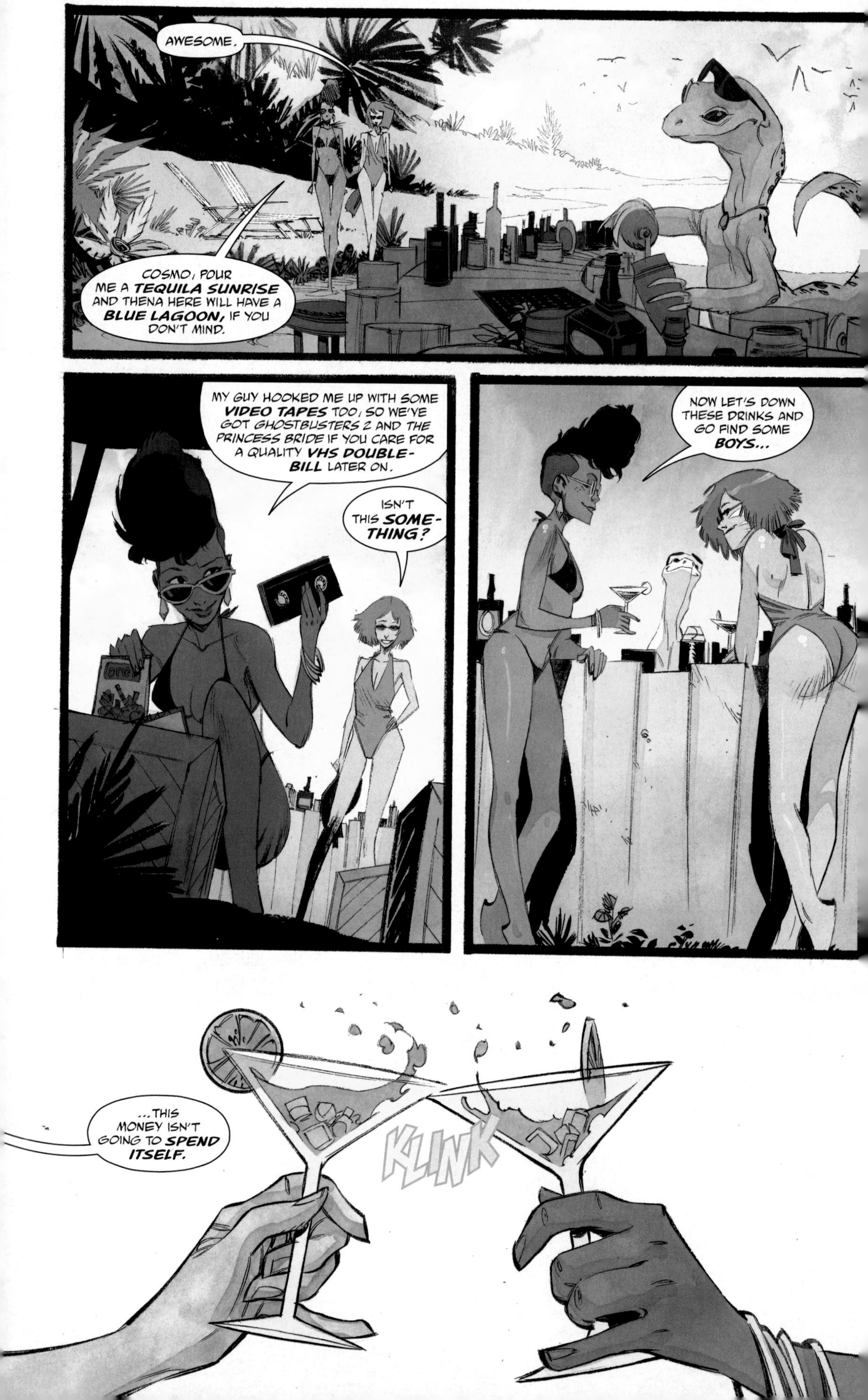
AWESOME.
COSMO, POUR ME A TEQUILA SUNRISE AND THENA HERE WILL HAVE A BLUE LAGOON, IF YOU DON'T MIND.
MY GUY HOOKED ME UP WITH SOME VIDEO TAPES TOO, SO WE'VE GOT GHOSTBUSTERS 2 AND THE PRINCESS BRIDE IF YOU CARE FOR A QUALITY VHS DOUBLE-BILL LATER ON.
ISN'T THIS SOME-THING?
NOW LET'S DOWN THESE DRINKS AND GO FIND SOME BOYS...
...THIS MONEY ISN'T GOING TO SPEND ITSELF.
KLINK

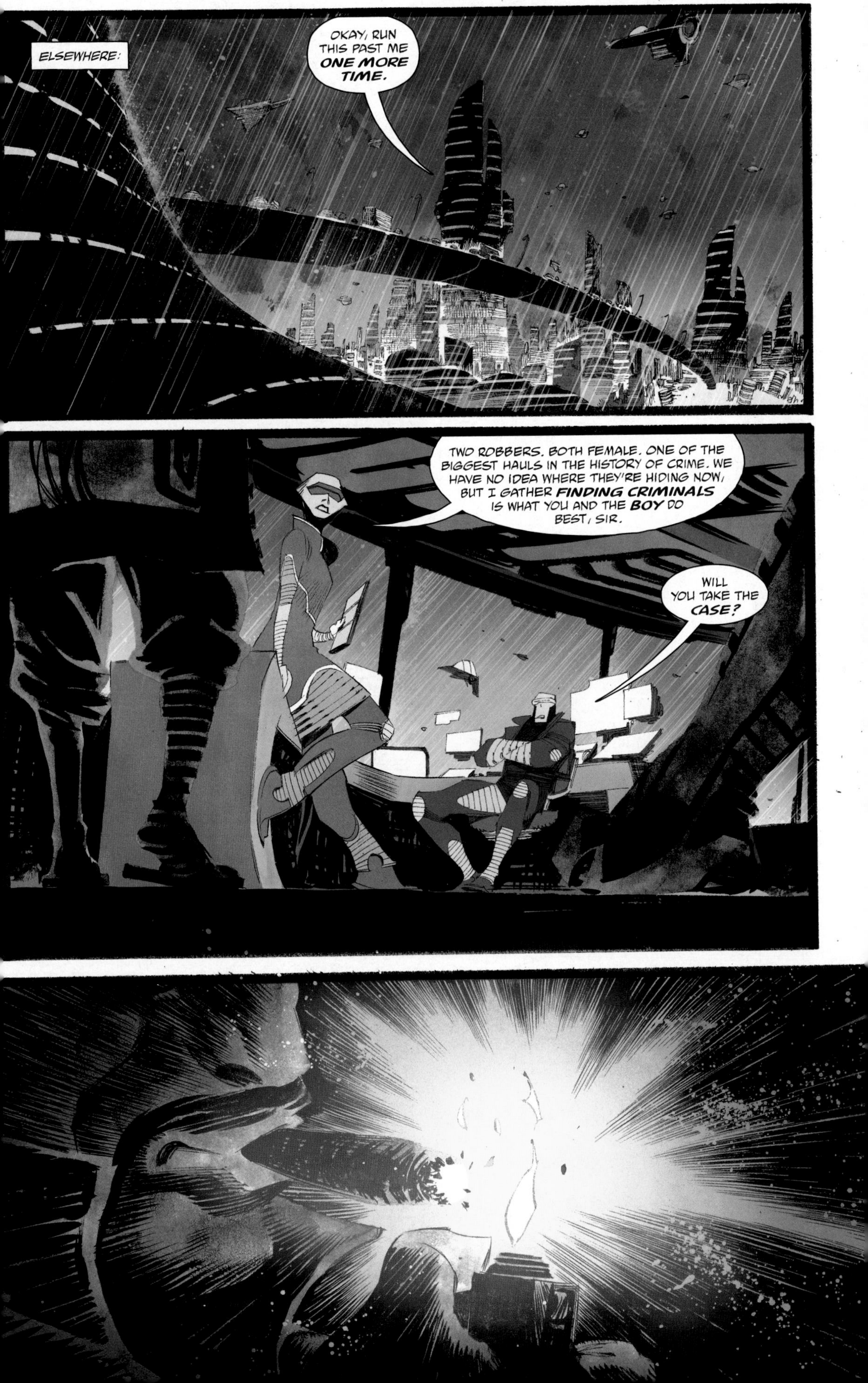
ELSEWHERE:
OKAY, RUN THIS PAST ME ONE MORE TIME.
TWO ROBBERS. BOTH FEMALE. ONE OF THE BIGGEST HAULS IN THE HISTORY OF CRIME. WE HAVE NO IDEA WHERE THEY'RE HIDING NOW, BUT I GATHER FINDING CRIMINALS IS WHAT YOU AND THE BOY DO BEST, SIR.
WILL YOU TAKE THE CASE?

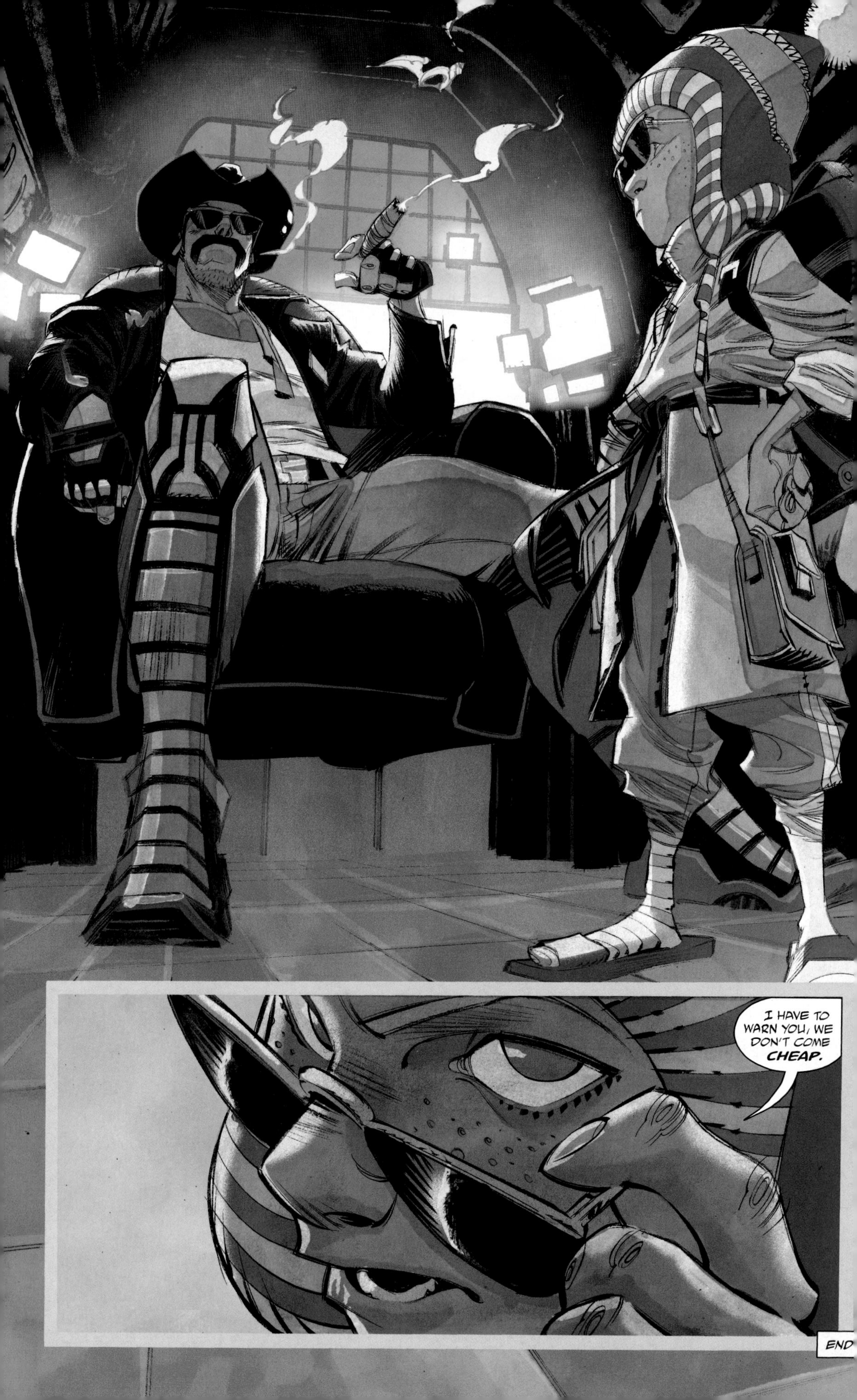
I HAVE TO WARN YOU, WE DON'T COME CHEAP.
END

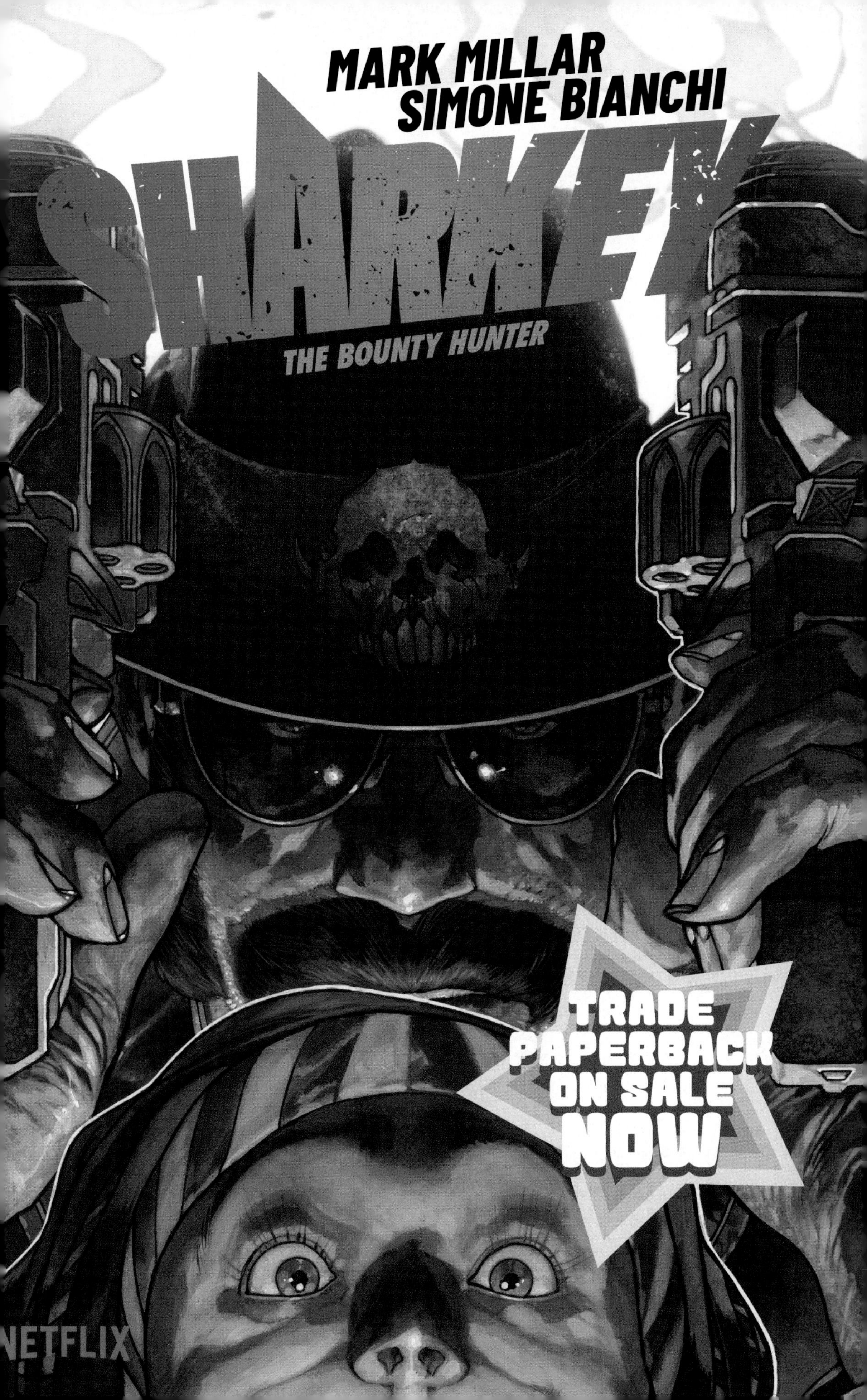

MARK MILLAR
SIMONE BIANCHI
SHARKEY
THE BOUNTY HUNTER
TRADE
PAPERBACK
ON SALE
NOW
NETFLIX

Mark Millar

is the New York Times bestselling author of KICK-ASS, WANTED, and KINGSMAN: THE SECRET SERVICE, all of which have been adapted into Hollywood franchises.

His DC Comics work includes the seminal SUPERMAN: RED SON. At Marvel Comics he created THE ULTIMATES, which was selected by Time magazine as the comic book of the decade, and was described by screenwriter Zak Penn as his major inspiration for THE AVENGERS movie. Millar also created WOLVERINE: OLD MAN LOGAN and CIVIL WAR, Marvel's two biggest-selling graphic novels ever. CIVIL WAR was the basis of the CAPTAIN AMERICA: CIVIL WAR movie, and OLD MAN LOGAN was the inspiration for Fox's LOGAN movie in 2017.

Mark has been an executive producer on all his movies, and for four years worked as a creative consultant to Fox Studios on their Marvel slate of movies. In 2017, Netflix bought Millarworld in the company's first ever acquisition, and employed Mark as President of a new division to create comics, TV shows, and movies. His much-anticipated autobiography, DON'T SASS ME, BATMAN, will be published next year.

Matteo Scalera

was born in Parma, Italy, in October 1982. His professional career started in 2008, with the publication of HYPERKINETIC, a four-issue series by Image Comics. Since then, he's worked on INCORRUPTIBLE, IRREDEEMABLE, VALEN THE OUTCAST (Boom! Studios), DEADPOOL, SECRET AVENGERS, INDESTRUCTIBLE HULK (Marvel), BATMAN, RED HOOD AND THE OUTLAWS (DC Comics), DEAD BODY ROAD, and BLACK SCIENCE (Image Comics).

Marcelo Maiolo

is best known for his work at DC Comics on titles such as I, VAMPIRE, GREEN ARROW, TEEN TITANS, and, most recently, JUSTICE LEAGUE OF AMERICA.

His work for other publishers includes TRUE BLOOD (IDW), KING (Jet City Comics), PACIFIC RIM (Legendary), ALL-NEW X-MEN and OLD MAN LOGAN (Marvel), LIBERTALIA (Glénat), and SPIDER (Delcourt/Soleil). He lives and works in Brazil.

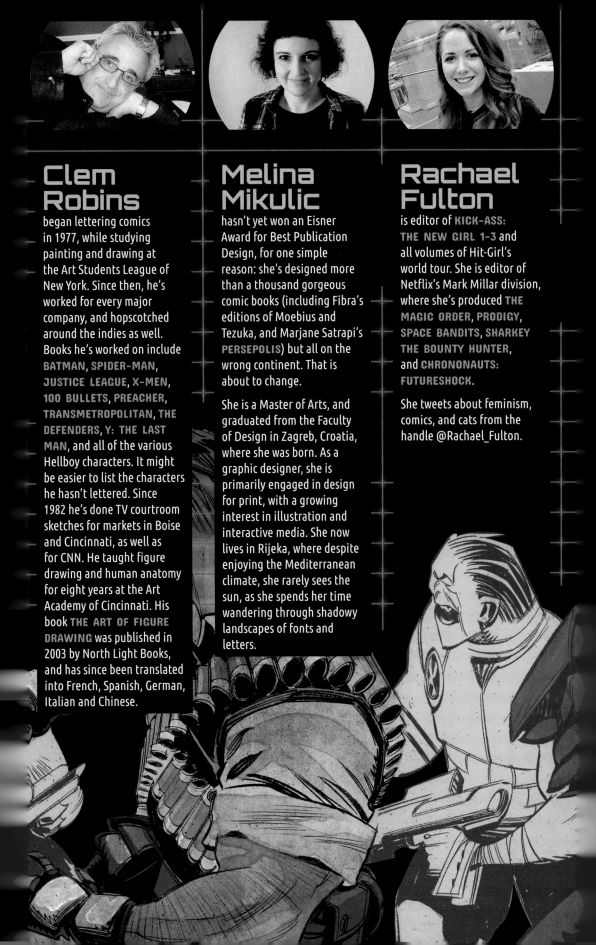

Clem Robins

began lettering comics in 1977, while studying painting and drawing at the Art Students League of New York. Since then, he's worked for every major company, and hopscotched around the indies as well. Books he's worked on include BATMAN, SPIDER-MAN, JUSTICE LEAGUE, X-MEN, 100 BULLETS, PREACHER, TRANSMETROPOLITAN, THE DEFENDERS, Y: THE LAST MAN, and all of the various Hellboy characters. It might be easier to list the characters he hasn't lettered. Since 1982 he's done TV courtroom sketches for markets in Boise and Cincinnati, as well as for CNN. He taught figure drawing and human anatomy for eight years at the Art Academy of Cincinnati. His book THE ART OF FIGURE DRAWING was published in 2003 by North Light Books, and has since been translated into French, Spanish, German, Italian and Chinese.

Melina Mikulic

hasn't yet won an Eisner Award for Best Publication Design, for one simple reason: she's designed more than a thousand gorgeous comic books (including Fibra's editions of Moebius and Tezuka, and Marjane Satrapi's PERSEPOLIS) but all on the wrong continent. That is about to change.

She is a Master of Arts, and graduated from the Faculty of Design in Zagreb, Croatia, where she was born. As a graphic designer, she is primarily engaged in design for print, with a growing interest in illustration and interactive media. She now lives in Rijeka, where despite enjoying the Mediterranean climate, she rarely sees the sun, as she spends her time wandering through shadowy landscapes of fonts and letters.

Rachael Fulton

is editor of KICK-ASS: THE NEW GIRL 1-3 and all volumes of Hit-Girl's world tour. She is editor of Netflix's Mark Millar division, where she's produced THE MAGIC ORDER, PRODIGY, SPACE BANDITS, SHARKEY THE BOUNTY HUNTER, and CHRONONAUTS: FUTURESHOCK.

She tweets about feminism, comics, and cats from the handle @Rachael_Fulton.

Behind The Bandits!

Here are some rad character sketches, drawn from designs by our in-house art team.

Matteo Scalera worked from these pics to draw the awesome '80s cast of *Space Bandits*.

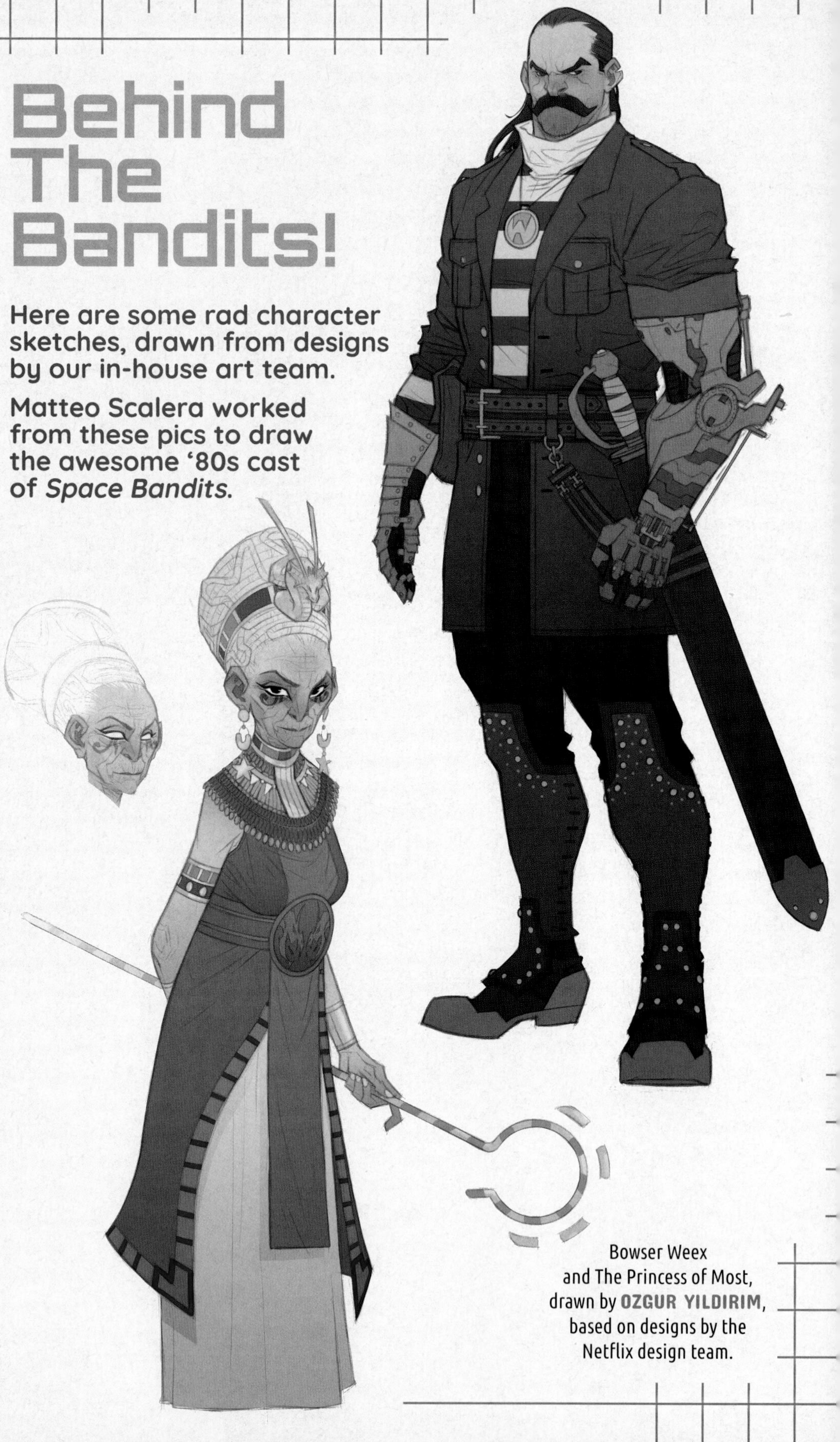

Bowser Weex
and The Princess of Most,
drawn by **OZGUR YILDIRIM**,
based on designs by the
Netflix design team.

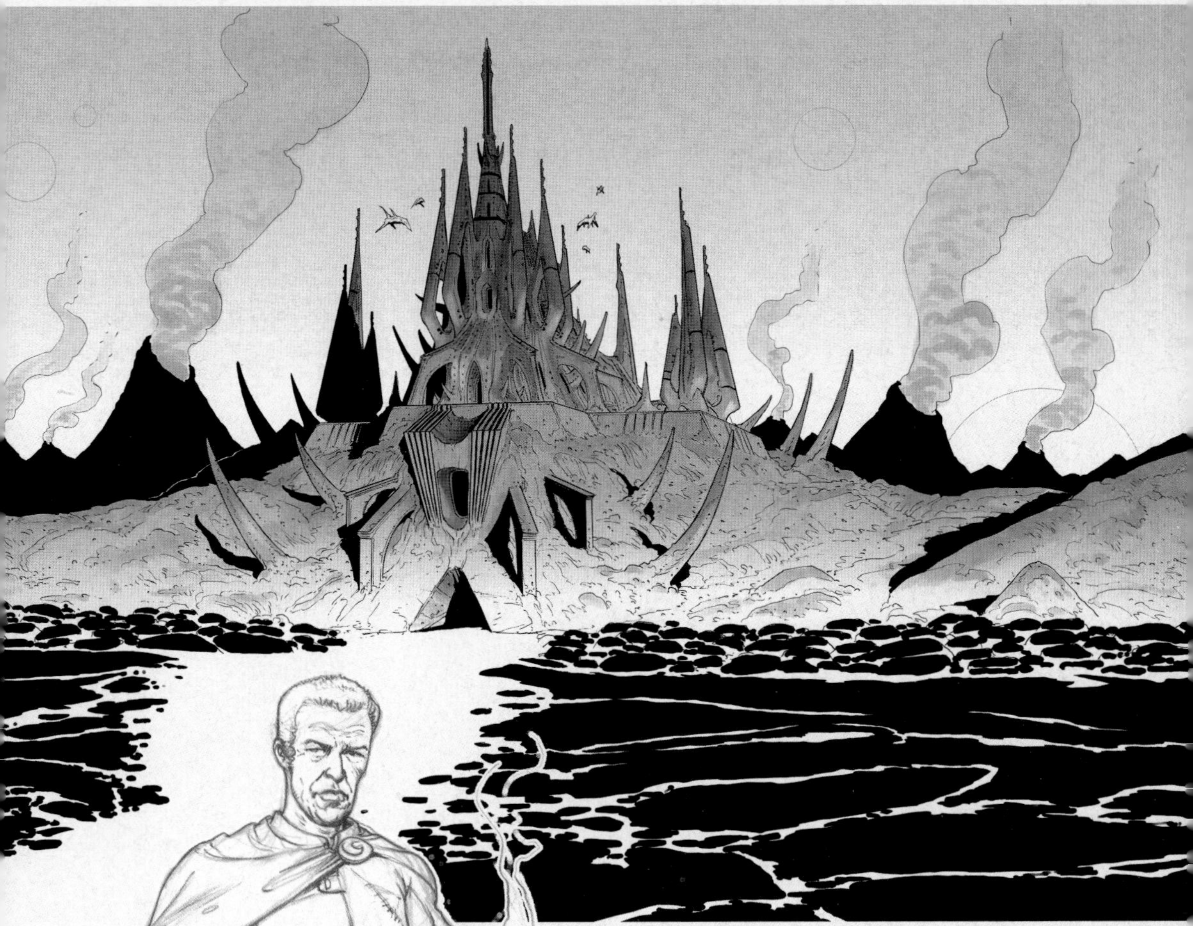

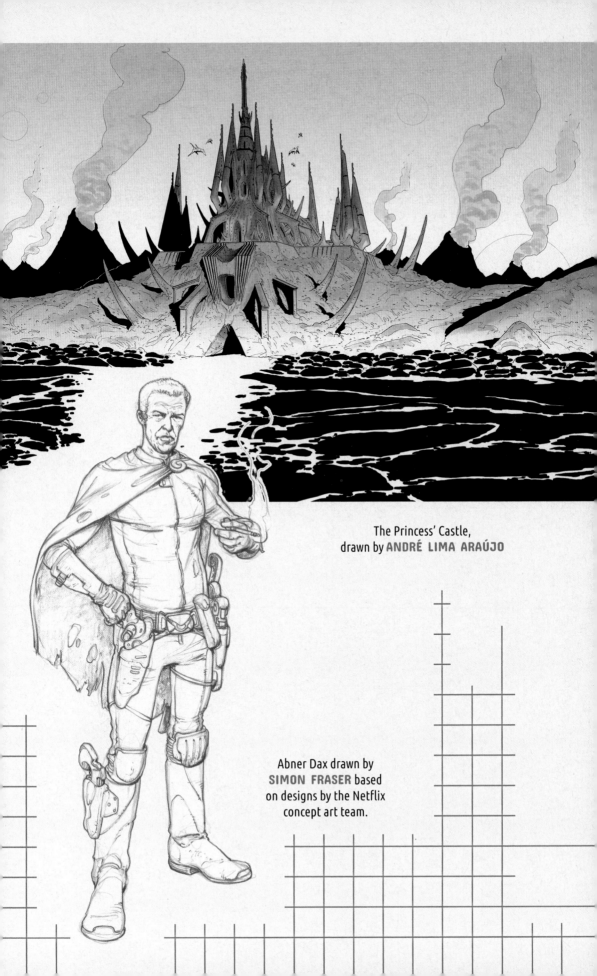

The Princess' Castle,
drawn by **ANDRÉ LIMA ARAÚJO**

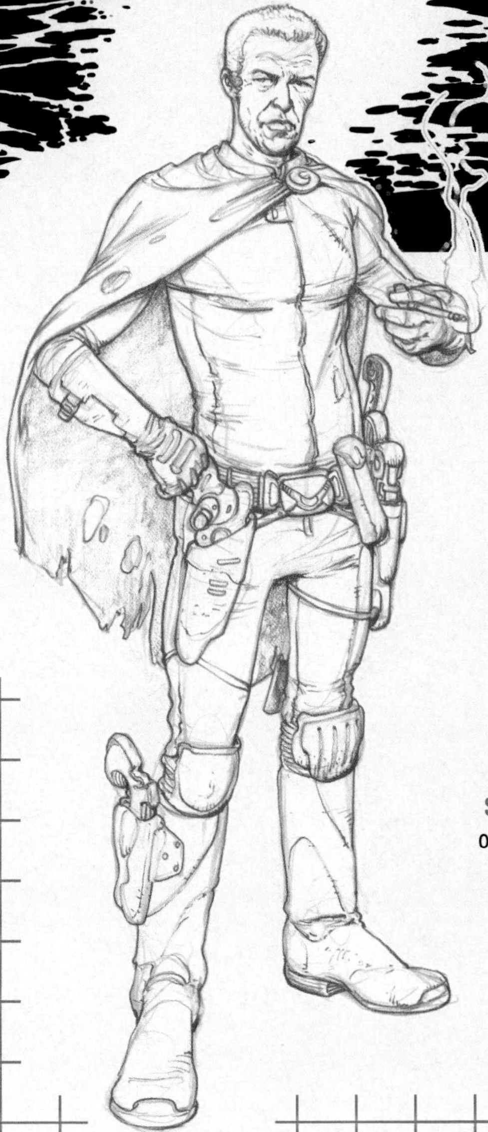

Abner Dax drawn by
SIMON FRASER based
on designs by the Netflix
concept art team.

VARIANT COVER GALLERY

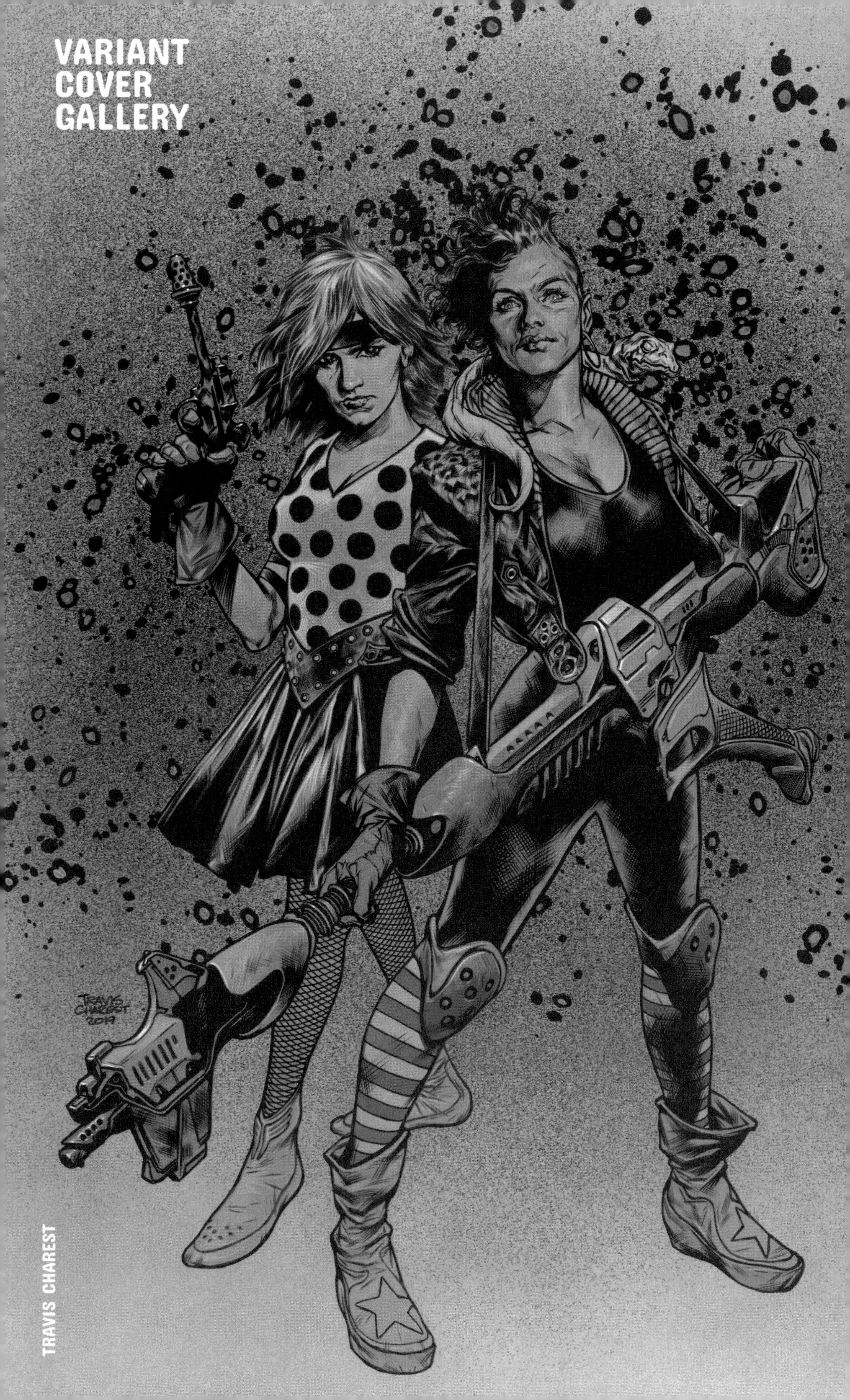
TRAVIS CHAREST 2019

TRAVIS CHAREST

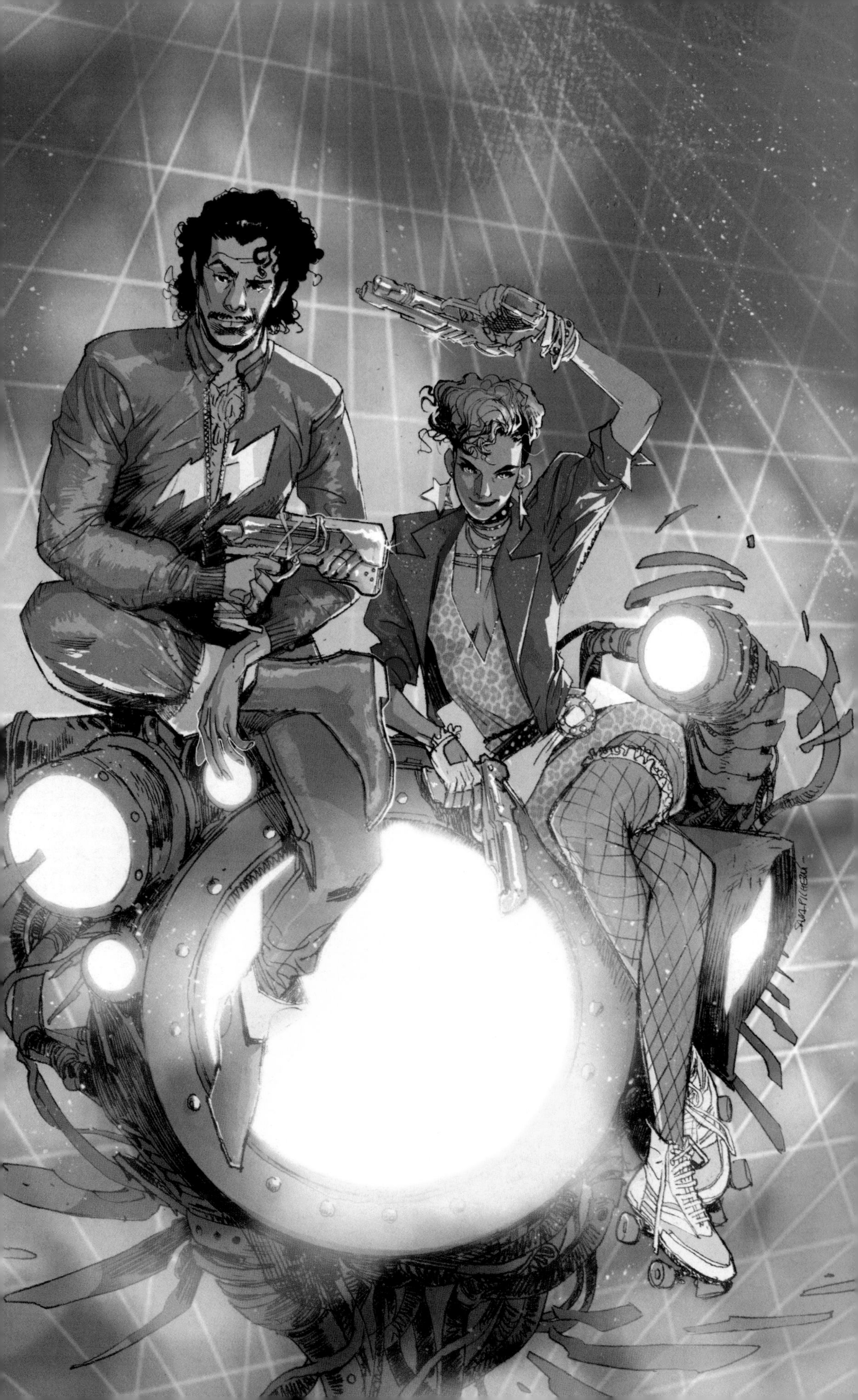

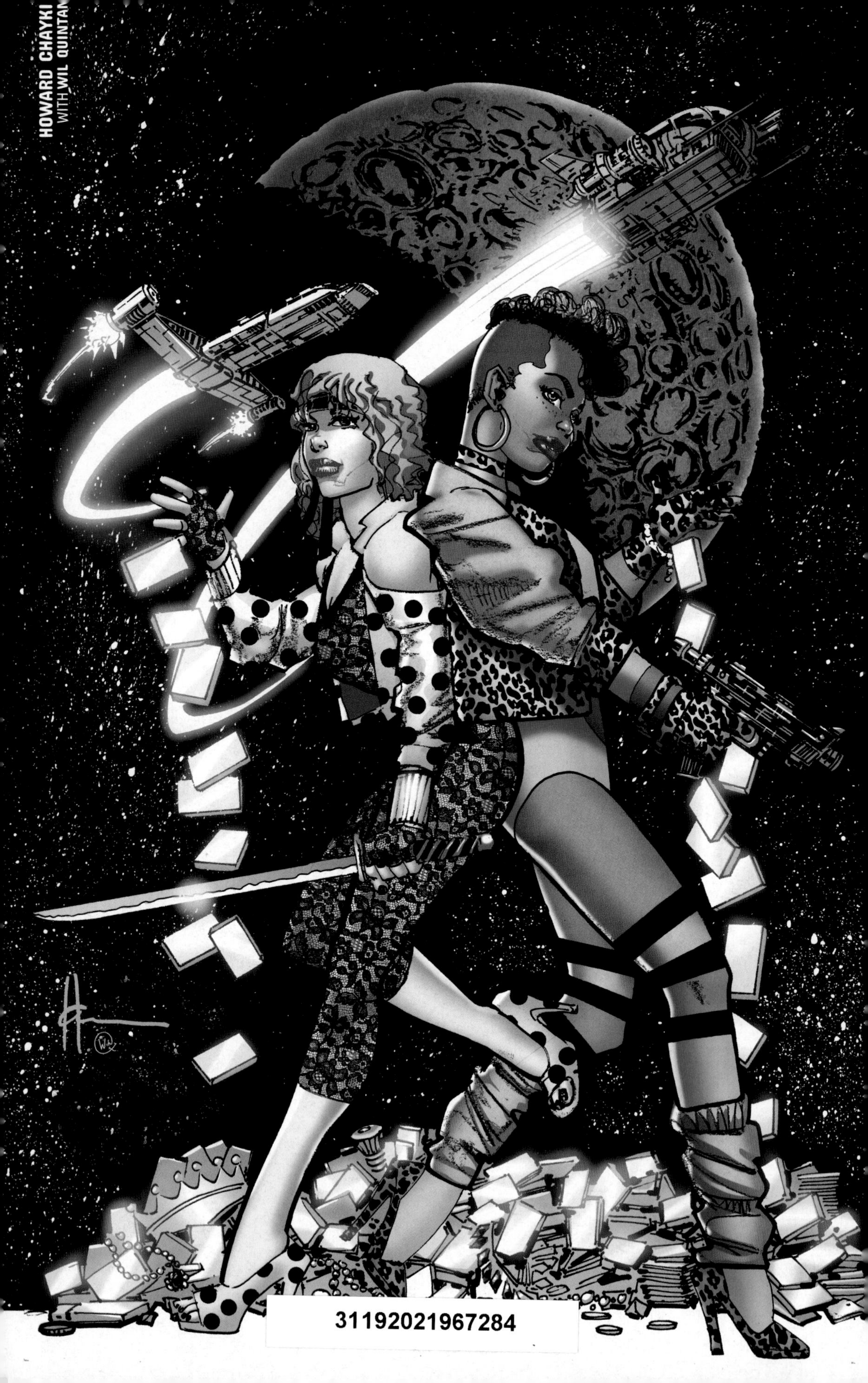
HOWARD CHAYKI
WITH WIL QUINTAN